SWITCHBACKS

2

CHAD LEHRMANN

Chapter 1

The dreadful summer heat had finally surrendered to fall's pleasant coolness along the western slope of the Rockies, and the aspens had turned, making the mountainsides look like a dragon's hoard of gold.

It was still a little early for the leaf peepers of the western United States to be out and about in droves, so Warren and Emilia Cornelius had the road to themselves. Their Arabian Grey Mercedes AMG G 63 glided around the curves of the switchbacks in the high altitudes of Garvin Pass in north central Colorado. The couple was enjoying a peaceful road trip to rekindle their struggling marriage fire.

'Peaceful' might have been the wrong word.

"I *told* you the exit for Eden Falls was back that way," Emilia said, rolling her eyes.

"Yeah. You said that. *Five different times!*" Warren shouted back. "I know where I'm going. The cabin is *outside* of Eden Falls. Not *in* it."

Tensions had been high in the marriage since Emilia discovered Warren's affair with his secretary. Of course, Emilia was having her own little dalliance with her yoga instructor, but what Warren didn't know wouldn't hurt him. He had suggested the trip, but Emilia only went along because the prenup stipulated that they had to stay married for five years for her to get half of his wealth in a divorce.

They were in year four.

And he had hundreds of millions of reasons to make her miserable enough to leave early.

Warren had made it big in crypto right before they met, and he knew she was drawn to him for his money more than anything. He had gone bald at twenty-two. Got the spare tire around the waist at twenty-three. Hit the monetary jackpot at twenty-five, got the wife at twenty-six.

She was out of his league. Physically, anyway. Beautiful and statuesque, long blonde hair and deep blue eyes. She had been a fitness influencer, and still was, but lately she posted more about her extravagant shopping sprees than her workouts.

Alas, she was not that smart, and the woman was mean to boot. He had worked hard to get fit, gotten hair plugs, and everything to please her, but nothing worked. Except his money. But his secretary fawned over him, telling him how smart he was and how much she admired him. So he fell for her.

Neither woman knew he was secretly funneling money from the company he had founded. Or that he was also embezzling money from some clients of his crypto investment firm. He told himself he was no Bernie Madoff, because he only stole from the richest clients.

For all the hatred he had toward Emilia for her extravagance, it turned out Warren was just as greedy and selfish as she was. And he had proposed the road trip because he knew all that time in the car would royally piss her off and hopefully make her take off before the five-year clause in the prenup. Plus, an investor's aide had offered the use of a remote cabin outside of Eden Falls for free.

She was pouting when he noticed movement in the trees to his right. They were on a curve with a near vertical drop into a valley on the left, and a tree-covered patch of steeply inclined land on the right.

At first, he thought it might be a herd of deer or elk, but then a single tree just fell across the road. Then a second. A third was instantly followed by an entire stand of trees. Warren slammed on the brakes and the Mercedes skidded to a stop just feet from the apparent landslide.

"What are you doing?" Emilia screamed at him.

He glared at her and replied, "Trying not to get us killed, woman!" He was breathing heavily and as the adrenaline faded, he felt terror rising in his chest. He had almost hit the trees. And had he tried to swerve, he might have taken them both down the side of the mountain. Who would get his money then?

Warren started to get out of the car, but Emilia taunted, "What are you gonna do? Move the trees with your bare hands?"

He looked back at her, arms crossed over her chest and sneering. "Well, we can't just go back, now, can we? Unless you want the trip to last longer?"

Her eyes grew wide, and he knew her answer. Maybe his gambit was paying off.

Warren walked to the trees to see if it was possible to go around, but sure enough, the trees covered the road all the way to the edge of the drop-off. He walked to where the landslide had come from, wondering if he could drive through that space. He smelled cobalt and saw heavy dust hanging in the air, but just assumed it was from the landslide. He knew finance, not geology.

Warren looked back and saw a truck approaching. He ran back toward his car, trying to wave them down and warn them. It was an older model Ford, beat-up and mud covered. It had what looked like a three- to four-inch lift with giant off-road tires.

It screamed redneck. Or mountain people. Warren wasn't sure what the proper term for them was in those parts.

The truck lurched to a stop, and as it did, it belched out an acrid cloud of black diesel smoke. But no one emerged from the truck. Warren could see a figure behind the wheel, but the window was filthy and he couldn't make out any of the person's features. He waved and shouted, "Road's blocked- you got a wench?"

The figure stayed put.

Warren began to walk closer, and as he did, Emilia scowled at him and warned, "Watch out. He might try to make you his girlfriend."

Warren flipped her off.

Finally, the door creaked open and a massive man hopped out of the truck. He sported cut-off sleeves displaying heavily muscled arms and had long red hair pinned back behind his head. His beard was well kept, a contrast to the oil-stained jeans he wore.

Then Warren saw the gun. A sawed-off shotgun was swaying from the man's left hand as he approached. Terror swelled up inside, and Warren wanted to run.

The man saw that, and then looked at his gun. "Oh, don't worry about that. It's just a precaution. We've been having some issues up here with wildlife." He looked at the trees, then the Mercedes, and then back at Warren. "I don't think that's the problem here, though. Names Rhett. Rhett Windsor." But he didn't put the gun away.

Warren still felt uneasy, but the man's demeanor was calm and intelligent. Not what he had expected. "Y-you think you can help me clear the road?"

Rhett looked around Warren and cocked his head to the side. "I can. But I need to go get my chainsaw. It's back up at my worksite. Take me about ten minutes, if you don't mind waiting?"

Warren smiled uncertainly, then looked at Emilia. Her jaw was hanging open looking at the muscular redneck/mountain man. "We can wait."

Rhett nodded, then lumbered back to his truck. He stopped, then turned back. A car approached from the other side of the downed trees, and Rhett seemed concerned. The car stopped, turned around and went back the way it came. Rhett relaxed. "I'd get off the road. Folks can't see around these switchbacks very well."

"Will do," Warren said. "Thanks!" He hopped in the Mercedes and pulled it off to the cut out on the side of the road. "He said it'd be ten minutes."

"I'd like ten minutes with that guy," Emilia said.

Warren muttered, "Devil woman," under his breath.

She chuckled maliciously. "You probably would, too."

He turned to face her fully, and was about to yell at her about how other women seemed to appreciate him, but he saw something that made him freeze. A large black vehicle with a metal grill guard plowed down out of the trees and into the side of the Mercedes. Emilia's body contorted and her head snapped forward and back so fast she had to have died instantly. Warren's door wasn't fully closed, so the force threw him out onto the pavement. The Mercedes was screeching toward him, and he had the presence of mind to roll under the vehicle. It stopped its progress when he was directly under the middle of the SUV. From his position, he saw three sets of booted feet drop to the pavement. "It's not one of Windsors," a gruff voice announced. "Too fancy."

"She's a goner," said a second voice. "Too bad. She was a looker."

"You're sick, Withers," a third voice said. "Now, find the driver. He has to be around here somewhere. See what we can get out of him."

The boots stomped around the car, then Warren felt an iron grip around his ankles. He tried to grab the asphalt, but his fingernails just peeled back and he screamed in pain. Light fell on him, and then he was rolled over. He saw a large African American man standing over him. He was dressed in military gear, dark, maybe black. A large rifle was strapped to his back, and he spoke in a deep voice. "Got him."

"Thanks, Benton," a dark-haired man said. He was wearing a beret and a khaki shirt, holding a tactical shotgun. The man knelt next to Warren and sized him up. "Name's Stone. You work for Rhett Windsor?"

"W-who? The big ginger?" Warren gasped.

Stone laughed maliciously. "That's him."

"I just met him," Warren said. "H-he was g-going to help me clear the road."

"He was here?" Benton asked.

"Just a minute or two ago."

Stone swore. "Then he might have seen us and will be coming back. Let's get outta here." He stood up, then looked down at Warren. "But first, what's your name?"

"W-why does that matter?" Warren managed.

Stone gave him a look that matched his name.

The third man, wearing a green beret over his close-cropped brown hair, stomped over and pointed his pistol in Warren's face. "Where I'm from, a man asks your name, you give it to him. Especially if he has a gun."

"W-warren. Warren Cornelius."

The men exchanged a look.

Stone spoke again. "Withers, take his wallet and any cash he has.

"You're robbing me?" Warren asked.

"Yeah," the man called Withers said flatly.

"I don't have any money."

The man looked at the wreck of the Mercedes. Then back to Warren. "Liar." Then he shot him in the face with the pistol.

"WITHERS!" Stone yelled. "What do you think you're doing? We could have gotten more out of him."

"He wouldn't talk," Withers replied, rifling through Warren's wallet. "C'mon Stone, you know the ending was always gonna be this. I just sped it up." He found a small slip of paper and waved it in the air.

Stone looked at the paper, and knew that- unfortunately, Withers had been right. He hated when that man was right. Stone turned to Benton. "Clear out the car. Check the woman for anything else we could use. Wipe it down. Just like usual. Withers- you keep an eye out for Windsor. We are gone in sixty."

Chapter 2

Remington Dean stopped and took a single aspen leaf between his fingers. The mid-morning sun shone down, giving the leaf a golden glow that almost seemed ethereal. His gaze turned to the peaks that surrounded the area, their tops covered in a whiter snow than they had been the day before. Despite it being only early October, winter was calling for the Rockies of northern Colorado. A breeze lifted a strand of his cheek length brown hair, and Dean squinted his hazel eyes against the wind. He rubbed together the fingers that had pressed the aspen leaf and took in a deep breath of the odor the leaf produced in the mountain air.

Summer in the Rockies was a pleasant departure from his time spent in Texas- which was most of his life. The winters were harsh, but Dean liked the cold and the isolation he often felt in the mounting drifts of snow that would come to lower altitudes soon enough.

But he loved the fall the most. The trees changed, the air *smelled* different. Cleaner. The mornings were frosty, the afternoons perfection.

There was a snap of a twig off the trail, and Dean turned just in time to see a deer bound off into the dark of the woods. He recalled a day, not that long ago, on a trail just like that one.

In his mind's eye, he saw a man. Shaggy blonde hair and bright green eyes. Grant Kolbe. The man was sneering, standing in a meadow. His hands at his side, staring down the gun drawn on him.

Remington Dean's Colt Python.

The man was not afraid, not repentant.

He was taunting.

There was a gunshot.

The roar of the Big Thompson River brought his mind back to the task at hand. Dean looked at his phone and checked his coordinates. He was near, and the sound of the river confirmed it. He knew the woods well enough he didn't need the technological aid, but he was looking for something specific.

A dead body.

Dean moved forward and felt the decline shift beneath his feet, growing steeper with each step. He turned a corner on the trail and saw an unnatural yellow fluttering in the wind.

Police tape.

His pace quickened and he reached the spot where he had to leave the trail. From that point, Dean relied more on the evidence left behind by hikers and Park Rangers who had trodden the grass and foliage as they made their way to the horrendous scene that awaited him. Dean thought again about how rough people were with nature. Even the Rangers, who were supposed to be good stewards of the wilderness left far more of themselves behind than they realized. Dean did it, too. All people did. Humans were just *that* clumsy and ignorant of the sanctity of undisturbed natural beauty in the wild.

Dean walked into a stand of trees, the sound of the river now deafening, and felt the temperature drop about ten degrees. He had eschewed his jacket for the hike in, but now almost regretted leaving it. He'd lived in Colorado for over three years, but still forgot that heat worked differently up there as opposed to his native Texas. Case in point, he had hiked almost three miles in wearing jeans, a long-sleeve henley, and a backpack yet had barely broken a sweat. In Texas, he would have been gasping for breath and soaked through his shirt.

"There you are," said the kindly voice of a Park Ranger. "You must be Remington Dean?"

"I am," Dean said. "Dudley?"

"That's me," the Ranger said. "Tim Dudley. I called you in when I was alerted to the body by some hikers. Figured it was a thing you might want to look into. Seeing as you are the official investigator for this region. I mean-"

"Tim, could you stop talkin'," Dean said curtly, as he knelt down next to the body. He brushed that same strand of hair back and briefly rubbed his bearded chin.

"Right. Forgot," Tim said. "You don't like talking. That's the reputation you-"

Dean turned his head and looked at Tim, who mimed zipping his lips shut.

The body had been there a few days, a week at the most. The torso was jammed under a rock on the edge of the water, and it was bloated, but Dean couldn't tell if that was from the stage of decomp, or the time spent in the water. Most of the clothes were torn away, and the body's chest was bare, which revealed to Dean the reason he got a call. Carved into the flesh was a large X in a circle. Dean slipped his pack off and reached in to pull out latex gloves. His eyes never stopped scanning the body as he pulled the black gloves on. Slowly, he reached out and touched the X, seeing that the edges of the wound were clean.

Then he looked down at the lower half of the body. The pants were still intact, which told Dean they were most likely a high-end brand of hiking pants. Men's hiking pants.

Turning back to the head, which was so swollen that the cheeks were pushing the eyelids closed from the bottom, and the eyebrows were pushing down from the top. With care, Dean pulled the flesh back to check the eyes for petechiae.

Dean started.

Twin hollow eye-sockets were hidden in the folds of the flesh.

"When did they find it?"

Tim didn't respond.

"You can speak now, Tim," Dean said without looking up.

"Uh, early this morning. I happened to be on my morning rounds, which is why they found me so-"

"Where are they?" Dean interrupted.

"Down by the bridge. With Kathy Tremont. A fellow Ranger," Tim said sheepishly. He started to say something else, then decided better of it.

Dean stood up, pulling the glove off of his right hand and placing it in the palm of the left.

Grabbing the bottom of the left-hand glove, he rolled them both up into a ball, then stuffed them in a plastic bag inside his pack. "I'm putting in a call to Abel Tolentino, Garvin County medical examiner. He will bring a camera and document the scene thoroughly. So I need it to be pristine. DO. NOT. TOUCH. THE. BODY." Dean said this last bit while pointing at Tim to stress each word. "And don't let anything or anyone else touch it, either."

"W-was it an accident?"

Dean sighed. "Know of any kind of accident that carves an X in a man's chest, and pops his eyeballs out?"

Tim Dudley went white. "His eyes are gone?"

Ignoring the park ranger as the man seemed to fight to keep his breakfast down, Dean turned to the body, pulled out his phone and took several pictures of his own. The vacant eye sockets were still open at him, the flesh around them having remained where Dean had left it. Without a word to Tim, Dean walked down the shoreline toward the bridge. His eyes watched where the small waves broke on the river rocks and spilled onto the brown soil. He didn't think he'd see anything, but he wanted to make sure.

The current wasn't too strong, and there had been no major storms in the last few days, so the body hadn't traveled too far. That meant the crime scene was right around where they were.

When he got to the bridge, he saw the other Ranger, Kathy Tremont. He had met her once before, a missing hiker case a year or so earlier. She knew his aversion to people better than Tim, and merely tipped her hat in his presence. "Dean."

"Ranger," Dean replied, then went to the two hikers. "I'm Remington Dean, Inspector with the Parks Service. How did you come to find the body?"

The girl, who looked about twenty, answered. "We were taking a picture on the bridge. Max set a timer and snapped us with our backs toward where the…where it was."

Max, a young man of about the same age continued. "When we looked at the picture, we saw what looked like legs in the water behind us. So Shelly and I, we went and looked closer."

"You touch it?" Dean asked.

"God, no!" Shelly exclaimed. "I screamed and ran. Max said we should call someone, so we called 911 and waited up here on the bridge. Ranger Dudley came by within thirty minutes."

Dean stared at them, sensing there was something missing. "Max, did *you* touch the body?"

Max swallowed hard. His mouth moved, but no words came out. Finally, he managed, "I…checked for a pulse. That's it."

"That's not it." Dean's face was stoic.

"And took a picture."

Dean nodded. Then he held out a hand. Max handed him his phone. He opened the photo roll, and said, "A picture?" as he glanced up.

"Or four."

Dean sent the pictures to himself, then deleted them. Then he went into the deleted pictures, confirmed they were the only four, and deleted them again. Then he handed them the phone back.

Turning to Tremont, Dean said, "Dudley is securing the scene and I'll call Abel. Let your bosses know you need to coordinate a high elevation rescue. Let these two go after you collect a statement and get contact information."

"I heard what you said about the eyes. Who would do that to a person?" Tremont asked sheepishly.

Dean paused and looked down the river to where Dudley stood next to the body. "Someone I don't want in the park." Without another word, Dean walked off the bridge and called Abel Tolentino. After explaining the situation, Abel said he'd be on the way as soon as they hung up.

"Will I get to ride in the helicopter?" Abel asked.

"Most likely," Dean said and hung up as Abel began to whoop and holler.

Dean looked out over the landscape, up and down the river and up to the mountaintops. People wound up dead in the mountains all the time. He knew that better than anyone. But the mutilation of the body down by the river was different. Dean knew there was a monster loose in the mountains. And unless Dean found them, they would kill again.

His phone rang and he looked at the caller ID It was unknown. "Remington Dean."

"This the Parks Investigator working the Eden Falls Organized Crime Task Force?" a deep voice asked.

"The same," Dean replied. "And this is?"

"Deputy Woodrow Quincey, Garvin County Sheriff," came the answer. "We have a crime scene we need you to take a look at. Appears to be a failed hit on your old friend Rhett Windsor."

"Failed as in no one died?"

"'Failed' as in the wrong people died," Quincey replied. "But we have two bodies, and Rhett Windsor is the man who found them and says he wants you to check it out."

"Where?"

"Garvin Pass. Half mile on the east side of the summit."

Dean checked his watch. "I'm at another crime scene on a trail. Take me a bit to hike out and get to you. Give me…two and a half hours?"

"We aren't going anywhere."

Dean hung up. He looked around the mountains, taking in the glorious view.

Why did so much beauty hide so much death?

Chapter 3

Colorado Bureau of Investigations Agent Ben Samuels was sitting in a room that had become all too familiar, at a table that he knew every square inch of, and next to a fellow law enforcement officer he had come to trust implicitly.

Sadie Donovan, detective for the Eden Falls Police Department.

Sadie was the only thing he liked about his current assignment. She was smart, determined, and tough. She had survived several potentially fatal gunshots during the case that brought them to the table where they currently sat. A murder of a local reprobate had exposed organized crime in the small vacation town, which led to an all-out assault on law enforcement as they tried to protect several key witnesses. Sadie had done so with extreme valor, facing down a half dozen armed paramilitary agents from a questionable security agency called Voight & Young Protection, Escort, and Reconnaissance- or VYPER- to protect a local reporter named Ashleigh Storms. She had taken some life-threatening wounds to protect her new friends, but she proved stronger than bullets. Storms had broken the story about the connection between an Eden Falls realtor and the Denver mafia, and by extension a group of VYPER operatives that had gone rogue, according to their company's 'operations commander.' That last tidbit had been one of the few things to come of their almost two month long investigation.

While he and Sadie, along with his partner with the CBI, Walt Marino, tracked down those kinds of leads, Remington Dean was out hunting those men down.

But Ben was in the interrogation room.

Asking questions.

Still.

Always.

That was the problem when your suspect turned key witness was an extrovert former realtor who loved the sound of his own voice. A man who wanted to "help" but didn't offer much of it.

"As I have said on numerous occasions, the Windsor boys ripped me off," Quentin Fletcher was exclaiming loudly and pounding the table with his cuffed hands. "They took my money!" The man was massive, sitting in an orange Garvin County Jail jumpsuit, his bald head gleaming. He had grown a bit of stubble, and lost a little weight. All of this made him a bit more intimidating- if you didn't know he was kind of a moron.

"And as *we* have said on numerous occasions, there is no proof of the money you claim is yours, or that the Windsors took it," Ben said calmly. He strongly suspected, as did his entire team, that Fletcher was stalling. For some reason. "Provide receipts of the money, and that's a start. And we looked all over the Windsor property before the Feds imploded their mine. There was no money, drugs, or anything."

"Never said anything about drugs," Fletcher said, crossing his arms. Despite promising to testify against VYPER for a deal with the U.S. Assistant District Attorney, Fletcher was reluctant to give any evidence of crimes that might help the Federal case. Especially crimes that might connect him to the Denver mob.

The man next to Fletcher leaned forward. He was the realtor's attorney. He was also the former lawyer for the late Horatio Bethea, the Denver mob boss that brought organized crime to Eden Falls. And who was but one arm of a large organization with a mysterious and unidentified head. "Again, my client has pleaded guilty to the much lesser charges of possession with intent to sell and we came here today to discuss more regarding the entirely false drug trafficking accusation," Edwin Jessup smirked. "And as he is willingly giving you testimony about Horatio Bethea's operation and connection with the rogue VYPER team Mr. Bethea hired to, among other things, order the murder of Carter Windsor. Please stop trying to entrap him in larger crimes."

Sadie was resting her chin on her hands, and she scrunched up her mouth, then asked. "Do you have to stretch before you contort yourself so much, Mr. Jessup?"

Jessup raised an eyebrow. "Excuse me?"

Sadie leaned back with a shrug. "You forget that you were Mr. Bethea's attorney until his death. His *mysterious* death in the custody of FBI agent Chris Starr, but allegedly at the hands of one of the very men he hired to kill Windsor, I should add. Then- and only then- did you start representing Mr. Fletcher. Now, suddenly, you are very willing to sell out your dead client for your new one."

Jessup chuckled mockingly and raised a finger. "I represented Mr. Bethea on behalf of my corporate client, and was unaware of his…extra-curricular activities. My corporate client has sent me to represent Mr. Fletcher because once his time is served here in the next few months, we intend to continue our business with him."

"And your client is?" Ben offered.

"Confidential," Jessup said flatly.

"So, you have no problem doing business with a drug dealer and man willing to work with organized crime?" Sadie asked.

"That…hasn't been proven," Jessup said.

"Yeah, I only helped Bethea move his drugs in and set up some money laundering," Fletcher said. "And tried to force Brent Chase to handle his illegal books."

"Quentin!"

Fletcher turned to his apoplectic lawyer. "What?"

"You just defined organized crime," Ben said.

Fletcher looked confused.

"Drug smuggling. Money laundering. Illegal books," Ben said.

"That's organized crime," Sadie said, drawing a circle on the table. Then she pointed to the middle of it. "And that's you putting Horatio Bethea and possibly Mr. Jessup's other *secret* client right in the middle of it."

The light slowly went on in Fletcher's eyes. "Oh. Well…did I tell you that the Windsors have other mines?'

Ben sat up. "What?"

Jessup also seemed surprised by the revelation. He tried to stop Fletcher, but the bald man was on a roll. "They bought up several old shafts a year or two ago. I never understood why…"

"There is no record of these mines under any Windsor," Ben said, looking over his files.

"Because they put it in an LLC," Fletcher said. "Red Beard Mining, I think. Named it after Rhett, but it was set up by Nigel and Zeke."

Ben glared at Fletcher. Jessup did, too.

"My client and I need to speak, so I think the interview is done for now," Jessup said, not taking his eyes off of Fletcher as he rose.

"Sounds good to me," Ben said. "Looks like we finally got something productive out of him."

Jessup scowled at him.

An officer came in and escorted Fletcher and Jessup to a separate area for them to speak privately.

Walt Marino, Ben's partner with the CBI, entered the room. Walt was in his mid-fifties, bald, and sported a salt and pepper beard. He was joined by a black-haired woman in a black suit-Assistant U.S. Attorney Elsie Kho- and Chris Starr. The blonde FBI agent carried the jacket of his three-piece suit over his right shoulder, and winced as he bumped into the door frame with his left. A residual reminder of his last encounter with Nathaniel Stone. The encounter where Stone killed an FBI agent and Horatio Bethea, but only wounded Starr before he could get away. Starr and Kho had been listening in with Walt. They were all working to build the case against VYPER, even if Starr was a tangential third party of sorts. AUSA Kho was keen on going for the Denver mob, Bethea's buddies, but Starr kept saying there wasn't enough hard evidence.

Stalling, like Fletcher, it seemed.

Ben could see wet plaster on the wall outside the interrogation room. The entire building was still being renovated following the shootout that had taken place there two months prior, so they had to sidestep tools and paint buckets wherever they walked.

Kho spoke first. There was hint of a British accent, as Kho had lived in Britain until she was ten. "Should be easy to find the papers to prove all that, but it will take legwork to check all the mines out. What do you think they would use them for?"

"Storage," Walt replied. "They had to move the stuff they stole- and we know they did- before the Parks shut down their minor operation at the homestead."

"Can't hurt to go check that out," Starr said. Then he looked at Ben. "Samuels, are we sure Brent Chase is clean?"

Ben looked at Sadie. "You're friends with his former barista. What does she say?"

Sadie took a deep breath, then said, "He doesn't come up. But I'm meeting her for brunch in a bit. I can see what she thinks. If it's possible he's dirty, that is."

"Walt and I will run the title on Red Beard," Ben said. "But I swear, if I don't get out of this building and outside, I am going to lose my mind."

Walt chuckled. "Did no one tell you the investigations involve lots of research?"

"Apparently no one told Dean," Ben said, half joking and half jealous that the ranger got to traipse around and actually hunt down the perps. Ben Samuels needed to stretch his legs, not just his thinking.

Kho smiled at Ben. "As far as I'm concerned, you're doing the heavy lifting on this case. Remington Dean is barely a blip on my radar."

Starr chuckled. In the months since the events leading up to Horatio Bethea's death, the bad blood between Starr and Dean had grown. Dean made it clear he thought Starr was crooked and…well, that was all that it took to turn that relationship sour.

Ben's phone buzzed, as did everyone else's. "Speak of the devil," Walt said.

"Sounds like VYPER is active again," Starr said. "I'll meet Dean up there." He put his phone away and made for the exit. "You guys run down the Red Beard Mining thing, and the Chase connection."

As the door closed behind him, Sadie commented, "He does realize he's not in charge of us, right?"

Ben chuckled, in spite of himself. Then they looked at each and smiled again. And the look lingered.

Maybe interviewing people with Sadie Donovan wasn't so bad after all.

Ashleigh Storms was walking down the main street of Eden Falls to her new office while listening to a true crime podcast about a serial killer on the Appalachian Trail. Her foot crunched the occasional golden aspen leaf beneath it, a sign that the peak of the leaf changing season was nearing.

The podcast was for research on the latest story she was writing for her new bosses. It was supposed to be about murderers who preferred to operate in the wild, places like the Appalachians or the Rockies. She would publish it with her magazine but the big-time publishers would syndicate it for real money. After writing the story that introduced the world to Remington Dean, and the earth shattering follow-up that exposed the organized crime movement into north-central Colorado's tourism jewel, Ashleigh was a hot ticket for a number of newspapers and magazines. The Associated Press had been the first to offer her a job, but she soon learned that it was more lucrative- and allowed more freedom- to freelance the news stories and funnel that money into a more consistent venture that would honor her late friend and editor, Laura Fielding.

Laura had run a local interest newspaper called *The Rocky Mountain Gothic* until she was killed for helping Ashleigh expose the criminal enterprises in Eden Falls. *The Gothic*'s offices were burned, but she was determined to raise it from the ashes. Not as a newspaper, but as a magazine, highlighting the beauty and the dangers of the mountains. She was interviewing quirky locals, contracting with photographers to do photojournalism highlighting the natural beauty of the Rockies and their wildlife, and was negotiating with National Parks to do a series highlighting their employees.

But as she listened to the podcast, she was waiting for a chime to tell her she got the call she had been waiting on. As she unlocked the door to the small office she was renting to run the new *Gothic*, that chime came.

"Dean?" she asked eagerly as soon as she clicked over to answer the call. "Is it?"

"Looks that way," came his terse reply.

"Dean, you know I appreciate your affinity to utilize minimal words more than most, but can you elaborate?" she asked teasingly. "Reporters need details."

"Body was dumped in a river, at least a few days ago. Abel will confirm later, after he's choppered in. There are wound patterns that would not…naturally occur. Namely, the 'X" carved in his chest, and missing eyeballs."

"Yep. That's murder-y sounding." Ashleigh had found a post-it and was frantically taking down the notes. Even if the murder Dean had called her about earlier that morning was a one-off, it would be a significant part of the story she would eventually pull together. "Where are you? You sound like you're in a car."

"I am."

"Dean…What's going on?" She had only known Remington Dean for a couple of months, but they had developed a friendship that defied Dean's history. He was a loner and had been since his wife's murder in Texas four years earlier. As such, he let no one get close to him. But after the events that suddenly made them both rather famous, they had bonded. She was drawn to the man, even if *he* was determined to keep their relationship platonic and professional. Perhaps she was drawn to him because of that. In any case, she had quickly picked up his tones and speech patterns. And at that moment, Remington Dean was hiding something.

"I can't comment on ongoing investigations."

"Dean, you *just* did."

A long pause. "Fair enough." Silence. "Well?"

Dean sighed. "Some folks were killed. Deputy Sheriff out of Garvin County called me in because Rhett Windsor found them. I think Rhett wanted him to call me because he thought he might have been the original target."

"Stone?"

"Maybe. On my way to meet with the Deputy."

"Does the rest of the task force know?"

Another sigh. "I'll text them. But they are doing interviews today. Might be busy."

"Excuses. By the way, we on for coffee later?"

"Depends on this, but I plan on it. How's the magazine going?"

Ashleigh smiled. He cared about her. She knew it. He knew it. Maybe someday he'd finally feel like it was okay to move their relationship forward beyond friendship. She was willing to wait. "It's going well…" and they talked for the rest of Dean's trip to the crime scene.

The morning rush was in full swing at the Book Brew, and Brent Chase was in over his head with coffee orders.

For the past few weeks, after the summer vacation crowd dwindled out and the temperatures started dropping, the coffee shop was full more often than it wasn't, and there was a line to and out of the door almost every day. And the promise- or threat, depending on one's perspective- of winter's inevitable arrival was also driving the book portion of the shop to significant profits.

All the fears Brent had harbored in August were abated and replaced by the fulfillment of long dormant dreams.

And one living nightmare.

They weren't always there, but from time to time, human reminders of the deal with the devil he had made to survive the mob, the military madmen, and the law dropped in. As he turned to hand a bespectacled young man in a beanie his latte, he caught a glimpse of one of them in the corner booth. It was not Horatio Bethea, or even Quentin Fletcher that glared back at him.

It was Nigel Windsor.

Nigel was drinking a bottomless cup of black coffee, waiting for the rush to die down so he could pass the bag in the seat next to him off. The bag contained cash, a lot of it. Drug money. Since the mob had been spooked away from Eden Falls, and Quentin Fletcher had been arrested, all of the drug trade in the Falls went through the Windsors and their ilk. Brent never touched the stuff.

But he did launder the money.

Did that make him part of their 'ilk?'

They brought it in to 'work,' because the Windsors were on his payroll. Of course, they never served anyone. They were his 'janitorial staff.' And they worked 'after hours.'

But the problem arose that the drug trade was *too* lucrative to just hide it in Book Brew funds. So, Nigel and Zeke, the brothers Windsor, had been using some old mining land they bought without Cousin Rhett's knowledge some time back to also hide the money. Rhett had been in on their initial agreement, but soon after the shooting died down, he seemed to almost disappear. Brent never saw him in the shop. Nigel and Zeke said he had bought some land up on the mountain. Land that had belonged to other generational mountain folks. And he was working to build mountain communes for Eden Falls natives that were finding themselves priced out of home buying in the valley after losing their land to the defunct machinations of the Denver mob. Brent marveled that Rhett had once been a calculating criminal mastermind and, on a dime, became a man who cared for his people. Brent was beginning to strongly suspect that Rhett Windsor was playing a chess game ten moves ahead of everyone. And that meant Rhett was doing far more than building budget mountain top homes out of the goodness of his heart.

Or maybe the man had experienced an epiphany that crime didn't pay, and Brent was just projecting.

Because as much as he said he loathed the criminal enterprise, it gave him an uncomfortable thrill.

Despite his partners.

Nigel was tapping a finger on the tabletop and when he caught Brent's eye, he raised the empty cup. Brent looked over to his new barista, Levi Montague, and said, "Booth needs a refill."

Levi looked over, his long brown hair shaking as he turned his head. "That dude just gonna keep drinking straight black?"

Brent shrugged. "He's the cleaning crew. Gets it free."

Levi poured a cup and walked toward Nigel. He was a local boy that had been a star football player in high school, but peaked way too soon. He worked several jobs around town, and was a good employee, but Brent's heart broke that the kid couldn't find a place in the world. He also worried that Levi would discover exactly why Nigel Windsor spent so much time in the coffee shop.

Brent turned back to the cash register to see that he had at last reached the last person in line. And he gasped.

She had shoulder-length blonde hair, dark blue eyes, and a kind smile. She was a little shorter than he was, wearing fashionable hiking gear and sunglasses on top of her head. But those eyes were so inviting and… entrancing.

"Can I help you?" he asked.

Her smile grew, and she said with a raspy but clear voice, "Pistachio latte, please and thank you."

Brent made the note on the coffee cup, and then he asked, "Name?"

"Charly," she replied. "Short for Charlotte. And you must be Brent Chase?"

He looked up, his eyebrow raised. "How-?"

Charly nodded at the plaque that was behind the bar emblazoned with the words 'Brent Chase, Owner and Proprietor.' "Ah," he replied.

"But that's not how I knew you," she said with that smile, and a flutter of those eyelashes.

Clearly flustered, Brent began to babble. "Oh…uh, well…um…How…do you know me?" He turned to start making the coffee, and she waited until he stopped steaming the milk.

"You turned state's evidence against Quentin Fletcher," she said matter-of-factly. "After you witnessed his part in the murder of Carter Windsor. And after his attempt to coerce you into working for the Denver mob. Who Fletcher then turned state's evidence for."

Brent smelled a lawyer. He'd talked with a lot of them over the last month. He deflated. "Oh," he said.

"I thought it was very brave," Charly said. "Not many would face the mob down, and fewer would do it without a gun. People make that ranger out to be the hero, but I think it was you."

"Look, Charly, I don't know what you're looking for-"

"I just wanted to meet you," Charly interrupted. "I've recently moved to the area as an employee of Xavier Voight. I'm his local ambassador. You know, meet the locals, look for business connections. Which, by the way, I am interested in for Book Brew. But no, I have no ulterior motives other than to meet a man I respect." She smiled again.

Brent was speechless. The coffee finished behind him, so he turned and finished preparing it. He turned back, and Charly was standing there patiently. He handed her the cup, and said, "Sorry…I just…I've talked to a lot of reporters and lawyers, so I just assumed-"

"I wanted something from you?" Charly asked.

Brent nodded. "Guess I'm cynical like that. Look, can I make it up to you? Want to get…something other than coffee…later?"

That smile again. "Love to." She slid a credit card onto the bar and Brent ran it. He handed her the receipt, and she filled it out, then slid it back. He read her name, Charlotte Addison. Beneath her signature was her number. He looked up at her and she mimed answering a phone. "Call me." With a final smile, she turned to leave.

Brent decided he would definitely call her.

When he looked back to Nigel, the redneck stood up and walked to the register. "'Bout time, brother."

Brent took the back of money and shifted it to the hand behind the counter. "I'm not your brother."

Nigel gave a half-grin that bore no warmth, and crossed his unsleeved arms. "Don't go thinkin' yer any better than us, Coffee Boy," Nigel sneered. "You can't be fergettin' that this whole thing was yore idea."

Nigel was right, he had suggested that the Windsor steal all the cash Fletcher had stored, then use it for their own good. In that moment, Brent had thought it was his only way out. The Windsors were a lesser of three evils- Fletcher and the mob being the other two. He had taken some of the money himself, to pay for advertising and some updates to the shop, but it was small compared to what the Windsors took. All it cost him was his soul.

And the friendship of the only person who had ever believed in him.

Ashleigh Storms.

Nigel, not being one for awkward silences or witty rejoinders, turned and left.

Brent took the money back to his office and put in the safe. He was closing it when Levi appeared at the door. "Boss?"

Brent jumped. "Jeez, Levi. You scared the crap out of me."

Levi made a face of regret and said, "Sorry- there's a guy that wants to talk to you."

Brent took a deep breath. "Lawyer or cop?"

Levi shrugged. "Feels like a cop, but not. Like…he has this air of authority, but in a scary way."

Brent pursed his lips in thought. Then he rose, his chair squeaking as he did, and followed Levi out.

The man waiting for him had black hair cut short and parted on the side. He wore a black polo shirt that exposed lean and muscular arms and a tribal tattoo just visible below his shirt sleeve. He leaned over the counter, his thin face with high cheekbones and deep-set eyes focused on Brent. Piercing, blue eyes. He rose to full height and smiled at Brent, but there was no warmth in the smile.

"Are you the owner?"

He had a deep voice that was not altogether an unpleasant one, but Brent understood what Levi meant. Something about the guy was scary.

"I am. How can I help you?"

"Does an Ashleigh Storms work here?" he asked, looking around the shop. "I'd heard she was a barista here?"

Brent bobbed his head. "'Was' is the key word. Hasn't worked here in a couple months. And you are?"

Those cold blue eyes looked back at Brent. He smiled coldly once more, then said, "Old friend from Denver. You know where I could find her?"

"She has an office-" Levi started to say.

Brent cut him off, "But she's not usually there. Likes to work outside. You might catch her having brunch with her friend. A detective with Eden Falls Police named Sadie Donovan. Red hair, young- can't miss her."

The man looked them over, smiled again, then turned to leave.

"If we see her, who should you say was looking for her?" Brent called after him.

He stopped at the door just long enough to say, "You shouldn't." Then he was gone.

"She doesn't work outside the office all the time," Levi said. "I see her there more than I do around town."

Brent wasn't listening. He was trying to text Ashleigh that a creepy guy was looking for her. He didn't know much about her past, and he knew she didn't really want to talk to him after…what he did…but this seemed like it would trump all of that.

"Who do you think that guy was?" Levi asked.

Brent looked out the window. "No one good."

Chapter 4

"Yeah, Samuels was complainin' about having to do all the interviews, but I told him he's the one that's always sayin' how smart he is. So it goes to show him."

Dean was steering his Jeep Gladiator up the incline toward the pass and continuing his conversation with Ashleigh Storms. To say that they had become friends was accurate, in his estimation. To suggest there was something more there? Well, Dean didn't let himself think about that. He knew Ashleigh had some sort of feelings for him that were not confined to friendship. He knew she stirred feelings in him he had not felt since…Amy. Dean could not, however, put her at risk. She was an innocent, and if his history was any lesson to him, that meant she was a potential target for anyone out to get him. He just couldn't do that to her. Like he had with Amy…

The case that brought him together with Ashleigh, Ben, Sadie, and Walt wasn't wrapped up yet. Nathaniel Stone was still loose and the head of the Denver mafia was still unknown. Not to mention the deep, unsettled feeling in the pit of his stomach that told him the gunfight in Eden Falls had been just the beginning of something. And even if the FBI was trying - and failing- to claim it as *their* case, Dean trusted no one but himself to solve it.

And he especially didn't trust the FBI agent in charge- Chris Starr.

Chris Starr, who was standing in the road chatting to an absolute mountain of a man with red hair, and a second behemoth in a sheriff's uniform. Behind them was a scene that clearly involved some sort of explosive. Trees and fragments of stone scattered across the road, and beyond that was a mauled ball of steel that might have once been an SUV.

"Hey, Ashleigh, I'll have to call you back," Dean said. "I'm here."

"Dinner later?" she asked expectantly.

Dean looked over the fallen trees and wrecked car, the dozens of law enforcement officers from numerous agencies, and the familiar faces Dean was growing tired of seeing, and he knew the answer to her question. "Not tonight. This is gonna be a big one."

Dean pulled his truck off to the side of the road and put the parking brake on. He slid out of the car, ran a hand through his brown hair, clipped his backup piece on his belt at the small of his back, then grabbed his green utility style jacket. It was cooler even than the hike he'd been on. Plus, at that altitude, there was a decent gust blowing at about twenty miles per hour with a decent chill.

Chris Starr was wearing his usual three-piece suit, but his left arm hung stiffly at one side. Dean wasn't a sadist, but Starr's pain made him smile. Aside from being an insufferably arrogant man, Dean suspected Starr was corrupt. And something else bugged him- Starr was reported to be in Texas at the time of his wife's death. Sure, Texas is a big state, but Starr also had connections with the man Dean *knew* was connected to Amy's death.

Grant Kolbe.

Rhett Windsor must have felt that the temps were cool enough to put on a black leather vest, but his tree-trunk arms swung free in the air. The sheriff's deputy next to him was also huge, but not nearly as big as Rhett. He wore a black baseball cap with a star on it, khaki cargo pants and a black polo shirt. He also eschewed a jacket. But one identifying feature- besides his size- that stood out was his mustache. It was a thick, black one, like Tom Selleck used to wear on Magnum

P.I. It reminded him of something else he couldn't put his finger on at the moment.

As Dean approached, he took in the scene. ATF was present, as was Abel Tolentino's new assistant, a young Hispanic woman he hadn't met yet. A few state police wandered around, seeming to be unaware of what to do. He recognized a few other LEOs from various state and local agencies, but he knew their faces, not names.

And there were already looky-loos. One group stood out in particular. Virgil Tolbert was standing there with two of his kin. Virgil was average height, with wavy brown hair and a scar running the length of his face on his left side. His brother had been Lenny, the man Dean had shot dead during a gunfight at the Windsor home a month earlier. Virgil's cousin Waylon had long blonde hair and wore all black, except for the brown leather belt that held his enormous knife. The same knife that had contributed to Waylon's defining feature- he only had three fingers on his right hand. He'd lost the pinky in a knife fight. Allegedly. Dean assumed he had just whacked it off while goofing around with the knife. The final Tolbert was Waylon's brother, with his mohawk flapping in the wind, black sunglasses covering his face, and a grin with far too few teeth. This was Travis Tolbert. "The Rocky Mountain Madman," he preferred to be called. His *legitimate* day job was 'Critter Catcher,' and he claimed to be able to wrangle anything from a marmot to a mama bear. Again, Dean doubted this claim's veracity.

In any case, he steered clear of them. He'd heard rumors they were looking to avenge their kin. And in the Rockies, that was no empty threat.

Dean reached the group he was headed for and made his introduction. "Starr, Rhett. You must be Deputy Quincey?"

The big sheriff nodded and offered a hand. It swallowed Dean's, and the strength of his grip made Dean wince. He hid it well. "Remington Dean. Your reputation precedes you." He tilted his head toward Starr, and Dean caught the insinuation. Starr was talking. He was good at that.

Dean looked to Starr. "Nothin' terrible, I hope?"

Starr smiled his phony smile and said, "Only that you are allegedly the fastest gun in the West. You and Deputy Quincey would make a good team. Fast Draw and the Linebacker."

Dean did a double-take. "Wait- Woody "The 'Stache" Quincey? Linebacker for Texas A&M in the aughts?"

Quincey smiled sheepishly. "Yeah. But I traded the helmet for…well…another type of helmet before the badge came my way. Did a tour or two in the desert, then came back here. Might should have accepted that third-round draft pick after all."

"I was in college back then, at A&M. Saw you play. You were amazing!" Dean exclaimed, letting out a rare show of excitement. Realizing Starr was looking at him funny, Dean reversed course. "But anyway. The scene?" Quincey motioned for them to follow him, and Dean kept an eye on the Tolberts. Why were they there?

"What I can surmise is that whoever did this blew out the trees over there-" he pointed to a twenty-foot gap in a wall of aspens. Some trees were broken, others simply uprooted. "I figure it was Tannerite. Or some other IED. Called in ATF to be sure. Heck, up here, it could be just old-fashioned dynamite."

"Or something military grade," Starr said. "We've been chasing a rogue paramilitary group, used to be affiliated with VYPER Securities. They have a beef with Mr. Windsor here."

"As I told the deputy, I was here just before whatever hit the car got down the slope," Rhett said. "I headed back up to get a chainsaw to clear the road. When I got back, I found this."

Dean looked at Rhett and judged his story was true. For what that was worth. Rhett had pulled one over on Dean before, but what did it benefit Rhett to kill two random travelers? "What are you doin' up there, Rhett?" he asked.

Rhett smirked. "Well, since the Parks imploded our mine, I've had to do other work to feed my people. So we are cutting timber on some land we bought. Completely legally."

Dean gave him a half smile. "Don't complain too much about the mine, Rhett. We coulda put you in the pen, if not for your help with those- what did you call them Starr? 'Rogue paramilitary' types?"

"That was a Parks call, Dean," Starr said, not looking at them. "Your Chief Walker has surprising pull for a glorified park ranger."

Ignoring the feeb, Dean asked Rhett, "You really building housing up here? For low-income folks?"

Rhett nodded. " Kinda have to. I tried to secure their land and keep in the hands of us up-landers. But, despite my best efforts, they got bought off their land by a developer." He saw Dean was about to ask, so he added quickly, "Not the mob. Something called 'Traditional Values Builders.'"

Dean took out his phone and made a note to check into the company. Rhett might believe it wasn't mob related, but a double-check wouldn't hurt. Then he turned to Quincey.

"Say, you thought it was Tannerite. Why?"

"Well, there was a delay from the time the trees blew- which Windsor saw- and the time the victims were hit," Quincey explained. "It suggests to me that either they used an unreliable trigger, suggesting IED. Or, they shot Tannerite from a distance and it took a bit to get their rig down the hill."

Dean walked over to the forest and looked into it. There was a steep incline up into the forest, but a path had been cleared straight up. He moved deeper into the woods and knelt down. The ground was damp, and as he brushed back some detritus littering the forest floor, he found a tire imprint. "Hey, get some crime scene techs over here. I got a tire tread."

Quincey whistled for someone and a young Hispanic woman came running up with a tool box. Dean saw Quincey tell her something, and she ran back to the CSI truck and returned with a bigger tool box. "Dean, don't know if you've met Grace Aguirre, assistant coroner and chief lab tech in Garvin County," Quincey said, walking over. "Don't know who knows who around here yet. Just started with the County about a week ago. Transferred in from Hinsdale County."

"Lake City?" Dean asked. "Heard it's beautiful."

"It is," Quincey replied. "But it's isolated. And the opportunity for upward mobility is limited, so I applied for a bigger county with bigger issues."

"Congrats," a woman's voice replied. "Got both! "Remington Dean? I'm Grace Aguirre. Abel has told me all about you!"

"Was it how your position was created because of all the people I shot a couple months ago?" Dean asked jokingly.

"Yep," she replied in a cheery tone. Then Grace knelt beside Dean and looked at the imprint. "Oh, that's a lovely print you have there," she said, a childlike wonder present in her voice as she tied her hair behind her head. She seemed really young.

Dean looked at her, but without looking up she answered his unspoken question. "Graduated high school at fifteen, college at eighteen. Doctorate in forensic science at twenty-two."

"I didn't ask," Dean said.

She looked at him and smiled. "Didn't have to." She looked him over. "You're shorter than I thought you'd be."

"I get that a lot," Dean said sarcastically. "I take it you read Ashleigh Storm's story?"

"I did," Grace said, mixing a gray powder in a clear baggy. "But Abel talks about you like you're a superhero. He idolizes you, you know?"

Dean chuckled. "Abel's good people." He began to walk back toward the road.

"He also tells me you don't talk much, but you're always thinking," Grace said. Something in her tone made Dean stop and turn back.

"Yeah?"

"If you start to think some about your murder down in the Park, the one you just called Abel in on," she said. "You might think about looking for others. He told me to cover this, and explained the details and the photos you sent him."

Dean looked at her with a raised eyebrow. "Why is that?"

"In addition to crime scene analysis, I do psychological profiling," she said, pouring the mix into the tread marking. "Abel reached out as soon as he got to the body. Someone who does that to a body, they don't just plan to do it once. Might have done it before."

"Huh." Dean looked off into the forest. "Contact other parks and see if they've had similar victims?" he asked.

"I would."

"Aguirre."

She looked up.

"Thanks."

She smiled, then went back to her work.

Dean walked back down to the road, and asked Quincey, "Anyone checked out what's up the slope?"

Quincey nodded. "Levels off about sixty yards up. Situated between the switchbacks with no way to see it from the road."

Dean thought for a second. "Can they see the road up there? I mean, more than just this down here?"

"I couldn't see anything in any direction when I was up there," Quincey explained.

Dean walked down to the road and looked across the chasm. The near vertical drop rose up again a hundred yards out. He squinted, and thought he might have seen something. A flash of light. Sun on metal. But he didn't see it again, and turned back.

"They had a spotter."

"What?" Starr asked.

Dean ignored him. "Rhett, you said you pulled up right behind them? The victims?"

"Almost as soon as they stopped. Why?"

Dean looked at Starr. "They weren't targetin' Rhett, but got lucky he was right there. I think they meant to kill these folks, and Rhett just happened to be here." Dean looked back at the volume of felled timber. "This would have been a big screen, but with the trees down, They could see exactly what was there. I guess once you start down that incline hidden up in the trees, there's no stoppin' you. Until you hit the car you're aimin' at." He looked back up the hill. "They meant to hit this SUV- but why? Any ID on them?"

"No ID on them." Quincey said. "But the plates came back to a Warren Cornelius outta California."

Another glint caught Dean's eye. It was coming from a slope next to where they were standing. He didn't see it again, so he walked back toward the others.

"Hey, Ranger! We'd like a word!"

Dean turned and saw the Tolberts.

As Dean started toward them, Quincey grabbed his shoulder. "Watch yourself. Those boys have been talking big about the ranger that killed their kin."

"I've met 'em," Dean answered. "They don't worry me much. Racist rednecks are, by definition stupid, and stupid always trumps dangerous."

"Fair enough, but their daddy isn't all that stupid," Quincey said ominously. "The previous sheriff put Joe Tolbert away about five years ago for drugs, but he's still calling the shots from prison. Word is, he wants revenge for all those involved in Lenny Tolbert's death."

"Of course he does," Dean said. "But Lenny wasn't his boy- Travis and Waylon are his sons."

"Yeah, but he raised Lenny and Virgil like his own after their daddy took a long snowmobile ride off a short cliff with a deep drop about fifteen years ago. Or so I hear,." Quincey said. "Before my time, obviously, but I heard it was a mess."

"Noted," Dean said as he sauntered over to the Tolberts. "Boys, how can I help you?"

Virgil glared at him, and spat at his feet. "You c'n die."

Dean half expected them to pull on him, but they didn't. Still, his hand went to rest on his holstered Colt Python. Just in case.

He squinted at them and said, "That kinda threat usually comes with some sort of physicality. Like, a draw, or at least an ominous flinch in my direction."

"We ain't gonna kill ya yet," Travis said. Then he cackled. "When ya least suspect it. Or when Daddy gets out of prison."

"Well, now, which is it?" Dean asked. "Cuz now I suspect it will be when Joe gets out, so I don't least suspect that. Does that mean you're gonna come for me *before* he gets out?"

Travis blinked. Waylon seemed to be doing mental calculations. Virgil just glared. "Jest watch your back, Ranger," he snarled. They turned to walk away.

"Hey Virgil?"

Virgil turned back. "Same goes for you. Oh, and what were you doin' up here?"

Virgil laughed, but Waylon answered. "Thought we'd done got lucky and got rid of Rhett Windsor. Had ta see fer ourselves."

Dean gave a thumbs up, and watched the rednecks walk away.

Returning to the small gathering of local and federal agents, Dean spoke to Quincey. "You have any idea where the paramilitary guys might be bivouacking?"

Quincey shook his head. "No. No reports of anything, no squatters or anything. Parks?"

Dean shook his head. "But if these folks were the target, I got a guy I can get to diggin' into Cornelius' background. Do it much faster than us Colorado lawmen."

"Faster than the FBI?" Starr asked condescendingly.

Dean ignored him. I can also check and see what new intel he's scared up on the VYPER team's movement."

The glint caught his eye again. He turned and saw it flash once more, hidden behind a large boulder on the nearest slope. "Quincey, Starr. I think the people we're looking for are watching us from over there." He pointed. "Of course, now they know we know, so they'll be gone before we get there. But why would they wait for us to show up, and then not take any of us out?" He looked at Starr. "Especially you, Starr. Since you're the one that got away."

"What's that supposed to mean?"

Dean shrugged. "I just found it odd that Stone- according to your story- killed your partner and Bethea, but you managed to get away. From a trained killer and military man."

"Careful with your accusations, Dean," Starr cautioned. "I'd hate for us to not be friends."

Dean smirked. "I've got enough friends, Starr."

"He spotted us."

Stone walked over to where Withers was squatting in a sniper position and looking through a scope down at the sight of their mayhem. "No worries. We will be long gone before he gets here. Just had to signal Starr."

"Why are we still working with that guy?" Withers asked. "The mob thing was a bust, and all it got us was wanted by all sorts of government alphabets. And you won't let me pop that ranger, even after he killed all our boys."

Stone didn't disagree with Withers' assessment, but as the commander of their group, he couldn't say that. Stone had bosses, too. And they had a mission that Withers wasn't fully read in on. Only Stone was. And it came from the top of the organization. From VYPER. It involved keeping friends close, and enemies closer.

"We follow orders, Withers, and they aren't complete, yet," Stone said. He watched as Benton hefted the gas tank up and filled their vehicle. "But soon, I'll have clearance to read you in. We will meet with Starr and the General. At Voight's hideaway. Maybe then we break with Starr and kill Dean."

Withers slid down from the rock. "It better be soon. I'm sick of bivouacking in nature. It's getting cold at night, and Benton refuses to cuddle."

Benton flipped Withers off with one hand and kept pouring the gas can with the other.

The rest of their team was hiking down to meet them. They had- as Dean had surmised- been spotting. Sharpe, their demolitions man, had been the one to blow the trees, which had been their signal. Sharpe, Simmons, and Trant had stayed in their perch atop the mountain until Stone and his men had cleared the scene with their vehicle, which they called the Behemoth.

"Soon as Benton finishes filling us up, and the others get here, we'll head to the meet-up point. Get the next orders." Stone hoped to himself that it would lead to them wrapping up the assignment.

He hated the mountains.

Chapter 5

Dean was driving again, having left Quincey with the cleanup of the road. The deputy seemed a trustworthy man, and especially since Starr had left, there was no concern about shenanigans at the crime scene. Starr left the scene around the time Dean did, but did not indicate where he was going. Dean chalked that lack of candor up to Starr's feelings of superiority as an FBI agent as much as Dean's own lingering suspicions of the Fed's corruption.

Dean still distrusted Starr. He had done more investigation of the man, and while he could not definitively say he was involved in the murder of Dean's wife, he couldn't rule him out either. Such was the nature of vast conspiracies, he supposed. They got vast because they had time to grow, and they had time to grow because they were well designed and hidden effectively. Perhaps his next destination could shed some light on that investigation as well as the one unrolling at the top of Garvin Pass.

The man Dean was going to see was another Fed. Homeland Security, to be exact.

They had met shortly after Amy's death, and in that meeting so began the long and winding road Dean was currently on toward avenging her murder.

A murder that seemed to be connected to the current events swirling around Eden Falls more and more each day.

Starr. The Denver Mob. The mysterious third man in Texas when she died, and *his* connections to a certain wealthy man residing in Eden Falls.

As Dean watched the trees blur outside his truck, his mind turned to those suspicions. To the possible links not only to organized crime but also to…

Amy…

The morning sun broke through the darkness of the bedroom as she threw open the blackout shades. The light caught her blonde hair and gave the appearance of a halo around her head. In spite of himself, Remmy smiled. "It's my day off, let me sleep, woman!" he groused playfully.

"It may be your day off from catching bad guys, but I have a long list of things you need to do for me today," Amy said in reply, her left hand on her hip and one eyebrow raised. Then she tossed a small notepad onto the bed.

"Ugh," Remmy sighed, and rolled over, covering his eyes with his arm. "Is it not enough I spend every workin' day puttin' away the worst of mankind? Do I also have to do-" he lifted up the pad and read, "Grocery shopping? And fixing the leaky faucet in the bathroom?" He groaned again, tossed the pad on the floor and rolled over, feigning he was trying to go back to sleep.

"You know, I put those same terrible people behind bars, too," she said, moving around the foot of the bed as she put her earrings in. She was dressed in a black pencil skirt and white blouse, ready to head into the district attorney's office. "And like we always say, no matter what we face, we got this. Just one breath at a time." She paused to let her favorite little phrase sink in. Then, with a smirk, added, "In fact, if not for me, most of your cases would never get a conviction," she teased.

She got too close to Remmy's reach, and his arm snaked out and grabbed her hand, pulling her onto the bed with him. She squealed in playful protest as he pulled her close. "I know this isn't on your list, but…"

She put a hand on his face and pushed him away. "I'm already close to being late." She held his face in her hand, leaned in, and kissed him. They lingered in the kiss, then she pushed herself up. "Later. Tonight." She walked toward the bathroom, paused and looked back. "*If* you get groceries *and* put them in the right places."

Remmy raised up on one elbow and cracked a half-smile. "You know how much I love you, right?"

Amy blinked and smiled. "You know how much I love *you?*"

The smile became a full one. But his eyes were no longer playful. They were kind, sincere. "I'm proud of you, Amy. You are fearless and have a genuinely good soul. I meet a lot of lawyers that are neither. On both sides of the courtroom." He knew she was in a hurry to get to work because she was trying a child abuse case that day. She was giving the closing argument that would put a really bad person away for a long time. It had been the kind of case that Amy brought home with her, the kind that gave her nightmares that had woken them both several times. But she had pressed on, fought for that child that no one else was fighting for.

A tear touched the corner of Amy's eye. She walked back to the bed, leaned down, and kissed him again. "Thank you," she said. "Remmy, I…" she paused. "Nevermind."

Dean sat up. "What? You know my detective senses just got set off by that pregnant pause."

Amy sighed. "Remmy, I don't want you to lose this. This…kindness. On your days off, I see it. The old you. Before the Rangers. Before the church stuff went down…when you were a minister who just wanted to love people, to encourage them, to make them smile. I don't see that much anymore."

Dean didn't say anything for a minute, so she continued. "It's just…I bring home some sick stuff sometimes. But you spend most days in the middle of it. And I see it working on you. Pulling you down." She looked at him. "You don't smile much anymore, Remmy. And it worries me."

"I'm fine," Dean replied.

"You can't do this forever, Remmy Dean," she said flatly. "Your soul is too good for that world you live in. I worry about what would happen to you if you dwelt in that darkness for a little too long. I don't want to lose you. *I've* seen too many cops go to that darkness and not come back."

Dean chuckled to himself. "But I've got you to bring me back to the light, don't I? My angel, right?'

Amy smiled. "Always." The smile slipped a bit. "But Remmy, if something ever happened to me, promise me something?"

Dean didn't like that line of thinking, but he bit anyway. "What?"

"If something happens to me, please…leave the Rangers. Leave law enforcement. Do something that brings light to the world- get out of the darkness."

Dean blinked and didn't answer.

"C'mon, Remmy. Remember. One breath at a time. Promise me, Remington Dean."

After a pause, he nodded. "Promise."

Dean pulled into the parking lot of the Homeland Security offices, which just happened to be housed in a small state prison.

Something about budget cuts.

The prison housed those convicted of drug crimes, usually with a bid of less than ten years to serve. That facility consisted of several drab concrete buildings and copious amounts of razor wire and chain link fencing.

It was minimum security, so there weren't walls, just chain link and barbed wire. It gave the men milling about the yard an animal-like quality that was almost sad. Some convicts were milling about in the yard, trustees, most likely. One of them seemed to note Dean's arrival, and stopped whatever he was doing to stare him down. A man of about fifty, he had a deep set tan from years working outside. His hair was thin and grayish brown, with thick mutton chops that wound around to a mustache. A deep scar ran across his forehead just under his hairline, and he glared with blue eyes filled with hate and intelligence. Though he bore a striking resemblance to the three rednecks who had been sightseeing up the mountain, Dean knew at once that he was not like his kin. He was a genuine threat, a man of mind and muscle. Even though he was older, Dean knew he was not someone to take lightly.

Joe Tolbert.

Joe smiled coldly, narrowed his eyes, raised a hand, and pointed at Dean. He made a motion like he was firing a gun, dropped his hand, and turned back to whatever task he had been doing before Dean arrived.

Ashleigh noted that Sadie winced a bit as she sat down at the small outdoor booth beside a salad shop where they had a weekly lunch date. "You still feeling that bullet wound?"

Sadie made a face. "Doctor says it might take a while. Going to rehab and making good progress, but not enough for my liking."

"Anything less than miraculous recovery is too slow for you," Ashleigh said, taking a bite of her kale salad.

"True," Sadie said. "But it doesn't stop me from doing my job, so I'm back at it. Sitting in an interrogation room. Every day."

"You sound disappointed."

"Dean gets to run all around and Ben and Walt and I are stuck," she ripped the cover off of her salad. "It's not fair."

"So, go out in the field," Ashleigh said.

Sadie threw up a hand. "Can't. Even though I'm medically cleared, Spitz won't sign off on me. I'm just bored. We can't get anywhere with these VYPER guys, and Fletcher thinks it's all a game. Which, by the way, he did finally give us something." Sadie paused, as if she was considering whether to ask her next question. Finally, she made her choice. "You talk to Brent since… everything?"

Ashleigh shrugged. "See him around, but after I quit, I think it made things weird."

"How so?"

Ashleigh thought for a moment. The idea that things between her and Brent Chase had been weird had never been spoken by her, and now she had to put logic behind the feeling she had gotten. "I think he thinks I don't trust him any more."

"You don't," Sadie said flatly.

"I wouldn't say that."

"I would. I did," Sadie said. "And you're right. He was involved in some shady stuff, and it put you in danger. The question is, do you think he still is?"

"Involved in criminal activities?" Ashleigh asked. It hadn't crossed her mind. "I don't think so. I know business really turned around for him, and there aren't any of those Denver mob guys around. The Windsors are, though. I see them around there a lot now. Especially the blonde one. Nigel?"

"Why do you think that is?"

Ashleigh shrugged again. "Maybe they are doing legitimate business there. I hear the Windsors are buying land and making some investments, and Brent has a realtor shingle in his window now."

Sadie laughed. "Guess Brent took Fletcher's old job, too."

The roar of a motorcycle caught Ashleigh's attention. It was a distinctive sound, a memorable one. The way the engine popped and whined…it was…familiar.

Too familiar.

"You okay?" Sadie asked, looking concerned. "Bad kale?"

Ashleigh shook her head. "Just old memories." She looked down and began playing with her salad.

"I haven't heard any word on his whereabouts, Ashleigh."

She looked up and saw Sadie's concern still etched on her face. "But he is out?"

"Robert Hesse was released six months ago," Sadie said. "He had been in for killing a guy while doing bodyguard duties, right?" Ashleigh nodded. "Apparently, he was a model prisoner, and the client he was protecting had good lawyers. He got out early, and hasn't been seen much since."

Ashleigh sighed. She was looking down at her plate and when she looked up, she gasped.

Robert Hesse- her ex-husband, her abuser- was standing across the street, looking at her. "Sadie!" she screamed.

Sadie followed her gaze and turned to look. "That's Robert!" The detective rose and began walking toward the street. A jacked up jeep pulled in front of Hesse as he waved at Ashleigh, but when it passed, he was gone. Sadie was looking up and down the street, but saw no sign of him. She returned to find Ashleigh breathing rapidly and trying to calm herself.

"He- he found me!" Ashleigh exclaimed.

Sadie sat next to her and wrapped an arm around her. "Maybe, but that also means we found him." She took Ashleigh by the chin and turned her face so they were eye to eye. "And now we get the law to protect you."

She appreciated Sadie Donovan, her friend, but was thankful that she was also *Detective* Donovan. But still…

"What if that's not enough?"

Sadie smiled. "Then we find another way to keep you safe. We still have yet to go to the gun range, right?"

Ashleigh returned the smile shakily. "It's way past time, isn't it?"

Dean was sitting in an office, waiting for the Homeland agent. His mind went back to his ranger days. The inter-agency give and take was never his favorite. Really, working with anyone was never his favorite. That much hadn't changed about his persona. As remembered the interesting folks he'd worked with, Dean thought of all the jailhouse snitches he had met with, trying to get a leg up on a bigger fish. The one that floated to his mind in that moment was a man who had been caught running guns for someone. A big player in Texas, the biggest case Dean had ever caught with the Rangers.

And the only case he ever worked with his wife.

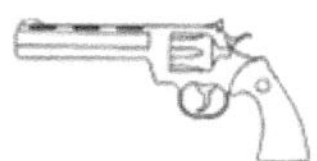

"Isn't it exciting?" Amy asked, sitting next to Dean in the interrogation room of the prison.

"Dealing with a scumbag? Not particularly," Dean replied.

Amy gave him a look, and he couldn't help but smile. She had been much happier since she got the conviction of that child abuser. And when she was happier, he was happier. But the promise she had made him make, to leave law enforcement- it had not left his thoughts.

"Amy, I've been thinking about that promise you made me make."

"To love, honor, and cherish me forever?" she said with a flirtatious smile.

"Well, it goes with that," Dean said, turning in his chair to face her. "The one about leavin' the Rangers. Gettin' away from all the darkness- after this case, why don't we both do it?"

"What?" she asked, surprise evident in her voice.

"There are consultant firms I could work at, you could do family law," he paused. "We could move to Colorado like you've always wanted."

"Remmy- this is out of the blue," she said, but not dismissively. "Can we get this interview done, and talk about it tonight? I just want to get this guy's information and agreement, get him released into our custody, and close this case." Her smile broadened. "But I like the sound of that conversation you want to have."

The door creaked open, and in walked the witness.

He had shaggy blonde hair, and bright green eyes. About average height, he had a scared look etched into his face. He was noticeably without a lawyer.

"Is your lawyer joining us?" Amy asked.

He shook his head. "Fired him this morning."

"Why?" Dean asked.

"Said the deal was bad for me. Shouldn't do it. But I wanna do it."

Amy and Dean exchanged looks. Then Amy said, "Alright. This conversation is being recorded. You are going to give us information on the organization you were running guns for in exchange for an early release- correct?"

"Yes, ma'am."

"Oh, almost forgot," Amy said. "What is your name, for the record?"

"Grant Kolbe- with an 'e' at the end."

"Sorry to keep you," Elmore Pickett said as he came into the room. Pickett was in his early thirties, African American, and sported a pencil thin beard. He was lean, Dean might go so far as to call him gangly. His jaw was angular, his chin pointed, and that always made Dean think about the devil. Elmore Pickett was a good guy, but not a *good* guy. Played for the right team, but played dirty.

Dean leaned back in his chair and crossed his arms. "Had a boss once, sat in an office a few floors above me. He was the 'big guy.' Loved to act all important and special. But us grunts, we never thought of him as a leader. Now, my CO, Company Major Royder, now he was a man who exuded respect. We loved him, and it drove the 'big guy' nuts. So, the boss started givin' Royder heck. Nitpickin' every little thing, micro-managing, and even started to give Royder junk assignments. Not the easy stuff- no, he gave him the stuff likely to blow up and end a career if it wasn't handled with utmost care. You know what happened?"

"Hello to you, too, Dean," Pickett said. "What does this have to do with the news you bring me today?"

Ignoring Pickett, Dean leaned forward and made a circling motion with his finger. "We grunts, we regular Rangers, started to rally round Royder. Now, we'd never openly talk poorly about the 'big guy,' but we all knew that our attitude had soured. *If* someone had given us a chance, we would have blown off all kinds of steam about how bad the big guy was. As we saw it, Royder was the only reason we stayed with the unit, and if he was hung out to dry? Well, we'd hang right there with him. If only someone who had the authority to set the 'big buy' straight would have asked us about the situation, we'd have unloaded. And not one of us would have felt like a rat."

"That feels like you're threatening me, But I have no idea why." Pickett sat heavily in his chair.

Dean smiled. "Couple got murdered this morning. All signs point to VYPER. All signs point to them being the target."

"Still not seeing the connection."

"*If* it was a targeted hit, then the person pulling the strings of these military guys just exposed them. And for what? Some part of the bigger plot- or a petty vendetta. If it's the latter, then those boys probably aren't feelin' so good about the big boss right now."

Pickett grimaced. "It's a stretch."

"Warren Cornelius."

Pickett sat up. "The bitcoin guy?"

"No idea, but that's who the car belonged to," Dean said. "No ID, it was taken. And neither the man nor the woman could be identified because of the trauma. But this fella was not what I would call a typical drug runner type. A little too…high falutin.'"

Pickett laughed. "Homespun. Love it. Look, if it is *that* Cornelius, then it would seem odd that he just *happened* to get whacked by the guys were are looking for. Especially considering what my friends over in the FBI white collar division have been investigating."

"About Cornelius?"

Pickett nodded. "Some clients reported irregularities. Things not adding up. They've built a decent case that he's defrauded at least two clients of north of a million each."

"Xavier Voight one of those, by any chance?"

"Nope," Pickett said. Then smiled broadly. "But he is a client."

Dean bit his lip in thought. "So, maybe Voight got scammed, but decided to handle it himself. Use his rogue black ops team that just *happened* to be in the same neighborhood to kill him, and then he could deny and say it was them on a rampage."

"It's thin," Pickett said.

"So are you, but I still recognize you have some value," Dean quipped. "Occasionally."

"Jerk."

"Speaking of FBI-"

"Nope- nothing there, Dean," Pickett said. "Everyone agrees that Starr is a grade A dick, but he's clean. No evidence of even a hint of bad faith there." Pickett put his elbows on the table. "I know you connected him to Texas when she died, but he's FBI. He gets around. And until you find evidence- real stuff, not just a vague feeling, tread lightly. Dude is decorated."

"So was Royder, if you recall," Dean countered. "It looks and smells a lot like to me."

"Yeah, but didn't you just tell me that you and your fellow Rangers would do anything for Royder? People have Starr's back."

Dean couldn't argue with that.

"Dean, when I pulled you in, got you that job at Parks so you could also liaise with me, I told you to keep your eyes on the case- THE case, not YOUR case. I can pull your interagency link if I think you're pushing the wrong buttons."

"What's Walker got to say about that?" Dean asked. Pickett squirmed. "People have my back, too."

Pickett considered this, then said, "Fair enough. You have a tiny bit of rope here. Don't hang yourself. Now, about those images I got. We commandeered a satellite to shoot some nice mountain shots recently, and we think we have a pattern of movement that could be your favorite little mercenary team.”

Pickett spun his computer console around, and Dean saw the familiar topography of the mountains just on the edge of Rocky Mountain National Park. The very area he had hiked that morning to find the body.

“Huh,” he said, pointing. “We had a body found there this morning. Eyes gouged out, big X cut across his chest. My M.E. is working on that one, too. Could be connected, but doesn’t seem like their typical tactic.”

“Sounds like cartel,” Pickett said. “But they aren’t active in that region because of our other problems. Serial?”

“Checking that.”

“I’ll run it, too. See if anything pops,” Pickett said, making a note. “The satellite seems to indicate some evidence of long-term habitation here- and here. One more there-”

“Wait,” Dean said. “That last one. That’s near a village or something?”

Pickett looked closely at a small scribble on the picture. “Yeah. Unincorporated town. No know name.”

"Send me the coordinates. I think I might know what it is- and if I do, then they are casing targets."

"For what?"

"Nothing good."

"Ah, vague Dean is back," Pickett said. "You and I have worked together for what, almost four years now?"

"More or less."

"I still haven't cracked you. I mean, you are one of the toughest- and quite frankly deadliest- men I've met," Pickett said. "You've killed a lot of men, haven't you?"

"Not today," Dean replied with a shrug.

"I'm serious. You think killing a lot of men might have an effect on your own eternal destination? Like, God frowns on killing, right?"

"Just because I'm good at it, doesn't mean I enjoy it. But to answer your question…yeah. I think about that all the time."

Pickett asked, "I've always wondered, why do you pray for the guys you killed? Do you, what…tell them about Jesus before they die?"

"Yeah."

"Why?"

Dean shrugged. "I believe that all souls go to Heaven or Hell. If I send someone there prematurely, I wanna make sure I give them the chance to choose the better of two options."

"So, guilt. Got it. And I suppose your previous employment has something to do with that?"

"I *was* a minister."

"Yeah, but 'was' is a heavy word. You really still believe in that stuff, after all you've seen."

"I have to, or what's it all worth?"

Chapter 6

He saw Ashleigh walk in, and a rush of excitement came over him. His friend had come back, and, he felt like they were all good again.

Then Brent saw her face, the terror in her eyes, and realized she wasn't alone. Sadie Donovan was with her, and she looked just as pissed as Ashleigh looked scared.

"What happened?" he asked, rushing forward to console her, but Ashleigh had made a beeline for the booth to his left.

So, Sadie replied, "Her ex showed up."

"Ex?" It wasn't something they talked about a lot, or much at all. He knew she'd had a bad break-up, but that was about it.

Sadie shook her head. "Yeah. She's pretty shook up. Could you get her-"

"Levi, get a double espresso with five shots of vanilla and five shots of caramel. And almond milk. Detective, I don't know your order."

Sadie smiled at him, her intensity fading for a moment, and said, "Make it two."

He caught Levi's attention and gave the order, pointing out their table.

Then Brent made his way over to the booth, looking around to make sure no Windsors were present. He slid in opposite the two women and his mind raced back to the man who'd asked about her. "I think he came in here, looking for you. Black hair, blue eyes and tats on the arm?"

Ashleigh nodded. Her eyes were red with tears, and for the first time since he'd met Ashleigh Storms, he thought she could be scared. What had this guy done to her?

Of course, he knew better than to ask. "What can I do? I'd call the cops, but I guess that's taken care of." He nodded to Sadie, who gave a grim smile.

"Why am I so shaken?" Ashleigh asked no one in particular. Levi set twin coffee cups on the table as the door chimed.

Brent turned to see not just the blonde ponytail of Nigel Windsor, but the faux hawk of Zeke, arguably the dumbest Windsor. They scanned the room, gave Brent a look, then went to their usual table.

They could wait.

Ashleigh continued to audibly process her thoughts. "In the last few months, I've been shot at, nearly burned alive, shot at some more. Never did I just fall into this…this sobbing mess." She took a sip of her coffee. "Why does that man have such a debilitating effect on me? Really-I'm genuinely asking."

Sadie looked at Brent, and he could tell she knew something Brent didn't. Cautiously, Sadie said, "It might not be normal for you, but it's normal for your experience. There is no easy workaround for it. But…you can- and should- distract yourself. Let me take care of Hesse."

Something in the way Sadie said those words gave Brent a chill. He was piecing together that this Hesse had done something terrible to Ashleigh. Worse than just a nasty breakup, sure. But he didn't like where his suspicions were going so he stopped following them. Instead, he tried to be helpful. "If it's a distraction you need, I may have one. I met a woman who works for Xavier Voight today. PR or something- I have her card. Maybe you could approach him about a story? Like why is he choosing Eden Falls as his base of operations?"

Ashleigh wiped her eyes. "He doesn't do interviews."

"I bet he would for Ashleigh Storms," Sadie said, taking up Brent's case.

"I'll get her card," Brent said, rising.

"Yo, coffee man!" Zeke called out. "Need ta talk ta ya."

"And two coffee blacks," Nigel added.

Brent walked to the front register and grabbed the card and the black coffee carafe.

"I'll get those guys, you talk to your friends," Levi offered.

Brent looked between the two booths and shrugged. "Nah. I gotta talk to those guys. It's fine." He walked to Ashleigh and Sadie and set the card on the table, then turned, snaked his finger between two coffee cup handles and went to the Windsor booth. "What?" he asked, letting his frustration show as he poured their coffee.

"Shipment comin' in tonight," Nigel said. "Gonna need ya to do your numbers magic and make it look like a- I dunno- coffee drop?"

"How much?"

"How would we know how much coffee is comin' in?" Zeke asked.

Brent sighed and rolled his eyes. "How much of *your* shipment?" *Morons.*

Nigel shrugged. "Twenty guns. Kilo of H. Buncha 'shrooms and LSD. So… twenty K?"

"Are you insane? No one orders twenty thousand dollars of coffee supplies!"

"How are we 'sposed to know the cost of coffee?" Zeke asked, irritated.

"Oh, that's right. You never pay for it. Why would you know?" Brent pushed right back. "Wait- I thought Rhett wanted no hard drugs?"

The Windsors exchanged a look before Nigel said, "What the cuz don't know won't hurt 'em."

Yeah, but it might kill me, Brent thought to himself. How was he going to hide that much product in the books?

After looking over the map some more, and discussing some possible investigation angles, Pickett suggested they go for a walk. They left the office situated in the prison and walked past the prison yard again. Tolbert was still out there, but seemed not to notice their passage.

Pickett put his hands in his pockets and sighed. "Dean, how long have we been working together?"

"Four years and some change, I figure."

"That's right. I came to you because I saw you as a valuable asset. And because you needed something to get you back on the right path," Pickett stepped closer to Dean, his tone becoming heavier, almost threatening. "*I* got you in with Parks. And you've fed Homeland info about threats to national security coming into the Rockies and in turn we've let you run your little side op. Even fed *you* intel to help. And let's not forget what went down with Kolbe. So, Dean, why don't I have your trust? I only ask because while I have been keeping tabs on you, you seem to be *very* trusting of those CBI guys and that Eden Falls detective. But you keep me at a distance. Why is that?"

Dean stopped and turned to look Pickett square in the eyes. "Trust ain't earned by favors and nudges. It's earned by bein' in the trenches with someone, and you and I've never drawn guns together. Sure, you help me out, but how do I know you aren't just using me to get what *you* want?"

"It's not what *I* want, Dean," Pickett countered. "It's what your government needs to put away a dangerous group of people. Xavier Voight has made friends with some questionable people. People that have agendas *not* necessarily in keeping with the good of mankind. And if Voight were a corner store robber, it wouldn't be a big deal. But he has infinitely deep pockets that buy crazy access. So I don't think I'm out of line in putting some pressure on you to build a case. Sooner rather than later."

"And why aren't you also workin' the case?" Dean asked. "I'm working this alone- and that means the people I trust, they don't know about you. Because you asked me to keep quiet. So if you want things to move faster, let me loop them in. If I'd wanted cloak and dagger stuff, I'dve joined the CIA."

"Fine," Pickett said, after a pause. "Bring them in, and that AUSA Kho, too. And get me that info by our secure channels so it's all above board. Then we'll see how to proceed." Pickett turned to leave, then added, "Man, you have got some serious trust issues."

Dean watched the man leave.

"I come by it honest."

Dean took a deep breath and slowly let it out.

He was anxious, but then, he always was before a breach. Surrounded by SWAT in tactical gear, loaded for bear with heavy weapons and about to go through a door that hid people armed with potentially even heavier weapons had that effect.

His nerves that day had less to do with the situation on the other side of the wall than usual. It wasn't even that Amy was waiting just out of harm's way to see the results. It wasn't the fact that the bust was a big one, ending a particularly virulent branch of an organized crime unit from snaking its way into Texas.

It was the specific target of the raid. The boss of that particular tentacle.

And he was a cop.

Grant Kolbe's information that there was a corrupt cop wasn't shocking in itself. It was *who* the cop was that made Dean anxious.

His partner, Jude Randall, looked back at him. He mouthed, "You okay?" and Dean nodded. A rivulet of sweat ran down from his cowboy hat. He hated that the Rangers made you wear the hat (it got *hot* in Texas without headgear), but he hated it more today.

Randall, the senior Ranger of their duo, shouted, "Go!" and the no-knock breach went down.

The door crashed open and SWAT poured in. There were shouts and yells, a few shots popped off, then Randall and Dean went through the door to the warehouse. It was dim and smoky inside, and Dean had to squint to see the people moving inside. SWAT had subdued everyone pretty quickly, but there were still a couple resisting. *Nothing to worry about*, Dean told himself. He walked over to a table with several bricks of heroin, some baggies with weed, and four automatic weapons. Six other tables were scattered around the space that looked more or less just like that and dozens of shelves with varying levels and types of illicit supply. Dean guessed the financial cost of the bust was in the low seven-figures.

He looked over to Randall, who was looking around the room. Not at anything in particular, just the room. Not the drugs. Not the guns.

Not the men.

And those men were looking at everyone but Paul Randall.

Dean sighed.

"Paul?"

Now it was Paul who looked nervous. "Huh?"

"Why'd you do it?" Dean's hand went to his holstered Colt. If it went sideways, he couldn't bring himself to blast his friend with the shotgun. It had to be personal- because the betrayal was personal. "How did they get you to go over?"

Randall was breathing heavily, his nostrils flared and his eyes widened. "W-what do you mean?"

"You know, Paul."

Randall's eyes narrowed. "What are you saying, Remmy?"

Dean didn't answer, but his hand rested on the butt of his gun.

Randall scoffed. "After all our years together…"

Dean took one more deep breath. "Paul Randall, you have the right to remain silent-"

Two SWAT moved to apprehend the Ranger, who was too focused on Dean to even try to pull. "This is a mistake, Dean! I want a lawyer!"

Dean finished reciting the rights, and Randall was escorted out, right past Amy and her guest- Grant Kolbe. Upon seeing Kolbe, Randall began to yell and curse. In the midst of the yelling, Dean heard his former partner say, "You set me up, Kolbe!" Dean's gaze fell on Kolbe, who was uncuffed. His deal got him time served on a lesser drug charge, so after the raid, he was free to go.

As Randall shouted at him, Dean saw a look on Kolbe's face. It was a look of…a man who just got away with something.

Remington Dean's stomach dropped.

Dean's phone rang and he brought it up to his ear as he walked out of the prison. "What's up, Mike?"

"I see you're at the prison. Wanna grab a bite for dinner?"

"While I am flattered at the offer, I am a bit concerned as to how you ascertained my location."

Mike laughed. "Fair enough. I have all the vehicles my agents use lo-jacked. You cover so much territory, I gotta keep an eye on everyone.

Plus, you aren't the only one with trust issues.(Dean wondered if he was listening in, too.) What do you want to eat?"

Dean thought. There was a surprisingly good Mexican food place in town, run by a couple from New Mexico. Dean liked it because it was hard to find good Mexican food north of the Red River, so he said, "Olde Sante Fe sounds good. See you in ten?"

Nathaniel Stone and his men pulled up to the rendezvous point and put their Behemoth in park. The giant Humvee was outfitted with extra armor and a road grader attached to the front end. Good for clearing trees and roads alike. Benton drove, as usual. He was their driver and heavy arms man. Withers was the sniper, and a smart-mouth arrogant SOB. The three other men from their team had finally joined them for the ride to the meet up. Sharpe, their munitions expert, wore a balaclava rolled up on his head like a toboggan. Trant and Simmons were the grunts, infantry men.

Good ones, too. Aside from the late Link Elliott, the VYPER elite squad was all there. The current line-up, anyway. There had been the one man who had been snatched up by Xavier Voight for personal security a few years earlier.

Robert Hesse.

Their team had seen action in the Middle East when they were in the military. Stone had been the Chief Warrant Officer for Trant, Simmons, and Benton during that time. Hesse had been the Master Sergeant for their squad when they were in-country. So they had been his first recruits to the team. Withers was a Marine, and that came with all the trappings of arrogance one would expect. He'd replaced Hesse when the call came down, and from the jump, Stone knew it was a mistake. Hesse was intense, scary, and probably crazy. But he was steady. Withers was wild, intense, scary, and definitely crazy. But not stable.

Link had been the only SEAL and a stabilizing influence for the team. A few other men had been in their initial ten-man team for VYPER, back when they did special ops overseas. Link had taken the lead on that part of the team when they came to Eden Falls.

All of them were now dead.

Most at the hand of Remington Dean.

Link had been Stone's favorite. The strongest of the team, but he had been no match for Dean's draw.

"Up there," Stone said, pointing to the parked gray sedan.

Waiting for them was Chris Starr, leaning against his government issue car, rubbing his shoulder and a scowl on his face. He barely waited for them to exit the Behemoth before laying into them. "What were you thinking, hitting the civvies?"

God, Stone hated Starr. He'd taken great pleasure in putting a bullet in the man, even if it was for show. Stone wished he could have done more damage. Wanted the SOB to feel it for a bit.

They were on opposite sides of a tenuous alliance. Stone was Denver mob muscle, and he thought he was elegant and James Bond like. He looked down on the VYPER team as brutes. Dumb military hammers to his refined FBI scalpel.

Stone sauntered over to Starr and put his hands on his hips. "We thought it was Windsor, coming down the mountain. Withers had clocked him, we set the charge, just like Sharpe said we should and we blew the trees. Didn't see the rich folks until it was too late." It was a lie. They had orders to hit the couple.

Voight's orders.

"And once the Behemoth gets going down hill, she don't stop," Benton added in his booming bass voice.

Starr glared at Stone. "Bull. Dean knows you hit them on purpose. Sussed it out at the scene while I watched. What's your play?"

"Our play is to follow orders. And not have to tell snotty feebs anything," Withers snorted.

"You know how to play nice with others? Withers, is it? Well, I don't either," Starr snapped back. "Stick to shooting that overcompensation you call a weapon and shut your mouth."

Withers turned red. "You want me to, I'll show you how good a shot I am. 'Specially from this distance."

Both men bowed up at each other, and Starr's hand was too close to his pistol for comfort.

Stone stepped between them. Starr was a dick, but he was a capable man with a gun. Withers was clearly underestimating the man. Any man who betrayed his government for the mob was a man you never turned your back on.

And the man who betrayed the mob, as well? That's one you never underestimated. If you did, it would cost you.

The growl of an engine caught their attention, and they turned to see a massive truck pulling up to their location. It was a deep blue American-made thing, lifted, and a dually.

A tall man dropped out of the driver's side, putting on a black cowboy hat as he did. He wore a black canvas jacket and jeans that dropped over black boots. Beneath the hat, a black-haired and bearded man was chewing on a toothpick and gazing at them through dark blue eyes.

For a multi-millionaire investor, Xavier Voight was not what you would have expected. Stone had known him for years, having been with VYPER from the small start-up it had been. Even then, Voight was hands off, preferring to let the man getting out of the passenger-side run the often-times gray area operations the paramilitary men engaged in. But hands-off didn't mean in-the-dark.

The man with Voight was Clayton Young, or as he liked to be called, "The General."

He wasn't.

He was a former JAG lawyer who led the team in name only. Especially the teams like

Stone's. The ones who got their hands dirty. Really, Young just set schedules and cleaned up legal messes.

Stone hated him. Voight tolerated him. Stone suspected the only reason Voight kept him around was because he needed the 'Y' in VYPER to mean something.

"Seems we have an issue, boys," Voight drawled. He was from somewhere in the south, Stone didn't know where. Had a ranch in Texas, once, then expanded to Montana. He was a smart guy, invested wisely, but made enemies. So he hired Stone as a bodyguard- along with Hesse. Pretty soon, he saw the lucrative nature of personal security, which led to a pretty hefty set of contracts to do security overseas. And so VYPER was born. "Now, you had a job, Nathaniel. Take out Cornelius, and leave as little trace of yourself as possible. You left enough for that infernal Ranger to sniff you out, and now you got collateral damage. See, Young here has already been contacted by ATF. Seems Dean suggested to them at the scene that it it might have been you guys. And some deputy sheriff said 'Tannerite,' so they started drooling, thinking they got something on me." Voight paused for a breath.

"And now I gotta loop Starr in. Wanted to keep him and the mob boys out of this one, but that ship sailed and sank." He turned to Starr. "I had investments with Cornelius. The dick was stealing from me, so I had our mutual friend, Hesse, send an invite to my cabin for he and the missus. God, Warren was a doofus. Stealing from and thinking that not only did I *not* know, but was so oblivious as to invite him for a relaxing weekend. So, they are dead, the cops-" he looked at Starr-" the *real* cops are onto VYPER and will see the connections I had with the Cornelius folks. Not lookin' too good for me." He paused again, then added as an afterthought, "Shame you had to off the girl, though. She was hot," Withers nodded lecherously and Benton shoved him.

Stone swallowed hard. He'd faced terrorists, IEDs, snipers, and tanks. But when Xavier Voight was angry, it was a different kind of fear. Somewhere along the way, Voight went from rancher to organized crime. Not for money, but for power. He bought politicians, ran protection rackets with other branches of VYPER. And he had his eyes on Denver. He'd turned Starr against Bethea, laid out the assassination plan. Wanted Starr to take over Bethea's branch of the

Denver mob, then find out the identity of the head man. Then VYPER was to take him out.

The reason they hadn't was that the man was impossible to identify, let alone find.

But as he was working that angle, Voight was also trying to acquire land around Eden Falls. He had made it his home, and wanted to bring other people who were like him to the area. So he began buying up land that was for sale. If it wasn't, he was driving people off land they had held for generations. He knew about the lithium mines the Windsors were working, but he also knew they were depleted. No, he didn't want what was under the land, he wanted the land. To develop into a community for rich, powerful, white men to be able to bring their families and hunt and collaborate. See, Xavier Voight was what you might call…a racist monster.

But he paid well.

"Sorry, Mr. Voight," Stone said, his voice fighting to stay strong. "We didn't know Windsor was going to be there. Got too far into the op to pull out, and Windsor was too far from the scene to track down and eliminate. Dean… well, he needs to be dealt with sooner rather than later."

"Rhett Windsor is not of our concern. I've taken steps to remove his resistance to our intentions without bloodshed." Voight bit his lip. "But Remington Dean? I'm personally far too familiar with that name. Haven't met the man, personally, but I've encountered his interference before. Dean is always right on your trail? You just one step ahead of him?"

Knowing better than to disagree, Stone replied, "Yes sir. That seems about the situation."

Voight looked at Young, wearing an aviator's jacket complete with that wool collar and some medals pinned to it that he had not earned. It looked like he was going to ask him a question, but thought better of it. Then he looked at Starr. "Chris, can you do something about Dean? Get him moved off the case?"

Starr shook his head. "His boss has pull, somehow. There is someone else keeping him in the mix, and I can't get a feel for it. But, I am being brought in to fill Bethea's role in Denver. Officially."

"Well, that's something. They don't suspect our connection?"

Starr laughed. "I've been a double-agent for ten years. I know how to cover my trail."

"But no ID on the big guy?"

The smile disappeared. "No. I don't think there will be for a while. He uses proxies to deliver orders. Proxies who get notifications from burner phones and dummy emails. He's the best I've ever seen. They call him the Ghost for a reason."

"I like that. The Ghost. Make that trend," he said to Young, who acted like he had no idea what was going on. It might be because Voight didn't know what "trend" meant, or that Young was just stupid. "So, Starr, keep doing what you're doing. Stone- you need help. And a new directive. I want Dean dead. He's the priority."

A rumbling sound interrupted them. Voight turned to see a motorcycle roll up to their gathering. "And here is your help."

The engine died and Robert Hesse got off, a pistol strapped to his thigh. He ran a hand through his jet black hair, and cracked rolled his head to crack his neck. As he walked toward them, he stopped and shook hands with Starr, saying, "Agent, it's been a minute."

"Hesse," Starr said.

When Hesse saw Stone, he broke into a huge smile. "Nate, old man- great to see you!" Hesse wrapped him in a bear hug, and when he pulled away, he said, "It has been too long. Taking that rap for the punk that hassled Voight kept the band from getting back together before now. But no more!"

Stone was glad to see his old friend, but something was nagging at the back of his mind. Why was he here? Was he just back to being Voigt's body man? Or was his role bigger? Because Stone knew full well what Robert Hesse was capable of. He was a friend, yes, but he was psychotic. Not just a military cold, a cold-blooded killer. And then Stone remembered- Hesse's wife was in Eden Falls.

"Say, Voight old buddy," Hesse said to the boss. "I got a call from a prison guard, fella I made friends with when I was in. Told me some park ranger was talking to one of the Homeland agents headquartered in their house. Says this Ranger- Dean- will probably be headed back home after dark tonight." Hesse looked at Stone. "Sounds to me like a perfect time to take out a problem." Hesse raised his eyebrows, and those deep blue eyes were as cold as ice.

Voight laughed boisterously. "See, now aren't you glad he's back? Starr, see if you can find out who this Homeland guy is, and why Dean is meeting with him. Stone, take the Ranger out. Hit and run, leave no trace. Then we make a move on that settlement up near the mountain top. After that, your squad could use a break. Someplace tropical, maybe." Voight leaned in close to Stone's face. "But if you fail- well…"

Voight didn't have to finish the sentence. Stone knew the score. He glanced over at Hesse.

So, that's why he's here, Stone thought to himself.

Chapter 7

Ben was sitting at the desk he shared with Walt in the Eden Falls police office, idly typing up notes from the interrogation of Quentin Fletcher when the door to the bullpen flew open.

Sadie stormed in, and immediately made a beeline for him. Her face was red, almost to the same shade as her hair. Ben almost made a comment, then stopped himself. "What's up?" he asked instead.

"Ashleigh's ex is in town," Sadie said, pacing beside their desk. "Robert Hesse. Real bad guy, and that's all I'm gonna say." She was moving back and forth like a typewriter, not looking at them.

"Can we help?" Walt offered. That stopped her.

"Can we see who his employer was when he went to jail? A manslaughter charge. About five years ago- killed a guy while acting as a security consultant."

"Bodyguard?" Walt asked, as Ben began to search the database for the case file.

"Something like that. Ashleigh doesn't talk much about it."

Ben found the file. "Doesn't say who he was protecting… but he was employed by a company called…Bastrop Arms."

"Can you look that up?" Sadie asked, biting her nails.

"I can look that up right now," Ben replied.

"Look, I know you are close with Ashleigh, but I have two questions-" Walt said, turning in his chair to look directly at Sadie, who had resumed pacing. "One, where is she now? And two- why are *you* so worked up?"

"At the Book Brew, with Brent Chase. She's working him for some information, but honestly, I think it's the only place she felt safe in town. Familiarity, I guess," Sadie stopped and looked at them both. "I shouldn't tell you this… and you can never say I told you. But you need to know. Robert Hesse was abusive. She's told me bits and pieces over the last month. And I've been… looking for him. Since he got out. For Ash. But today, he was just *there*."

"You saw him?" Walt asked.

She shook her head. "I didn't. Not really. But Ash did. I saw what *looked* like him, then he was gone. On a motorcycle, I think. Didn't get plates."

"Okay, well, it took a minute for the business records to process, and while I waited, I looked up things in Hesse's name. And since I assume he is not eighty-two-" he paused for Sadie to confirm with a shake of the head- "Then he owns a blue Harley. That's it. No homes, no rentals, no last known address. Hasn't checked in with his parole officer in about a month- and no one is looking for him."

"So we can pick him up on that," Walt said.

"If we can find him," Ben said. "Guy is good at hiding his trail, but…the business- Bastrop Arms- is a weapons manufacturer out of Texas. Owned by a holding company called "True Patriot," which is one of a dozen companies owned by… oh wow…Xavier Voight."

They all perked up. Looks were exchanged. "The same Xavier Voight that owns VYPER?" Walt asked.

"Yep."

"Well, let's go talk to him!" Sadie said forcefully.

"Talk to who?" asked the Eden Falls Chief, Bradley Spitz.

"Chief, we got a lead that might help us get to Xavier Voight. I want to go talk to him," Sadie said.

Spitz seemed to consider it, but also noted Sadie's agitated state. He took a sip from his coffee mug, and said, "Okay. But not alone. And just questions- do *not* push him too hard. He's got better lawyers than that doofus Fletcher has. What's his name again?"

"Jessup," Walt said with a chuckle.

"Yeah. Moron," Spitz said, turning. "Carry on. Carefully."

Sadie turned to Ben excitedly, "Can we go now?"

As Ben was nodding, Walt announced, "I'll grab my coat and start the car."

Ben noticed a slight deflation in Sadie's mood at that, and he couldn't help but smile. He too grabbed his coat and joined Sadie as they walked out the door. Walt was waiting in the CBI sedan they had assigned to them.

Since getting moved to Eden Falls full-time for the task force, they had eschewed the suits and now wore business casual wear. For Walt, that meant button downs and khaki cargos. For Ben it was jeans. He missed the suits occasionally, but the comfortable temperatures of that day, when added with the relaxed attire felt good.

Sadie slid in the back seat, and Ben took shotgun. "Where does this Voight live?" Walt asked.

Ben typed the address into the GPS. "About five miles east of town, it seems." As the device began to robotically call out directions, Walt took off.

"You know, it's a beautiful day up here," Walt said, looking around from the driver's seat. "Shelly and I are loving living up here. Might even make retirement seem more palatable. You liking it, Ben?"

Ben glanced in the back seat and saw Sadie looking at him, and he quickly replied, "I like it. I could see sticking around long term."

"Where are you staying, Ben?" Sadie asked.

"Got a little rental condo down on the river south of town. Glenmore Village?"

"Yeah, I live just down the street!" Sadie said, really smiling for the first time. "Aspen View."

"Those cute little cabins?" Ben asked.

"Shelly and I nabbed a house up on DeWalt Parkway, just across from the big hotel.

It's a real nice-" Walt was saying, then stopped cold when he looked back and saw Sadie's face. "Oh. I see. I wasn't *supposed* to go on this little adventure."

Ben was turned and looking at Sadie, who was blushing. His own cheeks felt warm.

"Awk-ward," Walt mumbled and turned back to the road.

The road that began to slowly climb out of town and up to the base of the mountains. Ahead there was an increasingly dense forestation, but peaking above the pines and aspens was a large roofline. It was still a good distance away, but the sheer size of the mansion was evident. A rustic wooden fence lined the sides of the road, and beyond it was a small herd of buffalo. Grazing amongst them were a handful of elk. A large blue dually truck turned down the driveway in front of them, and seconds later, they also turned into the driveway. They followed the truck to the front door of the house, where a man emerged and walked to the driver's side of the truck and opened the door.

A thickly built man in a black coat and blue jeans stepped out, putting on a black cowboy hat. His blue eyes fell on their car, and an engaging- if manufactured- smile split his lips.

Walt stopped the car as the man waved. "Did he expect us?"

"It's a show," Sadie said. "He's known for being an excellent host. To some people." They all got out of the car.

"Howdy folks," Xavier Voight said cordially, with a twang that reminded Ben of Remington Dean. But less sincere. "Can I help you?"

A second man got out of the car, and Ben recognized him as Clayton Young, "The General" of VYPER. The man who had come out of the door climbed into the truck and drove it away without a word. *People have valets at their own homes?* Ben thought to himself.

Walt replied first, "Inspectors Marino and Samuels with the Colorado Bureau of Investigations. This is Detective Donovan with Eden Falls PD. You are Xavier Voight, correct?"

Voight tipped his hat. "Inspectors. Ma'am."

Ben almost felt Sadie tense up at the refusal of Voight to call her by her police title.

"This is Clayton Young. He is my business associate," Voight said pointing to the man in the aviator's jacket. "Now, as I said, how can I help you?"

"Do you know a man named Robert Hesse?" Sadie said, stepping forward.

Voight made a thinking face. "No. Can't say as I do."

"Really?" Sadie asked, her voice growing louder. "He worked for Bastrop Arms? Was a security guy? You own Bastrop Arms through your subsidiary- True Patriot?"

"Ah. I see," Voight motioned for Young to come forward. "Mr. Young runs-"

"VYPER. Yes, we know that," Sadie said, her temper showing for all to see.

"What Detective Donovan is saying is, we already knew Mr. Young- by reputation- because of an investigation we have going on regarding the shootout last month in Eden Falls," Walt diplomatically interceded. "Mr. Hesse is a man who was released from prison and has missed check-ins with his parole officer. We just need to speak with him, and since, well, he was your employee, we thought we'd just start here."

"Mr. Voight has thousands of employees across his many businesses," Young said. "While he cannot be expected to know all of them, I do happen to know this man. Yes, he was protecting one of our clients- and no I cannot divulge who. But then, the court record should show-"

"It doesn't," Ben said flatly. "It was sealed. Can't get that without a warrant. Now, I don't think we need that here, do we?"

"If you want the client's name, you do," Young retorted. "But then, it won't be necessary for you know that to get Mr. Hesse's information. First, he was terminated following that incident, and while we did provide representation in his trial as a corporation, we have had no contact with him since he was sentenced. Second, if we did have any contact from this moment forth, we would gladly alert you with any information we have. Now, not only do I run VYPER, I am also an attorney, so here is my card. Any further questions for Mr. Voight can go through me."

"It really take two state inspectors and a detective to track this guy down?" Voight said, whistling between his teeth. "Must be a bad dude. Sure hate to be on his bad side. What did he do?"

"He got on my bad side," Sadie quipped, turning back to the car.

That's when Ben saw another car come up the driveway. It carried Brent Chase and Ashleigh Storms.

Dean folded up his third tortilla and took a bite, then set it down and took a sip from his second glass of Dr. Pepper. "Feels almost like I'm back in Texas. In a good way."

Mike Williams, his Chief at the National Parks looked at him over his own plate of Sante Fe style enchiladas, complete with egg. "Do you miss it? Texas?"

Dean took another bite and munched for a bit. "Sometimes," he said, swallowing. "The food, mostly. You know, not one person up here claiming to have Texas barbeque actually has it? They don't understand the concept of 'low and slow,' I guess." Dean's mind went to one of the best briskets he'd ever had, at a little dive outside of Brenham, Texas. "Ya gotta cook it no higher than two-twenty-five. One hour for each pound, at a *minimum*. Preferably twelve hours or more, total. Even for a tiny brisket. Mm. Good stuff. Melts in your mouth. And tender, too."

Mike laughed. "Who knew the secret to getting Remington Dean to talk was food?" He paused, then asked, "But other than food? You miss the Rangers? Miss home?"

Dean took a sip. "Don't miss the Rangers. What with how it all went down?" he shook his head. "No trust left there. And as for home? I've been thinkin' a lot about that lately. Texas ain't home anymore. All I loved about it is gone. Sides, home is wherever you feel it to be. I'm honestly much more at home in my cabin in the mountains than I ever was in Texas. 'Cept when Amy was with me."

Mike scooped up a bite of enchilada, a healthy dose of egg dangling off the fork. "First time I heard you say her name since I first met you. You ever talk to anyone about her?"

Dean thought of Ashleigh. He had talked with her, she knew the story. Most of it, anyway.

"Seems that reporter, Storms? She'd be a good listener," Mike offered, appearing to read Dean's mind.

"She is. But there are some things from that time that I won't tell anyone Mike. Not yet. I still got things to sort out."

"Like Chris Starr? That Hesse fella you've been looking for?"

Dean bit the inside of his lip, but said nothing.

Mike put his fork down and templed his hands beneath his chin, elbows on the table. "Dean, I've known about the side gig all along. Since Agent Pickett came to *me* with the deal. I know you work Parks' stuff, and you work Homeland stuff. And I know you work Remington Dean stuff. What has me worried is that it is all bleeding together now. Starr probably knows you're suspicious-"

"If he don't, he's a moron," Dean said. "I've not been subtle with my disregard for the man."

"Alright, fine. But why?" Mike asked, his eyes searching. "Just a gut feeling, or you got something else? Because if you have something else, that might be something worth bringing out of your deep, dark secrets."

Dean was quiet for a moment, watching the bubbles in his Dr. Pepper rising to the top. "Just a gut thing. Something about those tats Starr has rings a bell. But it's distant-like. Like it's hangin' on a memory, but I don't quite have it."

Now Mike sipped his tea. "Okay. Progress. What about Hesse? You suspect he was a hitter, but was also a security guy?"

"For Bastrop Arms. It was a company out of Texas, which was another bell ringer," Dean said. "It puts Hesse with Texas ties, and Kolbe ties. Kolbe was a 'consultant' for them- if you catch my drift. What I don't yet have is how Starr and his mob connections fit. What would the Denver mob want in Texas?"

Mike shrugged. "Expansion?"

Dean's phone rang. He saw it was Abel Tolentino from the M.E. office. "Gotta get this," Dean said as he took the call. "Abel? What's up?

"Dean! Dean! Dean! I got something!"

Dean pulled the phone away from his ear. "Abel, you gotta calm down. I could almost hear ya without the phone."

"Sorry!" Abel said, taking audible breaths. "Grace Aguirre is here, brought in those two killed up on the divide. Anyway, we were looking over the body from the forest- that was cool, riding in the helicopter, by the way. We swooped in and the trees were-"

"Abel. Focus."

"Hi, Dean, it's Grace," came a calmer, female voice. "What Abel is trying to say is, the wounds on the man found down by the river were really strange."

"Almost ritualistic," Dean added.

"Right," Grace said. "So I took the initiative to do what I suggested to you- and ran the details for similar instances."

"And you found others in RMNP?" Dean asked.

"No- that's the first weird thing," Abel said. "Nothing like that reported in the Rockies. Well, the Colorado Rockies. The Smokies, TR in North Dakota, Olympic, and Acadia. All with trees or mountains or both."

"And other than the Smokies, pretty far north," Dean added. "No one pieced that together- that it looks like a serial?"

"No," Abel said. "We think it was because no one park got hit twice."

"Right, but there's something else odd about our body," Grace said. "The marks were the same- the eyes and the big 'X' were present in all the others. But…"

"But what?"

"Well, there is one big difference, I just don't know if it's anything," Abel said.

"Well, I sure can't tell if you don't say what it is," Dean replied.

"Well, the other victims were all Caucasian males in their late forties or fifties," Grace said.

"This guy here in RMNP? He's Hispanic and about thirty-five," Abel finished.

"That's two big differences, Abel," Dean replied. He thought for a second. Serials didn't change victimology that significantly. Unless… "How long ago was the last body found?"

Papers rustled. "Six months ago. They figured the guy to have been dead no more than a few weeks when found."

"Identification on those bodies?"

More rustling. "Yeah, they know who they are. All hunters, big game types. Oh, our guy was named Miguel Collazo."

Ding.

Another bell.

"Hunter?"

Papers shifting.

"Nope. Got a record, though. Minor stuff," Abel answered.

Collazo. Why was that familiar? "Abel, that makes three differences. And that means something else."

"What?" Abel asked.

"It means there is a serial killer in the National Parks, but they're not in ours. Our body is a copycat. Keep digging, I'll alert the Parks network. Good job on the catch, Grace! Abel, you too."

He hung up before they could thank him.

"Mike, we got evidence of a serial killer operating in National Parks," Dean said, returning to the table. "Doesn't look like anyone has connected it yet, but my techs just did. Might want to reach out to Abel Tolentino and Grace Aguirre- they have the details."

"The body in the woods today?" Mike asked.

Dean shook his head. "Nope. But they found the pattern because of him. That body was a guy named Miguel Collazo. Hispanic, around thirty-five. That name rings a bell for me. You?"

"Nope," Mike said, dropping some cash on the table and picking up the check. "Think it could be from your Ranger days?"

Dean pulled on his jacket with a shrug. "Maybe. But I'll look into it tomorrow. It's been a long day and my bed is calling."

"You gonna make it home before dark?"

"Nah. But I did get a to-go Dr. Pepper, so I'll be good."

Why did he recognize Collazo's name?

Ashleigh got out of Brent's car, and Sadie came up to her.

"What are you doing here?" they asked in unison.

"You first," Sadie said.

Ashleigh looked over to Brent, and he gave her a nod of encouragement. "Well, Brent thought the best way to forget about Robert showing up was to go to work. Said he'd met someone who worked for Xavier Voight, so he thought we might try to do a brief interview with him." Ashleigh smiled broadly. "He's no shootout in a mineshaft, but he's a notoriously tough guy to get an interview with."

Sadie made a face that Ashleigh didn't quite understand or like, then she said, "Don't know how this fits into things, but Robert worked for a company that he owns. When he went to jail."

Ashleigh wasn't sure what to make of that, but she was determined to let nothing drag her back down. When she saw Robert, she lost all the strength, all the backbone she had built over the years he was gone. She had tasted what it was like to be independent and unafraid, and she was not going to let it go so easily. "Well, if it comes up, I'll ask Voight. Maybe he will tell me what he won't tell you."

Now Sadie smiled. "That's the Ash I know. Go get 'em." And with that she walked to the car that Ben and Walt were getting into. She turned and said, "Shooting range- tonight around eight?"

"If you bring me a gun!"

"You look better," Brent said. "Like the Ashleigh I knew."

She appreciated his support, and what he was doing to help at the moment, but she didn't like that comment for some reason. It was like he saw her as something of value only when he recognized it. And that was a little too… Robert Hesse. So she ignored him and called out, "Xavier Voight! My name is Ashleigh Storms, I run the magazine for the Eden Falls Valley-"

"The Rocky Mountain Gothic!" Voight exclaimed. "Why yes! I've read your stuff. Particularly liked the piece on the Ranger- what was his name again?"

"Remington Dean," she replied with a smile. She noticed Brent got uncomfortable, but didn't care if her relationship with Dean- whatever it was- bothered Brent. "That's a favorite of a lot of folks. This is my friend, Brent Chase-"

"The local businessman- Book Brew, isn't it?" Voight said coming down the steps and shaking Brent's hand, then turning to Ashleigh to shake hers. Then back to Brent. "My new public relations person, Charly Addison mentioned you to me just today. Said we should meet up."

"Did I hear my name?" a woman's voice called from the front door. The man with Voight was long gone, whoever he had been, but now a tall blonde woman was coming their way. She was beautiful in a very business-like manner even though she was casually dressed. Her hair was pulled back in a bun and she had on glasses that did little to make her look nerdy. A quick glance toward Brent convinced Ashleigh he was smitten. Which was good, given she suspected he had once had a crush on her. Or still did.

"Charly Addison," she said, offering her hand to Ashleigh. Then, turning to Brent, she said, "Brent- I didn't expect to see you so soon. But

I'm glad you're here." Then back to Ashleigh. "You're a reporter, Ms. Storms?"

"I am."

Charly turned to Voight, who was being far more approachable than she had expected him to be. It struck Ashleigh as a bit odd. "Mr. Voight, I have been encouraging you to do some press. Especially in light of all the VYPER mess. And from what I've heard about Ms. Storms- she would be a great interviewer."

Voight made a face that conveyed thinking it over, then he smiled. "Alright. But I'm busy right now-"

"Oh! I never intended to crash interview you right here," Ashleigh said. "I merely hoped to get on your schedule."

"That sounds great. But I want to one-up you. How about an interview and a dinner? I would love to meet with Mr. Chase here about some business opportunities I have in mind, what with his new venture into real estate. And I would dearly love to meet Remington Dean as well. You two are somewhat close, I hear?"

Now Ashleigh felt her face flush. "We're good friends, if that's what you mean. Are you saying you are inviting us to a dinner party?"

"I am," Voight turned to Charly. "Can you find a time soon? In the next few days?" Charly nodded. "I believe I'm free if you are?" he asked, turning to Brent and Ashleigh.

They exchanged a glance and a shrug. "Not a lot going on for us, so I'm sure we can make it," Brent answered.

"And I'll call up Dean," Ashleigh added.

"Great!" Voight said, clapping his hands together. "There are a couple other folks I wanted to invite, so I'll get in touch with them. You know, since I moved my operations to Eden Falls, I just feel so much more welcomed than any other place I've been. You folks are excellent at your hospitality."

Ashleigh smiled. "It is a great place to live."

Voight looked at her and said, "And I hope to do my part to make sure it stays that way. Listen, I have to take care of some business, but I'll have Charly reach out with the details soon. Have a great evening!" He waved and mounted the steps towards the doors of his massive home.

"That means I have to go, too," Charly said. "Brent, I have your card, but may I have your contact information, Ms. Storms?"

Ashleigh produced a business card and handed it to her. "Thank you for setting this up. It means a great deal! I've heard Mr. Voight is reluctant to do interviews."

Pocketing her card, Charly said, "Oh, that is completely true. It's why I got hired to change his image. Really lean into the 'cowboy wisdom' thing he had back when he was doing business in Texas. By the way, I must tell you, the whole VYPER situation, be careful bringing that up. He is about to make a big announcement about it, and it is just breaking his heart. He *might* talk about it with you- but I'd tread lightly." Charly's admonition didn't come off as a threat, but as professional courtesy.

"Duly noted," Ashleigh said, fully intending to broach the subject at dinner.

"Brent, I definitely look forward to seeing *you* soon," Charly said, flashing a gleaming smile of perfect teeth. Then she winked at him.

"Uh, yeah. Me, too," Brent managed. Then Charly turned and followed her boss up to the door.

Taking their cue, Brent and Ashleigh turned to leave.

"Someone has a crush," Ashleigh teased.

"I mean, she's gorgeous, but I don't think I have a crush," Brent said bashfully.

"I meant her, doofus," Ashleigh retorted.

"Oh…OH! No- she doesn't…"

Ashleigh gave him a look over the hood of the car.

"Really?" Brent asked in shock.

Chapter 8

The night was growing darker the higher in elevation he went, but Dean was driving on auto-pilot. His mind was trying to place that name. Collazo. If it had been a perp he apprehended, then it had been a long time ago, or very small-time. So, he didn't think that was the connection.

He took a sip of the Dr. Pepper in the to-go cup. Colorado was pretty serious about the environment, so they had done away with styrofoam cups in most places, replacing them with double insulated paper cups. Dean looked down at the imprint on the cup that read "Olde Sante Fe" and it hit him.

Not Collazo.

Collazo's.

"What's this place called?" Dean asked Amy. She was wearing a blue cocktail dress that fit her very well, her hair was done up how he loved, and her smile was even more intoxicating than ever. It was their anniversary, and he was finding it hard to keep his mind on anything else but his beautiful wife.

"Collazo's," she replied. "Miguel, the owner, was the victim in one of the first cases I tried. Armed robbery back when he was just a cook for a small restaurant. He'd had a record, so he was worried I'd treat him like a perp. When I didn't, I became his hero. He opened this place a few weeks ago, and he gave me a standing invitation to the best seat in the house any time I wanted."

Dean looked around at the well-appointed crowd waiting to get in, and watched as Amy glided up to the maître d' and said her name. Instantly, they were led to a table and seated. The waiter asked if they wanted any wine, and he informed them they were entitled to the top wine- on the house. Amy looked at Dean and asked, "I know you don't drink, but come on- it's our anniversary."

"Alright, fine. I'll get drunk with you."

The waiter went to get their bottle. "Why are you always so extreme, Remmy? Tea-totaler to drunk, pacifist to pugilist-"

"I ain't no fighter. You know that."

"Maybe not with your fists, but you fight, Remmy," Amy said, looking over the menu. She paused and looked at him. He met her eyes. God, she was so beautiful. "I know how hard it's been with Jude, but that's what I mean. You fight for what matters. As much as I hate how dark your work makes you, I love that you are such a man of integrity. One of the things I love most about you, sir."

Dean smiled. "Right back at ya. You aren't afraid to go after the big fish, even the ones that bite back."

Amy pursed her lips and set the menu down. "You haven't stopped looking into Grant Kolbe, have you?"

Dean sighed and shook his head. "I thought this was an anniversary dinner, not a working supper." She had on her no-nonsense face. "Alright. Yes. Something bothers me about it. Yeah, Jude was dirty. That's clear. But Kolbe passed himself off as a low-level guy that knew a high-ranking Ranger was on the take?"

The waiter brought their wine and poured it into their glasses. Amy sipped hers, and her eyes went wide. "Wow! That's amazing!"

Dean sipped his and made a face, but quickly hid it. Didn't want to dim any of Amy's enjoyment. "Could I get some water to go with this?" he asked the waiter. "And a Dr. Pepper?"

"So, what have you found?"

"That I don't like expensive wine, either," Dean answered.

"About Kolbe."

He sighed again. "He was not low level at all. In fact, he was makin' a move to head up a significant portion of the criminal organization here in Texas. There was only one person in the way."

Amy sat back in her seat. "Jude Randall."

"Yep." The water was set on the table, and they placed their orders. The waiter safely out of earshot, Dean continued. "I know we originally thought it was the mob, but I'm not so sure anymore. I mean, I think there is some organized crime group from Colorado, and maybe it's the mob. But I'm thinkin' it might be a new player, and Kolbe is double-agentin' it."

"Is double-agenting a word?" Amy asked, laughing as she sipped her wine.

"It should be," Dean replied, giving the wine another try. It did improve a bit when paired with Amy's laugh. "No more work talk, okay?"

She smiled that smile that melted him every time, and they fell into talking about life. About their dreams. About the future.

"I think I'm ready, Remmy," Amy said without context.

"We haven't gotten our food- not that I'm complainin' about it," Dean said, and was promptly kicked under the table by Amy.

"Not *that*," she said. "Although that is part of it."

"Oh," Dean said. "*Oh!* Really? Kids?"

She smiled. "Yep. We could start…tonight?"

Dean no longer cared about the meal, but just then it arrived. Carried not by their waiter, but by a middle-aged Hispanic man in chef's whites.

"Ms. Dean!" the man exclaimed. "So glad you came to my restaurant!" He began setting the food down.

"Miguel- of course!" she said as she motioned to Dean. "Miguel Collazo- this is Remington Dean, my husband."

"Ah yes, the Ranger! Ms. Dean told me much about you. Please enjoy the meal- and if you need anything, do not hesitate to ask for me personally. Your wife got me justice, and if not for her, I would not be able to own this place." Miguel beamed with pride and gratitude.

"She's pretty amazing," Dean agreed, looking at his wife with all the love in his heart brimming to overflow. Miguel excused himself and left them to eat their meals. "Okay, the wine was iffy, but this is excellent," Dean gushed as he took a bite of his carne asada.

There was the scrape of a chair across the floor, and Dean looked up to see a familiar face.

Grant Kolbe.

"Well, if it isn't the Deans," he said casually. "Enjoying a pleasant night out? Which, thanks to you guys, I am as well." He smiled that same smile from when Jude Randall was led out in handcuffs.

"Mr. Kolbe, I'm surprised to see you here," Amy said, putting on her most diplomatic voice. But Dean knew that she was upset beneath the surface.

He had no such filter. "What do you want, Kolbe?"

Kolbe looked between Amy and Dean, then settled on Dean. "For you to stop digging into my life, Ranger. I helped you get your guy, and in exchange, your lovely wife got me a suspended sentence. I'm a free man. And so far as I can see, an innocent man. So, stop digging."

Dean took a bite of his meal. "That a threat? Cuz if it is, then you ain't so innocent."

Kolbe smiled. Then he looked at Amy. "So, you're the more rational one, eh? Makes sense. Listen. You've gotten what you were looking for. A corrupt cop with ties to organized crime. He will *no doubt* cooperate, then you can take down the entire operation. Only reason he hasn't yet is he's probably looking for the best deal. Like I was. My hands are clean, tell your husband that."

"He has pretty good hearing and he's sitting right there, Grant," Amy replied. "So if you think I'm a pushover and can be threatened more easily than him, you're wrong. And let me tell you- if you are still elbow deep in illegal activities, trying to claw your way to the top of some dung heap, my husband and I will take you down just like we did Jude Randall."

"Hmm," Kolbe said with a chuckle. "I misread you both, I guess." He stood up, grabbing the chair as he did and sliding it back. "Well, I will leave you to your… anniversary dinner, I suppose? Congratulations. You know, finding the right partner for life is… so very difficult. Never take that for granted Mr. and Mrs. Dean." He turned and walked away. Two men peeled away from the bar to join him. One was black-haired with deep blue eyes and hollow cheeks, tribal tats just visible below his short sleeves. The other was blonde and was wearing a vest and white shirt with the sleeves rolled up. He too had tattoos, but they went all the way down to the forearm.

The most prominent tats were large stars.

That was it. Collazo was the owner of the restaurant. Starr had been with Kolbe, and the only reason he wasn't sure Hesse was there is that he had only seen Hesse in pictures. He had been on that trail for almost four years, and all it took was one brief memory for him to start making connections.

But why kill Miguel Collazo and drop him in the National Park? Dean's National Park? That wasn't Starr's style. And Hesse was- from all accounts- a cold killer. He wouldn't make it personal unless he already saw it that way. Was there some other connection that he was missing? Something that connected Dean and Hesse on a more personal level?

Headlights coming from the left blinded him, and he had just a split second to wonder why someone was driving down the slope of the mountain before the vehicle broadsided him.

The impact drove his Gladiator off the road and into a bank of pines. It was the only thing that kept him from rolling down the steep mountainside some three hundred feet to his most likely death. But the assailing vehicle didn't stop pushing him.

It was a black monstrosity- half Humvee, half road grader. It was armored, and as he looked out his side window, he saw an African American man sneering through what was most likely bulletproof glass. He decided to try to find out.

Dean grabbed the shotgun in the holder next to him and pushed himself away from the driver's side. Bracing with his feet on the door, he took aim and fired.

To his surprise, the windshield of the monster truck cracked. He racked another load and fired again. The window imploded, and the man driving threw his hand over his eyes.

That was all Dean saw because at that moment the truck's equilibrium shifted as the trees that saved him gave a bit of ground. He heard them groan and crack beneath the weight of his vehicle. Dean didn't have long to escape before he *did* end up at the bottom of the gorge.

"Okay, God, if you're listening, now's a good time for some help," he prayed.

Slowly, carefully, he moved toward the driver's side once more. The truck groaned and squeaked as his own weight shifted the stability of his precarious position. At least the other vehicle had stopped coming for him.

With no sign of the man- or men- who had ambushed him, Dean cautiously poked the shotgun through the window inch by inch. Without warning, it was jerked from his hands and a beefy gloved fist grabbed the front of his shirt. He was unceremoniously pulled through the window and dropped on the ground. A heavy boot kicked him in the head, and his vision began to swim.

"You've become a problem, Ranger."

The voice was familiar, but Dean couldn't quite place it. Probably the kick to the head.

"Fortunately, my boys and I are specialists at taking care of problems."

Dean managed to push himself up, then rolled over onto a kneeling position. His hand moved to his hip from his head, making the briefest of contact with his Colt as he made a show of checking for blood. There definitely was some.

He clocked three men in front of him. The driver, a man in a balaclava, and a man in a beret.

Nathaniel Stone.

All of them wore tactical gear, but nothing protected their heads. With his head swimming, any shot at their cranium was a waste. Aiming for shoulders or necks were also dicey propositions. And that was if he could even pull fast enough.

But then, Remington Dean on a bad day was faster on the draw than most.

He just needed to stall for a bit longer.

God? Miracle?

"Stone? I thought you'd taken off after you killed Bethea."

Stone smiled coldly. "No, you didn't."

"True, but I wanted to give you the benefit of the doubt."

"About what?"

Dean shrugged. "That you were smart enough to leave town before I got to you."

"Awfully arrogant for a man with a head wound, on his knees, and surrounded by armed men."

Dean smiled. "What can I say? I'm a Texan."

The Colt flashed forth, and the first blast hit the driver in the hip- a glancing blow. The second managed to hit the masked man in the chest, despite Dean aiming for his shoulder. By then, Stone had taken a defensive position.

That was when Dean heard the movement behind him. He rolled as a shot hit right where he had been, then brought the Colt up and fired at the man who'd been sneaking up on him. The first shot missed, but the second hit him square in the chest. Even with the body armor, a .357 at that range would put him out of commission for a bit.

Apparently, Dean's head wound wasn't that bad.

Still, Dean knew there must be more men he couldn't see, and standing his ground wasn't the best plan. So he ran for the trees. Wood splintered around him as either Stone or another unseen assailant took their shots.

He didn't have his backup piece on him, as he always took it off when he was in the truck. So he was down to two shots in the Colt, and one full reload on his belt. To his left, he saw a glint of a scope, so he turned and fired. He heard the bullet strike metal and a man yell out in shock.

Then he felt the bullet graze his shoulder.

Fearing a follow-up- and more accurate shot- he threw himself forward and rolled down the decline. He tucked his head and hoped he didn't strike a tree too hard as he made his descent. He came to rest against a scrub bush, rose to his hands and knees then crawled behind it. No real protection from bullets there, but it might hide him some in the dark.

He looked up and saw he had rolled about twenty feet. His truck was ten yards to his left, the trees cracking almost constantly. It would go at any minute. That might give him cover.

A beam of light began moving around his position. Dean looked up to see a man glad in dark-gray body armor, wearing a black motorcycle helmet. Unlike the others, he was not in military fatigues. Dean found that interesting.

Slowly, the man in gray descended toward Dean. The truck groaned, and the man turned his head quickly. Then back toward his search for Dean.

Dean, who had one shot before he needed to reload. Dean who was growing lightheaded. Dean who felt a thick branch under his right knee.

The man was about five feet from his position. Dean gripped the branch and waited. He looked for more cover further down the mountain and saw a small evergreen he was pretty sure he could make it to in time.

The man was three feet from Dean.

Now two.

Now standing on just the other side of the bush.

Dean stood up and swung the branch at the visor part of the helmet and felt a satisfying crack as it shattered. Then he ran.

Nervous gunfire erupted, spraying everywhere but at Dean, who thanked God for *that* minor miracle. And he reached his new hiding spot safely.

The man ripped his helmet off with a curse, and Dean recognized him immediately.

Finally.

Robert Hesse.

The third man.

Kolbe. Starr. And Hesse.

Involuntarily, Dean clicked the hammer on the Colt.

"Hesse- we got wounded!" Stone shouted.

Hesse ignored Stone, instead bringing his weapon to his shoulder and sweeping it around searching with the flashlight attached to the muzzle and moving toward Dean's exact position. He felt it- there was going to be a shoot out. Hesse's automatic versus Dean's final bullet. He had to be perfect, or he was dead. Hesse locked in on the tree Dean was behind, and moved in.

There was a deafening crack above him and Dean saw that his retreat had taken him right into the path of his wrecked truck's eventual descent. But 'eventual' had become 'immediate.'

Hesse seemed unaware until the truck shattered the last tree holding it and began to roll- fast.

Hesse turned to look and Dean rose and pointed his gun. In a split second, he weighed the risk of taking the shot. Killing a man he believed had a part in his wife's death but never getting those answers if he did fire.

Hesse finally realized the mortal peril the truck presented and dove for cover. It rolled past him and obliterated the small tree where Dean had been.

But Dean was racing down the hill with as much speed as he dared. He finally saw that a road lay at the base of the slope, and he made for it. In the distance, he saw a pair of headlights approaching. Truck headlights. Late nineties Ford, he guessed.

Which meant it probably didn't belong to his pursuers.

He hoped.

He reached the road and all his adrenaline dried up. He collapsed in the middle of the gravel and was bathed in the glow of the headlights. Dean lay there breathing jaggedly, blood pooling beneath him from the head trauma.

The truck stopped and he heard a door creak open. In the distance, the Gladiator came to its ultimate resting place in a mangled ruin.

Heavy footsteps approached and Dean looked up to see a giant of a man with red hair.

"Thank you, God," he mumbled.

As he lost consciousness, Dean heard Rhett Windsor say, "You look like roadkill, Ranger."

Rhett had been outside when he heard the unmistakable sound of a car crash. It happened pretty frequently on the switchbacks, what with the limited visibility of the hairpin turns and folks being more concerned with the steep slopes than the oncoming traffic.

He was on his way to the truck to go see if he could help out when he heard the gunshots. Had he been closer, he might have been able to tell the types of weapons beyond semi- and automatic. Gunshots up in the deep woods were almost as common as the car crashes, and Rhett usually paid them little heed. But when the wrecks and the gunfire were so close, it usually meant something else.

So he grabbed his shotgun and his hunting rifle.

When you spend most of your life living in the same place, you get a feel for your surroundings that might seem almost supernatural to outsiders. For instance, you can pinpoint where a sound is coming from on the mountain- how far away and how far up or down. The wreck was no more than a mile away, probably up on the main road from the eastern slope.

Rhett knew it was probably those VYPER guys. He'd heard the same noises that morning when the couple got killed. Got killed because of him. He hadn't acted that day because he wasn't sure what was going down.

But Rhett Windsor was a fast learner.

And despite his reputation as a mountain criminal, he was a good guy deep down.

Or he wanted to be, anyway.

Because things were changing in his life.

A picture dangled from his rearview of a small woman with chin length light brown hair. His girlfriend, a young woman named Tina that he had known since they were kids, was pregnant. He'd found out about a month and a half earlier. A sonogram taken by his sister, a doctor, was taped to the back of Tina's picture.

That was why he had handed off the running of the guns and drugs to Nigel. He was smarter than Zeke, but that was a low bar. Whatever came of it, he could wash his hands of the matter, and make a fresh start.

Rhett found he could justify using the funds from the ill-gotten-gains if he used them for something good. Like providing homes and a safe community for the mountain residents who had been displaced by the arrival of wealthy low-landers. By the Xavier Voights and the Denver mobsters as well as the East and West Coast elites that wanted to collect their nature badge. And they got it by purchasing ten or twenty acres of land for eight thousand square foot mansions that pillaged the forests for the wood and stone to construct their monstrosities.

As he drove toward the sounds of danger that night, Rhett grew angry.

If VYPER was murdering another wealthy person, so what? Maybe they'd take each other out. If not, one day Rhett feared he'd have to get his hands dirty again to protect his soon-to-be family. Maybe it would be that night.

He kind of wished it would be.

He rounded a switchback and gained some elevation, then leveled off and added speed. His headlights bounced down the washboard road as he kept an eye out for the wildlife that might be out grazing as well as signs of the conflict he was racing into. It would be just a few hundred feet up the ridge on his right.

A rumble and crash drew his eyes to a heap of metal rolling down the slope. Rhett couldn't make out what it was, other than dark colored. Maybe black or blue.

His eyes turned back to the road just in time to see a man laying in the road. He slammed on his brakes and the tires crunched to a stop.

He recognized Remington Dean instantly.

Rhett hopped out of the truck and grabbed his hunting rifle. He walked toward Dean, but kept an eye on the tree line.

As he got closer, he saw the blood running from the Ranger's forehead, and the pool beneath his head. A big head wound, but he was breathing. "You look like roadkill, Ranger," he said with a chuckle.

Dean didn't respond, his eyes closed and he went limp. Still breathing, though. Rhett was reluctant to move him but out of the corner of his eye, a glint in the moonlight made him reconsider.

He turned and brought his rifle up to sight. A man in green fatigues was taking aim at them from behind a tree, but Rhett drew a bead faster. The shot caught the man in the upper chest and he went down. Taking that moment, Rhett grabbed Dean up and ran to the truck. He thought first about dumping him in the bed, but thought keeping an eye on him was more important than keeping blood out of his upholstery.

It wouldn't be the first time for blood in that cab.

As he was putting Dean in the cab, a shot pinged off the roof. Rhett saw a dark figure emerge from the treeline, and decided not to waste time returning fire. He slammed his door and made a u-turn. Dust flew up around the truck as he raced down the road.

Rhett was determined to not let the Ranger die on his watch. And he knew just who could save the man's life.

"Dr. Feelgood, here we come."

Chapter 9

BANG!

"Whoa!" Ashleigh said, her hands trembling and her eyes wide. She was standing with her feet spread and both hands grasping a smoking pistol.

"Now, set your feet, take a breath, and fire again," Sadie coached from the stall next to her. Then she fired off four rounds in rapid succession.

Ashleigh shuffled her feet, took a deep breath and slowly let it out. Her shoulders lowered, her eyes focused, and she squeezed the trigger. Once. Twice. Three times.

Despite wearing protective gear, her ears were ringing. So it took her a second to realize she was laughing out loud.

"Feels good, huh?" Sadie asked.

"I'M SHAKING ALL OVER-"

Sadie motioned to remove the ear plugs.

"OH, SORRY," Ashleigh yelled, then pulled them out of her ears and cupped them in her hand. "That was…exhilarating!"

"Yeah, bullets are cheaper than therapy," Sadie said. She shifted her shoulder and winced a little.

"You still feeling your gunshot wounds?"

"I think I always will, at least a little," Sadie replied. "But I haven't been shooting as consistently as I should. So the recoil gets me a bit. How do you like that pistol?"

Ashleigh turned it over in her hand and nodded. "A lot. What's it called? The number or the…um…"

"Caliber?"

"Yeah, that."

"You've got a Sig Sauer P365. It's a 9mm. What I carry. In fact, that one is my old one," Sadie said, showing Ashleigh her weapon. "Small but effective. If you like it, I can loan it to you. With…him back in town, you know. Just in case."

Ashleigh shifted the gun in her hands indecisively. That thought hadn't crossed her mind. That Robert might show up again. "Maybe…"

"Yeah, just hold on to it for a bit," Sadie said, relieving Ashleigh of the burden of having to make that decision. Then she asked, "You want to try something else- since we're here?"

Ashleigh looked back at the bulletproof glass and the large, hairy man that managed the range. "What kind of gun does Dean use?"

"Colt Python," Sadie replied. "That's a much bigger kick. It's a .357."

Ashleigh shrugged. "Means nothing to me."

Sadie laughed. "Bullets are about the same size around, but the .357 is much longer. Carries a bigger load-" she saw Ashleigh scrunch up her nose in confusion- "More grains, bigger boom."

"Ah." Ashleigh looked back at the manager again. Then smiled broadly with wild eyes. "I wanna try it!"

Sadie laughed and pointed toward the door. "Let's see what he has that might work."

Ben had just sat down to his dinner when the phone rang. He snagged a quick bite of the burger he'd gotten from the local joint and looked at the caller ID.

Elsie Kho.

"Yeah?" he mumbled around a mouthful of beef, cheese, and bread.

"Catch you at a bad time?" Kho asked.

"Not for a telemarketer."

"Wish that was why I called," she said, then silence for a moment. "Quentin Fletcher is getting released tonight."

"What!" Ben yelled, nearly choking. "How?"

"Jessup made an argument to the judge that since he's a local celebrity of sorts, he's in danger of being mistreated at the jail. On top of that, he has nowhere to go outside of Eden Falls, so Jessup pushed for house arrest, pending trial."

"He's just as at risk outside of jail as he is in," Ben argued. "Won't Denver be wanting to silence him?"

"Um, yeah. About that."

It began to occur to Ben what was about to happen. "No. Elsie, not that."

"He's requested protection," she said flatly.

"That's a marshal thing," Ben offered, hoping that was true.

"Normally it is, but he requested you and Walt."

Ben swore. "Walt know?"

"Yeah, called him first. I wanted him to tell you, but he insisted I tell you myself," Elsie replied. "I think he wanted me to be the one to get yelled at."

"Well, he was right," Ben said, rubbing his head. "When do we report?"

"Tonight. In about an hour, he will be processed. You are supposed to escort him home, then flip for who stays tonight."

I know how that will go, Ben thought to himself. *"I'm old and need to sleep in my own bed, kid."*

"On my way," he said with resignation.

Ashleigh immediately felt the difference in the weight of the two guns. The Colt was decidedly heftier, and the longer barrel made it more difficult to find her balance. When Sadie moved behind her, she was confused. "What are you doing?"

"Spotting you."

"Like in weightlifting?"

Sadie shrugged. "You'll see."

Once again, she set her feet, gripped the pistol, and squeezed. Nothing happened.

"Pull the hammer back," Sadie advised.

"The what?"

"Thing above your hands, kinda like a T?"

"Ah."

Click.

She squeezed again, and felt a tremendous weight press back on her, and her feet came out from under her. Sadie caught her, of course. And once again, she was laughing.

"Well…ha ha…think I've had enough for tonight," Ashleigh managed between giggles.

"So, wine time?" Sadie asked.

"Definitely."

Walt was standing at the door to the jail with his arms crossed, and a scowl on his face. Elsie was there too, still wearing her professional clothing while Walt was in shorts and sandals. Ben was still wearing jeans, and had packed his overnight bag, which was in his left hand.

"Read my mind kid," Walt said. "I'm old and need to sleep in my own bed."

"Why are you so predictable, Walt?"

"Because I'm old and set in my ways," Marino replied. "And since I'm still your superior, it's good for you to know what to expect. Keeps you from making mistakes."

"Elsie, how did this happen?" Ben asked, ignoring Walt.

She raised her hands. "No idea he was even presenting this to the judge until the judge called me. From my end, that's not protocol."

Walt cut his eyes at Ben. "You thinking what I'm thinking?"

Ben rolled his eyes. "Got to the judge with threats or money. Either way, Fletcher may think he's getting to walk, but he's really just being ushered into a trap. You think they'll send big city hitters?"

"Wait, you really think Fletcher is important enough for the Denver mob to put a hit on him? Here?" Elsie asked.

"Fletcher may be a moron, but he's a realtor, too," Walt answered. "He keeps information. Definitely a liability. Even if he doesn't know who the big guy is. And no, Ben, I think they'll go local for the kill squad."

"You think they'd leave it to the hillbillies?" Elsie asked.

"Did once before," Ben answered. "That shoot-out at the Windsors. What was the family? The Tolberts?"

"Think so. Wanna call Sadie and ask her if she remembers?" Walt asked teasingly.

"She's hanging out with Ashleigh, don't want to bother her. I could call Dean?"

"Works for me," Walt said.

Ben dialed Dean's number, but it went to voicemail. "He's not answering." Ben turned and saw the door open. The hulking frame of Quentin Fletcher stepped into the night, closely followed by his attorney, Edwin Jessup.

"Well, hello, gentlemen," Fletcher said boisterously. "I hear you get to be my bodyguards."

They were sitting at a small wine bistro on the edge of the river that ran through town, sipping their wine and talking about their favorite spots around Eden Falls.

"I love the drive up to through the park," Sadie said. "I'm not a big four-wheel-drive girl, so the fact that it's paved is good for me. And the wildlife is used to the people, so the little ones come right up to you- it's adorable."

"That's a good one," Ashleigh said. She looked around cautiously, almost automatically, for her boogeyman.

"He's not here, Ashleigh." Sadie said. "And if he was, I'd get rid of him. Or you know, you could. With his history, you'd get off as a battered spouse."

Ashleigh made a face, knowing that last part was a joke, but still finding it hit too close to home. She looked down at her glass and swirled it. "I know. And thank you for being there for me. Today, tonight. Always. I just… why did it have to go sideways?"

"You mean your ex showing up?"

"Yeah. I mean, it's been years. Nothing, no contact, no indication he even knew where I was."

"Hey, that's a question. Did you change your name?" Sadie asked. "You know, to hide from him?"

"I dropped Hesse. Went back to my maiden name," Ashleigh said. "Why?"

Sadie sat forward. "It's just that you didn't hide much- not like some people do. And he's been out for a bit, almost six months. It seems strange he waited until now to come find you."

Ashleigh sipped her wine. "The Ranger. That story went wide. I was so caught up in the moment, with Laura being killed, the whole thing that went down with you and Dean and the CBI and the mob. I didn't even think he'd put it together."

"Not a reader, was he?" Sadie asked with a laugh.

"No, he was. Actually, Robert was really smart," Ashleigh said wistfully. "That was what attracted me to him at first. He was witty, funny, and said exactly what I wanted to hear. I knew he had been military, and had seen some stuff, so I learned to not push those buttons. For a time, that worked. But then… it was like he got bored."

Sadie made a face. "Bored how?"

"It wasn't that he hit me for not doing what he wanted. He hit me because he *wanted* to. To show he was dominant, and to break my will. I don't think he loved me, I think he needed me to be afraid to live without him."

Sadie just looked at her. Ashleigh was used to sympathetic looks, but Sadie was trying to understand. Her cop mind was working overtime. "I know what you're thinking. 'He's a sociopath.' And I've thought that, too. But then, why even date me? Why, for God's sake, marry me?"

Sadie was quiet and thoughtful. Ashleigh loved that about her. She had thoughts- everyone did. But she wouldn't say anything until she was sure of what she wanted to put out into the world. Finally, Sadie said, "Maybe it was a cover."

Ashleigh furrowed her brow. "Like, he needed a wife for something?"

Sadie leaned forward and set her glass down. "Yeah. Remember, I said he worked for a company that was part of another company that Voight owned? Well, what if all of that was a ruse? Just something to hide what Hesse really did for Voight. Did he travel a lot?"

Ashleigh shrugged. "Yeah. Couple times a month."

"When he was home, did he go to an office or something?"

Ashleigh wracked her memory. "Not much- once a week."

Sadie rubbed her chin. "Would you, by any chance, have a record of the dates he was gone? Like, did you keep a diary or anything?"

"Why?"

"If Hesse was really doing… underground work for Voight, and we could tie his absences to unsolved murders… maybe we could nail them both."

Ashleigh smiled. "I have my journals at home. Let's go."

Ben hated corrupt rich people.

Fletcher's home was massive. Not nearly as big as Voight's, but a sight to behold, nonetheless. It was a beautiful rock and cedar mansion with custom furniture and an enormous television over a gigantic river rock fireplace. Pretentious- but quality- art hung all around, and Fletcher had a fully automated system set to his voice command.

Ben thought of his sad little apartment, and felt the green monster of jealousy rise up.

"Ah, my home! How I have missed you!" Fletcher said loudly as he moved into the sunken den. "I will be needing a shower first, then I shall sleep like a baby in my bed."

"Easy there, your majesty," Walt said. "Before you do anything, Ben and I have to check your home for safety."

Fletcher made a pouty face, then plopped on the couch.

"I do appreciate you doing your due diligence, Inspectors," Jessup said, taking a seat next to Fletcher. He reached over and fumbled with a lamp next to the couch, finally bringing an amber glow to the seating area.

"I could have just spoken that on, Edwin," Fletcher said, mildly irritated.

AUSA Kho was the last to come in, and she moved toward a couch opposite Fletcher and Jessup. Ben knew she would keep an eye on them while he and Walt checked the house. As he moved from room to room, checking closets and under beds and other furniture, he wished he'd requested local PD to help. But outside of Chief Spitz and Sadie, there weren't too many people Ben and Walt felt they could trust locally. And Spitz was still kind of iffy. Dean could be trusted, but two more calls to the man had gone to voicemail. It wasn't like Dean to miss calls, so he was either out of range doing what the Ranger did, or something very important had come up.

After sweeping the upstairs, Ben went down to the kitchen, where he met Walt. "Basement and ground level are clear," Walt informed.

"Upstairs is good. Should we check the outbuildings?"

Walt shrugged. "In the morning. I doubt there is a squad of killers hanging out in a dusty garage." Walt rubbed the bridge of his nose like he had a headache. "This fishy to you?"

Ben laughed sarcastically. "Corrupt judges always are, Walt."

"Not that. Why would Jessup agree to getting him out?" Walt had lowered his voice and leaned toward Ben. "I mean, the guy was Bethea's lawyer. And he always struck me as a weaselly little turd, but not stupid. Town lock-up isn't County, and sure isn't State or Federal. He had a cush- and safe- stay lined up. Now? Now he's exposed. And he's gotta know we're gonna try to talk to him. Or is that his hope- we question without Jessup present and the case gets dropped?"

"You think it's what Jessup wanted?"

168

"I think it's what whoever runs that mob in Denver wants. And I think it just might give us the leverage we need to find out who they are- and what their connection to Voight is."

"Gentlemen- are you done yet? I want my shower," Fletcher called.

"Get the lawyers out of here and take a run at Fletcher without them, anyway?" Ben asked.

"It's like we are of one mind, kid."

"That's eight dates, so far," Sadie announced. She had a cup of coffee in her hand, trying to push away the wine fog- just like Ashleigh. "I can't verify if there were any crimes on those dates right now, but the last one was just a little bit before he went away three years ago."

"That was the one where I left," Ashleigh said. "He said he was going to be gone for a week or two, so I cleared out my stuff and went to stay with Laura and her husband. They had already

169

moved to Eden Falls, so I came here and never looked back.”

Ashleigh saw Sadie looking at her with that sort of understanding that was rare to find in the world. Sadie may have had a similar experience in her childhood, but it wasn’t the trauma that bonded them. It was their survival instinct.

Deciding the night had gotten too heavy, Ashleigh changed the subject. “So. About you and Inspector Samuels.”

Sadie blinked rapidly, as if her brain had to restart. “That came out of nowhere!”

Ashleigh shrugged. “Not nowhere. You too have been flirty since you got out of the hospital- what a month and a half ago? We all see it.”

Sadie scrunched up her nose. “Really?”

Ashleigh nodded.

“Well, nothing has happened. Lots of longing glances and failed attempts to spend time alone outside of the interrogation room,” Sadie said, sliding off the chair to the floor. “If we are going to do some girl talk, it’s going to be a long night. Because if I have to talk about Ben, you’ve got to talk about Remington Dean.” She said his name with her interpretation of his drawl, and both of them began to laugh.

"On that, there is nothing to tell. Just friends. Close friend, but at a distance. We see each other occasionally, but he has walls."

"You think it's his wife? Was her name Amy?"

"Partly," Ashleigh looked into her coffee cup. "But I also think he's digging deep into her case. He believes- or I think he does- that her death is connected to the Denver mob and those VYPER guys."

"How?"

Ashleigh weighed whether or not to mention what she had found in Dean's basement during their first meeting, and decided she might as well. "He has a crime board- one of those corkboard things with pictures and strings. He thinks there are possibly three men who killed Amy. I think he's eliminated one as a suspect. There was a big X over his picture. Another spot was there, but he didn't have a name or picture. I think for the third guy, he suspects Agent Starr for some reason-"

"I get that vibe, too. Nothing I've seen, but Dean doesn't trust him."

Ashleigh scoffed. "Does he trust anyone?"

"He trusts you."

Ashleigh looked at Sadie and smiled.

"I think you need to trust him, too. Tell him about Robert."

"He knows about my past. I told him I had been married and it was abusive."

"Tell him who Robert is, what we think might be happening. And that he's here."

For a second, fear ran down her spine. Ashleigh had a terrible thought, and before she could stop herself, she blurted out, "What if Dean goes after him?"

Now Sadie shrugged. "So?" The room grew quiet, then they nervously laughed. "Wait, you said Dean had three suspects. Who else?"

"No idea. He's kept that one close to his chest."

Ben roughly set the just showered Quentin Fletcher on the couch as Walt dragged a chair up to face him.

"You get our protection, we get answers," Walt said. "You've been playing with us since the shootout, now you're here. And we're here. And no one else is."

Fletcher swallowed hard. Walt glared at him.

Then he laughed. "Just kidding, we can't do anything to you. Heck, we can't even legally question you about the ongoing case. We're cops. But you know who isn't?"

Fletcher looked from Walt to Ben and back. "L-lots of people?"

"Your attorney," Ben said, walking beside Fletcher's couch. "Now, what Inspector Marino and I can't figure out is why he wanted to get you out of the local jail. And *that* we can ask you about."

"I-I wanted to go home and sleep in m-my own b-bed. You guys are creeping me out."

"Good," Walt said flatly. "Because we find it odd that you are jerking our chain about intel on the Denver mob, and your attorney was one lawyer for said mob. Why would he want to help you over his much more powerful- and connected- Denver friends?"

Fletcher had begun to sweat. "You didn't realize Bethea was making a play here because he was trying to make a move on the leadership of the Denver mob."

Ben and Walt exchanged a look. They hadn't asked directly, so technically Fletcher was offering of his own free will. "Of course we did. But why use Eden Falls? It's small potatoes," Ben pointed out.

Fletcher chuckled nervously. "It may be small, but it's an excellent hub for distribution. Guns, drugs, people. I found some of those old moonshine networks and trails to run things through, and Bethea tapped me to head his organization here. The plan was to build the business side so much that he had some clout with the Denver boys. But he never had enough manpower to go gun for gun with them."

"So he hired someone?" Walt asked.

"Link Elliot was the point person for VYPER. Now, I think they were doing it off the books from the official VYPER group," Fletcher said. "Voight wasn't in on it, to my knowledge. I did sell him his house, though. Have you seen it? That was a big commission." He seemed very proud of himself.

"So, VYPER- Nathaniel Stone and Link Elliot- they were doing freelance work for the

Denver mob *outside* of their work with the legitimate security business?" Ben asked.

Fletcher seemed to run it through his head, bobbing it side to side. "Yeah. Except it wasn't the Denver mob, just Bethea. Remember, he was going rogue."

"Did he have an inside man anywhere?" Walt asked.

"Yeah. A federal somewhere. No idea who."

Walt cast a strange look at Ben. Then he returned to Fletcher, asking, "Did Bethea ever have dealings in Texas? Any attempts to expand his venture there?"

Fletcher gave an odd look. "No. He was a Colorado man through-and-through. Why?"

"Just a theory," Walt said. "So, who is the big guy? The head of the Denver mob?"

"No idea."

"Really?" Walt pressed. "You got into business with just Horatio Bethea- and he never mentioned the name of the man he was going after?"

Fletcher laughed. "I don't think he knew! That man- whoever it is, is a ghost. No one has ever met him, and very few men even mention that a guy like that exists. He's like Keyser Söze."

Chapter 10

"He 'Keyser Söze-d' us," Dean said as they pulled into their driveway. The garage door began to open and his 68 Camaro sat idling as they waited.

"Who and what?" Amy asked.

"Keyser Söze. *The Usual Suspects?*" Dean asked incredulously. Amy gave a how-should-I-know look, so he explained. "It's a movie. The big bad is a guy named Keyser Söze, but he's like a myth. This one guy is telling the story, and Söze is this unseen thing driving the story. In the end, the guy telling the story is Söze, and he had been playing the cops all along. Just to get away."

Amy stared at him blankly. "And what if I wanted to see that movie? Now you've ruined it," she said with a deadpan delivery.

"Aw, it's been out for thirty years. If you haven't seen it yet, you ain't going to."

They pulled into the garage and climbed out of the car. No sooner had Dean gotten out than his phone buzzed. He checked and saw it was the office calling. He put the phone away.

"Something important?"

"Naw. It's my night off, and I have a beautiful wife to spend the evening with."

The phone rang again. He switched it off again.

They walked into the kitchen and Dean tossed his keys on the table, grabbed Amy by the waist and pulled her close to him. Her back was to him, so he spun her around until they were face to face. He leaned in and kissed her.

The phone buzzed again.

Amy broke away. "Take it. If the office is calling you that persistently, it must be important."

Dean made a disappointed face.

"I'll make the wait worth the while, I promise." She smiled seductively.

"Fine," Dean said. He hit redial. "Major Royder? You called?"

The Major's voice was cracking. "Dean, it's Jude… he- he's dead."

"What? How?"

"Someone got to him in prison. Shanked him."

Dean shook his head in disbelief. Amy looked at him with concern, and he mouthed *Jude's dead*. Her hand went to her mouth.

"Wasn't he supposed to be in protective custody?"

"Someone messed up, Dean. Maybe on purpose. We need you down here, ASAP."

"I- I understand. I'll be right there."

As he hung up, he looked at Amy. "I'm so sorry-"

She held up a hand. "No- he was your partner. He may have been corrupt, but he didn't deserve to die in prison like that. Go- do your thing."

Dean sighed, then crossed the room and kissed her again. "I love you, Amy."

She smiled. "I love you, too, Remington Dean."

Dean's eyes opened to a fuzzy scene. There was an uncomfortable bed beneath him, pain in his shoulder and head and a person was hovering over him with long, blonde hair.

"A-Amy?" he asked, disoriented and still reeling from that memory.

"Don't try to get up, Ranger, your stitches are still raw and you have a mild concussion. I want to do some checks before I let you sit up. So lay still." The voice was a woman's, firm but kind.

Was he in a doctor's office? The last thing he remembered was… falling into the road and then seeing… Rhett Windsor? Windsor had said something about… "Dr. Feelgood?"

The woman chuckled. "That's what they call me up here. I hate it. Open your eyes as wide as you can and look into the light."

Dean complied, and a sharp pain struck the back of his head. He must have winced, because the woman said, "That's what I thought. You've got light sensitivity. Wear these until it calms down." She handed him a pair of wraparound sunglasses.

He slid them on, and the fuzziness faded considerably, but not totally. The woman before him was blonde, with bright blue eyes and deep red lips. He thought he saw a faint sparkle in her nose that would indicate a nose ring- the small kind. She wore a white tank top that exposed her shapely figure and well-toned arms as well, and khaki cargos. She did mildly resemble Amy, but the hair was thicker and the face a bit more stern. But beautiful.

She leaned back against a table, and Dean saw they were in a well-lit room of a cabin with medical charts, some machinery and medical instruments. "You can sit up- slowly," she said. "I'm Rhiannon Windsor. My brother brought you here last night about bleeding from the head and unconscious. Fortunately, I am a doctor, and a pretty good one. So, aside from a painful shoulder for a bit because of the stitches, and a massive headache, you should be okay."

Dean sat up and the world swam. His left hand went to his head, and pain shot through that shoulder. He shifted weight and put his right hand to his head. "Did you say… that you were… Rhett's sister?"

She scrunched up her lips, popped her eyebrows, and nodded. "Yeah. I get that a lot. Even up here in the Switchbacks where we grew up. I guess it's the hair. And the fact that I'm five foot two and he's decidedly taller."

"How does that happen?"

"Genetics are weird," she replied. "And Rhett is a mutant."

In spite of himself, Dean chuckled.

It hurt so bad.

He began to take stock of himself. He was shirtless, and he moved his right hand over to his left shoulder to confirm that bandages covered the wound.

"It was a scrape, but a deep one," Rhiannon answered without him asking. "You got extremely lucky. The big threat was blood loss from the head wound and the other minor bangs you got from apparently falling off the mountain. Your adrenaline was pumping all your blood out. That's why you passed out. Here. Take this shirt." She tossed him a black t-shirt. "Couldn't save the shirt or the jacket you were wearing, but it's warm enough today the t-shirt should work."

"What time is it?"

"Time for you to get up and get moving around. About mid-morning."

Dean looked over and noticed for the first time that Rhiannon had twin guns on her hips. "Never met a doctor that carried," he observed, sliding the shirt over his head with a wince. Then she tossed him a sling.

"Sling will help rest the arm while we walk around. And yeah, I carry. Up here, it makes sense. Wildlife alone is cause, but with the local flavor- including my family- guns are kinda necessary."

Dean stood up and found his footing unsteady. Rhiannon rushed to support him. "What kind?" he asked. She smelled of flowers and wood and smoke- like a campfire.

"The perfume or the guns?" she asked with a smile. "You sniffed loudly. But I assume you meant the guns. Two Lugers. From World War II. My grandfather served and brought them back as souvenirs. When I came back here to do medicine for the community, figured if I had to protect myself, they'd work fine."

"Community?"

She guided him toward the door and said, "I'll show you."

The door opened and Dean was thankful for the sunglasses. It was a bright, beautiful day, and even with the protection, he felt pain in his head. When his vision cleared again, he was looking out on a mountain top. To the left there was land being cleared and small homes going up. To the right, he saw homes- some little more than shacks- littered around the weaving road down the mountain they were on. It opened to a small valley, still hidden in the shadow of the forested mountain to the east even at the late morning hour. Scattered around the valley were homes and what looked like shops and work sites. "What is this?"

Rhiannon shrugged. "It's a refuge. The Denver elites have been buying up all the old land these folks had on the western side of the mountain. These people couldn't afford to go down into the valley, so they moved up here. Some built their own homes, started their own commerce, tried to live off the grid. Over the last few weeks, Rhett has been buying up the land over there-" she pointed to the left- "And preparing to build more homes for the displaced mountain folks. He's taken to calling it the Switchbacks. His little play on words about switching the land back to its rightful owners."

"Some of these have been here for a lot longer than that," Dean observed.

"Yep. For generations, in fact. Our family was one of those that lived here for a time. But there were just a handful. These are a welcoming people, Mr. Dean, if the people who come to them understand their ways. Honest people, too. But dirt poor. That's why I came back."

Dean turned to her and looked her over. "You're an actual doctor?"

She laughed. "What? You thought I was just a hillbilly medicine woman using herbs and rusty knives?"

He liked her laugh- reminding him of Amy.

"No. I just…well, the whole Dr. Feelgood thing."

"Right. The bane of my existence," Rhiannon said, turning and looking down the slope. "See that lush, green space there? That's where I grow the marijuana. Completely legal- I have my state grower's license and everything. It pays for me so I can provide free- or really cheap- medical care to the people up here. And before you ask, no I didn't slip you any ganja for pain. And no, I do not partake myself."

They were walking down a gravel road toward a work site. In the distance, Dean saw a red-headed giant cutting some timber into usable wood for a house. A small woman with short brown hair was helping him. "Rhett and Tina. His girlfriend," Rhiannon explained. "He's become a bit of a local hero up here. That stuff you all went through changed him." Rhiannon turned to Dean. "You know that mess with the drugs and the guns he was involved in is done for him, right?"

Dean saw concern in her face. Fear that her brother was going to get in trouble. Her brother that seemed to be trying to find a better way in life. "I didn't. But I can see a different Rhett than the one I first met."

"He give you the whole 'people see what they want to see' bit?"

"Yeah. As for why he played dumb all the time. He said everyone thought he was dumb just because he was big. And they never respected him for going to school. But here you are, a doctor."

Rhiannon looked off to the rising sun. "We were a very different branch of the Windsor family all along. Rhett desperately wanted to fit in, so he played that game. I never cared. Plus, I was a girl. Girls went to school in our world."

"Why did you come back, if it was so bad?"

She sighed. "After mom and dad were gone, someone had to look after Rhett." She looked back at Dean. "And I did my residency in Boulder, hated the city and realized I was always a country girl. Came back to visit about a year ago, saw the situation up here, and made some choices. Haven't regretted them yet." She was smiling with pride, and Dean noticed that the sternness she had when he first woke up had melted. "You know something about choices, don't you, Ranger?"

Behind his glasses, he blinked. "What do you mean?"

"I read. Rhett talks. I know your story, why you came out here from Texas," Rhiannon said, turning him around and heading him back toward her house, where he had been treated. "Who is Amy?"

Dean looked at her quickly. "My wife. Why?"

"You called me Amy when you woke up. Figured that was the case," she put a hand on his back to steady him as he stumbled a bit over a small stone. "Rhett told me a little about that, too. For what it's worth, I am sorry."

"Much appreciated," Dean said. "Forgive me if I don't talk much about it."

"Hey, no pressure from me." She opened the door and helped him inside. "But I do have some questions. About how you got shot- and who shot you. And just how much of a firestorm is coming for this little community?"

Dean sat on the bed, feeling pretty wasted from the short walk. "Hopefully none. If I can help it. Now, is there any way I can call someone about what happened last night?"

She reached into the bloody mound of clothing that was his jacket and shirt, retrieved his phone and tossed it to him. "Yeah, but make sure it's people you can trust. These mountains have eyes and ears that are not altogether friendly. As you have clearly seen."

"He's alive," Withers announced, looking through his binoculars. Dean had managed to take out his sniper rifle in the action the previous night.

Stone was leaning against the Behemoth, watching Hesse patch up his team. Benton had taken a shot to the hip- glancing, but it still needed stitches. Sharpe had been hit in the chest, but the body armor took most of the blow. Simmons had his shirt off, showing the deep bruise from the shot Dean got off on him. Stone was unharmed, as were Hesse and Trant. It had been Hesse who got the shot off on Dean, but they hadn't known if it was fatal or just a wound.

Stone swore, and he saw Hesse pause in his stitching for a moment. The man was pondering when to make his move. To clean up the mess just like Voight wanted. And the mess was Stone and his team.

"So, he lived," Stone said aloud. "And now we know where Windsor has been spending his nights. Anyone else think Voight might want to take this land up here, sooner rather than later?"

Hesse, knowing the question was for him, turned and said, "There isn't much Voight doesn't want. You thinking we make a run for this place tonight?"

Stone smiled. The one thing Hesse enjoyed more than killing was creating chaos and terror. The idea of trying to run a hundred or so people off their land with threats and violence would plant a seed in the sociopath's mind. He'd argue for another chance for the VYPER team with Voight. "I am. But my guys need to make a plan."

"What about Dean?" Hesse asked. "He's still a problem."

"Yeah, but he's human, too," Withers said. "He's moving slow, got a sling, and looks like he's wearing sunglasses to help with a concussion. He won't be coming after us too quickly. But we do need to change up our hideouts."

Stone stood up and looked out over the valley from the mountain across from where they had seen Dean. "This looks good to me. For now."

Behind his back, Hesse and Withers exchanged a knowing glance.

"What happened?!?"

Dean had just told Ben what had gone down the night before and asked for a pick up. Ben couldn't believe what he was hearing.

"VYPER came after me. I got away. But my Jeep didn't. What else is there to explain?"

"A lot. But, I can't come get you," Ben said. "Walt and I got tagged with providing protection for Fletcher- who got released."

"What? Why?"

"See, doesn't feel too good not getting all the details, does it?" Ben said snarkily. "Look, when you get back down here, we can fill each other in on all the good stuff. Can't you call Sadie or Ashleigh?"

"They didn't answer."

"Sure, I'm your second choice. Makes sense."

Silence. "I'll find someone else. Let you know when I get back down the mountain."

Click.

Walt walked in the front door with coffee and donuts and saw the frustration on Ben's face. "What happened?"

"Dean was ambushed by VYPER. He managed to get away, but he lost his truck. And he's up on the mountain, somewhere, but didn't say where."

"Does any of what you just said surprised you?"

Ben sighed. "No."

"Then let's get to work getting the moron upstairs to reveal more intel," Walt said. "Coffee?"

"No rides for me," Dean said.

"Ask Rhett," Rhiannon said as she brought him a cup of coffee. "He would gladly do it.

When he brought you in, he was really concerned about you."

Dean screwed up his face in confusion. "Why?"

Rhiannon shrugged. "You'll have to ask him. But what I do know is that after that business down in the Falls, he cut ties with Nigel and Zeke's criminal stuff. Not immediately, but he's been clear of it for at least a month."

"That's not long."

"When Rhett decides, he doesn't go back."

"Hmm," Dean said taking a sip of coffee.

"He gives you credit, by the way," she said. "Something about your interactions with him changed things. He said you were a man of integrity. Something about a man of faith?"

Dean chuckled.

"Do you really read the men you've killed last rites?"

Dean chuckled again. "I'm not Catholic, and it's not last rites. I just pray for them. How'd you know about that?"

"Like I said, I read, Ranger," Rhiannon said. "And you were all over the news- especially with that Storms lady's story. It intrigued me, and with Rhett talking about you, I did my own research. Something about a man you killed about three or four years ago outside of Denver. A Dmitri Koskoff? What was that all about?”

Dean hesitated. He hated talking about that time in his life. He’d only really talked about it with Ashleigh. But that internal signal that told him she was okay was saying the same thing about Rhiannon.

“If you don’t want to talk, that’s fine,” she said.

“No. It’s okay. He was a suspect in my wife’s death. Wasn’t him, but he told me there was something to look for here. In Colorado.”

Rhiannon bit her lower lip and took a deep breath. “Do you know who *did* kill her?”

“It’s one of three men. Well, two. One was just involved in the plan to kill her. He’s…not a problem anymore.”

Rhiannon was silent, seeming to understand what that meant. Then she asked, “What happened to her?”

Dean had not talked about that night with anyone else, other than investigators. Not even Ashleigh. Not Mike. Maybe it was the wooziness of his head, maybe it was the pain, or maybe he just needed to get it all off his chest…

"It started when I got a call that my old partner who had been arrested for working with the mob had been killed in jail…"

Chapter 11

Dean drove to the prison in less than twenty minutes. Traffic was light at that time of night, especially for Austin. As he got out of the car, he put on that blasted hat again and flipped his badge out of his suit coat pocket.

The guard saw the badge and waved him through, but not before making a comment along the lines, "Kinda fancy tonight, Ranger." Dean was in no mood for good humor, so a cutting look shut the man's laughter down. He walked toward the warden, a man he recognized from visits to Grant Kolbe.

"Ranger, I am so sorry, he was-"

"Supposed to be in protective custody," Dean said sharply. "Why wasn't he?"

The warden hemmed and hawed a bit, and Dean knew what that meant. Incompetence or corruption. The warden was wearing a rather expensive suit, so Dean guessed corruption.

"Look, Ranger, I know he was your partner, but he was a bad guy. Not for nothing, but bad guys die in here all the time."

In a flash, Dean was in the man's face, a finger pointed at his chin. "Then you aren't doing your job, warden. And yes, he was my friend, and I don't know why he turned like he did. I was gonna find out, but now I never will. Ya know why? Cuz you screwed up- either on accident or on purpose- and now my friend is dead. And a promisin' lead on a major criminal enterprise is gone, too. *Not for nothin'* Warden, but you suck at your job." Just as fast, Dean spun away from the warden and went toward the morgue. Major Hank Royder, his boss, was in the room, standing over Jude's body, silently analyzing him.

"Boss," Dean said to announce his presence.

Royder didn't turn. "It was a set-up, Dean. Someone on the outside got the hit set up. Someone who knew the right people. You know who it was?"

Dean looked at his shoes. "Suspect it's Grant Kolbe. Figure he set up Jude to take the fall and get himself out of prison. And we fell for it. Hook, line, and-"

"Jude was dirty, Dean," Royder said flatly. "That wasn't a lie from Kolbe. He's been on someone's payroll for a year. Someone out of Colorado."

Dean's mouth hung open in surprise. "How did-"

Royder turned. His face was gaunt, his eyes sunken. He looked ten years older than he was. "Because I am, too. And now, they are coming for me because I just sent all my files to you. I doubt I'll make it home tonight. But you- you gotta take 'em down, Dean. You were the best of us, the only one clean. It killed Jude to hide it from you, but he had debts. Truth be told, man, the rot in the Rangers is deep. How you managed to avoid it, I'll never know."

Dean shook his head. "Wait- why now? Why come clean, why give me the info now?"

Royder took a deep breath. "When they killed Jude, I knew I was next. I'm a loose end. Won't take them long to realize I sent my evidence to you."

"In an email? I could check it-"

Royder held up a hand. "Courier. Should have arrived just after you got in the car. Told them to wait until you left."

Dean looked at him askance. "Why?"

"So I could apologize before you saw how dirty I was."

A silence fell on the room. The two men stared at each other, unsure of what to do. Finally Royder said, "Let's go to your house. I'll go over the files with you, and you can take me."

They began to walk toward the exit. "I still don't get why you didn't just bring the files to the house instead of having me come here," Dean said, running the illogical situation over in his head.

Royder didn't respond.

Dean's bells were going off. "Your apology's reasonin' don't add up, Boss. Why did you really call me down here?"

Royder looked at him with tears in his eyes. "I-I'm sorry…But I have faith in you. You're not just fast on the draw, you know."

Dean's mind was racing. What was he getting at?

"They made me. Threatened my wife. I-I had no choice. But if you go to Amy fast-"

BANG!

The Major fell backward, blood pouring from his forehead. It was all in slow motion. Royder struck the ground, Dean turned and saw a figure in black move across the street from the jail. Sniper. He jumped into a dark sedan and peeled away.

Royder's last words rang in his head. *They made me…I had no choice…*

Amy.

Dean raced to his car even as the guards were swarming to Royder's body and calling for Dean. He thought about calling for an officer to go to the house- but then he remembered more of Royder's words. *The rot in the Rangers is deep.*

No one. No one to trust.

He called Amy.

No answer.

He began to sweat, and no amount of air conditioning would cool him. His heart raced, his left foot tapped rapidly on the floorboard of the car. A thousand thoughts raced through his head for every white line that zoomed past the left side of his car.

What kind of danger was she in?

Who had been sent to his house?

Could Amy defend herself?

And the one that sent cold shivers down his already sweat-soaked back:

Was she already dead?

The Camaro raced through those empty streets at a breakneck pace, dodging in and out of lanes on the rare occasion he crossed a fellow traveler. In the days and weeks after that night, Dean had no recall of the drive. No memory of what he saw, what he passed. The only reason he knew it started raining was that it was falling hard when he skidded into his driveway.

The house was dark. Quiet.

Stepping out of the car, he barely noticed the downpour falling on his shoulders. His brown hair immediately fell into his face and he absently swiped it away with the back of his left hand.

Dean drew his Colt.

His breathing was heavy, and he forced himself to take slow, deep breaths. He was no good to Amy if he hyperventilated. Dean entered through the open garage door, and immediately saw that the lights were out. The motion sensor light in the garage didn't react to his presence. Someone tripped the power- the storm wasn't that bad. His breathing picked up- he forced it to slow down.

Again

The door to the house was open, just a little. He approached it slowly, gun at the ready.

He took his steps one at a time, lightly.

Holding his gun in his right hand, Dean reached across his body with his left to open the door.

Then the door opened on its own.

A man clad in all black, with a black ski mask was standing there, gun in one hand, knife in the other. The only other thing Dean saw was the blue eyes behind the mask. Dean hesitated out of surprise- just a split second- but the man barreled over him and ran out of the garage.

Then his instinct took over.

Dean rolled with the impact and came up in a crouched position. He turned and fired at the assailant- and he saw the man's shoulder jerk with impact. The man reached the street and a black sedan- *just like or the same one as at the jail?-* screeched to halt and flung the door open. Dean fired repeatedly as the car peeled away, the force closing the door behind the wounded man in black.

The hammer clicked on empty cylinders, but it took a moment for Dean to register it.

No plates. No identifiers.

Then.

Amy.

Dean ran back into the house and called out, "Amy! Amy- where are you?"

No response. He went from the den to their bedroom, and there he saw a bloody blanket thrown on the floor. "Amy!"

"R-Remmy…" a soft voice called.

Dean looked for the source, and realized the blanket was Amy- covered in blood. He dropped to his knees and cradled her broken and bloody body in his arms.

"Amy! Oh my God!"

"B-broke in…t-took t-the file…"

"That doesn't matter now, honey," he said, stroking her hair and looking into her glazed over eyes.

His heart screamed that he had to try to help her.

Even if his brain told him rationally that it was too late.

Dean fumbled with his phone and dialed his emergency number. "This is Ranger Remington Dean, I need emergency services at my location forthwith. Severely injured female-"

Amy was shaking her head. "It's t-too late, Remmy," she managed, confirming his brain's understanding. She pulled back the robe he had mistaken for a blanket and he saw what she meant. Her wounds were extensive- stab wounds and a gunshot to the chest that was somehow not instantly fatal. "F-files from Royder got h-here. B-barely had t-them in my hand when he sh-shot me. T-took them from m-me. S-said he w-wanted to t-take his time…"

"Oh, Amy…" Dean began to cry as the sound of sirens that would arrive too late reached his ears. "I'm so sorry."

"R-Remmy? P-promise me t-two things?" Her blue eyes were weak and pleading with him.

"Anything, love."

"Catch them," she said with as much assertiveness as she had left. "And promise me-you'll learn to smile more again? Get away from this dark life. F-find y-your hope again." She gasped, then, "Remember…One b-breath at a time…"

He smiled faintly. "I promise. And I love you, Amy."

"I love you, too…"

Her last word was drowned out by the siren pulling into the driveway, and the room was flooded with red and blue flashing lights.

But Remington Dean only saw red.

"Oh my God," Rhiannon said, tears at the corners of her eyes. She wiped her eyes and her hand went to the pistol on her hip. Dean saw it, and assumed she was seeking comfort from something familiar. "Did you catch the man who did it?"

One of them. Got him good, Dean wanted to say. But this part, Dean wouldn't share with her. Or anyone. "No. But I will."

There was a knock at the door, and Rhiannon composed herself and answered it. Rhett was standing there with a short woman with light brown hair and big doe eyes. She wore a pleather jacket with a wool collar and big work boots. She had an impish look, and Dean assumed this was the infamous girlfriend of Rhett Windsor.

"You making my sister, cry, Ranger?" Rhett joked.

"He told me about his wife, butthead," Rhiannon said.

"Never told me, Ranger. And here I thought we'd been through some stuff. Had to read about it on my own. Haven't I earned a good, sad story?" He smiled again, and Dean was struck by the change in his demeanor from when they'd had their little shootout with a VYPER kill squad. He seemed…lighter.

"Well, you never told me you had a sister," Dean replied. "Or a girlfriend." He smiled at the young woman, and she returned it with a boisterous laugh and a slap on Rhett's back.

"Well, you aren't telling folks about me, huh?" she asked, her voice high, but not shrill. Girlish, maybe. "Maybe it's time I evaluated the worth of *our* relationship."

Rhett blushed and his face- for a moment- matched his hair. "Remington Dean, this is Tina Boyle. My girlfriend."

Tina stuck her hand out and shook Dean's hand forcefully. "Known Rhett most of my life. Broke my heart when he took off for college, but he came back for me, didn't you Big Red?"

"I thought I was the only one who called you Big Red," Dean said.

"I guess I *do* need to evaluate our relationship, then!" Tina exclaimed and began to laugh uproariously. She may be small, but her personality matched Rhett's physical stature just fine.

"Tina, would you tell Todd and Dell to go harvest the crop for the day?" Rhiannon asked. "Tell them to take about seven people with them. The dispensaries are expecting our shipment in Trinidad tomorrow morning."

"Todd Bolton and Dell Dumas?" Dean asked, surprised. "First, when did they get out of

County lockup? Second, how can you trust those morons to not smoke up half your inventory?"

Rhiannon seemed a bit perturbed. "Work release," she said flatly. "County trusts that I monitor my crews, and they know I do good for the folks up here, so they let me choose who I want. And I wanted those boys because they deserve a second chance."

Dean scratched his temple. "I'm all for second shots, but those boys are on about their tenth shot. Can't tell you how many times I've busted them for Park violations."

Rhiannon's hands went to her hips, and Dean knew she was angry. Amy did the same thing when she was pissed. "You assume because they are 'mountain people' that they are dumb and criminally inclined. They are just simple, Ranger. They work hard, and do as they're told. The problem for them is when someone takes to bossing them around that doesn't care about doing the right thing. That's how they ended up in County. And wasn't it you who put them there?"

"It was. Because they had come to kill *your* brother and cousins with a team of Tolberts," Dean said, keeping a measured tone. "It was an unfortunate night for Lenny Tolbert, but those boys had enough sense to surrender. And I don't think they're morons cuz they're mountain people. I think they're morons because I've talked to them."

"Typical lowlander," Rhiannon scoffed. "Lower elevation equals higher status."

Dean was confused by her sudden shift in demeanor. They had seemed to be getting along quite well. "Look, sorry about the comment- I didn't mean anything by it."

She sighed, crossed her arms and said, "Sure. Okay."

"Eh, Rhi- he's on our side," Rhett interjected. "Maybe ease up on him a bit. Those boys are slow- by a lot of different standards." Then he turned to Dean. "But they are good boys deep down, just easily influenced. Rhi is helping them. Promise."

"Aaaanyway," Tina said. "I'll get them and we'll get the harvest going." She turned and left.

"Rhett, can you take Ranger Dean down to town, then come back and help them get the plants harvested, loaded, and down to Trinidad by tomorrow morning?" She grabbed a bottle of pills and tossed them to Dean. "For the pain. It's ibuprofen, don't worry. Take as needed and see your regular physician." Her tone was still curt.

Dean was confused- was she that angry at him because of what he said about Dell and Todd? "Look, if I offended you-"

"You did," she said. "But it was my fault. I expected too much of you. You seem like a good guy, Dean, but you aren't really one of us. That's not your fault, you just don't really know us. No matter how much my brother vouches for you. You may live in your cabin outside of town, you may be a loner, you may share some of our sensibilities- but deep down, you are one of them. A lowlander. I doubt I will see you up here again. Unless it's to hassle us." She stalked across the room to a door and barged through. Leaving Dean and Rhett alone.

"She's a bit strong willed, sorry," Rhett said. "And moody. For what it's worth, I think you are the closest to one of us we've met in a while. And I think she'll come around."

Dean walked over and grabbed his belt and gun. "Doesn't sound like she expects to see enough of me to allow her to change her mind."

"Eh- you never know."

"Looks like they are cutting weed," Withers announced. "Getting ready to ship it somewhere. Maybe we could hit the transport? Then go in and take the village? I'd sure like to take that blonde- or heck, that tiny chick a message. If you know what I mean."

Stone looked at Withers with disgust. Something in that man was growing more and more detestable with every day, and it bothered him. Something about the whole affair he was tangled up with was making him feel unsettled, if he was being honest.

He made eye contact with Hesse, who shrugged and said, "Up to you folks. I gotta do some stuff for the boss." No comment on the misogyny? Well, okay.

Stone looked around at his men. He didn't want to use them all for the transport ambush, just in case. So he decided to hit with a small group. "Simmons and Withers, you come with me tonight. We'll take their truck and their supply. The rest of you set up for the assault on the village. We take it- minimal bloodshed- and leave a message to anyone else up here who resists Voight's offers."

Looking at a leering Withers, he added,
"*My* message, Withers."

Chapter 12

Ashleigh woke to the sound of her doorbell and the instantaneous pain in her head.

Sure, they had done some investigating, some digging. Good leads had been unearthed in their endeavors the night before.

But there had been a lot of wine, too.

The thought that telling Dean about Robert Hesse being her abusive ex-husband might send the Ranger on a path of vengeance had been too stressful, so Sadie suggested they have something to calm their nerves. And there were a lot of nerves to be calmed.

A groan from the couch opposite her reminded her that Sadie had chosen to stay the night rather than drive home. "Who is dumb enough to keep pressing the doorbell when we are clearly not answering," the detective grumbled. Ashleigh wasn't sure if that was the hangover talking, or if Sadie was just not a morning person.

She got up to go to the door and felt the world spin. Ashleigh paused, steadied herself, then took a few more steps only to have to repeat the process twice more before she got to the door.

Upon opening it, light flooded in and the world spun again.

"Whew, you look awful," a man's voice said. Ashleigh squinted against the light and first saw the bald, hulking form of Quentin Fletcher- the owner of the voice. But that made no sense, and she screwed up her face in confusion.

"Yeah, we feel the same way about Fletcher being out," Walt Marino said- his voice coming from a blurry shape to the left of Fletcher.

"Is Sadie here?" came the third voice. Ben Samuels.

"Ugh. Why are you so loud?" Sadie moaned from the den. "I can hear you from here."

"I'll take that as a yes," Ben said. "You heard from Dean yet?"

Ashleigh, now sitting on the floor (because, why not?) shook her head, and found that also set the world in motion. "Why?"

"This should be fun," Marino said sarcastically.

Samuels sighed. "Dean was ambushed last night- he got shot."

Suddenly Ashleigh was extremely clear-headed. "What?!?"

"So, how long've you two been together?"
Dean asked as they drove, the Ranger still
wearing the sunglasses and looking for all the
world like *he* had a hangover. Unbeknownst to
him, they were driving back the same way he'd
come the night before, when he had been
unconscious.

Rhett smiled as he recalled meeting Tina
in the first grade. One of only four mountain kids
in the class at Eden Falls Elementary (most
uplanders homeschooled- or rather,
"homeschooled"), they immediately clicked.
They'd been best friends since- except for the
period when Rhett went to college and Tina was
so hurt she refused to speak to him. "Friends
forever. *Together,* I guess for about five years."

"You seem to fit together," Dean said,
looking out the window. Rhett picked up a hint of
sadness, and he recalled the conversation he had
walked in on up at the Switchbacks.

"We do. She's small but loud, and I'm big
and quiet," Rhett said.

"'Cept you ain't so quiet."

Rhett chuckled. "I am around my people. Talk more around you and your cop friends than anyone else."

Dean turned and really looked at him for the first time since they got in the old truck. "Why is that? The whole, bein' quiet around your people, thing?"

Rhett knew Dean was reading him, trying to understand him, the giant genius. The need to understand him had to stem back to when Rhett pulled one over on the Ranger- and everyone else, too. He'd played at being a simpleton and let everyone assume his less intelligent cousin Nigel ran their criminal enterprise. Everyone- even Dean- fell for it. Apparently, not too many people could fool the man. "Well, they still aren't too comfortable with the idea of one their own being well-endowed in the thinking aspect of life. I suppose I keep quiet to make them feel more comfortable."

Dean smiled. "People see what they want to see, huh?" he said, calling back to their encounter in the interrogation room about two months prior.

Rhett chuckled again. "Yep."

"They don't seem to mind Rhiannon being smart, though. For what it's worth."

Rhett considered this. "I've noticed that myself. I suppose there is a bit of a double standard up there. Just like there is down in the valley and the rest of the world. Only…flipped. Women are supposed to be intelligent and loquacious, men are powerful and reserved. A brilliant woman doesn't scare folks up in the mountains because she still needs a big, strong man to take care of her. But if a man is big and strong and smart…well, he might just get too big for himself and not be one of 'us.' Whatever that is."

"Hmm," Dean said, then looked back out the window. "Guess nothing is simple anywhere, no matter how much we idealize that simpler places still exist."

"You and I need to talk philosophy more often, Ranger," Rhett said. "I appreciate the intellectual gymnastics from time to time."

"Alright," Dean said, turning again to Rhett. "Why'd you clean up your act so fast? I fully expected you to take over the drug and gun running after last month's events, but you disappeared. I never see you around town, never with your cousins."

Rhett thought about telling Dean that Tina was pregnant. He didn't know why, but he wanted to trust Dean. Maybe there was a sort of kindred spirit, a genuine friend that he could never find 'with his own people.'

He decided to take that risk. "Well, it started when Tina found out she was pregnant-"

"What?" Dean exclaimed, then winced in immediate regret.

"Yeah, knowing fatherhood was looming hit me square between the eyes about my choices in life. I suppose I came to see the error of my ways. Didn't want to set a poor example for any little one I might soon have charge of. And I wanted to live a lifestyle that would allow me to be there for the kid," Rhett said, looking off into the distance. The switchbacks that took them down to where Dean's car had ended up were just ahead. "I saw the outcome for those mercenaries, too. Those men came to town to do violence, and had violence done unto them. And I began to think that down that way lay only death and pain. So, I finally listened to Tina and Rhi- there's that intelligent woman thing again- and took a different path. If I'm being honest, seeing you in action helped too."

"How so?"

"Well, you're a good man, Remington Dean. Honorable. Loyal. Just. Merciful. You don't just talk about good and evil, doing the right thing, you try to live it. I appreciate that." Rhett paused for a beat. "Plus, I *did not* want to be on the receiving end of your quick draw. That is downright terrifyingly fast."

Both men laughed, then grew quiet as they descended into the foliage and began the back and forth of the next set of switchbacks. After a moment, Rhett asked, "How come you didn't go vengeful after what happened to your wife? I mean, I'd be inclined to hunt down and kill the man who did that to Tina. Not that I think you're wrong not to."

Dean looked at him again and said, "What makes you think I just haven't found the guy yet? And that when I do, I won't put him down?"

Looking over at Dean, Rhett sensed that was no lighthearted banter in that response. Dean was serious, but Rhett also knew that didn't change his estimation of the man. Remington Dean was still a good man- maybe a bit old-school in the justice area, but what he did, he did for righteous reasons. "That's a bit Old Testament of you, isn't it? I mean, I hear you were a reverend once upon a time."

"It is, and I was," Dean said. Once again, he turned to the window even though there was little to see besides the stone of a valley wall just feet from the truck. "Things change. Man's plans, our interpretation of justice. But it's always been wrong to do murder, and once done, murder is always met with murder. In a manner of speaking."

"Eye for an eye?"

"Not necessarily. When you take a man's life, you lose a bit of yours. Now, you take a bit of his, too. But takin' on another man's burden like that is sort of like a square peg in a round hole. It turns and tears and wears you down until all you once were is changed. Maybe even gone forever." Dean looked at Rhett. "You killed a man back in the shootout. Tell me you don't feel different because of it."

Rhett grew quiet. He did. Even though his actions saved the lives of some good people, he felt that weight. It did change him. But for the better. "I do. And that's why I don't pursue the same life I once sought."

Dean gave a half-smile, then turned to the window.

At that moment, the cliff side fell away and a small open meadow appeared. Just ahead, Rhett saw the wreck of Dean's jeep, and standing next to it was that big Sheriff's Deputy Quincey.

"Looks like I might be able to get a ride with the Sheriff and save you some time, Rhett," Dean said.

Rhett was both sad to lose out on a good conversation, and glad to have some quiet time to think over what they'd discussed.

Ben had found the coffee pot and begun brewing the stuff that would hopefully get Sadie and Ashleigh a tad more clear-headed. As soon as enough for a cup was ready, he grabbed it and took it to Sadie. While the news about Dean had been helpful for Ashleigh, Sadie was less shocked.

"I got shot. I'm fine," she had explained. "Dean didn't even have to go to the emergency room. Let me sleep this off."

"Sadie, it's not so much that he got shot, it's that VYPER is showing itself for the first time," Ben explained handing her the cup. "And that they went after Dean *purposefully*. That means they may come after any of us."

"A- they were both up in the mountains and we are not," Sadie said, sipping the coffee disinterestedly. "And B- Dean has a way of finding trouble. I'm still technically not medically cleared, either."

Ashleigh looked up, "I thought you said-"

"Shhh!" Sadie hissed.

"Yeah, but I don't want anything to happen to you," Ben said. He immediately realized what he'd said, and tried to cover with, "Because, you know, you are still recovering and all."

Sadie looked at him over the rim of her cup, and he could see a hint of a smile curl up at the corner of her mouth. "Aw, you care about me," she teased.

Ben felt himself begin to smile, and a warmth spread to his cheeks. "I mean…"

"Bout time. Now get in here you two, stop flirting," Walt said, thoroughly ruining the moment.

Sadie stood, cradling her cup in both hands and Ben allowed her to go first into the living area. Ashleigh was in the kitchen, waiting for there to be enough coffee for the second cup, and Fletcher was on the couch, looking around the room. "Ms. Storms, this place has great resale value if you are ever interested."

"That's cute you think you'll be able to go back to your old life, Fletcher," Walt said. "Even with the sweetheart deal your mob lawyer is working on, you're still gonna be a felon."

Fletcher smiled smarmily. "We'll see."

"Fletcher, why is it every time I look at you, I think of Jabba the Hutt?" Ben asked.

Sadie spit out her coffee.

Fletcher's smile didn't fade as he said, "Something tells me I'll serve less time than you think."

"Provided you survive until trial, big boy," Walt countered. "Remember, you got released. Mob will think you talked. They might just come gunning for you, and if it's just us here to protect you? Well, might not be enough."

"That a threat, Inspector?"

Walt shrugged. "Just an observation. See, looks to me like you are a loose end, Fletcher. You thought getting released was a win? I think it was a set-up. You realize your lawyer *willingly* put you in our custody. Even if we didn't ask you questions, the odds are good you'd say something dumb to get yourself in trouble. He doesn't care about that because he never expects you to make it to trial."

Now the smile was gone. As was the bravado.

"Sucks to be a loose end, huh?" Sadie asked, her words enshrined in sarcasm.

"I want to call my lawyer," Fletcher said flatly.

Walt tossed him a cell phone. "Go for it. Ten bucks says he doesn't answer."

Ashleigh walked back into the room at that point, and Ben could tell she was a bit more pulled together. She held a large mug with both hands close to her face, and walked over to Sadie and sat.

"Alright, while Fletcher over here learns the fruitlessness of hoping for loyalty from the mob, let's catch each other up," Walt said. "Dean will be down from the mountain shortly with his intel, but in the meantime, we can compare *our* notes. And since you were visiting Mr. Voight with Brent Chase last night, how about you start, Ms. Storms?"

Ben looked over to Ashleigh and saw Sadie give her a pat on the back for encouragement. She opened her mouth to speak and-

"Answer the phone!" Fletcher screamed.

Walt leaned forward and held out a hand.

Fletcher was ghostly white and flabbergasted. "It's not funny, man! What if they are trying to off me? You gotta protect me!"

Ben and Walt exchanged a look, and Ben said, "I'm so confused. What have we *been* doing all night?"

"You gotta get me out of town- like right now!"

"Ah, can't do that," Ben said, quite enjoying the realtor's fit. "You have to stay in the city limits."

Fletcher looked at the two men, then to Sadie. "Don't look at me- I was having a girls' night out when you got sprung," she said.

Ben saw in Fletcher's eyes a look of abject fear. He was breaking into a sweat, and suddenly Ben felt pity for the man. Here was a guy who had always come out on top before. Bought low, sold high. Made the light just in time, every time. Always got away with it.

But suddenly, he couldn't get away.

Trapped.

Like a rat.

And you know what rats do?

"Fine. I'll talk. Whatever you want to know, I'll spill it to your AUSA. Just don't let them kill me."

Ben looked to Walt, and the older man nodded. "Deal. I'll call her," Ben said.

"Then we might ought to wait for her and Dean before we share our various sides of the story."

Rhett pulled up next to the deputy's SUV and parked. "Bet he wants to talk to you, too," Dean said when he noticed Rhett wasn't moving.

Woodrow Quincey waved and started over to them. When he saw Dean in glasses and wearing a sling, he said in his deep, bellowing voice, "Guess that answers my first question."

"Was it 'who is dumb enough to roll their truck down that hill?'" Dean asked.

Quincey half-smiled. "More or less. Now, the second question is one I also think I know the answer to, now. Who helped you make such a poor decision?"

"VYPER," Dean said. "Six by my count this time."

"Seven," Rhett said, slamming his creaking truck door. "There was one more that showed when you were unconscious."

Quincey reached out and shook Rhett's hand. "Your sister patch the Ranger up?"

"It's what she does," Rhett replied.

"So, you know what Rhett and company are actually up to, Deputy?" Dean asked.

"It's my job to know about the Switchbacks," Quincey said, shifting his cap on his head. "Just as much as it's my choice to keep my knowledge about them quiet. But as you now know about them, we can speak freely."

Once again, something was being kept from Dean. He hated that. "Alright, so why does a LEO not tell a Federal about an entire community living atop a mountain just a few miles from a major crime scene?"

"Two," Quincey said. "Two crime scenes now. And I keep it quiet because of the feud. I might be new around here, but feuds are feuds no matter where you are. Add to that the recent events with outsiders like VYPER and I think my silence is justified."

"Feud?"

This time, Rhett answered. "The Tolberts and the Windsors. Been bad blood for generations. Back to the mines. Then during prohibition- rival moonshiners. That's when both families fell to the criminal lifestyle, by the way. Well, the organized kind. Always been shooting and killing, but when that demon water and later the devil weed came along- well, things really got nasty."

"The Windsors are a rough bunch, but a few branches have shown promise over the years. Like Rhett and Rhiannon. Though Rhett was tempted with the dark side for bit, I've heard."

Dean looked at Rhett. "I knew there was some vitriol there. Didn't realize how deep it ran. So, the people up in the Switchbacks, they're what- refugees from your little Hatfields and McCoys show?"

"You can put it that way," Rhett said.

"But it's more than that, Ranger," Quincey said. "Rhiannon has been working up there for years consistently. It's not just Windsors- there's folks from the valley who got bought out or priced out by people like that Bethea fella. Or Xavier Voight. And there's Tolbert kin, too. Or Tolbert friends."

"Todd and Dell?"

Quincey laughed. "Ah, so you do know the boys. God love 'em. Already learned a lot about these folks in my time."

Dean cracked his own smile. Todd and Dell were those rare criminals you almost felt sorry for. Like, if you could just help them a little, they might go straight for a bit. Not for long, but then, they weren't smart enough to do any one thing for too long.

He wondered what Rhiannon would have to say about that thought.

Dean started walking toward the wreck of his truck, and then he heard Rhett say, "I got work to do, boys. I gotta head back."

"I'll swing by later tonight," Quincey said. "I gotta get your statement since you apparently witnessed some of this. Besides, Lorey baked some cookies she wanted me to take up to Rhiannon."

Dean tuned out their voices as he looked from his truck to the path it had taken down the mountain. He remembered so little of the night before- just patches and flashes. He remembered Stone, remembered encountering five others- just not that last one Rhett mentioned.

And he remembered Robert Hesse was one of the five.

A man who had only been a set of blue eyes and a tattoo that might have been involved in his wife's murder now had a name and now he had a body. He'd come across the name a month earlier when the whole mess he was wrapped up in started. He'd put that name in a circle, stuck the mugshot to the board and begun to look for him. But the man was a bit of a ghost. He'd stopped showing up at his parole office, and aside from some sketchy employment history and a marriage that quietly ended in divorce, there wasn't much. The divorce was pretty shadowy, leading Dean to believe the woman was hiding out from him. He hadn't even found her name, but then, he hadn't really looked. If she wanted to escape the monster, who was he to dig her up and potentially expose her to him?

"I guess you need a ride down to the Falls?" Quincey asked, breaking Dean's concentration.

"Yeah, thanks, Quincey," Dean said. "I can give my statement while we drive. I really don't want to hang around here, too long."

"Sure, I get it."

Dean walked over to the ruined truck- which was upside down- and leaned in the shattered window. He looked around, saw what he was searching for, and grabbed it.

"Something important?" Quincey asked.

"I prefer not to go anywhere without my back-up piece," Dean said, inspecting the Glock for damage.

"If half of what I've heard about you is true, I doubt you need it much."

"If half of what you heard about me was true, I wouldn't be needing a ride right now," Dean replied.

Chapter 13

Brent was coming out of his office when he saw the man from the day before standing at the counter, Levi taking his order. Brent didn't think the man saw him, but he paused and made a heel turn to check stock. If the man was going to ask about Ashleigh again, Brent didn't trust his poker face when it came to lying.

Glancing from his hidden position, he waited until the man- he assumed Hesse- left. Then Brent brought out some cups from the supply closet.

But Hesse hadn't left, he'd taken a seat by the window. And he was boring holes in Brent with his eyes.

"What'd he want?" Brent asked, tilting his head toward Hesse.

"Uh, coffee," Levi replied sarcastically. "It's usually why people come here, boss."

"Right." Brent turned and saw that Hesse was still staring. Smiling, too. But it was not an inviting one.

When Levi had the coffee ready, a strange feeling of bravado welled up in Brent and he said, "I'll take it to him."

"Awesome. Saves me steps. Plus, dude's creepy."

Brent walked slowly toward Hesse, but didn't say anything. He set the coffee down, and out of nowhere, asked, "Why are you here, Mr. Hesse?"

That dark smile again. He was a severe-looking man, his eyes a dazzling blue but dead. "So. You know who I am, Mr. Chase. As I know you," he took a sip. "Mmm. That's good. As for why I am here? Well, business and pleasure, I should say. Got a job here in town. And as for pleasure? I'm looking to make amends with someone I hurt."

"And if she doesn't want those amends?"

Those dead eyes locked with Brents, then he smiled again and chuckled. "You her protector? Cuz I had heard it was the Ranger that was trying to steal my girl."

Brent felt disgust rising in his throat. "She's no one's property. And they are just friends. I *know* she wants nothing to do with you, though."

"Ouch, struck a nerve there, *Brent*?" Hesse asked. He cocked his head to the side, as if looking at Brent differently. "Jealousy. You wish she felt about you like she once felt about me.

Like she *might* feel about the Ranger. See, I read people pretty well, Brent. I know the kind of man who will talk tough and run. The type of man who won't talk at all, but cut you deep when you least expect it. And I know the type who steps too far over a line and regrets it instantly. Which one do you think I suppose you are?"

Brent said nothing for a moment, then said, "Please finish your coffee and leave. The management retains the right to refuse service to anyone." Brent turned to leave.

"Yeah, but you aren't the only management, are you?"

Brent turned back, and as he did, the door chimed. Glancing over his shoulder, he saw Nigel and Zeke Windsor walk in. They looked toward Hesse, and waved. Then they turned to Brent, and Nigel gave a derisive snort.

"Get used to seeing me, Mr. Chase," Hesse said. "Looks like we're going into business together."

"Sounds like you got lucky," Deputy Quincey said after Dean finished relating the story of the night before. He clicked off his recorder and dropped it back on the console between them. "I mean, you are still a legend, but sometimes legends come from a lot of luck."

Dean laughed a bit, and his head didn't hurt. Progress. "That's about right. If Rhett hadn't showed when he did—"

"He's good people," Quincey said wistfully. "I mean, I know he was in some stuff, as you know far better. But I swear he has made a true turn for the good. Now his brothers- they seem to be amping up their drug sales. Got wind of some arms sales, too."

Dean nodded. "Our task force is looking into it. Lots of suspicions, no hard evidence. Can't catch them in the act, can't find a paper trail."

"Huh."

"That was a weighty grunt."

Quincy rubbed his chin with one hand while the other rested on the wheel. "It's just that they don't strike me as criminal masterminds. And I know Rhett has cut professional ties with them."

Dean was intrigued. "Go on."

"They got a third? Someone doing the thinking for them?"

Dean had to admit the idea had crossed his mind. And the idea was Brent Chase. It made sense. He had been the guy Fletcher was trying to rope into the Denver mob. When that whole operation fell apart, it was as if the drug trade didn't skip a beat. At first, the assumption had been Rhett- but like Quincey, Dean saw him as reforming. Not reformed- but getting better.

The problem was that Brent Chase had always been a reluctant participant. Why would he suddenly go all criminal mastermind?

"Huh." Dean grunted, instead of sharing his thoughts.

"I'd heard you keep things close to the vest," Quincey said. "Heard you don't even trust other LEOs much."

Dean looked out the window. "Made that mistake before."

The bustle of a late night police station is always chaotic.

But when that night has included the murder of two high-ranking Texas Rangers and another Ranger's wife? Forget about it.

Dean sat in the interview room for what seemed an eternity. Cops came in. Rangers came in. FBI came in. Dean told them what he knew about how Royder had died, what he had found when he got home to find…

Amy…

But he never told them what Royder had said.

The rot in the Rangers is deep.

At the moment, Dean didn't care. She was gone. His beloved. His hope. Torn from life by a monster.

A monster you couldn't stop.

And for all he knew, a monster he worked with.

Rot in the Rangers.

The door opened and a tall, stoic man in a white cowboy hat walked in. Chief Gavin Rauls, head of the Ranger Division. Rauls sat across from Dean and took his hat off, exposing a head of buzz-cut, close gray hair. His face was lined and his eyes were gray, but they bore no sorrow. No sympathy. Just business.

"Ranger Dean, I am sorry for your loss," he said, his voice a slow drawl. "For Major Royder, your partner, but mostly for your wife. I understand she was a deputy District Attorney?"

Dean nodded, his bloodshot eyes focused on Rauls' crystal clear ones.

"Dean, you need to understand that this investigation is at its infancy, and as such we do not have much information. Anything else you can tell us-"

"I've told you everything. I went to see about Ranger Randall's death, met Major Royder, we talked about what might have happened- why it happened. Then he was shot. I raced home-"

"Why?"

"What?"

"Why did you decide to race home? Did Royder say something before he died that made you think your wife was in danger?"

Instantly, Dean's mind cleared. Rauls was probing. He suspected something.

The rot in the Rangers is deep.

Or was the better term, *high*?

"Chief, my partner was murdered in jail after I took him down for corruption. A case I was workin' with my wife. Someone then killed my boss- who was standin' right next to me. Maybe they were aimin' for me? I don't know. But is it such a leap for me to assume everyone involved in that case was a target?"

Rauls leaned back.

"No. It's not a leap. But I have to say, this is a dark day for the Rangers. A lot of blood spilled, not a lot of answers," Rauls stood up, and put his hat on. "I am sorry about your wife, Dean. But if I find out you are keeping things from me out of some chance at vengeance- or worse, you're tied up in this- I'll be on your tail personally."

And he left.

The door hadn't even closed when a young-looking black man stepped in. He was wearing a utilitarian jacket, green or brown, Dean couldn't tell. He had on black slacks and a black tie. His hair was thick, and he had a pencil thin beard and mustache.

Unlike Rauls, he smiled.

"Ranger Remington Dean," he said, his voice low and calm. "My name is Agent Elmore Pickett. Homeland Security." He reached into his pocket and pulled out a round, black fob- which he pressed. Dean heard a whirring noise and looked up to see the camera in the room's red light stop flashing. "I think you've stumbled onto something I've been chasing, and I really want to talk to you without prying eyes. I assume you don't trust law enforcement right now, and you are right not to. The rot in the Rangers is deep. That sound familiar?"

Dean looked into Pickett's eyes. "What did you say?"

"Thought it would. You didn't think Royder *only* sent that packet of information to you? He's been my man on the inside for a while now. And you know what he told me to do if anything happened to him?"

Dean shook his head.

"Find Remington Dean, and point him in the right direction."

"This is it," Dean said, pointing to the red and forest green cottage with three sedans parked in front.

"Must have company," Quincey said.

"About that," Dean said, turning in his seat. He was still wearing the sunglasses because when he had attempted to remove them he was met instantly with stabbing pains for his trouble. "We are talkin' about the case from this summer- and how it connects to what happened to me. And apparently some other stuff that went down while I was otherwise engaged. I think you should sit in."

Quincey scoffed. "Why me? I'm just a Sheriff's Deputy."

"You have good will with the folks up in the Switchbacks. And I figure they are bein' lined up in VYPER's crosshairs- if they weren't already in 'em." Dean opened the door and slid out. "And you're right. I don't trust cops. Blindly. I learned the hard way to get a feel for the good ones." Quincey smiled sheepishly. "And…I kinda wanna hang out with my favorite Aggie linebacker of all time."

Now Quincey laughed. It was a deep laugh, and genuine. "Since you put it that way," he said, killing the engine and getting out of the vehicle. It shifted as he did.

They walked to the door, and as they passed under the shade of an aspen grove, Dean dared to take off the glasses. He winced, but it wasn't too bad. It wasn't too good, either, so he put them back on. He knocked on the door when they got to the stoop, and after a beat, Ashleigh answered the door. She reacted slowly, her eyes bloodshot and red, but when she finally recognized it was Dean, she threw her arms around him and gave him a hug. Had she been crying over him?"

"Whatever possessed you to take on VYPER by yourself?" she said angrily as she tightened her grip on him.

"Well, I didn't *plan* to get ambushed," Dean said, making his voice tight like he couldn't breathe. "Much like I didn't plan on you suffocatin' me here at your doorstep."

"Ambush?" Sadie asked, walking to the door. She didn't hug, she punched his arm. Like Ashleigh, her eyes were bloodshot and red, too. "Getting slow on the uptick, old man?"

"Looks like I'm not the only one who can't do things like we used to," he said, finally breaking Ashleigh's embrace and pointing to his eyes.

Sadie squinted at him with an accusing- but friendly glare. "It was a rough day."

He looked down at Ashleigh, who subtly shook her head toward the red-headed detective. Then she asked, "What's with the sling?"

He looked down and shrugged with his good arm. "Just a precaution, keeps me from pulling at the stitches from the graze wound."

Ashleigh's eyes got big. "And the glasses?"

"Got a little headache," Dean replied. "You need some, too, it seems."

She gave him a playfully angry look.

"If you kids are done commiserating, we got work to do," Walt announced from the den.

Ashleigh led the way in, and Quincey shut the door behind them. As they entered the den, AUSA Kho let out a shocked, "Oh my!" at the sight of the deputy. "Sorry, I just wasn't expecting anyone else."

"Everyone, this is Deputy Woodrow Quincey with the Garvin County Sheriff. He's got some intel on who the VYPERs are maybe going after," Dean explained, waving toward the deputy.

"All well and good, but we've got a more pressing matter," Kho explained. "Mr. Fletcher has decided to waive counsel and tell us all he knows about the machinations of the Denver Mob in Eden Falls. But we have to get that on tape, so everyone have a seat. Ms. Storms, if you will run the camera. And, this goes without saying, but as a reporter, please remember discretion here."

"Why does she have to stay?" Fletcher protested. "She's not involved in the case. Not a law officer."

"It's her house, she stays," Walt said.

Ashleigh read the room and said, "Actually, I can just step outside. Fresh air is good for a hang- my condition." She grabbed her coffee cup and opened the back door to the porch. Dean greatly respected that even though she was a reporter, she knew the lines of integrity that far too many crossed for the sake of a story.

And she knew Sadie or Dean would tell her everything later, anyway.

With the door closed, Kho turned to Sadie. "Detective, will *you* turn on the camera?"

Sadie complied while Kho read out Fletcher's rights, and he waved them.

"Please state your name for the record," Kho said, adjusting a notepad on her lap as she turned toward Fletcher.

"Quentin James Fletcher."

"Thank you, Mr. Fletcher. And for the record, you will be signing an affidavit waiving counsel of your own free will at this time? It states you understand your rights and choose to speak openly and honestly with us?

"Uh, yeah."

She slid the papers to him, and he scribbled his name. "Now, will you explain the nature of your business and how that led you to cooperation with one Horatio Bethea?"

Fletcher began to run down how he went from real estate agent to drug runner and mob stooge. Dean looked out at Ashleigh, and saw her rubbing her forehead and sipping her coffee. He'd heard- or knew- all about Fletcher's past, but he knew Kho had to establish all of that for his testimony. He turned to Sadie, who was leaning against the wall next to him, and said, "Let me know when we get to the good stuff."

"Checking on your girl?" Sadie said teasingly.

Dean gave her a look. "I don't have a 'girl.' And you know Ashleigh and I are just friends."

"You sure about that?"

That made him blink. "What?"

"Just saying, you two are perfect for each other. And you both know it, but won't act on it. Just go for it, Dean."

Dean grimaced, then turned and went to the door to the porch.

Ashleigh looked up as he came outside, and she gave a weak smile. "It was a rough-"

"Day. Yeah, Sadie already said that. Wanna tell me why?"

"You first. What happened with VYPER?"

Dean went through the events of the day, explaining the trip to the jail to meet with Pickett, explaining that Homeland had interest in their investigation, but leaving out his much longer relationship with the man. He detailed the ambush, the interactions with Stone and the state of his Gladiator. Then he paused. He did trust her. And yet there were things he had never told her. Things he had told Rhiannon freely. Why had he told one woman his darkest moment, but his friend- maybe even the closest thing to a best friend he had- he kept it hidden from? "You remember the board in my basement?"

"Vividly."

"Well, you recall there was the guy with the red X over him?"

She sat forward, her interest piqued. "Yeah."

Dean took a deep breath. "Amy, my wife, was working with me on a case in Texas. She was a prosecutor. We found corruption in the Rangers, and cut a deal with one of the criminals we had arrested. Grant Kolbe. The guy with the red X. Only he wasn't a low-level guy like we thought. He double-crossed us, and then some people got killed. Amy was one of them. Now, Kolbe had two friends, who I knew only by sight, not by name. I've since found the name of one man, and I have strong suspicions that our mutual 'friend' Chris Starr is the other."

"Whoa," Ashleigh said. "I knew you didn't trust him, but…man."

"Starr or the other guy- one of them killed Amy. I don't know which one."

"How do you know it wasn't Kolbe?"

"He was more of a planner, a plotter. A mastermind, not a gun." Dean paused, weighing whether or not to say the next part. "And he told me before I killed him."

Ashleigh gasped, but didn't recoil. "Let's come back to *that*," she said, keeping her tone level. "Who is the other man? What's his name?"

Dean shrugged. "I doubt you've heard of him. He was a onetime member of VYPER- but only tangentially. He worked for Xavier Voight as a bodyguard, but I think he was also a freelance hitter. Got locked up a few years back, but just got out. He was there last night. I looked him in the face. A real sociopath named Robert Hesse.”

Ashleigh dropped her coffee cup and it shattered on the wooden deck below. Her eyes were wide and her hand went to her mouth. She looked as she was about to have a panic attack.

Dean rushed to her and put his arm around her. “What is it? You know him?”

“You could say that,” she said. “He’s my ex-husband.”

Dean shot up to his feet like a bullet. His mind reeled. “Y-your what?”

Ashleigh looked up at him with plaintive eyes. “My ex. I divorced him when he got sent up for manslaughter. On a bodyguard job, he killed a guy. In self-defense, supposedly. But…but I knew he was a dangerous man.”

An irrational anger rose up in Dean’s chest. “You knew? You knew he was a bad man, but didn’t turn him in?”

“It’s complicated.”

“If you had turned him in, maybe he wouldn’t have been involved in Amy’s death. Maybe she’d still be alive!” His voice grew louder and angrier.

Ashleigh stood up, her own face a mix of indignation and fear. “He abused me, okay? Beat me. Tore me down. Assaulted me. I wasn't in a good place, Dean. He victimized me. Don't you *dare* try to put this all off on me!"

Dean realized he'd overstepped, but he couldn't control the rage inside him. He wasn't angry at Ashleigh, but she was there and he had to lash out at *someone*. "I'm not puttin' anything on you. But my wife is dead, and the man who might have taken her from me was *your* husband. I mean, it's ridiculous to think that the same man might have ruined both our lives, and somehow we found each other."

Ashleigh narrowed her eyes at him. "Found each other? Like some sort of warped 'meet cute' where my psychotic ex tore both our lives apart and now we find solace in each other?"

"That's not what I meant, Ashleigh," Dean said firmly. "You know it."

"Do I? I mean, you share this surface level version of you, so I only *just now* heard the story of your wife's death and we've talked almost every day for the last two months. No, Dean, I don't really know you. I know what you *let* me know. Which isn't much." She crossed her arms and turned away.

"Well, ain't that the pot callin' the kettle black?"

She turned back, her eyes flashing unhinged anger. *"Excuse me?"*

"I knew you had an ex, but you never told me he abused you."

"Dean, that is intensely personal information, I like to keep *some* things to myself. You keep *everything* to yourself. Everything real, anyway."

Dean sighed. "I need to think for a bit," Dean went back inside.

Sadie was looking at him with raised eyebrows. "What was that about?"

"Did you know Ashleigh had an abusive ex?"

Sadie blinked rapidly. She didn't respond for a second, and Dean could tell that not only did she, she was afraid of his reaction. "…Yes…"

"How long?"

Another weighted pause. "Since we met…"

Dean gritted his teeth. "Well, he might have been the man that murdered my wife."

Sadie's jaw dropped.

"Now, Mr. Fletcher. Can you tell us how Bethea could stay ahead of the FBI, Denver PD, and the CBI for so long?"

"He had a man on the inside," Fletcher said. "Chris Starr with the FBI."

There was a gasp throughout the room.

"Do you have proof of this? I mean, we cannot simply take your word, Mr. Fletcher."

Fletcher smiled. "I have tapes."

"Where?"

"In my house. Safe behind the big painting in my office. The code is 114587."

Walt looked at Dean and Sadie, then at Ben. "Go get them."

Dean stomped past Sadie toward the door. He needed to get some fresh air.

Chapter 14

Hesse and the Windsors had chatted in hushed tones at the Book Brew for about half an hour, then they got up and left.

Without paying for coffee, of course.

"Levi, you mind covering the store for a bit?" he asked. "It's pretty light, and I got some errands to run."

"You got it, boss," Levi replied. Brent didn't see Levi's look of concern, nor did he see the young man pick up the phone.

Brent walked outside and looked around for his erstwhile customers. They were chatting around the Windsor's jacked up old truck, and Hesse was motioning toward a cherry Harley with the name "The Hessian" emblazoned on the body.

Brent moved toward his car, trying not to look as if he had seen them. From what he could tell, they had not noticed him.

He sat in his car and watched them get in the truck and on the bike. A roar filled the empty street and Hesse pulled out and headed down the road. The Windsors followed. Brent put his car in gear, and slowly pulled out behind them. He kept a suitable distance, thankful the Windsors were in back because he suspected Hesse would notice a tail pretty fast.

They wound around the small town, past the waterfall that gave the town its name, around the rock dome that jutted up in the middle of town, and began to climb up the street that led to one of the half dozen wealthy neighborhoods in Eden Falls.

Brent had recently sold a house in the neighborhood they were entering as a part of his new real estate side gig, so he knew that most houses there were between three-quarters of a million and a million and a half.

He also knew it was home to some local celebrities. Chief among them, the incarcerated (as far as Brent knew) Quentin Fletcher.

But they drove right past his house when they saw another junk of a truck parked in front of it. Instead, they drove up the street, and began winding up to the street that sat on the hill above and across the street from Fletcher's house.

In his rearview, Brent saw a dark sedan pull up to Fletcher's house. He recognized it as the one Ben Samuels drove.

What was going on?

"Well, crap."

Ben looked back at Dean, who was sitting in the back seat with Sadie. The deputy named Quincey was jammed into the passenger seat next to Ben. He'd decided to go along with them after Dean had stormed out. "What?"

"That's the Tolberts' truck," Dean explained. "They were drivin' it yesterday. Up at the sight of that hit and run killing."

"Yeah, those boys are never up to any good," Quincey said. "Didn't take me long to learn that."

"How do you keep track of the hillbilly trouble-makers up here?" Ben asked. "There seems to be a never ending supply."

"It's called a most-wanted list," Quincey replied. "You state boys ever heard of it?"

"Great. Now there's another Dean," Ben said, shaking his head.

Quincey and Dean exchanged a look, then Quincey added. "It's an Aggie thing."

"A what?" Sadie asked.

Quincey shifted back, as Dean was still quietly stewing over something, and said, "Texas A&M University Aggies. Dean and I are both Former Students."

"Ah," Sadie said. "So you guys also keep track of the rednecks because like recognizes like?"

Quincey laughed. "I like her," he said to Ben.

So do I, man, Ben thought, casting a look back at Sadie. She met his gaze in the mirror.

Ben had barely pulled to a stop when Dean was out of the car marching toward the house. "At least let me put in park, Dean!" Ben shouted. "What is up with him today?"

"He did almost get murdered last night," Quincey answered.

Sadie began sliding out of the car, and she did, she said, "It's something else. And that something else means we need to keep an eye on him."

Ben got out and called after her, as she was already jogging to catch up to Dean. "You know, I *like* being kept in the loop on things that might get me shot at."

Quincey got out, and the car shifted as his weight left it. "I don't know Dean well. Just by reputation. But he seems pretty determined right now. That gonna be a problem?"

Ben shook his head. "Remington Dean is always a problem." He followed Sadie.

"Now, see, I don't know you well enough to recognize if that was good-natured sarcasm or an indication I need to have my gun pulled," Quincey said, following Ben.

"Probably both," Ben replied.

Brent was sitting in his car, his eyes on the Windsor truck, when his passenger door opened. Robert Hesse slid in.

"Shouldn't follow us, man," Hesse said, his deep blue eyes staring at Brent.

Brent felt his stomach drop. "I wasn't-"

"Shut up," Hesse said gently. There was no yelling, no force. But Brent sensed a definitive threat. Hesse waited to see if Brent challenged this declaration, and when he didn't Hesse said. "Go back to your little shop. Stay there. And when we need you to do something, do it. Other

than that, keep your nose out of our business."
Another pause. "And just for good measure,
because I know she talks to you, keep out of
Ashleigh's business with me, too. We got history
we need to work out, and there are already too
many people messing around where they don't
belong there." He chuckled. "But dealing with
that will be both business and pleasure for me."
Hesse got out of the car, then before closing the
door leaned back in. "You can go now." The door
slammed and Hesse was gone.

Brent sat for a second, trying to gain
control of his shaking body. When he looked up,
Hesse stood in front of the car, tapping his watch
and pointing for Brent to leave.

He started the car and put it in gear.

Dean hadn't found them in the front of the
house, so he went around back. Sure enough, he
saw the mohawk of Travis Tolbert bobbing as he
tried to pick the lock of the back door. Virgil was

watching him work, but it was Waylon who first saw Dean. His hand went for that huge knife on his hip, but Dean just tapped his pistol. "Mine moves faster," he said.

Virgil started at the sound of his voice, and Travis just froze.

"You boys here to hurt Fletcher?" Dean asked. "Cuz he ain't here. Now, if you're just here to break in and steal some stuff, well, that's still not good. But I'm not as likely to blow you away. Except I'm in a bit of a foul mood, so I might just do it to make myself feel better. Sure, I got this sling, but I shoot right-handed. So, it's best you just stand up and walk away."

Sadie had walked up behind him, and that meant Ben and Quincey were nearby.

Travis chuckled nervously, but Virgil spoke. "You won't shoot us for just breakin' and enterin' will ya? That ain't legal."

Dean cocked his head to the side. "True. Unless you threaten me with deadly force. And Waylon ain't moved his hand off that Bowie knife. So, I'm within my rights. Just so ya know, Waylon, you go first."

Ben and Quincey *were* there, and Dean wasn't looking, but he assumed they, like Sadie, had their weapons drawn. "Now, I might take

Travis next, cuz I know he also carries a hillbilly toothpick. But in any case, I save you for last, Virgil. Cuz I want it to be you that has to tell your uncle you got your cousins killed. And by the same man that killed your brother."

Slowly, Waylon's hand dropped away from the handle of the knife. Travis stood up, sheepishly tucking his lock-pick kit in his back pocket.

But Virgil was having none of it.

"You think you're so much smarter than us, Ranger? So big and tough with your loud gun and your shiny badge? Well, I think you ain't nuthin' and I intend to show you." Virgil shifted his weight so Dean could see the gun strapped to his leg.

Dean cracked a dismissive half-smile. His fingers tapped the butt of the Colt.

"Virgil," the deep tones of Quincey called out calmly. "I know you only finished the tenth grade, but I'm pretty sure they had taught basic arithmetic by then. We got three guns on you right now. And from what I hear about Remington Dean, he'd get his shot clean before we could pull our triggers and you'd cleared your holster."

"And he's in a bad mood," Sadie added. "I think he *wants* you to pull."

"I just don't want to do the paperwork," Ben said.

Virgil was staring at Dean, but his eyes flicked over the Ranger's shoulders, confirming Quincey's warning.

A nervous smile crossed his face. "Aw, I was just messin' around. Trav, Waylon. Let's go. I think we got the wrong house." He started walking toward Dean, who was unmoving. "See someone called and said they needed a critter removed from their house, and Trav asked us to come help. But they said they'd leave a key, and whelp, this house didn't have no key where they said it was."

They walked around the house, and Dean followed.

"Let it go, Dean," Ben cautioned.

"Not them. I heard something," Dean replied. He had. An engine. Not a car or a truck.

A motorcycle.

Sure enough, they came around the front and saw Nigel and Zeke Windsor standing on either side of a man in blue jeans and a black polo. Black hair, blue eyes, and tribal tats on his exposed arms.

Robert Hesse.

The Tolberts stopped in their tracks, but Dean charged forward. Behind him, Sadie saw Hesse and ran to catch up to Dean.

She passed the Tolberts and matched his pace. "Dean, what are you doing?"

"Havin' a chat."

"Now, is that Remington Dean? Famous *former* Texas Ranger? Current…*Park* Ranger? Man, I heard you were larger than life- or did I read it somewhere? Anyway- you're shorter than I expected."

Dean stopped about twenty feet from Hesse. His right hip jutted out just a bit, his hand near the Colt, and every muscle in his right arm was relaxed. He'd been bluffing about shooting the Tolberts.

He was prepared to follow through with Hesse.

The Tolberts cautiously walked up about ten feet behind him and Sadie, while Quincy and Ben had sidled up next to them.

They were set.

No one moved.

"Yeah, I guess it's hard to gauge a man in the dark, when he's on his knees at gunpoint," Dean said, an edge in his voice.

Hesse cocked his head to indicate confusion. Then he shrugged, frowned, and shook his head. "You must have me confused with someone else. We've never met."

"We've met at least twice, Hesse," Dean said. "Last night, with Stone and his men." His hand brushed the butt of his Colt as he brought it up to gesture. "And about four years ago. Saw you in a restaurant with Grant Kolbe…and Chris Starr."

Hesse's eyes squinted ever so slightly at the mention of those names, but he kept a smile on his face. "Never heard of them."

"Might've met you one other time, but I'm not so sure," Dean paused. "June fifteenth, four years ago. Outside my house. You were wearing a black mask. I put one in your back as you ran out- my wife's blood on your hands."

"Whew- that's dark, man," Hesse said. "Like I said, you got the wrong guy. My friends and I were just here to see if Mr. Fletcher wanted to hire some bodyguards. Heard he got out and that there might be some folks-" he looked around Dean and waved at the Tolberts. "Howdy boys! Anyway, might be some folks looking to do him harm."

Dean kept his breathing slow and shallow, he was hyper-focused on the man in front of him.

"Listen, if you law boys need any help, we'd like to offer our services. Xavier Voight is looking to start up a new protection firm here in town, and he hired me. Gotta replace those worthless paramilitary boys since that whole debacle from a couple months back. Say, there has been a lot of death in town lately, hasn't there, Ranger Dean?"

"You want there to be some more?"

Hesse chuckled, making a show of clapping his thigh. "God, I love your dark sense of humor. No, I heard there was a body found in the Park yesterday. Some guy from Texas. Sounded like some weird ritual killing. Think maybe that should be taking your attention more than hillbilly breaking and entering?"

How did Hesse know about the body? Moreover, how did he know where the man was from? Unless…

"You killed him. Because he knew me in Texas. At the restaurant that night- but why?"

More sarcastic laughter. "Man, you must think very poorly of me. You've just accused me of no less than two murders and one assault in the five minutes we've been here. Look, I can see it's a bad time, so my friends and I will take our leave. Just let me know if Fletcher wants some protection. Something tells me you'll know where to find me."

Hesse turned and climbed on his motorcycle and revved the engine. Over the roar, Hesse called out, "Tell Ashleigh I'll see her soon."

Dean felt his body tense, but it was Sadie that rushed toward Hesse. Dean saw her stride by, and he instinctively reached out and grabbed her arm, holding her back.

"Let me go, Dean," she hissed back at him.

"He's goading us."

"He's goading *you*," she spat back. "And he's going to hurt Ashleigh if we don't stop him. So I'm gonna stop him."

"Sadie- stop."

Dean turned to see Ben standing there. His eyes were sad, concerned. "We will get him. But not right now. We do our job, and this whole thing, this entire nightmare, goes away. But we do our job. And it's not vengeance."

Sadie took a deep breath, pulled her arm from Dean's grasp, and walked to Ben. She paused for a minute, looking him in his eyes.

Then she wrapped her arms around him and embraced her right back.

Dean shook his head as if clearing the cobwebs. "Did I miss something?"

Chapter 15

Rhett bounced along with his truck as he pulled within sight of the Switchbacks. The road was rougher than the road to Hell, but the view was worth it. While Eden Falls sat at just over seven thousand feet, the Switchbacks were at 9,212. And still, a couple peaks reaching twelve and thirteen thousand towered above them. But they were close. Like the road where Dean had encountered his problem the night before. Mountains had a way of always looking closer than they were, but up there it was just different.

He passed a small cabin and an older man in overalls and a flannel shirt waved at him. Dale Fugate. Good man. Lost his home to an entrepreneur that wanted to make a tiny home village for the tourists. They shortchanged him, of course, and left him with nowhere to go. That had been just over a year ago, and it had been the start of Rhett's plan.

He'd wanted out of the criminal stuff almost from the get-go. But he had so much anger. So much hate for the low-landers and even his own people for rejecting him. Because he was smart. Because he was big. And because those two things didn't go together.

So he sold those people drugs. He saw it as justice, in a weird way. Dumb people who judged him for his intellect and wanting to make something of himself got hooked on the drugs he was smart enough not to take.

Then he met some of the other people who had been hurt by his work.

Like Dale Fugate. Lost his wife to opioids. Lost his money trying to save her.

Then he lost his home.

So Rhett Windsor made some changes. While he'd always feigned being the dumb guy, the people he grew up with knew the truth. So he just let Nigel actually make some choices, then he started doing research. He had money from the drugs, so he used it to buy up the land, acquired some building permits, then started creating the hillbilly utopia that was the Switchbacks. He'd been building the town up from the small tracts that had been in his family for generations long before the end of his criminal ways.

Dale was his first client.

Rhiannon soon followed.

Rhiannon, who was standing at the door to his house with her arms crossed. Her scowl told

Rhett she was pissed. She may not have inherited his red hair, but she got the red-head temperament just fine.

"You get your boyfriend home?" she taunted as he opened the door.

"Rhi, what's your problem with Dean?" he slammed the door to truck. "You seemed willing to help him and even make friendly with him at first. What changed?"

"He mocked Dell and Todd for being stupid."

Rhett shrugged. "Well…"

"Oh c'mon, Rhett. He's a lowlander. The disdain for us was dripping as he mocked them. Tell me you didn't hear it!"

"I didn't, Rhi," he said. "Todd and Dell are not the smartest. He was just making a comment-"

"He doesn't get to mock us, Rhett," she said, uncrossing her arms to point at him with accusation. "Those people down there have- forgive the wording- looked down on us all our lives, and now you brought him up here."

"Oh."

"What's that mean?" Oh?"

"When he said that, you realized it. That by bringing him here, I'd exposed our little world to people like Dean," Rhett paused. "People you see as a threat."

She nodded. "Dean was nice enough, but when he said that, I knew it was over. This. What we've built."

"Rhi, it's not like we brought Voldemort to Hogwarts," he said with a smile. They had been huge fans of Harry Potter when Rhi was in college and Rhett was still in high school. "He's a good guy, and he wants to help us. Heck, he helped me get out of my charges. He's willing to support my attempt to get out of the crap I was in with Nigel and Zeke."

"But they'll come," Rhi said. "With guns. With drugs. They'll take it all again, Rhett. You know it." She reached into her pocket and drew out a piece of paper. "Some woman came with this, Rhett. It's an invite to dinner at Xavier Voight's house tonight. For you. She said he wants to meet the men who faced down his rogue VYPER unit, or some other BS."

Rhett took the paper and read it. It looked cordial enough, but something twisted in his gut. Maybe the rich man wanted to chat about the daring-dos of local heroes, or maybe Rhi was right and it was a ploy to get their land."

"You go. I'll handle the delivery tonight," Rhi said definitively. "This Voight guy- you just have to know that he's got those men that tried to kill Dean looking for you, too. No way they went *that* wrong and he has nothing to do with it. He'll try to schmooze you at that dinner. So, you let him. You let him think he's won you over, and all is well. Because he *has* to think that. Because if he thinks you're suspicious or obstinate, he'll send them out. They'll come here, Rhett. And then what do we do?"

Rhett took a deep breath. She was right. VYPER would come for him. Voight would come for the land. It's what men like that had always done in the mountains. And they wouldn't care about collateral damage. And once Voight knew they'd created a community up there, he'd want it. Xavier Voight, Horatio Bethea- men like that came to take what others had worked for. They built their fortunes on the blood, sweat, and tears of others. Deep down, Rhett knew that what Rhi was saying was true. They'd have to defend their home.

Because the last time a well-suited man came bearing gifts, it was the end of their happy little family. Their parents had been poor, living on the land a little lower down the mountain, where their mine had been for their brief lithium scam. While that house and a handful of acres remained Windsor land- Nigel and Ezekiel's- it had once been nearly fifty. A man came with promises, bought the mineral rights for a song, then stole the land through shady deals and deceptions. Drove their father to drink and drugs, mother to die and premature death. Left Rhi and him with debts and broken reputations. No paths forward that didn't involve desperate choices.

How does a man stay innocent in a world like that?

"When they come," he said finally, with resignation. "We fight."

"You know why they sent us in, right?" Sadie asked as they made their way into the home of Quentin Fletcher.

"Figure it's cuz we're the hotheads at the moment," Dean replied.

Sadie nodded as she rounded a corner toward where Fletcher had said his study was.

"Yep. Cuz if Hesse came back, he'd get at least two in the chest right now." She paused as she and Dean stood outside its door. "So, why're you so pissed at him?"

"Mighta been the guy who killed my wife," Dean replied flatly.

Sadie's jaw dropped. "You're kidding."

Dean's lack of facial movement indicated he wasn't.

"What are the odds?" Sadie asked.

"What, that the man who killed my wife might be the man who was married to Ashleigh? Who beat her?"

Sadie bit her lip. "You know?"

"She just told me," Dean said. Then he pointed ahead. "Better get this and get goin' on back." Dean walked past her and she didn't move. He stopped and turned. "What else?"

"She likes you Dean. A lot. She didn't tell you about Hesse because…" Sadie looked away, and Dean thought she might have wiped a tear. "Because a woman who has been abused and hurt by a man she loved carries an unfair burden of shame. Of guilt. She shouldn't because it wasn't her fault. None of it was. But now, I assume you stormed out all pissy because you found out she was married to the man who *may* have killed your wife. Well, now she carries *that* guilt, too. You think about that?"

Dean dropped his head. He hadn't, of course. "You're right. I just…wasn't expecting that. I mean- what are the odds?" He cracked a half-smile.

Sadie returned it. "Yeah. Like we're on some bad soap opera, right?" Dean chuckled. Then Sadie added, "But you'll talk to her, right?"

"I will," Dean said. Seeing Hesse had shifted any anger he had toward Ashleigh for not telling him about her past to the man who deserved it. Now Robert Hesse had his anger- and apparently Sadie's as well. "You wanna talk about why you're so pissed at Hesse? That lunge was more than just a want to defend your friend."

"Let's just say Ash and I have a lot in common and leave it at that." She started walking past Dean.

"Agreed. But what's this with Samuels? You two…you know, a thing?"

She didn't turn around, just kept walking. "Not sure- but I like him. He likes me. And we get to spend a lot of time together since you leave us to do all the office work and interrogations."

"I think that was a good natured jab at my not bein' around Eden Falls, and I'll just leave it at that assumption."

Sadie was already moving the picture to get to the safe, so Dean looked around the room. Pretentious art, a lot of books on the bookshelf. He walked over and found one- it looked to be a first edition of a Hemingway novel. Pricey stuff. He walked over to the other wall and found a pair of pearl-handled pistols encased in glass. The placard read that they were replicas of the pistols General George Patton had worn in Italy in World War II.

Making his way over to the desk, he found a ledger. Lifting the front cover, he began to look through it. He found a bunch of names of wealthy families in Eden Falls, names he often saw as donors to Rocky Mountain National Park's various charities. He'd met some at events Walker made him attend.

Then he saw a name that made him freeze.

Bastrop Arms.

"You know Kolbe worked for a company named Bastrop Arms, right?" Pickett asked as they sat in a government issued black SUV. The sun was rising and shedding light on the Flatirons, letting the world know it was time to rise and shine.

Dean and Pickett had been up all night.

They were staking out Kolbe's new address in Boulder, Colorado. It had been less than a month since Amy's death, and the Rangers were keeping him on bereavement leave. Which meant that they didn't know he was in Colorado.

And Dean didn't care.

"Read that somewhere. A consultant?"

"You know what he consulted for?" Pickett asked, thumbing through a file.

Dean shook his head without taking his gaze from the building. "Nope."

"Here," Pickett said, placing the file in Dean's lap. "Take a look at what federal government digging can get, Ranger."

Dean began to peruse the files, annoyed at Pickett's condescension. For the last month, more or less, Dean had been working with Pickett to track down Kolbe and the men Dean had seen- but did not recognize- at Collazo's the night… the night Amy was murdered. In that time, he had learned that Pickett was a rising star at Homeland, and had the ego to go with it. He was going to make the case, and he was going to need Dean to do it. Taking down a corrupt cop shop was one thing, but the size of the feather in his cap that taking down the Texas Rangers would net Pickett was unfathomable. Dean knew he was just a tool being used by the man who thought he was his better.

Dean let him think that, and even played into the 'aw shucks, I'm just a dumb ole country boy' guise a bit.

Because Dean was using Pickett, too.

He never could have gotten his hands on files like the one Pickett had literally just dropped in his lap with Ranger resources. In the pages before him, he saw that Bastrop Arms was a company within a company- which they knew. But *that* company was a company within another and another. And one of those had a government contract. Big deal with a Senator out of Texas named Reese for fracking rights in a previously closed region south of San Antonio. A deal that stood to make the owner of that company- or rather, the company that owned that company- very rich.

Or richer, as it were.

And Dean had encountered Reece- or rather his circle of influence- before. A real politician- and all the negative trappings that go with that title.

"Xavier Voight?" Dean asked.

"You heard of him?" Pickett asked, that smug smile on his face.

Of course I've heard of him, you dick, Dean wanted to say. Instead, he replied, "Yeah, rich guy. Cowboy version of Elon Musk with his fingers in lots of pies. Nothing illegal."

"That we can prove. *Yet.*"

There it was. Pickett's angle. Not just the Rangers, he wanted to take down a billionaire. Thing was, reading the papers before him, Dean kinda felt like Voight needed taking down. "So, just because Kolbe contracted with them, doesn't mean he can connect any dots with the big guy. And wasn't Kolbe workin' with organized crime outta Denver?"

"He was. He is. Kolbe is part of a group of players I've been after for more than a hot minute," Pickett explained. For once, he was just chatting- not talking down to Dean. "FBI usually handles organized crime, but this new generation treat their connection to the big families like mercenary contracts. They go to the highest bidder like the contract killers used to do. But here's where it gets real interesting. See, Kolbe seems to be amassing loads and loads of intel on everyone he works with. Denver, Texas, Voight. Not just blackmail stuff, stuff about how businesses run. Like he might want to take over all of them, and combine the resources left over into his own massive op."

Dean shook his head. "Can't believe we missed all that."

Pickett shrugged. "I can." *Dick.* "See, at Homeland, I can pull your files, FBI files, local PD from all over. Heck, if it's connected to the Justice Department anywhere- I can get it. I even get CIA stuff from time to time."

"The Patriot Act- the gift that keeps on giving," Dean said sarcastically."

"You know it!"

"Then why ain't you shut them down yet, Pickett?" Dean said. "If ya got such an advantage?"

Pickett's smile vanished. The corner of his mouth twitched. "Every time I make a move, Kolbe is one step ahead of me. Until now."

Dean smiled. Then he chuckled. "He's got inside people much higher up than the Rangers. Can't believe you missed that."

Pickett stared blankly, realization washing down his face from his eyes to his mouth. Which let out a shocked curse.

Dean looked out and saw Kolbe emerge from his house and climb into an SUV of his own. "Let's follow, Agent Pickett."

Slowly, after winding up and down the streets of Boulder for almost half the morning, Kolbe's SUV turned and headed for the mountains outside of town.

Brent shoved the door open to the Book Brew and stomped in sullenly.

"You okay, boss?" Levi asked as he walked back to the counter from cleaning a table.

"Yeah," Brent said unconvincingly. "Just doing stupid stuff, as usual."

Levi made a confused look, shrugged, and went back to work.

Brent leaned over the counter and thought over the encounter with Hesse. The man was cold, terrifying. Brent was no tough guy, but he'd seen some tough characters over the last month. Seeing the real Quentin Fletcher- and then meeting the man in the suit- Chris Starr. The crooked FBI agent. Yeah, Brent had figured that out- but he still wasn't sure what Starr's play was. Now, he worked with the Windsors. Brent sold drugs and guns, or rather, cleaned up after those who did. He never dealt with the buyers- that was Nigel and Zeke's job, but he knew the kind of people they dealt with. All that to say that Robert Hesse was terrifying. Remington Dean was intimidating, and that quick draw was something to see. But Brent didn't fear the Ranger. Because Dean meant him no harm.

Hesse did.

The idea- no, the nightmare- that he'd wake up to see those blue eyes staring down at him with a knife floated to his consciousness.

"Why did I follow them?" Brent mumbled to himself.

The door chimed and he felt his body tense.

Was it Hesse?

"Oh, good, you're here," came a somewhat familiar female voice. He turned to see the statuesque figure of Charly Addison. He felt a nervous smile cross his face, and she scrunched up her nose. "You're not disappointed to see me, are you, Brent?"

He blinked quickly and nervously scratched the side of his mouth as he said, "Uh, no. Just wasn't expecting you."

She raised an eyebrow. "Someone else? Should I be jealous?"

He blinked again at her brazen flirtation. "Definitely not," Brent said before thinking. "I mean, what brings you here? Coffee?"

"Sure, but to-go if you can. Let me try the Amaretto Avalanche today," she replied, reaching into her jacket pocket to retrieve a piece of paper. "I know we mentioned getting together with Mr. Voight later this week, but he's had a situation arise. I know it's short notice, but he really would like you to come tonight for that dinner. If you can?" She looked at him hopefully.

He took the invite and looked it over. "Ah, sure. Yeah. I can make it."

"Great!" she exclaimed. "Wear a dinner jacket, he likes to have some mild formality at his dinner parties." Levi set her cup on the counter. She moved slowly past Brent, reaching so that her body was close to his. He could smell her perfume- he thought it might be Chanel. He knew he liked it. "See you then- I've got more invites to send out. You know where Ashleigh Storms and Remington Dean might be?"

Ashleigh had come back into the house to get more coffee, her eyes still red from crying, to find that while the camera was still up, they seemed to be on break.

Fletcher was regaling Marino and Kho with the tale of the time he almost sold Clint Eastwood a house. Kho was feigning interest effectively, but the older man was clearly looking for an out.

"Coffee, anyone?" Ashleigh asked. "I can make more if you want some."

"You know I would mainline coffee if I could, sweetheart," Fletcher bellowed. "Want me to help?"

Ashleigh ignored him.

"I'm not drinking coffee, but if you have some green tea, I'd appreciate it," Kho asked kindly.

"I do."

"Great," Kho said. "And Mr. Fletcher has contacted his former attorney to inform him of our situation, per Detective Donovan's suggestion. So we are taking a break from the video interview. Just so you know."

Ashleigh nodded, then went to the kitchen.

"I'll help you," Marino said, rising quickly upon making eye contact with Ashleigh. When he got to the kitchen, he said in a low voice, "If we don't find a way to get that man out of my presence, I might be saving the mob some money."

Ashleigh smiled sweetly and opened the pantry. Marino leaned back against the cabinets and looked out the window over her sink. "Thank you for allowing us to have our questioning session here. I know it's quite unorthodox, but, well, I think you get it. Too many unfriendly ears around this town. And on that- thanks for not being a…well… reporter… about it all."

She turned on the tap and filled the kettle with water for the tea. "Oh, I'll write the story. But after I have all the info. Besides, people here want fluff from the *Rocky Mountain Gothic.* Well, not fluff, but personal interest stuff. Or action. Like with Dean's whole thing last month. This just isn't boring *or* exciting enough."

"Lukewarm porridge?"

She looked at him with confusion.

Marino smiled. "Goldilocks. Just in reverse. You don't want *just right,* you want the extremes."

She affected a thoughtful grimace, considering the comment as she set the kettle on the stove and clicked the flames on. "Yeah. That's about how news is. It's why you get the hard stuff at the start of the local news. The controversy, the murder, the tragedy. And you end with the fluff. In the middle is the weather and sports- important stuff, but usually nothing that's appointment television." She chuckled to herself. "The news is just a nothing burger within a bun of interest."

Now Marino laughed. "I've been a cop for thirty-plus years, and I've never met a reporter I liked. But I like you. And for what it's worth, Dean does, too."

Her hand shook just a little as she dropped the tea in the water. Ashleigh just watched the water bubbling, and said nothing.

"My wife and I- been married almost as long as I've been a cop, by the way. Anyway, we clash a lot. She says it's because we are both passionate people, and passionate people who end up on opposite sides of an issue tend to butt heads. But she also says it's better to care so much you fight than it is to care so little you don't' even talk."

Slowly, she turned. Tears were stinging her eyes again, but she fought them back. "Is it weird that besides Sadie, Dean is the person I trust more than anyone? I mean, I've only known either of them a month, but they- especially Dean- are so dear to me. And the fight we had this morning-"

"Is none of my business," Marino interrupted. "But it's not weird. It's human. We all went through something, you three and Brent Chase more than us. That whole thing up at Dean's cabin- whew. Glad I missed it. But that drew you together, bonded you. The bigger question is why you mentioned Sadie and Dean, but not Chase."

Despite the kindness Brent had shown that morning, she knew the answer. She had *lost* trust in Brent because of what he had gotten himself into. But it hadn't been his fault- he'd been trapped. Forced into it. But then, why did something in her mind- no, her heart- tell her Brent still couldn't be trusted? Then she realized something. "That was a cop trick, wasn't it? Testing to see if I knew something about Brent. If he was up to something."

Marino shrugged. "Force of habit. Yeah, I think the guy's got something else cooking. But I will say this- I know Dean only slightly more than you do, but he is a good man. To his core. He has his secrets, but I don't think he has secrets to protect himself. He has them to shield us. Those he dares to let get close to him. He lost everything, but the way he's been with us for the last two months, I think he's getting ready to re-enter the world again."

"We don't see him much. Just talk on the phone."

Marino nodded. "How often?"

She sighed. "Almost daily."

"I don't claim to know his thoughts and feelings. Only a fool would do that with anyone, let alone a man like Dean. But if he's calling you that much, he cares. Not sure what kind of care- but for him, it's probably a lot."

There was a pounding on the door.

Ashleigh excused herself and went to the door. Marino reached out and stopped her. "Wait a sec. I'm not expecting anyone, and they wouldn't be back yet. Kho- you expecting anyone?"

"No. I'll get Fletcher out of sight," she replied.

Marino pulled his gun, then motioned for Ashleigh to go to the door.

She looked through the peephole and saw an FBI badge.

Chris Starr.

"It's Starr," she said.

Marino's eyes narrowed. She noticed he didn't put his gun away. "Go ahead."

She opened the door to see three men there. Starr, looking arrogant as usual. Edwin Jessup in that same rumpled tan suit. And Captain Spitz. Spitz looked frustrated. Jessup was angry.

Starr smiled.

"We need to see Mr. Jessup's client," Starr said confidently. "Now."

"We got company," Ben said as they pulled up to Ashleigh's house.

Dean saw Spitz and Jessup clearly, but he couldn't make out the third man at first, as he was already muscling his way in the door. But he didn't need to see the man. It was Starr. Had to be.

The car wasn't even fully stopped when Dean opened the door and walked out, slinging the door shut behind him. He walked quickly and decisively toward the confrontation at the door. He could hear the argument, Walt saying they were doing as Jessup had told them, Jessup saying they were trying to corrupt the witness, and Kho trying to explain they were videoing everything.

Oh, and Fletcher shouting, "Don't let them take me!" or something from inside.

"What's goin' on?" Dean asked, sidling up to the group.

Starr leaned back against the wall, Jessup sneered. And Spitz spoke. "So, after the orders given to us last night, and the release of Mr. Fletcher into our protective custody by Mr. Jessup's direction, it seems Mr. Jessup's employers decided they didn't like that arrangement."

"That is not what I said," Jessup protested. "I said upon further consultation with my partners, I believe in the best interest of Mr. Fletcher to *not* remain in police custody any longer."

"Don't let them take me, Ranger!" Fletcher yelped.

"Seems two things are happenin' here," Dean said. "One, you are a piss poor lawyer, Mr. Jessup. And two, it seems your client is currently- and loudly- refusing counsel. And seein' as all the law enforcement officers with Mr. Fletcher are out here with you, it seems he's making said claims of his own volition."

Jessup squinted at Dean, and for a brief second, the generally harmless demeanor of the bumbling lawyer disappeared. In that moment, Dean saw a flash of genuine rage, genuine malice.

Then it was gone.

"How am I to know you didn't coerce him before I got here?" Jessup countered.

Dean shrugged. "Well, I wasn't here, or much involved in the discussions with Mr. Fletcher. As for my fellow officers of the law, I believe Ms. Kho is tryin' to tell you it's been recorded, and verified by non-LEOs. Am I right?"

"Correct," Kho said. "Ms. Storms has been witness to this encounter-"

"She's a friend of theirs- of course she corroborates their story!" Jessup protested. "And a reporter!"

"Again, we're back to the fact that- as I understand it- you released him to their care," Dean said. "Bad lawyerin' right there."

Starr was trying to hide a smile.

Jessup huffed, then finally said, "Ms. Kho, may we speak privately?"

Kho made her way out the door and led Jessup to the front yard, away from the door.

"Sorry Dean," Spitz said. "He showed up at the office making a stink this morning, bringing Starr here along. Threatening federal investigations and all."

"Nice one about the bad lawyer bit," Starr said with a nod.

Dean just glared.

Cocking his head to the side, Starr asked Dean, "What is your deal with me? I paid you a compliment."

"You ever been to a restaurant called Collazo's? Down in Austin? 'Bout four years ago?" Dean continued to stare at Starr, but his hand, his good hand, was inching toward his Colt.

Starr seemed think about it, but gave no indication he knew the place.

But Dean saw the corner of his mouth twitch.

Ever so slightly.

"Can't say that I have. Why?"

"Oh, I was there with my wife, on our anniversary. Saw a man there, Grant Kolbe-" Dean paused, and saw the twitch again. "He made some veiled threats toward us, and he had a couple friends there. One had tribal tats on his arm." Dean dropped his chin to his chest, and nodded at Starr. "The other had stars."

Starr laughed. A little too loudly. "So you don't like me because I have tattoos that thousands of other men have? But they just so happen to remind you of a very bad night in your life?"

"I never said it was a bad night."

Now the mouth twitch was accompanied by rapid blinking.

Dean chuckled. "Why so jumpy, Starr?"

"Okay, we have this worked out," Kho said, returning. "Mr. Jessup has contacted a private security firm who will provide protection for Mr. Fletcher- under the guidance and direction of Eden Falls police and the CBI until such as a time we can get Mr. Fletcher to a secure location outside of Eden Falls. A matter we hope to resolve ASAP. Both sides get what they want, and Mr. Fletcher will be safe in his own home until then. Monitored, but *not* questioned by CBI agents and local detectives. Now, let's tell Quentin the good news." Kho and Jessup walked through the tense atmosphere none the wiser, motioning for Spitz, Ben, and Walt to follow her.

"Oh, the atmosphere here is really tense."

Dean turned slowly at the sound of a new voice. A tall blonde woman holding some envelopes had walked up behind Sadie and Woodrow..

Not getting a response, she continued. "I was told this was Ashleigh Storm's residence, and when I arrived and saw Remington Dean, I thought I could kill two birds with one stone." She smiled broadly.

"Who are you?" Dean asked flatly.

"Uh, Dean, that's Xavier Voight's secretary," Sadie said.

The woman made a mildly aggravated face and corrected her. "Personal assistant and legal counsel. My name is Charly Addison, and Mr. Voight would very much like to meet you for dinner tonight, along with Ms. Storms and some other guests. He is very interested to hear from the people involved in the incidents of what he calls the 'Battle of Eden Falls' directly, and he had a standing appointment with Ms. Storms."

"I thought that was later?" Ashleigh asked, coming out the door.

"Mr. Voight had something come up and hopes you can still make it." Charly walked up to Dean and handed him an envelope, then went to Ashleigh. "The time is on the invite, and it is semi-formal, so wear a suit, Mr. Dean."

Jessup and a very aggravated Fletcher came out of the house, and Charly beamed. "Mr. Jessup- I have an invite for you, as well. It's in the car. If I had known you were here, I would have brought it out." She turned and went to the car.

"She's bubbly," Woodrow said, having watched the interaction quietly.

Dean turned the envelope over in his hand, opened it, and saw the inscription. He looked at Ashleigh, who was looking at her own slip of paper.

"I guess getting shot doesn't merit an invite," Sadie said sarcastically. "I don't know that I've ever felt more like a side-character in my own life."

Ben came out just in time to hear the exchange, and said, "Well, Spitz has you and I on first duty with the private security guy tonight. So, you had plans anyway."

"Oh, that's so much more exciting than a fancy dinner party at a mansion," she quipped. Then she quickly caught herself. "I mean, I'm kidding-"

Ben smiled and Dean saw him give her a wink. Then he glanced over at Ashleigh, who was looking at him. She mouthed, "I'm sorry."

He half-smiled. Then he mouthed, "Me, too." Then he walked over to her and asked, "Since we both have to go to this thing, how about we go together?"

Her eyes brightened and she smiled. "I think I'd like that."

"Me, too," he said. Then he remembered. "Wait, my truck is wrecked. Do you mind riding with me in the Camaro, provided someone takes me back to get it?"

She smiled. "Why would I ever mind that?"

Maybe the day was going to be okay after all.

Chapter 16

Deputy Quincey took Dean back to his house to get his car, Walt went home to his wife, Kho went back to her office, and that left Ben and Sadie with Spitz, Starr, and Jessup.

And Fletcher, of course.

All standing on Ashleigh's lawn.

But the reporter was ready to be free of them, so Ben and Sadie started getting Fletcher ready for transport. With all of them out of the house, Ashleigh closed the door and bolted it. Ben had to chuckle at that little added emphasis.

Kho had not informed Jessup of the files they had acquired. Partly because Ben had quietly slipped them to the AUSA out of Jessup and Starr's view. And partly because the prosecutor knew that Fletcher wouldn't want them to know the files were in her possession. It was beyond the matter of disclosure at that point, what with Fletcher waving his right to counsel and the fact that said counsel might just be part of the group out to get him.

Still, watching Starr and Jessup made Ben nervous. They were sequestered away from everyone, chatting in low tones. Jessup in particular didn't seem too concerned about his client not only firing him, but turning State's evidence against the men Jessup represented.

Starr was stone-faced, thoughtful.

"So, this company they found- we know who they are?" Ben asked Spitz, who was standing next to Ben and Sadie. Fletcher was standing between the two groups, grinning for no apparent reason and casting frequent, furtive glances toward the attorney and the FBI agent.

"Some company out of Fort Collins. The guy's name is Garland Wagner. I had the office run him, he's clean," Spitz said. "Or at least, he seems clean."

"What do you think they're talking about?" Ben asked.

Spitz turned and looked, so of course they noticed. Their tones grew even more hushed. "All I know is they were none too please that Fletcher wanted to talk to you without them. Good call having the man call them himself, by the way."

"That was Sadie's call," Ben said, making sure she got credit.

"I just know Jessup may come off like a slimy moron, but he can twist a legal situation better than any attorney I've encountered," Sadie said. "Why are they still here?"

"Wagner is on his way," Spitz explained. "Don't want to leave Fletcher here without him to oversee you."

"I thought we were overseeing Wagner?" Sadie asked.

Spitz gave her a look that indicated he did not agree with that assessment.

"So how long is this gonna take?" Sadie asked.

Spitz looked to Ben, and said, "That's more in CBI's wheelhouse. It's your safe house."

Ben looked at Jessup and Starr, then in his own hushed tone replied, "Could be days. Could be tonight. But when we move him, based on what he's told us so far, even Jessup won't know. It'll be pretty cloak and dagger."

"But Wagner will have to know," Spitz said. It was almost a question.

"Not until we move him. Last minute."

Spitz nodded.

Ben could feel Sadie getting fidgety, and finally she asked, "Can we take him to his house, now? We're kinda infringing on Ashleigh's space here."

Jessup grew red-faced and raised an accusatory finger. "Fletcher goes nowhere with just you two."

"Man, I fired you," Fletcher pointed out. His eyes darted nervously toward Starr.

Jessup glared at Fletcher. "That's what you think."

"No, I did!" Fletcher protested.

Now Jessup smiled. Ben did not like that smile. "Well, fine then. I will text Mr. Wagner to meet you at your home, Quentin. Where I will follow you to pick up Agent Starr."

"Why?" Ben said slowly, thinking he already knew why.

"Well, he's riding with you two and Fletcher. He may have fired me, but until the ink is dry and the paperwork is in the court, I will do my duty to protect my client," Jessup said proudly. Ben thought he was about to put his hands on his jacket and stick out his chest like some old movie character. He was a bit disappointed when the lawyer didn't.

"Yeah," Sadie said under her breath. "Which client?"

Jessup heard it, and an uncharacteristic calm came over the man. The man who just a couple months before had been punched in the nose by Ashleigh for coming onto her at the wrong time. The nebbish and nervous attorney that often cowered in the presence of more dominant personalities. He walked toward them and said flatly, coldly, "Young lady, to cast such aspersions on my character, that I would sell out my own client for personal gain- or worse, to purposely harm or solicit harm upon one client to benefit another- is beyond the pale. Watch your step- or I could file a slander suit on you." His lips spread in a wide grin, then he turned on his heel and marched to his car.

Sadie, unfazed by the man she had clearly already decided was no real threat- physically or legally- chuckled. "Was that supposed to intimidate me?"

Starr walked up next to her and said, "Whether it was or not- it should. That guy isn't all there."

Ben watched Jessup get in his silver luxury SUV and wondered if that was true. Or if Edwin Jessup was the kind of lawyer who played whatever role fit in the moment. The kind of lawyer who you took for granted.

The kind of lawyer that had more layers than you could count.

Rhett was putting on a jacket he hadn't worn since his college football days when they made the players dress up for the meal the night before the game. It still fit, and the spots that were surprisingly the most snug was his chest and arms. He'd stayed fit in the last ten years or so, something he took pride in. Sure, he let his hair grow long, and for a time had the shaggy beard, but kept his body sharp. It had little to do with vanity and everything to do with watching former athletes stop working out and start falling apart. Rhett had read the studies, seen the stats. Plus, heart disease ran in the family, and Rhi was constantly on him about eating right and staying fit.

"Looking good, bro," Rhi said, walking in as he admired himself in the mirror.

"Shut up."

"Seriously," she said, looking him over and brushing a tiny bit of lint off his shoulder. "Cut that mop of hair and you might pass for civilized."

He'd kept the long hair out of a need to feed that mountain man image. He looked like a biker and a thug, and combined with his size it made people ill-inclined to approach him. But he was going respectable now, maybe Rhi was right. "You think Tina would go for it?"

Rhi laughed. "Tina loves you *in spite* of your looks."

Rhett laughed, too. "You wanna cut it?"

"What? Seriously?"

Rhett shrugged. "I'm going to the rich man's house tonight. Gotta look presentable."

At that moment, Tina walked in and nearly screamed, "He's finally gonna cut it? Woo-hoo! At last! Give me those scissors."

Rhi smiled at Rhett and Tina and made her way to the door. He knew she was anxious about the delivery that night, she always was. And despite her angry defense of them, she knew Todd and Dell as her 'shotguns' were not the most reliable. Tina would go- which worried Rhett a great deal- and a fairly formidable young man named Hank Pinsky would, too. Pinsky wasn't as big as Rhett, but few were. He was, however, good with a gun. Pistol or long gun. But the route through the mountains at night, transporting a big shipment of legal weed was bound to be fraught with potential calamity. From illegal drug runners that made their homes in the mountains to the treacherous terrain, danger was all around.

And VYPER was out there…

As Tina grabbed the scissors, Rhett called after Rhi. "Hey sis? Be safe. See you tomorrow."

She smiled kindly at him. "Love you, big little brother."

He smiled at her, by way of the mirror. "Love you, little big sister."

"The blonde chick is moving," Withers reported. "Man…she's fine."

"Enough, Withers," Stone barked. He was tired of the man's lecherous outlook on life, and tired of the man in general. Sure, there was the bond of men in combat, but sometimes that brotherhood faded when the bullets stopped flying. Benton was a good man, as were Trant, Simmons, and Sharpe. Link Elliot had been, too. The kind of men you'd fight beside with no questions. Men of honor.

But Withers was a different man. Cut more from the cloth of a Robert Hesse. Less intense than Hesse, but just as unhinged. Stone had planned to cut Withers loose before things went down in Eden Falls.

Now he was stuck with the man.

Stone walked over to Simmons, who was the only man with them at that lookout spot. The rest were bivouacking at a secure location to recuperate. Out of earshot of Withers, he asked, "You think this is a good idea, hitting the transport?"

Simmons, looked at Stone with the respect Withers so often lacked. "Permission to speak freely?"

Stone sighed. "We aren't in the service anymore, Simmons. Just a bunch of grunts working on something we never should've been doing in the first place."

"Then it's important, sir," Simmons replied. "We have a mission. And whether we like it or not, we need to fulfill it. If that means hijacking this transport, we do it."

Stone looked out over the horizon, at the peaks that glimmered with the early fall snow that fell at that altitude. "I just… I think maybe we've gotten lost. Our mission has creeped. Remember when we used to just go after the bad guys? Cartels and terrorists? Now we go after, what, redneck weed growers because the guy we work for wants their land?"

Simmons looked at his boots and kicked a rock. "Still speaking freely, I don't much like Voight, myself. Didn't like it when we hooked up with that crook, Bethea."

"Bethea was a bad man, and we had been given intel that the woman- Storms- was a threat as well," Stone hated thinking about that night. In the paper's offices. He regretted what went down, knowing what he knew now. That he'd been fed bad intel by Voight's men. "That's why Link and I went and burned down the paper and killed the editor. Following orders. Then that shoot-out with Dean, that was FUBAR from the jump. But it was an order."

"Sir, whose order?"

"VYPER command. Why?"

Simmons looked over at Withers, then lowered his voice. "Then we follow those orders, sir." He leaned closer to Stone. "Scuttlebutt is that if we don't, we will become…expendable. And I wouldn't put it past Withers to make a move to rat you out. ."

"To who? Voight?"

Simmons shook his head. "Not sure. But think about it. We only used to get called in for overseas stuff. The black ops, wet work on bad mofos trying to hurt folks on foreign soil. Still sketchy work, but a man could sleep sound at night. This is different stuff, and Withers seems to like it just fine. But I got some friends in another unit that said the old school bodyguard stuff was starting to do back alley deals and move merchandise that wasn't exactly legal. I may not like it, but I wanna stay alive."

Stone looked over at Withers. "He heard that talk?"

Simmons' face was a stone. "Yeah. And he wanted in. Told me he reached out to Hesse, who was working for Voight again after he got out. Hesse said he'd look into it."

Stone began to think about the call to work the Eden Falls situation. The mission came through the usual coded channels, but it was domestic, and it involved taking out a mob guy. But it had to look like they were working with him. No biggie, they'd done that sort of bait-and-switch before. And taking out a mob guy, even if it was on home turf, was still doing good work. Subsequent coms mentioned corrupt cops- which was why Stone had made the call to go in hot at the police station. Were they being set-up? By one of their own, no less?

"They're packing up, gotta get ready to move," Withers announced.

"Change of plans, Withers," Stone said. "We aren't hitting the transport. It's mission creep. Not wasting resources or taking risks."

Withers cocked his head to the side. "'Mission creep?' Are you kidding me? We are supposed to hit the Windsors, right? Well, those are Windsors."

"Yeah. Those are the orders. But do they make sense? Why hit the Windsors? Heck, why were we told to go after Ashleigh Storms? Or Brent Chase?"

"Orders are orders, Stone, you know that." Withers' face grew dark. "Or are you going soft?"

Stone bowed up to Withers. "Have you forgotten who is in charge of this team, Withers? I can remind you!" he barked.

Withers laughed. Then he looked at Simmons. "He take the bait?"

Stone turned to Simmons. Simmons nodded and said to Withers, "Yeah. He's not comfortable with the new mission we've been given. Played the sympathetic card and he opened right up."

Stone looked from one man to the next. "What's going on?"

Withers smirked. "What's going on is that we felt you were dragging your feet after the shootout in the Falls. Lost your nerve or something. Then, when we hit that SUV- that rich couple? Well, you really started to hesitate. Started to think the work we were doing wasn't the *right work.* But we had orders to kill them- Warren Cornelius had embezzled and lost money from Voight. So the big guy sent a fake invite to Cornelius to come visit. You knew it, and you went along with it. Why the sudden change of heart?"

"Doesn't it bother you that we are becoming what we used to hunt?"

Withers tapped his head. "No- because we are going to be getting rich off of it. And if you go with us, you will, too."

"You've been playing me this whole time?" Stone asked, his mind reeling.

Simmons patted him on the back. "It's not personal, Stone. It's financial. Voight paid us all well to hang around and mess some stuff up. Now, we have to finish the Windsor job so it looks like collateral damage and no one suspects the Cornelius job was a hit. Let word get out the hit was an accident- a mistake, not a hit. Then Hesse and Voight get us outta the country to a non- extradition locale loaded down with cash."

"So, what happens to me?"

Withers walked over slowly, drawing his sidearm and screwing on a silencer. "Well, we hoped you'd come around- which you still can. But if not-" he looked down at the gun, then back up to Stone's eyes. "So, what's it gonna be?"

He was trapped, and he knew it. He wanted no part of hurting innocent people- but to resist right then was death. He knew it. They knew it.

"I guess I'm in."

Dean pulled up in front of Ashleigh's house and walked up to the door. He was wearing a black suit and white button down, sans tie. He had also eschewed his sling, recognizing the loss of mobility was more a detriment than the pain.Plus, surely eight hours was enough time for stitches to set, right? He wasn't trying to be tough or macho, he was trying to be practical. The sunglasses were gone, too, but then the light was starting to soften anyway, so they didn't matter too much.

He knocked on the door and it suddenly struck him how date-like everything was. He was all dressed up, picking a woman up for a fancy dinner. All that was missing was the flowers.

Then Dean realized it was the first time he'd picked a woman up like that since Amy had died.

Before he could dwell on that thought, Ashleigh answered the door. Her auburn hair was pulled back on the sides with two tendrils curving around her face. She wore a red sleeveless cocktail dress with a pearl necklace and matching earrings. Though she often wore makeup, that night she had added eyeshadow that made her green eyes pop. As she smiled at him, he realized his jaw was hanging open.

"So, you like the dress?" she quipped.

"Ah, um…"

"Taking that as a yes," she said as she locked her door, turned and glided past him.

"You look beautiful," he finally managed. "I just wish we weren't havin' this dinner with Voight."

"So, you'd prefer a proper date to our working dinner?" Ashleigh shot back.

Dean blinked quickly, caught off-guard by the comment. "No, I- well, I mean, if we were to go out on an actual date I would prefer it just be the two of us. Not that I want to go out on a date with. I mean, you're beautiful and a dear friend, and I suppose if I was to date someone-" he stopped talking, and held up his hands. "That's probably a conversation for a different time."

Ashleigh laughed. "I'd like to have it sometime if you would. But yes, tonight, I need to get a story, and you need to get some answers. Any idea who else is going to be there?"

"The invite mentioned the Eden Falls events of last month, so I guess maybe Brent. I'd be surprised to see Rhett there. And of course, Fletcher, Marino, Samuels, and Donovan won't be there. Suppose it's too much to ask that Nathaniel Stone make an appearance?"

Chapter 17

Brent was the first to arrive, parking his conspicuously cheap car in front of the three story cabin. He wouldn't call it a mansion- it wasn't…fancy enough to be a mansion. Bur 'cabin' also seemed to miss the point. Tree trunks were used for the pillars flanking the entrance, the massive wooden doors were obviously some exotic species of tree, and the stone floors were obsidian. The wood was all stained dark brown, and the accent pieces were black or dark brick. He had seen the grand picture windows upon his arrival that looked out on the peaks to the east- Long's Peak was out there somewhere, but he had never been good at telling the difference in the rocky crags that surrounded Eden Falls.

Charly met him at the door with her usual smile and perfectly appointed hair. She wore a sleeveless, long blue dress that showed off her tall, athletic figure. "Welcome, Brent! Come on in. You are the first to arrive, so why don't you and I chat in the entry vestibule while we "

Brent chuckled to himself, and she heard it. "Something funny?"

He shrugged. "Entry vestibule. My house's 'entry vestibule' is a three-by-three square of linoleum." They entered the house, and the lighting went from the pale hues of sunset to the warm orange glow of the house lights. "In fact," he said, looking around. "My house could fit in this entryway."

Charly nodded. "Mr. Voight likes to express his wealth. Sometimes, a little too much for my taste."

Brent looked at her. "How did you come to work for him?"

"Same as you, I suppose," she said. Then quickly added, "Not that you work for him, I mean. Same as how you came to own a coffee and book shop. Your old job left you unfulfilled, so you struck out at something new. I was at a law firm, but was little more than a paper copier and coffee retriever. After all my years in law school. I met Mr. Voight when my firm handled one of his cases, he seemed to like me, and offered me the job."

"He liked how you got coffee and made copies?" Brent said, attempting humor poorly. One look at her told Brent why Voight noticed her.

Charly didn't take the comment as offensive. "Actually, yes. He assumed I was a secretary, and we got to talking. He realized I was a lawyer, and asked if I was happy there. I told him I knew I had to work my way up, then he offered a rather colorful reply, and asked me to send my resume. He called me a week later and said he wanted someone who could be his personal attorney and fixer."

"Fixer, huh?"

Charly smiled demurely. "Not like that. All the rich folks have fixers. It's just the nature of things these days. An accusation is as good as a guilty verdict in social media, so they need someone who catches and deals with the more salacious false accusations."

"Ah."

"And what about the true allegations?"

Brent turned and saw Dean and Ashleigh standing in the doorway. The question had come from Ashleigh. Ashleigh, in her red dress. Her hair done up. Her eyes sparkling.

Dean's arm around her waist.

"You got any alcohol?" Brent asked.

Stone leaned back against the tree with his arms crossed, watching the people down in the little village scramble to get the last of their cargo on the big box truck before the sun went down. He was also watching his team- make that his *former* team- make their preparations for the ambush.

Benton, Trant, and Sharpe had arrived, they had taken the Behemoth to scout out a good ambush location. Apparently Withers was communicating with them unbeknownst to Stone. There were a lot of things Stone didn't know, it seemed.

But the one he was most concerned with was his inability to get himself out of the situation immediately before him.

"About five miles up," Sharpe was saying. "The road narrows through a canyon. We set up to block their forward progress with the Behemoth. I can rig some explosives to blow the trees behind them, and we surround them before they know what hit them."

"Casualty rate for the weed farmers?" Simmons asked.

"Your choice," Sharpe said nonchalantly. "100 percent, zero, or somewhere in between. I personally vote for leaving at least one alive. You know how stories of survivors tend to spread."

"Do we have to kill them?" Benton asked. Stone perked up. The big man had always been the most compassionate of the team, and the one who least liked Withers. Maybe he could still be swayed. "They are innocents in this."

"No innocents in war, big guy," Withers replied. "They are on land that our boss- who is paying us very well, I might add- wants. They refuse to sell. They are entrenched. Insurgents. And you remember what we do with insurgents, right Benton?"

Benton nodded silently. "Don't feel right. Killing women."

Withers rushed Benton and grabbed his vest, pulling the man with him as he marched down to the rock where his scope lay. He snatched up the scope and shoved it in Benton's face. "Take a look. See that blonde? See what she has on her hips? See that kid? See what he has slung around his back? And that little chick? Isn't that shotgun she has in her hands? They look innocent to you?"

"N-no."

Wither leaned in and arched his back so he was almost face to face with Benton. "No, what?"

"No, sir."

"That's better. Anyone else got a problem?"

"No, sir," they responded in unison.

"Man, it is so freeing to say what I've been wanting to say for two whole months," Withers said. "Whatya think about that, Stone?"

Stone stayed silent. But he saw a way out.

Fletcher had gone down to his basement, and upon confirming that there were no exits for him to use- or for assassins to enter through- Ben and Sadie settled into the den and waited for the pizza they had ordered to arrive.

"So, what are we to do with ourselves now?" Sadie asked coyly.

Ben smiled. "Well, we are still on duty, so how about we just get to know each other better?"

"Oh, you took what I said in totally the wrong way," Sadie said, again playfully. "Pervert."

"Fine. I grew up here in Colorado. Down at the Springs. You?"

"Outside of Estes Park. Little place called Ward. Doubt you've heard of it."

He had, but it had not been positive. "Yeah, a little. Heard it has a lot of-"

"Hippies?" Sadie interrupted. "Yeah. That and drugs and drunks and terrible parents. I saw it all. Hated it. Ran out as soon as I graduated high school, did a couple years at a community college in Ft. Collins, then to the Police Academy, then Denver PD. Never been back."

"Wow. Opposite for me. Family was upper middle class. Dad was a former Air Force pilot who taught at the Academy- Air Force, not Police. Mom was an accountant. Brother went into the Air Force, sister went to UC Boulder."

"Older, middle, or youngest?"

"Middle. But without all the drama of a middle child angst. I felt seen. You have any brothers and sisters?"

She shook her head. "Nope." Ben sensed there was more, but not to know at the moment. "So, why a cop?"

He leaned back on the couch and replied, "It's silly. You ever see that old movie from the nineties with Pacino and De Niro? *Heat*?"

"Oh, my God- I love that movie!"

He chuckled. "Pacino was so cool. I wanted to be just like him. Minus the failed marriage and suicidal step-daughter."

"Makes sense you'd connect with the cop," Sadie said. "I actually identified with Ashley Judd."

He had to try to recall who she had played. "Val Kilmer's wife, right? Wanted out of the life of crime, but had a hard time ratting out her husband?"

"Yep. That one," Sadie stood and walked around the room. "My dad was a criminal. Mom overdosed when I was little, so it was just him and me. He made and sold meth. It was his batch that killed mom. And my little brother, who had crawled up to mom's body and got into her leftovers. We were poor, so the cops didn't look too hard into his involvement in their deaths. I hated him. And I think he hated me, too. And as bad as it got, as much as he beat me, as much as he used me to make his deals, I couldn't bring myself to rat him out when the cops came knocking. I got him off the hook."

Ben was sitting up, drawn into her confession. "Sadie, I had no idea."

"No one does," she said, turning to face him. Her face was stoic, strong. "That part of my life is dead and buried, even if Daddy isn't. I mean, he could be, but I have no intention of going back to find out. I'm telling you, Ben, because I like you. And I think you like me. The me I let you see, anyway. Well, this is part of me, too. And if we are going to be anything more than partners on this task force thing, I need you to know the full me."

She crossed her arms, and fixed her eyes on him. Waiting to see what he would do.

Without hesitating, Ben rose and crossed the room. He wrapped his arms around her and looked down into her eyes. Then he lowered his face to hers and they kissed.

Ashleigh could tell that Brent was unnerved by her arrival with Dean. She knew he had once- and maybe still- had feelings for her. Seeing his face when they walked in, Dean's arm around her waist, she knew he was crushed.

She couldn't help it. Brent had been a friend, nothing more. Dean was a friend, but maybe more. She knew he came with baggage, but then, so did she. It just so happened that their baggage apparently came in the same brand of Robert Hesse suitcases.

Charly pointed Brent toward the open bar, where a bartender stood at the ready. Seriously, how rich was Voight? And just what kind of dinner were they heading into?

"Well, Ranger Dean, Ms. Storms, pleasure to have you with us. Can I take your coat and gun, Ranger?"

"No," he said flatly.

"Oh. Well…uh…would you like a drink while we wait? If not, I can show you to the dining hall?"

Dean looked at her for her choice. She vaguely remembered him saying once that he didn't drink, and she was fighting off a bit of a headache from the bender the night before. "Dining hall is fine."

"Right this way."

She led them down a hall that seemed to stretch forever, then turned to the left. The hall was about thirty feet long, and a twenty foot live edge wood table made with tree trunk legs. A vein of blue and turquoise epoxy ran down the center, and ten place settings were evenly spaced around the table.

"Who else is comin' to this little shindig?" Dean asked.

Charly smiled, but didn't answer before the doorbell rang. "I'll answer that in just a moment." She glided out of the room and went to answer the door.

"Ms. Storms, you look lovely!" Voight called out as he entered the room. She turned to see he was wearing his black cowboy hat and a black suit, not unlike Dean's. It was just a much more expensive version. "Ranger, I see we have *similar* taste. And I must say I am pleased to finally meet you," he said crossing the room to offer his hand.

Dean took it and said flatly, "We've met."

Voight seemed surprised. "We have?"

Dean nodded. "In Texas. I was working a case that involved one of your holdings, and we briefly crossed paths- didn't exchange names, though. That's why I didn't place you until just now. You recall Bastrop Arms?"

Voight snapped his fingers and pointed. "You were a Texas Ranger then- didn't recognize you without a hat. You know, it wasn't until just now *I* put that all together. How did that case pan out?"

Ashleigh saw Dean's eyes narrow. He was searching Voight for a tell. "It's not over. But I got some of the culprits. Only a matter of time for the rest."

Voight pursed his lips. "Well, best of luck. By the way, you may also know my other guest. Senator?"

A black-haired man- in another black suit- walked in with a pretty blonde on his arm. They looked to be in their late forties, but both were well kept. He offered Dean his hand. "Braxton Reece, Senator from Texas. I've heard amazing things about you. And Ms. Storms- your writing is so vivid and real. I see big things for you. Ever considered running PR for a campaign?" Dean had shaken the Senator's hand, and after Reece had taken hers and demurely shaken it, he introduced his wife before Ashleigh could answer. "This is Gwendolyn, my better half. Now, are you two an item?"

Before they could answer the abruptly asked query, Charly returned with the next guest. Ashleigh saw a giant of a man walk in, red-hair and beard both closely cropped, and a true deer-in-the-headlights look in his eyes.

"Mr. Voight, just in time to meet your latest guest," Charly said. "This is Rhett Windsor."

Dean chuckled. "Nice haircut."

Rhett good-naturedly rolled his eyes.

Brent entered the room in the company of Clayton Young and a man in a white suit. Ashleigh felt her stomach turn. It was that lecherous lawyer, Edwin Jessup.

"Well, the gang's all here," Voight announced. "Why don't we all take our seats?"

Ben and Sadie broke their embrace, but kept looking at each other in silence.

Finally, Sadie broke the silence. "About time."

Ben laughed. "Well, you know, I am a modern man. I do *not* want to come across as a predator or a misogynist."

"So, it was me calling you a pervert that gave you the go ahead?"

He laughed again. "Yeah. That did it." He sighed. "Look. I know it can be complicated, but for the last month, working with you- I just feel like there's something there. Something I've never felt before."

"With Walt?" Sadie asked.

"Ha, ha. You know what I mean." He gave her a funny look. "Will our relationship be built on your mocking me?"

"All my relationships are built on mocking. Ask Dean. And Ash. Spitz. Do I need to go on?"

There was a knock at the door, and suddenly the fun stopped, and work took over. Ben went to the door with his hand on his gun, Sadie was backing him up. "Who is it?" Ben asked.

"Pizza."

"And Spitz."

Ben peeked through the window to confirm, then opened the door. The nervous pizza delivery guy handed over the pizzas, took the payment and ran to his car. Spitz glared the whole time.

"Ordering pizza? At the home of a witness? A witness we are to be protecting?"

"I mean, we gotta eat," Sadie said. "C'mon, Chief, we did this all the time with witnesses in Denver."

Spitz barged in, looking more anxious than normal. And, Ben noted, sweatier. "This isn't Denver, and you are no longer a beat cop, Donovan. For now, anyway."

"Flattery only gets you so far, Chief."

He ignored that. "Samuels, is the witness secure?"

Ben gestured to the basement. "See for yourself. He's down in the basement. Watching television. No phones, no windows, no doors."

Spitz went down into the basement, and immediately returned. "Okay, good. Donovan, I need you to do something for me."

"Aside from watching Quentin Fletcher?"

"No jokes, Donovan. Not now," Spitz barked. "I need you to run down to the office and file the appropriate paperwork with the AUSA office for this little 'at-home-monitoring.' Just got word it has to be done in case something goes wrong. And your paperwork is the best."

Ben looked at Spitz with confusion. "That can't wait until tomorrow?"

Spitz shook his head. "No. Needs to be done now. Donovan, I'll cover you."

Sadie deflated before Ben's eyes, so he gave her a wink behind Spitz's back. She smiled. "Fine. But I'm taking a pizza. I'll be back in an hour or so."

"Great," Spitz said, ushering her out the door. "They are on your desk." He closed the door swiftly.

"That really couldn't have waited?" Ben asked.

Spitz looked him in the eyes, and Ben saw fear. "Samuels, I have a confession to make."

"Almost there?" Withers asked, riding shotgun to Benton. Stone was smashed in the middle seat of the middle seat- the prisoner position. He knew it, they knew it.

Benton raised his right hand and pointed to a side road about a quarter mile up the road.

"We should be far enough ahead of them to dive down that road, drop off the back route squad, and hide around the corner." Benton did not seem too excited, and on that Stone was hanging his hopes. He just had to get himself assigned to the back route team because they would be closest to the mountain folk. He could get them clear from that position.

"Sharpe, you'll lead the back route team," Withers announced. "Set your charges to block the retreat, then drop out when they try to make a run. Trant, Simmons, you're with Sharpe." Turning in his seat, Withers gave Stone the smug smile he had come to loathe. "You stay with me, Stone. Benton and I have to keep an eye on you, right?" He slapped Stone's knee.

On to Plan B, then.

Benton glanced back in the rearview, and gave Stone a look. It was fleeting, but Stone hoped it confirmed his suspicions.

They bounced down the rough road, then emerged on a slightly more developed gravel stretch. To their left was a thin passage between two cliffs. A few miles back, behind a hill or two, occasional headlights emerged over a distant hill. "All out for ammunitions," Withers said, and the three soldiers disembarked. Stone did not try to move. Once they were clear, Benton turned left and angled the Behemoth through the gap. Just barely. Stone remembered that. He needed to remember that. He didn't know why, he just did.

They didn't go far before Benton pulled off to the side and then backed the vehicle into a little alcove. "They can radio us when the others get into position," Benton said. "Until then, we stay in the car."

"Screw that," Withers said, getting out of the car. "C'mon Stone, let's talk."

Slowly, Stone moved to exit. Benton coughed, and he looked back. "Sorry," Benton said. "Dust." His eyes looked down toward the ignition switch. Then to the canisters on the console. Their eyes met, and Benton nodded. Stone assumed he would be able to take the car and use the smoke grenades..

Stone emerged from the car and went to stand by Withers. He considered pulling his sidearm and ending Withers right there.

"Don't even think about it, Stone," Withers said, without taking his eyes off the road, where the headlights briefly emerged again before disappearing. Much closer now. "They all know you're here against your will. In fact, I'd wager

Trant or Simmons has you in their sights right now. Just in case, of course."

"If you don't trust me, why am I here?"

Withers turned to look at him. "I'm in charge now. I need to make sure they know it. Me forcing you along shows I am not afraid of you. Not intimidated by you. Plus, I want you to see these hillbillies die, Stone. To know that because you got weak, I had to step in. Voight is going to remake these mountains in his image."

"Drugs and guns from peak to peak, huh?" Stone asked.

Withers laughed. "Such small thinking. I can't believe you ever led this team. Sure, that stuff. But do you know what all Voight has his finger in? Hesse and an inside guy with the mob outta Denver are making a play to wipe them out. Take over all the criminal enterprises in northern Colorado. He wants the land up here to bring his buddies. The rich and powerful who think this country is gone to hell in a handbasket. Put all of those wealthy, gun-toting, patriots in one spot and then round up a bunch of vets that still have an itchy trigger finger, and you know what you have?"

"An insurgency."

Withers shook his head. "Insurgencies are poor and poorly weaponized. It's why they may get a few wins, but in the end, they fall. Every. Time. No, Stone. This is a revolution."

"It's madness. Because of politics?" Stone said, barely believing what he was hearing. That one of the wealthiest, most connected men in America was just an anti-government nut and wannabe mafia don. "And why would he tell *you* that? You're still just a foot soldier."

"First, it's not about politics. Voight uses both sides for his plan. He just wants power. Control. And I can vibe with that. As for me just being a foot soldier? Well, I'm about to do what you couldn't. Take out the Windsor family holdouts."

"Holdouts?"

That smile again. "Zeke and Nigel turned over their operation to Hesse yesterday. They went to take out Fletcher- that realtor connected to the mob. See, he has sensitive information that links some of Voight's holdings to this entire operation. Of course, Voight likes to control all of the pieces, so he's playing the lawyer of the Denver mob to make a run for the fat man, too. Gonna be a lot of blood spilled in Eden Falls tonight." He clicked the walkie he was holding and said, "Almost there, once they get past your position, blow the trees. Move in, but *do not* fire until I give the word. We need to get the go-ahead before the shooting starts."

"Go-ahead?" Stone asked.

Withers dropped the walkie to his side and turned back to the Behemoth. "From Hesse. He's got a little business down in the Falls to cover before we get the clearance to kill them all. Just in case."

"You're not just taking the weed, are you?"

"Nope. Kill these folks, then move into their little village and burn it to the ground. Preferably with the people sleeping soundly in their homes at the time. Oh, I can see by the look on your face that you are surprised. Well, this has been the plan from the jump. The attack on Dean-while killing would have been nice-was only about getting us a fix on the Switchbacks. That's what they call that hovel, by the way. Knew it was up here, hoped the shooting at Dean would bring them out. And it did."

"This is madness," Stone muttered again.

Withers turned and grabbed him by the throat. "No," he said, his face mere inches from Stone's. "It's war."

Chapter 18

As the dinner was being brought out, Senator Reece and Voight were holding court, tossing out questions to their guests. Dean was uncomfortable, and not just because he had worn a suit. The two so-called powerful men gave off an air that made Dean feel like all of the guests were spectacles for them to admire, take pictures with, and attempt to understand their primitive lifestyle on a surface level.

In short, Dean felt like an animal in a zoo.

Looking across the table at the current focus of their attention, Rhett Windsor, Dean felt a surge of pity. The poor mountain man was also wearing a suit, and had cut his hair to look…professional?

Unrecognizable was a more apt description.

"Now, you used to be a criminal, am I correct?" Senator Reece asked bluntly and without a hint of subtlety. Dean remembered the Senator from his Texas days. He had been a dick, then. Now, he was a dick with a long tenure in Congress and big aspirations.

"Well, now, I see it as doing what my family and I needed to do to survive," Rhett replied calmly. Sometimes Dean forgot the big man was an academic, and had defended a thesis at one point. So, he was familiar with condescending and offensive questions. "The law, of course," he nodded to Dean and then at Jessup, who was seated next to Reece in his role as- was it legal counsel? Dean wasn't exactly sure. "Well, now they saw it differently. I am not ashamed of the activities I partook in that I might care for my kin, but I am grateful for the second chance Remington Dean and his friends were able to help secure for me. In large part due to my service in the affair that no doubt brought us all to your attention."

"Ah yes, the *Battle of Eden Falls*," Voight said with a smirk, shadowed beneath his ever-present black cowboy hat. "I'd have liked to have had a go in that engagement. My Desert Eagle might have made a name for itself that day. Unfortunately, I was out of town on a safari."

"Yes, unfortunately," Ashleigh said, disdain evident to all at the table except the hosts.

"I think we had more than enough guns in town that day," Dean said flatly.

"Ah yes. Remington Dean. The hero Ranger riding in to drive off the outlaws," Senator Reece said, spreading his hands out like he was displaying the words for all to see as he turned to look at Dean. Brent Chase rolled his eyes. Partly because of the insincerity Reece was putting on, but Dean suspected it was partly because Chase was tired of the story always coming back to "hero" Dean at the center of it all. Dean wanted to tell Brent that he wished he wasn't. "Remington—may I call you Remington?" Reece asked.

"No," Dean said curtly.

"Um, Dean, then?"

Dean raised an eyebrow.

"Ranger?"

Dean nodded.

"Ranger, Ms. Storms presented you as quite the hero in her fascinating articles from that situation," Reece said, mustering as much fake respect as he could. "America loves its heroes, don't you agree?"

"No," Dean said again. "They tend to run them outta town when they speak out against corruption, right, Senator?"

Reece turned red. Another thing Dean remembered about Reece was that the senator had been one of the powerful people that spoke openly during his last days with the Rangers about the need for Remington Dean to retire, despite it not really being his business as a United States Senator. But only after Dean had kept digging around.

Voight chuckled nervously. "Not being very respectful to the Congressman, are we Dean?"

Dean's eyes narrowed at Voight and said, "First, I didn't say *you* could call me that, either. Second, I don't think it's disrespectful to disagree."

The facade of the politician had vanished, if only for a moment, but Reece had regained his composure. He asked, "So, you don't think America loves heroes?"

Dean shrugged. "For a moment. Then someone else catches their fancy. I figure that old saying about fifteen minutes of fame is about right. Then, say a few years go by, and if the 'hero,'" Dean made air quotes, "Is lucky, the world forgets them. If not, the world will remember just enough to start lookin' for a flaw. For a mistake. Something they said one time and society now finds those words ill-fittin' for polite society. They sacrifice that hero, in the same public spotlight they lauded them in. Then it's on to the next big story."

He felt Ashleigh's eyes on him and knew she was hurt. *She* had made him a hero in the eyes of the public, and *she* didn't deserve his harsh words. But he hated the way Reece and Voight were treating them like show ponies, there for entertainment only. His beef was with them.

Reece must have seen Ashleigh's face and turned to her. "How does that make you feel, Ms. Storms?"

She scoffed, then said, "Like my job is unappreciated."

"See," Dean said. "Here's that flaw I mentioned." He meant it as a joke. Ashleigh clearly didn't see it that way.

"Dean, I gotta say," Reece said. "That's a pretty bleak look at heroes."

"It's a pretty bleak world, Congressman."

"You don't think you're a hero?" Voight asked.

Dean shook his head. "No. Maybe I was to Ashleigh during that- what did you call it? Battle? Whatever. What you rich fellas glorify was just a bunch of folks tryin' to survive. Maybe I was some hero to some other folks. But I was just doin' my job. And while I need to make it clear that I respect Ashleigh's job to tell the stories, and regret that my previous statement offended her, I stand by it. Mostly because I see what you're doing Senator. And you too, Mr. Voight."

Feigning offense, Reece asked, "Oh? What are we doing?"

"You want people who played a part in what happened in Eden Falls, people the locals look up to for savin' their town, to support you. Congressman, your party lost this state in the last presidential election, am I correct? And you've been making noise about runnin' for the big chair pretty soon, right?" Reece swallowed hard. "And Mr. Voight, you've been helping raise funds for him, and my guess is you're doin' that because he made some promises about government contracts. Or maybe government support of some of your special interests. Which are what, exactly, Mr. Voight? Cause as I see it, you don't do much to support the likes of Rhett Windsor, or Brent Chase, or Ashleigh Storms. No, you just take from the mountains- or wherever you plant yourself for the moment- and give little back."

Rhett smiled broadly and gave Dean a wink.

Brent took a big drink from whatever liquor was in his glass.

Reece smiled, but pushed himself back from the table a bit. Voight kept a straight face, but Dean thought if he looked close enough, he could see steam coming from the rich man's ears. "*I* do little for the mountains? Son, I have brought *millions* to these mountains. Jobs. Investments. Infrastructure. I was here before you rode in on your dusty horse from Texas-"

"But not by much," Dean interjected.

"Excuse me?"

"You used to be based in Texas. Until your company started getting too much heat for illegal practices. A couple subsidiaries linked to dark dealings," Dean said, then paused for effect. "Some involving one Grant Kolbe, I believe. Who made a deal, then had a district attorney murdered." Another pause. "Amy Dean. My wife."

Instead of blowing up, Voight smiled. Ever so slightly. "I was cleared on that matter. Just because a branch of the corporation is corrupted, doesn't mean the roots are. No connection."

Dean reached out and took the goblet in front of him that held water. He took a sip, tilted the glass at Voight, then said, "Yeah, but sometimes the rot is deep, isn't it? And you don't always see it until the tree needs to be cut down." He concluded with a sarcastic half-smile.

"I don't appreciate that insinuation, sir," Voight said coldly, but with a volcanic anger just below the surface.

Dean sipped his water. "I didn't appreciate my wife bein' murdered. Or bein' driven outta Texas by the likes of your politician friend here only to find that you both were tryin' to get your claws into my new home."

Voight cocked his head to the side. Then he looked at Jessup, then over to Brent and across to Rhett. "*His* home. You hear that? Edwin Jessup has lived here his whole life- mostly in Denver, right?" Jessup nodded. "Mr. Chase, you have as well." Brent looked up drunkenly with surprise. "I do my research, good sir," Voight replied knowingly. "And Rhett Windsor. Standout student in high school, all-star football player for the Orediggers down in Golden. And holder of a doctorate. Which you used- for a time- to make a mint off of the last remaining lithium stores in these here mountains surrounding Eden Falls." Voight lingered on Rhett a moment. "You knew they were gone when Mr. Jessup's clients came looking, claiming to be in search of lithium. You knew they were looking for land, not minerals.

You know I'm looking for it, too. Because you know these mountains, you know this land. It's *your* home." Voight kept his eyes on Rhett, but pointed at Dean. "He thinks it's his. What do you say?"

Dean looked at Rhett, who shifted slightly in his seat. Not a sign of discomfort, Dean noted. A sign of a man preparing his argument.

"Well, it is," Rhett said finally. "As much as it is mine. Or yours. A home is where a person sets their roots. Where they defend their keep from attackers. As I see it, Remington Dean defends these mountains. He may not have been here as long as us, but what he's put on the line for the people of this area is more than enough of a claim to it being his home. He may not be the gentlest of souls, but by my estimation, he's a good and honest man. He's tough, he puts up with very little, but he's always done right by me. More than I deserve. He's tough, yeah. But he's gracious."

Voight laughed. "Gracious- that's rich!" He turned to Dean. "You were a minister, right?" Dean nodded. "Then how can you kill so freely, without compunction? What was it- ten men you killed? Twenty? The legend grows all the time. By next spring, Remington Dean will have killed a hundred men with just the six bullets in that Colt he carries."

"Are you accusing me of embellishing his story," Ashleigh interjected. "Or of Dean being some heartless monster? Because both of those are false accusations, and I won't stand for the slander on either of our names."

Voight scoffed, and Reece looked on smugly. Brent drank more. Jessup leaned in, elbows on the table, while Reece's wife and Charly were watching Ashleigh closely.

"Did I offend the lady and her special friend?" Voight mocked.

Now Ashleigh smiled. "I came to get an exclusive on the man who was coming to offer so much to Eden Falls. The philanthropist, the businessman, the 'boardroom cowboy' I think you were called by Forbes. And what I see is a man of opulence, a man who surrounds himself with useful things. Useful people" She nodded at Reece. "But a man who no one really knows, because being known to you is a weakness. You thrive on your mysteries and secrets and keeping people at a distance." She looked at Dean, who was a bit surprised at her forcefulness. "Remington Dean is much the same. Except people are not 'useful' to him like tools or chess pieces to play. It's the one thing that sets you two apart. That and extreme wealth. And that Remington Dean is a *good* man. Maybe you are, too, Mr. Voight. But right now, you paint yourself as more of a bully than anything. Now, is that the copy you want to go to press, or would you like to stop antagonizing and start being civil?" She looked at Dean and said, "That goes for you, too." She gave him a wink with the eye opposite of Voight. She turned back to Voight.

The man sat there, his face a mask of unknowability. Slowly, he smiled. Then he laughed. "She's got spirit- I love that! Bring out the next course!"

The mood began to loosen just a bit, but Dean suspected that Voight was still looking for a way to take another shot.

"They got to me after my divorce," Spitz said, looking down at his feet. "Promised me no hard crime would come to Eden Falls, just drugs and guns."

Ben scoffed.

"No guns would *stay* in Eden Falls. I just had to let them pass through. And it worked for a long time. I mean, I had let Fletcher slide on drugs for years, because it was all recreational stuff. No heroin or crack. Just pills and stuff."

"That's how you justify it, I guess," Ben said. "But why come clean now?"

Fletcher emerged from the basement and froze. Uncharacteristically, he was at a loss for words.

"He knows, Quentin."

"Oh. Just as well, I was going to have to tell him, eventually. And those papers the lady lawyer has will say stuff, too."

"That's why now," Spitz said, pointing absently at Fletcher. "That…and Jessup called. That guy from Fort Collins- Wagner? Not a bodyguard."

Ben stood up straight and swore. "He'll be here any minute. Wait- Jessup called? Of course, he's not just a mouthpiece is he?"

Spitz shook his head. "More important than that. Made-man, maybe? Look, I don't know any more than Fletcher who the big man is. Other than they call him the Ghost."

"Uhhh, well…now that you mention that name…"

Spitz and Ben turned to Fletcher. "See, I had some…data. I kinda sent emails that skimmed from the recipients."

"A phishing scam?" Ben asked.

Fletcher shrugged. "I got some stuff about a guy named 'G.Host,' but I guess maybe it was Ghost? Anyway, what I found out about him kinda scared me, so I never looked too hard. But I'm pretty sure the actual name of the Ghost was in that paperwork you sent over to Kho."

Ben swore again. He pulled out his phone to call Walt, but got no signal. "You have a landline?"

"Kitchen," Fletcher said.

Spitz followed him, trying to explain. "I sent Sadie away because I knew he was coming. I don't want her to get hurt."

"But I'm just a state boy, so no one cares?" Ben said, picking up the phone. No dial tone. "Your phone hooked up, Fletcher? And paid for?"

"Yeah, why?"

The lights went out.

"Fletcher- down in the basement- now!" Ben yelled, pulling his gun. He saw Spitz draw his, too. "You think I trust you after what you just told me?"

Spitz grimaced. "You think you have a choice? Look, I'm gonna make this right, starting now. I go to jail with Fletcher, go into witness protection- so be it. I just want to make it right."

Spitz was right about one thing- Ben had no choice.

Fletcher was walking toward the basement when there was a loud crack and the back window shattered. Fletcher ducked, then ran the rest of the way to the basement. Another shot followed, but it just cracked the tile on the floor behind the realtor's fleeing feet.

Ben moved to try to gain a view of the shooter, but the failing light outside and the lack of light inside made that an impossible task. But Ben saw a red beam tracing the floor and moving toward him, so he followed it back and saw a dark shape behind a tree fifty yards from the back door.

"Would they send two teams?" Ben asked.

"No, they only sent Garland Wagner. He works alone."

That didn't make Ben feel better about their situation. He stayed low and creeped closer to the back doors, but stuck tight to the wall for defense. At the door, he peaked out. He couldn't see the shape behind the tree, but that didn't mean he was gone. It probably meant he was on the move. "Why would they risk killing a police officer and a state agent just to kill the realtor?"

"Oh, that's easy" Spitz said, realization coming over his face. "Land. It's always been a land grab for them. Land means more places to produce their drugs, and better hiding. It's what they came for Rhett Windsor's parcel for. Fletcher was helping make the deal, but they found out he was playing both ends against the middle. Rhett did, too. The Windsors shut them out, so they turned to the Tolberts. They'd heard the Tolbert boys were not the brightest, but their daddy is a sharp guy. With Joe Tolbert about to get out of jail, they rushed to make a deal with Virgil that allowed Denver to take advantage of the hillbillies. Virgil proved smarter than they thought, so they hired the Tolberts on as gun thugs. Either they help run off the competition- Xavier Voight- or they die trying. So, getting Joe's boys killed would likely make the man go off his rails. Do something dumb and die or get sent back up to the pen. Land goes up at the sheriff's auction for a song."

"That's a lot of finagling to get some dirt."

Spitz smirked. "It's prime dirt, Samuels. And a lot of it."

Things grew quiet, and Ben peeked out. Wagner was still out there, but not even trying to take a shot. Or hide. Close enough for Ben to see him, the assassin had set his rifle down. "Listen. I think we have our best shot of surviving this if we go down to the basement. Only one way in, we can funnel him down."

"Hey, statey, that also means we only have one way in and out."

"Can't win 'em all," Ben said, running across the room for the basement.

Stone saw the explosion before he heard it.

The trees fell behind the box truck, which immediately began to speed up. Withers nodded, and the two of them stepped in front of the truck. Benton gunned the Behemoth's engine and pulled in behind them.

The box truck kept coming.

Withers fired a warning shot into the windshield, not anywhere near where a head should have been.

That stopped them.

Simmons, Trant, and Sharpe came up to the back of the truck, guns drawn. Stone watched as Trant hopped up on the back bumper and opened the door. There was a gunshot, a couple yells, then two more gunshots.

"All good?" Withers asked.

"Yeah," Sharpe yelled back. "Had a wannabe hero. He's down."

The attractive blonde woman they'd seen in the village was in the driver's seat, and upon hearing that, she opened the door and jumped out. Her hands went for her hips, but Withers was on her too fast for her to pull whatever she was carrying.

"Whoa, now, babe, hold up there," he said, leering. He reached around her waist, under her coat, and pulled out a pistol with his left hand while cradling his rifle in his right. He held it up and whistled. "Is this a bona fide Luger?"

The woman said nothing.

"Aw, c'mon sugar, this is just business. Give us a name."

"Who did you shoot?" she asked instead. "Then I might give a name."

Withers looked her up and down, then called to the men at the back. "Who is it?"

"A dude. Young fella," Simmons said. Then quieter, to one someone else. "They said his name is Hank."

"Now you," Withers said, casually pointing the Luger back at its owner. "Rhiannon Windsor."

Withers turned back to Stone in surprise. Then he looked at Rhiannon. "You mean to tell me that something so fine and so tiny is from the same blood as that ginger giant?" He looked her over again, but she kept her steely gaze fixed on him. "Who else is with you?"

"Tina's up front with me. Todd and Dell are in the back. Is Hank okay?" Stone heard the concern in her voice.

Simmons hoisted a bloody young man up and pushed him forward. He was walking, but holding his gut. Not a good sign. Behind Simmons, Trant and Sharpe were herding two rednecks decked out in mullets and trucker hats- and not the fashionable kind. A slight, but fiery-eyed woman dropped out of the truck next to Rhiannon.

"Well, seems the gang is all here," Withers said, waving that Luger around."So, here's the plan. We are going to take your product, and the truck it's in, and kick-start our own little venture. Any of you going to have a problem with that?"

The kid was turning gray, and the rednecks were sullen and had their heads down. The tiny woman, Tina, Stone believed was her name, was looking at Hank.

Rhiannon was staring holes in Withers.

And Withers noticed.

"Whew, you are getting me all hot and bothered with that smolder, Rhiannon," Withers said, walking over to her. He put the muzzle of the Luger to her head. "Walk with me for a minute."

As if she had a choice, she began to walk in step with Withers. "Join us, Stone. But hang back a bit."

Stone did not like that tone. He didn't think Stone would try anything truly sinister with Rhiannon (only because it was a waste of time), but then he hadn't thought the man capable of mutiny until that day.

"You hold these people's lives in your hand, Rhiannon," Withers said calmly. "You give me what I want, without a fight, and they live. You do one little thing to stop me and my boys from taking your truck, BANG!" he yelled, motioning with the pistol. Rhiannon's eyes were on the gun, and Stone could see clearly she was having none of this. She and Withers stood in the glow of the truck headlights, and that was when Stone saw the thing Withers missed.

Rhiannon had a second Luger.

Stone began to position himself back by the Behemoth, but not too close. He also tried to get himself in Rhiannon's sight line.

"You think I'm stupid enough to believe you'll let us live?" Rhiannon asked. Stone knew she was right, Withers wanted blood. But the others…maybe they didn't. At least, not the blood of those particular people. He moved his hand to his temple, and made a small signal. He thought Rhiannon's eyes briefly flicked to him, but he wasn't sure. He'd have to rely on hope.

At the door to the Behemoth, he looked in. There on the seat was the flashbang Benton had left there. And from the look the man had given Stone earlier, it meant he might have that miracle he needed. But distracting them wasn't enough. He had to disable their ability to follow Rhiannon and her people. And the Behemoth was the better vehicle for escape. So he had to get them away from it.

Stone knew what to do.

He moved back to the interaction between Withers and Rhiannon in the middle of Withers' second threat.

"-make it hurt, like your boy Hank is feeling right now," he sneered. "And I'll really take my time with you and what's her name? Tina? Yeah, that will be…fun."

No one was watching and it was dark enough to hide his movements, so Stone chunked the flashbang up over the truck and into the trees behind it. A few seconds later, there was a pop and white light came from the side of the truck. Withers turned and yelled, "Simmons, Trant, Sharpe, Benton- check it. Stone- guard the others." As Stone walked up into the headlights, he warned, "And if you try to let them go, I'll kill this one first."

"Yes, sir," Stone said sarcastically. Then he gave Rhiannon a wink and nodded toward her friends. He hoped she got *that*.

Walking up to the others, he decided that Tina was the most in-charge. "When I give the signal, go for the military vehicle back there. It's a push-button-"

"I can drive it," the one with the mullet said. "Drove in the army. Or sumthin' like it."

Tina nodded. "You'll help Rhi, too?"

Stone looked and saw her with her hands on her hips, and one hand very near that second, hidden Luger. "I think she's got it herself."

"And the signal?" Tina asked.

"This." Stone drew his K-Bar knife and slashed the tire on the truck. "Withers, we got a problem. Tire is blown."

Withers turned from Rhiannon and looked back. With his back turned, Rhiannon pulled the other Luger and shot him in the back. Withers let out a cry and went down.

"Go!" Stone yelled, and Tina ran for the Behemoth. The rednecks- Dell and Todd- carried Hank as fast as they could. Stone could hear the others coming back. "Hurry!"

Rhiannon was walking up to Withers, intent on finishing him. Stone rushed over and put his hand on the pistol. "Go, get your friends' help."

She pulled her phone out. "I have the number of my brother- and that Ranger- Dean- in here. Call them. They can help you."

Stone nodded, and took the phone. That was when the first shot struck Hank in the back of the head. Todd and Dell were covered in blood, but they knew he was gone and dropped the body. The one with the longer mullet jumped behind the wheel and Rhiannon ran to Hank.

At that point, Withers, who had body armor on, raised up and took aim. Stone couldn't get there fast enough and he fired.

But the bullet didn't hit Rhiannon.

Tina jumped in front of the shot and took it in the gut.

Rhiannon turned and caught the woman as she fell. The other redneck leapt out of the Behemoth and helped drag Tina into the back seat. Stone fired at Withers, knowing it was protected but that it would still hurt quite a bit.

Before the door was closed, the vehicle was lumbering away, shots pinging off of its thick metal hull.

Sharpe took aim at Stone, who was standing over a writhing Withers. There was no where he could go, that was just it. But Benton gripped the muzzle of Sharpe's rifle and pulled it down. "Give him a head start. He was a good CO." Then Benton saluted Stone, who returned the gesture.

Withers snarled, "I'll kill you, you backstabbing son-of-a-"

He kicked Withers in the face. "Gotta find me first, Withers," Stone said running past his former team and into the woods. "And you suck at tracking."

The dinner had concluded somewhat… amicably. Ashley got to ask the fluffy questions she promised Voight she'd lob at him, and that seemed to calm the mood. He talked of his 'humble' beginnings, the hunts he went on all over the world, and the businesses he built that were thriving. She stayed focused despite Dean's simmering next to her and an increasingly loud- and inebriated- Brent across the table. She wasn't sure why Brent was there, he had said very little. She also wasn't sure why that slime ball Edwin Jessup was there. He kept giving her looks, no doubt recalling their last encounter that had left him with a black eye. She returned his looks by cracking her knuckles, as if her hands were growing tired of writing. She had a pen, but she was recording the conversation on her phone.

When the dinner and conversation died down, Voight stood up. "Ladies and gentlemen, despite a…rough start, this evening has concluded quite well. Now, I must insist that you all take a tour around the house, see the wonders that my adventures have brought me. Mr. Chase, Ms. Addison, would you join me in the study?"

Brent rose, unsteadily, and Charly was there to help him. Ashleigh noted that she was a stunningly beautiful woman, and seemed far too intelligent to just be Voight's assistant. She made a mental note to look into that.

"Mr. Voight, I was told that I would have an audience with you as well," Jessup said raising a finger of protest.

Voight grunted and gave a look of disdain. "In due time. Senator, Mrs. Reece, would you entertain Mr. Jessup while I have my conversation?" And with that, he left.

"I kinda wanna see the lion," Dean said as Rhett walked over.

"Same here," he said. "Say, you really went after the Senator and Voight. There really some bad blood there?"

Ashleigh listened intently as they walked past the bar and into a long hall with dozens of creatures frozen into a position some taxidermist found interesting. There were birds and small cats, wolves and even a bear. At the far end, under a spotlight, was a male lion with his full mane seeming to blow in the wind. Then Ashleigh saw the small fan that gave that appearance.

"Like I said, Reece tried to get rid of me when I was lookin' into his businesses. Didn't take much likin' to me."

"And the case disappeared when you left?" Ashleigh asked.

"Yep," he said.

They walked up to the lion, and marveled at its majesty. *Such a beautiful, proud creature struck down by an ugly, proud man*, Ashleigh editorialized, wishing she could put that line in print.

"You ever think that lion's kinda like us?"

Ashleigh turned to Rhett with a curious look.

"How so?" Dean asked.

Rhett pointed at it. "This thing was the baddest thing around. All it did was protect its kin, try to get its food, and everyone looked to him. Kinda made him the King of the Mountain. The guy to shoot for. Literally, for Voight." Rhett stepped closer. "People look to us, too. I mean, think about tonight. Voight brought us here to meet because of what we did. Protect our kin, make our living, and we got everyone's attention. I don't know about you two, but when I walk around town, people stare like I'm some celebrity. They did that before, on account of my size. But this is different. This is…"

"Respectful," Ashleigh said, nodding. She had seen it. Her articles had made national headlines, and that meant that Eden Falls made national headlines. She was keenly aware of the looks and the pointed fingers following the words, *That's that reporter.* She hadn't thought of it as bad.

"Yes! Exactly. I just worry that with all the eyes on us, we might make a mistake. Lead folks wrong. Or, like this guy, become an even bigger target.

"Huh," Dean said. "Are you also implyin' that Voight's wantin' to put our heads on his wall? Metaphorically, of course."

Rhett chuckled without humor while he looked at the lion. "Maybe I am."

Ashleigh heard raised voices, but they were muffled. Behind a wall. She broke away from the men and wandered to a door in the same room. She leaned in close, and heard two voices. Voight, and Jessup.

"-will not be put off, Mr. Voight," Jessup was saying. "My organization's leadership has made it abundantly clear that you will either need to join our ventures here in Eden Falls, or get out of the way. And by out of the way, I mean out of town."

"That a threat, Jessup?" Voight growled. "Cuz I've been threatened by scarier folks than you. You tell your bosses, whoever they may- especially that fool who calls himself the Ghost or whatever- any of our past interactions are to be seen as the completion of our deal. I am done with the Denver mob and their foolishness. Tell the Ghost that. Seriously, what kind of limp-dick wannabe hard-case calls himself that kind of nickname?"

Jessup, more forcefully, but with a calm that almost scared Ashleigh, replied, "My boss is, I assure you, no empty suit. There is a reason he has found himself atop the pyramid of organized crime in the Rockies. And don't you go by Darkness in these interactions?"

A grunt. "But he can't show his face? He scarred- or just scared?" Voight taunted.

"The Ghost will reveal himself when he feels the situation warrants. He finds the mystery adds to his power," Jessup said. After a pause, which Ashleigh desperately wished she could see, Jessup added, "It's called subtlety. I doubt you'd understand the concept."

There was a sound of movement, and when Voight spoke, it was clearly through clenched teeth. "Get out of my house. And tell the mob that Eden Falls is off limits. It's *my* town."

More movement, then Jessup said, "For now, Mr. Voight. We will be seeing you. Soon."

"What's got your attention?"

Ashleigh jumped at Dean's question.

"Eavesdropping?" he asked,

"'I ain't been droppin' no eaves, sir, honest,'" Rhett said with a chuckle. Ashleigh and Dean looked at him. He shrugged, "Lord of the Rings? What- didn't you read? Or watch the movie?"

Dean's phone rang and he reached into his jacket to answer it. His nose wrinkled in confusion. "It's your sister, Rhett."

"She calling to check in on the patient?"

Ashleigh felt a surge of unexpected jealously, then asked, "Patient?"

"Rhi is a doctor," Rhett explained. "She patched him up, but she was supposed to be busy with something tonight."

"Say again?" Dean said into the phone. Ashleigh thought she heard gunshots. Dean listened, then turned to Rhett. "Big rock formation, funnels the road down to a single lane on the way through the mountains to Boulder- where is the closest spot a person can find cover?"

"What happened to Rhi?" Rhett asked, suddenly tense.

"It's not her, it's Nathaniel Stone. She's fine, he said."

"Uh, due east, three-quarters of a mile. Old mine shaft. Couple small shafts off the main, just don't go too far down."

"You hear that?" Dean asked the phone. "Good. Stay safe- we will come recover you." He hung up. "Nathaniel Stone turned on his men- wants to come bring us intel on VYPER and Voight. They did not take it well. Rhett-" Dean turned and looked the man in the eyes. "I need you to be calm. Rhiannon's group was ambushed. She, Todd, Dell, and Tina got away. But Tina got hit pretty good. Call her phone, or Todd and Dell's if you have it. Tell them to go straight to the hospital. I'm calling Abel Tolentino to meet them there."

"Wait- what? Why call the coroner?" Rhett asked, panic rising in his voice.

Calmly, Dean said, "Because he has hospital privileges, and I'd trust Abel Tolentino to assist your sister more than any doctor in the ER. I'm calling him on our way there."

Rhett's hand went to his mouth, and Ashleigh felt his pain. People he cared about were in danger, and he was helpless to do anything about it. She was surprised that the name he said next wasn't his sister's. "Tina…"

"Rhett," Dean said forcefully. "Call. Her. Now."

Rhett nodded and went for the front door, pulling his phone out.

"What can I do?" Ashleigh asked.

Dean grabbed her hand and began to follow Rhett. "Tell me what had you so interested behind that door while we make sure Rhett gets where he needs to go? And I'll tell you the secret I know about Rhett."

Chapter 19

Ben and Spitz had made it down to the basement without a shot being fired to find a surprisingly calm Quentin Fletcher. He was sitting in a big recliner, idly rocking back and forth.

"How are you so calm?" Ben asked angrily.

Fletcher shrugged. "I'm not in danger. They just want to get me out. *You* guys are the ones in trouble."

Ben looked at Fletcher like the man was the dumbest thing on earth. Because at that moment, he was. "You *moron!* They are not sending a babysitter, they are sending an assassin. *For you!*"

The wheels slowly turned in Fletcher's thick head, and then his eyes flooded with panic. "We gotta get out of here!"

"You want to just give him to Wagner when he shows?" Spitz asked. "Not because I want to get out of my own predicament, I'm just tired of dealing with that man."

"Tempting, but duty and honor and all that," Ben said. He looked around the room and confirmed his suspicion. One way in, one way out. No windows. It was a fortress.

And they were under siege.

As long as Wagner didn't decide to try to flush them out, they could definitely stay until help arrived. Which could be soon, if Sadie came back.

Sadie.

"Sadie could come back and not have any idea what's going on. She could walk into a trap-" Ben said.

"What I sent her to do will take hours. Unless she grows suspicious, she won't be back any time soon."

There was the sound of glass crunching under foot from above. Wagner was entering the glass door he'd shot through from the patio. "He's coming in," Fletcher whined.

"Yep, boy genius," Ben replied. He nervously checked his weapon.

Steps came to the top of the staircase. "I am coming down, and I am unarmed." Patent leather shoes and white slacks came into view first.

"You Wagner?"

A small, thin man came into view. He was bald, his cheeks gaunt, and his eyes too big for his face.

He looked like Death personified.

Ben wasn't sure if the man was going for that look, or was just lucky in a dark and twisted way.

"I am. And I come to offer a proposal," he said, stopping halfway down the stairs. "There is no way you two are leaving this basement with Fletcher. So, if you two want to leave this basement- a poor choice of defense, I should add- give me Fletcher."

"He's a witness against the Denver mob, and we are duty bound to protect him," Ben replied.

Wagner pursed his thin lips. "I suspected that from the boy scout. But Spitz- we have had an agreement in the past, have we not? Between you and my organization?"

Spitz looked at Ben and shook his head. "Deal is broken. I intend to honor my oath to the law."

Wagner cocked his head to the side and squinted. "Why the sudden emergence of a conscience, Spitz?"

Spitz looked at Ben. "I've been around some good people who showed me a better way. And if I have to go out, I want to go out right."

Wagner took a deep breath. "Very well." With a flick of his wrist, Wagner produced a small gun from his sleeve. He fired at Fletcher, but Spitz leapt in front of him, and the bullet struck him in the chest. Ben began to open fire on Wagner, who fled up the stairs.

"Omygod, omygod, omygod he's dead!" Fletcher screeched.

"Shut up," Ben barked. "You've had your hand in killing people before. Weren't you there when Link Elliott killed that Windsor cousin?" Ben went to check on Spitz, who, despite being declared dead by Fletcher was still breathing.

"Yeah, but this guy is dead because they want to kill *me!* Totally different deal!"

"Spitz, you still with us?" Ben asked.

"He's alive?" Fletcher screeched.

Spitz moaned and took a rasping breath. He handed Ben his weapon, coughed up some blood, then went still.

"No," was all Ben said as he looked down at Spitz. Then he turned to Fletcher and asked, "You got liquor?"

"You really shouldn't drink right now!"

"It's flammable, stupid. I can make a Molotov cocktail!" Ben yelled.

"Oh. Yeah. In the fridge behind the bar."

Ben ran to the mahogany bar and found some vodka. It was 180 proof, and he smiled because it was unopened. Definitely not Quentin Fletcher's preferred drink. Rummaging through a few drawers, he found a dishcloth and crammed it in the neck of the clear alcohol. He found a silver lighter in another drawer and pocketed it. Shaking the bottle to soak some alcohol up into the rag, Ben walked to the edge of the stairs, making sure he was out of the line of sight.

He looked back at Fletcher and said in a whisper, "When I throw this, you run behind me. I'm not looking back. If you stay here, then he will come for you. Understood?"

Fletcher nodded.

Ben took a deep breath, lit the rag, and tossed the bottle. The tinkle of broken glass was followed by the *whoosh* of the flame catching fast, and Ben ran.

He heard the heavy footsteps of Fletcher behind him. At the top step, a bullet whizzed past his head, and Ben returned fire. Wagner was behind a couch, so Ben put two in the plush cushions where the man was most likely ducking down. "Out the back," Ben commanded, and Fletcher ran, head ducked and covered with his arms out the back door.

Wagner popped up and fired a few shots, and Ben dropped to a knee and fired back. Then he walked backward until he was outside. Seeing Fletcher hustling around the side of the house, he followed. It didn't take much effort to catch up to the big man, but it did take effort to help him keep up.

They came around the front of the house, and when he looked back, Ben saw flames rising from the house already. Someone would come soon. Surely.

But someone was already there.

Sadie was out of her car and coming toward him when she pulled her gun and fired. Ben turned to see that Wagner had emerged from the front door of the house and was about to take a shot, but Sadie saw him and fired first. He ducked back into the house and was gone.

"What happened?" Sadie yelled. "I leave and it all goes to sh-"

"Spitz is dead, Sadie," Ben said, cutting her off. "I'm so sorry."

She blinked rapidly and shook her head. "What?"

He took her into his arms and held her tightly. "He saved us. But there's a long story with it. I'm just so glad to see you." She squeezed him back.

"I'm fine, by the way," Fletcher huffed, climbing into the back seat of Sadie's car uninvited.

Stone had called Remington Dean, and surprisingly, the Ranger was quick to help him find an escape. Stone knew telling the lawman he wanted to spill about VYPER and Voight meant he was going to go away for a while. Maybe a long while. But he'd earned it- he saw that now. He had always thought men like Withers were the ones who came back from the war damaged. Their moral compass rewired and askew. Almost unhinged.

But Nathaniel Stone saw that he was messed up, too. And maybe worse. Because the things he did, while not driven by some manic need to spill blood, were wrong. And he had done them with what he thought was a clear head. A rational and well-adjusted mind.

Stone had killed in cold-blood. And he had done it out of a sense of duty. Had he been lied to? Sure. But he hadn't checked the mission too closely. Hadn't asked the questions a moral man would ask. Even now, even as he was prepared to do something his training told him was wrong, he realized he broke ranks too late. Stone had let that boy die. He could have opened fire on his menhis *former* men. Instead, he let a sense of loyalty and duty stay his hand while those men killed an innocent boy. And maybe an innocent woman.

Ahead, Stone saw the cave as Rhett Windsor had described over the phone. He was managing to move a bit faster than his pursuers, but they had his trail. He only hoped that they'd deem chasing him into the old mine was too risky. But then, wouldn't they just wait him out?

As he ducked into the shaft, he saw the multiple small openings on either side of him. He wanted to pick the first one, because if they came in, he could slip past them as they went deeper in.

They knew him, though. They'd know he chose the first one.

Behind him, the snap of a tree branch warned of their approach. Stone jumped into the second opening.

"Withers, wait up!" Benton called out.

"You pick up the pace!" Withers barked. "We're losing him."

"Look, Withers," Sharpe said calmly. "Does it matter? He doesn't know these woods- we don't either. Let him get lost, and we finish the objective."

"How Sharpe?" Withers said, turning on the man like a rabid dog. "We got no vehicle, we got no more ammo, and we got a man that knows the mission objective somewhere out here that can still turn this thing FUBAR if we let him."

"Withers-" Benton interjected.

"And another thing," Withers said, wheeling to face Benton. "Where did he get that flashbang? Or the idea to take the Behemoth? You helping him, Benton?"

"No-"

"No, *what?*"

Benton hesitated. Then, "No, sir."

Withers took a breath. He looked around, looked right at the mineshaft. It was too dark for Stone to be seen, but he still inched back just a bit. He could no longer see the interaction, but he could still hear.

Withers: "How much ammo do we each have? I've got three spare clips. Plus two mags for my sidearm."

Benton: "Gotta belt for the M60 and two clips for the sidearms."

Trant: "Four clips and two mags."

Simmons: "Same."

Sharpe: "Six clips, three mags, and three grenades. Few small C4 charges and detonators."

Silence.

Sharpe: "I'm demolitions, I come prepared."

Nervous laughter.

Sharpe: "If the question is, can we take the village, then yes. I think we can. Assuming their heavy hitters were on that truck, and I think it's a good bet, then we walk in and take the place with little effort. But we have to move. If those folks get back and alert the authorities, the odds shift fast."

Silence.

Withers: "If you can hear me Stone, you better hope you die of exposure- because if I find you, I'm gonna take it out of traitorous hide *slowly*." Pause. "Mount up, men. Make for the village."

Stone listened as the sound of their heavy presence in the forest dwindled. He sat in the dark, in the quiet for a moment. Thinking.

What would a good man do?

The part of Nathaniel Stone that believed he had completely lost his soul laughed at the notion of last-minute heroics.

But a glimmer of the man he wanted to be whispered, *Defend the village.*

"I might die," he said to himself out loud. "But then, maybe, I can die for something decent." He stood up, checked his gear, and marched into the forest after his former teammates.

Rhett was pacing back and forth in the vestibule of the city hospital with an anxiety that did not fit his normally composed persona.

It worried Dean when he walked back into the room after having changed out of his suit into his jeans, henley, and the spare green utility jacket he'd grabbed after losing the last one to blood stains.

"You always carry a change of clothes?" Ashleigh asked him.

"Yes," Dean said matter-of-factly. Why wouldn't he want to be prepared for anything? He didn't say that out loud, of course.

Abel Tolentino came bustling in from the morgue with Grace Aguirre right behind him. The smiling lab tech waved at Dean, and he couldn't help but smile back. "Long time no see, Dean," she said brightly.

"You could say that," Dean replied.

"Dean!" Abel yelled, seeming to just realize Dean was there. The Filipino medical examiner, with a youthful face and demeanor equal in joy to Grace beckoned him over with a wave of his hands. "Room is ready for them when they get here. But why are we here, again?"

Dean looked over at Rhett, who was still pacing. "Rhett's sister is a doctor. Practices up in the mountains in a little village called the Switchbacks. She'll want to help, but the hospital won't allow it without a person with privileges-that's you, Abel. I need her busy- and I need Rhett to know his family and friends are okay."

"Afraid he might do something rash?" Abel asked.

Dean shook his head. "Afraid he might *not.* I need his help to go after these guys. I think they might be goin' to the Switchbacks to finish the job."

"Yeesh," Grace said, having walked over. "Hey, sorry to interrupt, but did you tell him?"

Dean looked from Grace to Abel. "Tell me what?"

Abel took a deep breath. "First, the man you found in the Park-"

"Collazo."

"Yeah. He was emaciated. Like he'd been held for a few days. Also had ligature marks on his wrists," Abel explained. "Unlike the other victims in the other parks."

Dean nodded. "A copycat. I think someone killed Collazo to send a message to me, and the copycat part was just to throw us off for a bit. Pretty sure a guy named Robert Hesse did it. Or Chris Starr."

"Man, you know how to ruin a surprise, Abel whined.

"Wait, the FBI Agent?" Grace asked with wide-eyes.

"Catch her up later, Abel," Dean said. "You said, 'first,' before all that. What else?"

"That's actually Grace's thing," Abel said, turning toward a smiling Grace.

"The victims up on the Pass- Warren and Emilia?" she asked, as if he had already forgotten. She paused, and when he didn't say anything, she kept going. "Well, Warren was a big-time investor. I'd seen him on some of those cable shows about the stock market. Anyway, I got to digging into his reason for being here in Eden Falls when he was based in California. Couldn't find anything."

"That's not helpful, Grace," Dean said.

"But it is, just wait," Abel said, giddy with excitement.

"But finding nothing *was* something. See, there were, no reservations at any hotels in Colorado, no itineraries," Grace said. Dean had to admit, that was odd. "So, I started wondering if they *knew* someone here. And guess who is one of Warren Cornelius' biggest clients?"

It hit him. "Xavier Voight."

Grace nodded rapidly. "Right! So, I dug even deeper. And things weren't going too well between the two of them. I found a few angry- but vague emails from Voight to Cornelius. Lots of 'You owe me' messages. Then, an invitation to come stay at Voight's cabin came out of the blue. So, I wondered- why would Voight invite him out here if they weren't on good terms?"

"Trap," Dean said. "He set a trap. Cornelius was stealing from Voight?"

Now Abel couldn't help himself. "At least two million!"

"Abel, let me tell it!" Grace said, shoving Abel playfully. "At least two million!"

Dean pursed his lips. "That's enough to kill over. And there is no digital trail connecting their visit to a request from Voight?"

"Nope," Grace said. "Not directly, anyway. But the invite they *did* get was from Robert Hesse. On behalf of Voight."

Now Dean smiled. "That's enough to bring him in for questioning. But it'll have to wait. Tonight we have to finish this VYPER thing once and for all."

The doors to the hospital burst open and Dell Dumas and Todd Bolton came barreling through, carrying a bloody woman between them. Right behind them was Rhiannon Windsor, covered in blood and yelling.

"Get her on a table, now! She's pregnant!"

Rhett heard those words and fell to his knees. He watched as Tina was rushed back into the operating suite. The place where dead people were. The place where the woman he loved was either going to join those folks, or be saved by a medical examiner and a mountain doctor.

But he was going to be a father.

It had been his Damascus Road experience- the thing that finally made him want to go straight. To get right. The universe couldn't just tease that and yank it away. Could it?

Everyone else was focused on Tina and the effort to get her taken care of, so Rhett just sat there on his knees for a moment. He was tormented by the swirl of emotions in his head and heart, and was only stilled when he felt a hand on his shoulder. He looked up to see the green eyes and auburn hair of Ashleigh Storms looking down on him kindly. Actually, they were almost eye to eye, as he was so tall and she was not.

"She's in the best hands, Mr. Windsor," she said kindly. "You trust your sister, don't you?"

Rhett couldn't form words. His *sister*. She held Tina's life in her hands. His baby's life. It wasn't fair to her. To him. To anyone.

"Rhett?" Ashleigh said, patting his back.

"Y-yeah. I trust her."

"How long have you and-?"

"Tina."

Ashleigh smiled. "How long have you and Tina been together?"

Rhett shrugged. "Forever. Since we were kids. Only person who ever saw me for what I really was. Except Rhi, anyway."

"Is Tina a strong woman, Rhett? A good woman?"

Rhett thought of their fights- with each other and against others. He couldn't help but smile. "She scares *me,* she's so tough. And she's such a good person. Hated what all I used to be wrapped up in."

Dean emerged from the other room and walked toward Rhett. "Nothin' to report. She's shot in the abdomen, looks like it's in a spot they can get to. Even so, wouldn't hurt to pray."

"The baby? What about the baby?"

"Like I said, nothin' to report," Dean said. What Rhett didn't see was the eye contact between Dean and Ashleigh- or the subtle shake of his head.

Dean knelt next to Rhett on the side opposite of Ashleigh and placed his hand on his shoulder. "Lord, we pray for Tina and those workin' on her. May you guide their hands, clear their minds, and still their anxieties. We pray for healin' and protection."

"And retribution," Rhett added, his voice stronger than he felt at the moment.

The doors to the outside burst open and in ran Ben Samuels, Sadie Donovan, and Quentin Fletcher. Samuels announced, "We have a problem."

Dean listened as Ben recounted their ordeal. Dean then filled Ben in on the situation with Stone.

Then a quiet fell on them.

"We have to get Fletcher somewhere safer. Out of Eden Falls," Ben finally said.

"Agreed," Dean said, rubbing his chin. "Have you called Marino?"

"No, Wagner's cell blocker knocked my phone completely out," Ben answered.

"There's a safe house in Fort Collins that Homeland Security has," Dean said. "No time to get into that right now, but I have a contact I…don't completely distrust in that agency. But I don't think it's wise to go alone."

"I can go with you," Sadie offered.

"That okay with you?" Ben asked Dean.

"I mean, I need some help up at the Switchbacks, but if you need her," Dean replied.

"I'd really like her with me," Ben countered.

"Um, I'm right here, *boys,*" Sadie said, pointing to her face. "Jeez, it's the twenty-first century, let a woman pick her death for herself. And if he's riding into a firefight, I pick Dean."

Ben looked startled. "But-"

"Yeah, it's more dangerous. But I'm not a rare vase. Dean will need extra guns, despite how much of a superhero Ashleigh makes him sound like in her articles."

"Hey!" Ashleigh protested from across the room.

"Sorry," Sadie offered.

"Sadie, I'd love you to come, but I don't need you ridin' into a gunfight if you aren't one hundred percent," Dean said.

"But *I* need it," Sadie said. "The last time I met these guys, I nearly died. I want a chance to even the score."

Dean looked at Ben who shrugged. "Fine. Sadie, give Ben your cell so he can call Walt. I'll call Agent Pickett with Homeland to see if he can get some folks up there. Maybe Deputy Quincey, too."

"I'll stay here," Rhett said, now standing off in a corner.

Dean looked at him. He needed the big guy to fight, but looking at him told Dean that he was not in any condition to be of use. "Probably best," Dean admitted. "I will need some directions or coordinates, though.

He looked around and found some paper on an end table with a pen. Rhett began to scribble directions.

Dean turned to Ashleigh and Sadie. Quietly, he said, "Ashleigh, can you keep an eye on Rhett? I'm worried he won't deal well with the news."

Sadie raised an eyebrow. "News?"

Dean and Ashleigh exchanged a glance. "His girlfriend was pregnant," Ashleigh said.

"You said was," Sadie said knowingly.

Dean nodded.

"What if he finds out, and wants to go up there?" Ashleigh asked.

Dean looked at the giant of a man, then back at Ashleigh. "If you think you can stand in his way, go for it. Otherwise, I probably could use his help."

Chapter 20

Brent was bleary-eyed and wobbly, but Charly was on his arm, propping him up.

Voight had led him to what the billionaire called a 'small study' behind the bar. Of course, 'small' was very relative. The ceilings were twelve feet high, the walls ordained with all manner of taxidermied creatures, including a rather intimidating boar that stood on a stone outcropping behind the ornate desk centered on the back wall. Voight moved behind the desk and Brent's perspective made it look like the boar was looking over Voight's shoulder as he opened a ledger. Brent stifled a giggle, and Voight looked up.

"I didn't call you here to talk about the shooting. I called you here to talk business," Voight explained. "See, I do my research on people. I learn their strengths, weaknesses, and…" he paused and smiled. "Pressure points." He looked down at the ledger and said, "You got a substantial cash infusion about two months ago. Looks like the late Horatio Bethea dropped a pretty penny on your little coffee shop.”

Brent nodded. “Saved my <hic> shop.”

Voight looked up with a stoic face. “No. He prolonged the inevitable. See, his cash influx helped, the patronage of his Denver associates helped. But those have both dried up. Winter is coming, and the numbers you’ve been seeing the past two months will shrivel up. You have not banked enough profit to offset the upcoming downturn that is inevitable in the winter months. And people have a short memory. Come spring, if you are still here, the customers very well may not be.”

Brent blinked rapidly, then looked at Charly with confusion. “Listen to what he has to say,” she encouraged.

Brent didn’t like that. Not one bit. “I’ve got a side business-”

“The realtor thing? Or the drugs and guns?” Voight asked. “Because how many homes have you sold? And as for the other- well, you’ve been bought out.”

A door opened and Robert Hesse walked in. He was wearing gray military fatigues and had a motorcycle helmet under his arm, with a gun on his thigh. Zeke and Nigel Windsor walked in behind him.

Voight continued. "See, you let the Windsors run the business, and they took on Hesse, here because you seemed…disinterested. Hesse convinced them to cut him in, and effectively they cut you out. Now, Hesse works for me, so I now own your little side business. But I see you are concerned, and that's to be expected. So…I have an offer."

Brent wobbled more, but his mind was clearing up remarkably fast considering the amount of liquor he'd consumed. "The same as what Bethea offered?"

Voight smiled. "More or less. But more less. See, Bethea's mistake was letting you think you could keep your hands clean. Your mistake was *thinking* you could. You had no skin in the game. So, I'm giving you skin." He nodded to Zeke Windsor, who ducked into the room he'd come from and returned with a man whose head was covered with a black bag. He shoved the man to the floor, but kept the bag on his head. Brent heard the muffled sounds of gagging protest beneath the black cloth.

Voight pulled open a drawer on his desk and removed a large wooden box. He opened it, looked down and admired the contents, then reached in. He drew out a huge pistol, Brent thought it might be that Desert Eagle Voight mentioned at dinner, but he wasn't sure. Voight nodded at Hesse, who drew the pistol from his thigh and shoved it into Brent's hands. Confused, Brent reluctantly took it. He looked up and saw the enormous black emptiness of Voight's gun barrel staring at him. "The man before you is a rat and a thief. He snitched on my associates on my newly acquired business. The one that used to be yours. Seems he saw a local businessman- you- making deals with some disreputable people- the Windsor brothers. Thing is, this guy called the wrong LEO."

FBI Agent Chris Starr entered from that same room. If Brent was still drunk, it didn't matter. Fear for one's life had a way of clearing your head.

"Now, Agent Starr has been a friend of mine, and an associate of Mr. Hesse's for some time. He called me up and told me this dude was about to mess things up for me. And by extension, *you*." Voight moved around the desk and came toward Brent. "So, you get your skin in the game. Kill the rat. Right here. Right now. Or I kill-" Voight shifted his aim and put the gun right on Charly's forehead. "Her."

"What are you doing?!?" Charly yelped, but Voight merely pressed the gun into her forehead even harder.

"Applying pressure to one of his points, dear," Voight said. "You think he cares enough about you to kill a man? Every guy says he'd die for a lady, but few would kill for her. What say you Brent- save Ms. Addison? Or protect whatever shred of morality you have left?"

Brent was shaking, looking down at the gun in his hand.

"She not motivation enough for you, Brent?" Voight asked. "What if I threatened…Ashleigh Storms?" Brent looked up, and as he did, he saw a flash of pain cross Charly's eyes.

"I can't kill a man for anyone," Brent said, his voice cracking.

"Any*one*? So how many would you kill for? Let's start with Charly and see how many of your friends and loved ones have to die to get you that skin in the game."

Brent saw Voight's finger begin to squeeze the trigger, and he screamed, "No!" then turned and fired the gun into the man on the floor. Once. Twice. Three times.

The body fell over and twitched. Then it was still.

Brent dropped the gun and stood there, frozen. Hesse walked over and picked up the pistol, wrapping it in a cloth. Then he turned and walked to the body. Hesse removed the black bag and Brent felt all the air leave his lungs. He fell to his knees and began to weep.

The man he killed was Levi Montague.

"Don't cry for him, Brent," Voight said, dropping his pistol to his side. "He sold you out. And *now*, you *really* have skin in the game." Voight knelt down next to Brent, reached out and grabbed his chin, turning his head so they were face to face. "Because you can be connected to him. Hesse is gonna put that gun in a safe spot, with your print all over it. You become a problem, it turns up along with your old employee's body. *If* they find him." He stood up, and said to the Windsors, "Take Brent and Charly to dispose of the body. Starr, you know your job- make tracks fast. Hesse, I need you to clean up Nathaniel Stone's mess. Withers sent his coordinates and their plan for the raid. Should be going down any time now. Once they do their job, you know what to do."

Hesse nodded, then asked, "Is there time for me to see Ashleigh?"

Voight sighed. "Robert, let it go. She moved on. You don't own her anymore. And if you keep poking that bear, she'll get Dean on your trail. And since Stone botched that hit, we aren't ready to go down that trail. Yet." Voight paused to think, then added, "Unless he impedes another of our operations, of course. Then all bets are off."

"You say you know pressure points?" Hesse pushed back. "Well, she's Dean's now. And I know what happens when you press Dean's points. He gets angry. Makes mistakes. Gets distracted. We could use that."

Voight sighed again. "Fine. Threats. Vague. And make it fast so you get into position.. I want to be free of this VYPER mess tonight."

Hesse nodded and left.

Voight stopped and looked back at Brent. "Make the hole deep, son. Wouldn't want you getting found out, now would we?" As he walked out of the room he shouted back, "Got some *good* skin in the game now."

"Starr is in the wind," Pickett said over the phone as Dean drove his Camaro as fast as he dared up the mountain toward the Switchbacks. The Homeland agent had secured the safe house for Fletcher and sent the codes they needed to get access. Dean had called again to see if Pickett might be able to support their operation in a more physical nature. No dice.

"Why'd he rabbit all of a sudden?" Dean asked into the phone, which was set to speaker. Sadie listened on in the seat next to him.

"My contacts say that AUSA Kho shared that evidence from Fletcher with FBI brass, and they put a BOLO out on him," Pickett replied. "Someone tipped him off, and he was gone. That means a coordinated effort to find him across various agencies, and that means Homeland takes point. I'm tied up leading the manhunt for him, so I can't help you with the VYPER thing right now. But Dean?"

"Yeah?"

"Try to bring at least one of them back alive? Not like Kolbe?"

Sadie looked up at Dean, her brow furrowed.

"Remember when I said you were on speaker?" Dean said.

"Yeah. Why?"

"That implied someone else was in the car with me, Pickett."

"Hey, Agent. Sadie Donovan. We haven't met."

Click.

Dean's eyes stared forward, but he felt Sadie looking at him expectantly.

No one talked for two solid minutes.

"I can wait, but it's only gonna get harder to tell me the longer you wait," Sadie said. "And you *will* tell, eventually."

Dean let out a long breath.

"Fine."

"God, I hate the mountains," Pickett complained as it became clear Kolbe was heading toward a parking lot near a trailhead that led up into the higher, rougher country.

"I'm pretty partial to them, myself," Dean replied. "Somethin' about how they make me feel so small. So insignificant. Reminds me of my place in the world, I suppose."

"Gets too cold up here as it is," Pickett grunted. "Why would I want to go up where it gets colder faster and for longer? Besides, you're a Texan. Don't you people love the heat?"

Dean shook his head. "I've been through summers with more than forty days of hundred degree highs. I'd like a shot at a winter with dozens of feet of snow and forty days below freezin' to see which I prefer. He's stopped. Next to that car."

Pickett pulled over under the cover of trees and killed the engine and the lights. Kolbe climbed out of his SUV and tapped the window of the luxury sedan next to him. From their vantage point, they saw the window roll down. Kolbe shoved his hands in his pockets, and they could see his breath in the cool of the morning. "Who's he talkin' to?" Dean asked.

Pickett pulled out his phone and snapped a picture of the sedan. Then he typed the plate number into the laptop that was fixed to the dashboard. Seconds later it came back to a Laslo Koskoff. "Huh," Pickett grunted. "Laslo and his brother Dmitri are hitters for the Denver mob. And that means we have a standing warrant to surveil them." Pickett reached into the back seat and pulled out a small black box. He opened it to reveal a parabolic microphone, which he turned on, clicked a button to record, and rolled down the window. With his free hand, he turned on the sound so they could listen.

"- getting nervous, Laslo," Kolbe was saying. "They don't know where he is. But they are pretty sure he knows I'm involved in her death."

Dean and Pickett looked at each other. "Think he means me?" Dean asked.

"Don't worry, man," Laslo said in a slight Russian accent, and muffled from being inside the car. There was shuffling as Laslo got out of the car. Pickett shifted slightly to better catch the conversation. "He shows, we pop him. The Ghost and the Darkness says so."

"God, I hate those nicknames," Kolbe muttered. "I mean, I get it. Better than using real names. But they sound like bad supervillains from some D-list movie.”

“Hey, that *was* a movie. About lions in Africa,” Laslo said. “Killed a bunch of railroad workers before Val Kilmer killed them. I think Michael Douglas was a hunter in that, too.”

“Huh. Makes sense. The whole hunter thing, I guess,” Kolbe said. “Still dumb.”

The two men began to laugh. Laslo lit up a cigarette. “Ghost and the Darkness?” Dean asked.

Pickett shrugged. “Has been some chatter. Ghost is the name of the dude who runs Denver mob operations. We think he might be a Horatio Bethea- or some other guy. Maybe some guy who acts low level to conceal his identity. Darkness is new. First I heard of him.”

The other two were talking again. “Why did you go after the woman, anyway? You were free and clear, right? She’d cut you a deal.” Dean gritted his teeth. It was about Amy.

“She had, but people could still talk, you know?” They were walking to the back of the sedan. “Like that Ranger boss of Dean’s- he had papers. Sent them to Dean. We weren’t trying to kill her- she was just…in the way.”

Before he knew it, Dean was out of the car. He flipped his jacket back so his hand could reach for the Colt and he strode toward the two men. Pickett was scrambling to get out of the car and stop him.

But nothing was going to stop him.

"Grant Kolbe," Dean announced. "I'd like a word."

Kolbe went white.

Laslo went for his gun.

Dean was much faster.

As crimson spread across his chest, Laslo sunk to his knees, and his eyes rolled back in his head.

Kolbe ran for the trail.

"Dean- you idiot! What do you think you're doing?" Pickett yelled.

"I'm going for a hike," Dean replied as he quickened his pace to keep up with Kolbe. Didn't matter if the man got ahead of him. Remington Dean knew how to track his prey.

"Wasn't Koskoff the name of the guy you blew away outside of Denver with Walt and his old partner?" Sadie asked.

"Dmitri," Dean said. "The brother."

"Man, you were rough on that family," she quipped.

"I'm rough on a lot of families," he replied. Dean steered the Camaro off the slightly paved road and onto the decidedly unpaved road that led to the Switchbacks. They passed the wreck of Dean's truck, which still hadn't been picked up, and kept going. He checked the instructions Rhett had written out. "Almost there, so I'll finish the story later."

"So there will be a later?" Sadie asked. "I only say that because you and I are riding into God knows what kind of shootout with trained Black-Ops military men. By ourselves- I might add."

Lights flickered in the rearview mirror. "Not by ourselves. Quincey is gonna meet us-" he pointed to a Sheriff's SUV just ahead- "And I'm pretty sure we got other company, too."

Sadie turned in her seat. "Who is that?"

"Looks like Windsor decided he was gonna join us after all. Wonder what went down after we left."

Ashleigh sat across from Rhett Windsor, a man she was connected to through their circumstance, but not a man she'd spent any real time with. She knew his reputation as a giant oaf had been a fabrication from her talks with Dean. She knew he was actually an incredible intellect, and a man who was trying to turn his life around from bad choices he made trying to survive in the mountains.

She knew he was a tough man.

So seeing him weep was breaking her heart.

"Can I get you anything?" she asked.

"I'll take a soda, if yer offerin' one up," one of the other men there said.

Ashleigh cut her eyes to him. "Todd, is it?"

"Nah, I'm Dell," he replied.

Ashleigh nodded.

"And I'm Todd," the other answered without being asked. "We ain't related, but folks think we are."

"Because you look so much alike?" Ashleigh asked.

The two men- one tall, thin, and blonde and the other a stocky brunette- exchanged looks. "Maybe that's it," Todd said.

Ashleigh pursed her lips and rose. "Todd, you want a drink? To go with Dell's?"

"Two cokes," he said.

Ashleigh turned to Rhett and knelt in front of him. Seeing the tears stream down his face made her feel a sting in her own eyes once more. "Anything for you?"

He shook his head.

The doors that led to the operating room opened and a beautiful blonde woman walked out and pulled her mask off. Her eyes were red, but not a fresh red. Abel and a Hispanic woman Ashleigh didn't recognize followed.

Rhett rose so fast he almost knocked her over and he ran to the woman. "Rhi- tell me she's okay."

The blonde woman- Rhi- licked her lips. "Tina is stable. We got the bullet out. She'll be fine. But Rhett, the baby…we did all we could…she wasn't far along and-"

A roar of rage and hurt erupted from the red-haired man as he fell to his knees.

And Ashleigh lost her own composure. She would almost have preferred to see Rhett punch a wall or kick over a chair. To see him weep, to see him mourn with such vulnerability was harder than to see him mourn in a terrifying rage. Ashleigh turned from the scene as Rhi knelt to comfort Rhett. Her tears fell freely, and her hand went to her face. Brutes. Savages. Who else could wreak so much havoc? She hoped Dean found them and they put up a fight so he could put them down like the dogs they were.

The door chimed and a figure dressed in gray camo and a biker's helmet came in. Even before he slipped off that helmet, Ashleigh knew who it was.

Robert Hesse.

He didn't smile when he saw her, and she thought he might have even had a flicker of compassion in his eyes. Eyes that barely fell on her before another roar from Rhett caught his attention.

Moving faster than a man his size should have, he rushed past Ashley at Robert, who drew his gun (different from the one he'd given to Brent)- forcing Rhett to stop.

"I'm not here to fight you, big guy," Robert said.

"Then leave," Rhi said, joining Rhett and holding forth a pistol of her own. "You may not have been up there, but these men work for your boss, so you are just as guilty."

Robert bit the inside of his lip, a nervous tick he had when they'd been married. Then he lowered his gun. "Not anymore. VYPER is disbanded as of tonight. No questions asked. Voight is drawing up the dissolution papers as we speak. I came to offer my condolences, and to ask a favor."

"We don't owe you sh-" Rhi began.

"Where did they hit you?" Robert interjected. "Coordinates?"

Rhi and Rhett looked at each other. "I don't know them. The coordinates that is. Rhett can show you. It's just a few miles from the Switchbacks."

Robert shook his head. "Doesn't work that way. And I bet *he* does know the coordinates," he said, pointing to Rhett.

Rhett, who had stopped crying, stood silent and still.

"They'll be dead before you find them, Robert," Ashleigh heard herself say. The strength in her voice surprising her.

Robert turned back to her. "What's that mean?"

"Remington Dean and Sadie Donovan are already on their way to the Switchbacks. They'll find them before you can get up the mountain," she replied, her eyes fixed on his.

He pursed his lips, then licked them. "That so? You got that much faith in your Ranger boyfriend? Yeah- I know you got a thing for him. Too bad he won't be around for too much longer. Bad things happen to people who poke their nose in the wrong business."

Ashleigh laughed. And she couldn't stop. She doubled over, put her hands on her knees, and guffawed. She raised up and wiped a tear from her eye.

"What's so funny?" he asked, that telltale anger she recognized all too well present in his voice.

"I never saw how small you were until now. How insecure. How much you hide behind your guns and your aggression and that overcompensation you call a motorcycle," she chuckled again. "I mean, that threat? Grow a mustache so you can twirl it, Robert. So cliché. But then, you never were all that smart, were you?

Of course that makes me a fool for staying with you as long as I did."

Robert nodded and smirked. "We'll see who's laughing when the smoke clears tonight."

Ashleigh took in his smug look, and something inside her clicked. He *was* a small man. A *weak* man. But he was still was- and perhaps even more so because he was small and weak- a dangerous man. And dangerous men would be violent men when they felt it could mask their deficiencies.

She made a choice.

She walked to Robert- mustering years of a desire to stand up to her abuser, years of repressed rage, and her newfound boldness. She shoved him in the chest and stared into his deep-set blue eyes that had long haunted her nightmares. Then she said flatly, "If Dean doesn't kill you, I will."

He laughed, but it was a short, uncomfortable laugh. He sensed what she was feeling- that his spell over her was broken. She had no idea if she could actually do it, but she was more sure than ever before that he would never lay another hand on her without it costing him dearly.

And Robert Hesse seemed to sense that.

"Switchbacks, huh?" he asked no one, backing away. "Guess I'll start there." He turned slowly, and walked out the door, shoving his helmet back on his head..

It was quiet for a moment, then Rhett asked, "Who shot Tina? Which one?"

Ashleigh turned and looked at Rhett and Rhi, and she saw the resemblance in their profiles. Siblings, for sure. Both with strong jaws, intense eyes. Rhi was small but imposing and Rhett was large but graceful. "Brown hair with buzzed sidewalls. Square jaw. I think he had a beret- but not the Stone guy. Withers, I think they called him. Cocky little prick."

Rhett nodded and walked past Ashleigh, then stopped and turned to her. "If that man shows his face near Dean, and the Ranger doesn't kill him, I will." Then he marched out the door.

Ashleigh felt a hand on her shoulder, and she turned to see Rhi standing beside her. "That man, who was he to you?"

Ashleigh looked out the door where Robert and Rhett had left and said, "The man who made the mistake of thinking I'm still the same woman he used to push around."

Dean pulled over next to Quincey's SUV, and Rhett's square body truck followed suit.

"You really gonna let Windsor go up there with us?" Sadie asked as Dean killed the engine.

"Way I see it, the man is defendin' his home," Dean said, gesturing out the front windshield. "And we are short on support, so I take what I can get. Plus, I know he can handle himself in a situation like this."

Dean got out of the car to find Quincey sizing up the Camaro with a shotgun on his shoulder. "This is slick, Dean. You do the restoration yourself?"

"Mostly."

"Gonna restore the truck?"

"Nope."

Quincey smiled. "These old cars are worth saving. New stuff was built to be replaced."

"Don't talk like that," Sadie said. "Old man Dean will get a big head. You saying old things are better than new things."

Quincey laughed. "I *really* like her."

"I used to," Dean replied.

Rhett walked up, his head down, unwilling to look at them. "I want to fight with you."

No one responded for a beat, then Quincey said, "Look sharp." Then he tossed the shotgun to Rhett. "Dean told me what went down. If it was my wife and kids, I'd be here, too." Then he went to the back of his SUV. "I figure you brought your side-arms, but if you wanted some long guns, I got a choice."

"Sadie will probably want one. I brought my own," Dean said, opening the trunk of the Camaro. To one side of the trunk was his Remington M700 in a case and to the other was his Heckler & Koch MP5/10. It was night time so the sniper rifle would require a night vision, which he did not have. Plus, any shooting to be done would likely be close quarters, so he grabbed the H & K. Shutting the trunk, he saw Sadie hefting an M4 Carbine while Quincey was hefting an identical M4. Rhett was shoving a pistol into his waistband with the hand not holding his tactical shotgun.

"Let's walk in," Dean said. "Cars make a bigger target, and these fellas might have ordinance. Rhett- how far out are we?"

He shrugged, his colossal frame shaded red in the taillights of Quincey's SUV. "Quarter mile, little more. Just over that h-"

The pop of automatic gunfire erupted from over the hill where Rhett was pointing, and without another word, they broke into a run for the Switchbacks.

Ben steered the sedan up the mountain, leaving Eden Falls behind to the south. He had called in CBI agents to cover the scene at Fletcher's house, informing their unit chief of the need to get the witness secured. He hadn't known Spitz well, but Ben felt a pang of sadness at the thought of him lying there dead. But he'd made a choice in the end, and that meant Ben and Fletcher were alive. And maybe, if they got Fletcher to Fort Collins safely, Spitz's sacrifice might have even more meaning.

As they rose in elevation, the sun was all but gone behind the mountains. Ben loved to drive at that time of night- it almost helped him find peace about the events of that day. Walt was riding shotgun, and Fletcher was cuffed in the back seat. For once, the big man was quiet.

Walt wasn't, though.

"This has all the signs of a major cluster," he said, looking at his phone. "Dean texted to say that Starr was outed in those papers Kho took. And the agent bolted- long gone with no idea where to. And if they sent that hitter in, there is no way they let this guy go so easily."

"You think I don't know that, Walt?" Ben asked, irritated. "You want to hand the man over to the mob? That in *your* character to do that?"

Walt looked out the window. "No. Don't guess it is. But I am getting too old for this sort of thing. The late night witness drops. Mostly the late night parts."

"It's nine o'clock, Walt."

"That's really late for me," Walt retorted. "I need a desk job. Ride out my twilight years in safety. Getting fat off donuts."

"You look to be on the way there, already," Ben observed.

Walt flipped him off.

Then he sat up. "Car. Coming up fast."

Ben looked in the rearview. "See it."

It was a big vehicle, likely a truck, but he only had headlights to go by. It came up behind them, got right on the bumper, then swerved and passed in a no passing zone. It raced past them, swung around the turn ahead of them, and roared away.

Walt drew his gun. "That's for us."

"Doesn't look like a Denver mob ride," Ben said.

"Didn't you say they had the Tolberts on retainer?" Walt asked.

They came around the turn and Ben cursed. There, blocking the road, was the truck parked sideways. Three shadowy figures stood around it, guns drawn. Well, guns and knives.

Ben slammed on the brakes and screeched to a halt.

"Stay in the car, and stay down," Walt said to Fletcher, who made himself as small as he could in the back seat. No effortless task.

Ben pulled the shotgun from the rest in the console, then looked at Walt. "Ready, old man?"

"As always, kid," he replied.

They opened their doors and drew down on the men before them.

"Easy now, boys," a voice called out from the driver's side of the truck. A large man with gray muttonchops that turned into a mustache and a rough-looking cowboy hat walked around from the driver's side of the truck. He wore a brown leather vest over a t-shirt and had a gun belt, but the sidearm wasn't drawn. "We're just here to talk," the man said.

"And you are?" Walt called out.

"Joe Tolbert. You've met my boys here, but our employers have asked us to speak with you. See if you can see reason. Before blood is shed."

Ben looked to Walt, who kept his gun raised. Walt spoke again. "And your employer would be?"

Joe chuckled. "You know. Folks down in Denver. Runs some drugs and guns and other unsavory things. Calls himself the Ghost or some foolishness."

"You met him?" Ben asked, genuinely curious.

"In a manner of speaking, I suppose."

"What's that mean?" Ben asked.

"Well, he secured my release from prison earlier today. Now, I've never spoken with him personally, but I do my research on people I work with. I have connections that will talk to me and that won't speak with you. And despite what you may have heard to the contrary, the Ghost's identity is not as much of a mystery as he wants it to be," Joe said. "But I have no gain from spilling that particular secret right now."

"You sound like an intelligent man, Mr. Tolbert," Walt said. "Why would you be foolish enough to fall in with the Denver mob?"

Joe smiled. "The world up here is changing, Agent Marino. Yes, I know you. And Agent Samuels. The Ghost knows you, too. And that might not bode well for you. But the truth is, he isn't after you. And I'm not either."

"You're after Quentin Fletcher?" Ben asked.

"I'm not," Joe said. "But he is a means to the end I seek. I want Remington Dean, but I have to play my part with Mr. Fletcher, first."

"You here to kill Fletcher?" Walt asked.

Joe looked at his wrist, at the watch on his muscular forearm. "Nope."

Ben and Walt exchanged a glance. "What are you here for? Ben asked.

"To talk. See if you'll hand Mr. Fletcher over to us. If not, you're free to go. After we chat."

"We aren't giving him up," Walt said.

"We chat then," Joe said. "You've met my nephew, Virgil here." Virgil stepped up next to his uncle, leaving the mohawk and mullet to remain by the truck. "But you didn't get to meet Lenny, I don't believe. Poor soul was gunned down because he engaged in some foolish actions. See, tonight is not the first time we Tolberts have worked with the Denver folks. Though it wasn't my choice the first time. Or this time, if I'm being honest." Joe gave Virgil a look, and the nephew dropped his head.

"Dean killed him, right?" Ben asked.

Joe nodded and waved his hand across the open air, then held up a single finger. "Only him. None of the other boys were there that night. They walked free, after a short stint in jail. But my boy—and though he wasn't my son, he was my kid, you know. Well, he's lying cold and dead in the ground." He walked closer, not in a threatening way, so Ben didn't shoot. Joe licked his lips. "My family is from a rough line of outlaws. Back in the times of the gunslingers they robbed stagecoaches and trains. In Prohibition, they made shine. My daddy grew weed, and for a time, I did, too. Now it's legal, and the fun is gone. I dabbled in some other drug manufacture, and I got put away for a bit for it. Previous county sheriff put me away for that, but I don't blame him. He was just doing his job. That's why I wasn't there to save my boy, by the way. I was in jail. So, while I'm in there, I discover my other boy, Virgil here, has gotten us tangled up with the Denver mob- the same organization that sent Lenny to his death. Like I said, just got out this morning. One of the Denver boys sent a lawyer up with wavy hair, beady eyes, and a tan suit. Ol' beady eyes said that was part of why they got me early release. Atonement. Make sure my kin got the job done right, this time. Heh. Now, I was not too happy to learn of this…entanglement, but I am a man of honor. I keep my word- and the word of my kin. Until the contract is complete…" he smiled. "Or the death of the parties in the contract."

Ben thought he saw what Joe Tolbert was up to. Double-crossing. Back-stabbing.

Tolbert looked at his watch again. "One more time, you want to hand Fletcher over?"

"No, sir," Walt said, shaking his head.

"Fair enough," Joe said. He pointed a finger skyward and waved it in a circle. The other three climbed into the truck. "Have a safe trip to Fort Collins, gentlemen. And if you see Remington Dean, tell him I'll be seeing him. Soon."

Joe Tolbert walked around to the driver's side, hopped in the truck, and started the engine. The truck roared to life, turned and headed back the way it had come. Joe stuck an arm out the window and waved as they went by.

"What was that about?" Walt asked, completely bewildered.

"A warning? A threat?" Ben offered.

"They were stalling," Fletcher said from where his head was stuck between the front and back seats of the sedan. "Letting the hitmen get ready for us down the road."

"Well, that sucks for you, Fletcher," Walt said, getting back in the car.

Ben waited a moment. Tolbert was going to make a play on the two entities he blamed for his son's death. He was willing to go to guns with Remington Dean because the lawman had pulled the trigger on his son. He would play the long game with the Denver mob, get in close to drive the knife into their heart..

And that made the old redneck ex-con a serious problem for everyone.

Brent had thrown up.

Again.

They were deep in the woods, and he was still wearing his suit. But his hands were caked with dirt and mud from digging a grave.

For Levi.

The Windsors looked on, cackling about how weak he was. How hard it was for him to split the ground with the shovel. Calling him 'city boy' and other less than complimentary names.

But Brent didn't hear them. He just looked at the slowly deepening pit where he would put Levi, a young man that was his friend. A young man he had *killed*.

Why? To save Charly? Would Voight have killed Charly? Or was she just playing a role, too?

She was there, sitting in the truck to stay warm from the cool night air. She had been awfully quiet, either to keep from giving away her complicity or because she was shocked at what Brent had done.

Murdered a man.

For her.

Or was it for himself? Had Brent pulled the trigger because he was afraid to die? Probably. And Voight was right. The man now owned him in a way the Denver mob never did. Got him drunk, got him scared. Just plain got him.

"Hey, stop leanin' on it and start usin' it!" Zeke barked, waving a pistol.

"Rhett know you're in with Voight now?" Brent asked, gasping for air, much more sober than any man should have been after consuming so much alcohol. Well, killing will wake you up, he guessed. And make you bolder. Calling out Zeke like that when he never would have said a cross word to the man for abusing his free coffee privilege.

It was Nigel that answered. "Big Red went soft when he found out he was gonna be a daddy. Not long after we set up our deal. Far as we're concerned, he's got no say in what we do."

Brent struggled to lift a heavy load of dirt and stone. "He know you're gonna sell out his land?"

Nigel spat on the ground. "Nah. But even if he did know, wouldn't matter. Them VYPER boys are hittin' that Switchback place right about now. Won't be no one left up there soon enough."

"Weren't they your family?"

Zeke smiled, exposing a missing tooth. "Family don't pay the bills, son. We got a new family now. They pay good."

"Loyalty? Not a fan?" Brent asked.

Nigel chuckled coldly. "You're one to talk. Remember whose grave you're diggin?'"

Brent looked at Levi's body, then back at the hole. "Yeah," he muttered to himself. "Mine."

Chapter 21

Dean hadn't really seen the village from the entrance, so its size surprised him. The winding gravel road they were on dipped down in between small cabins on either side of the path before it began to rise again and turn to the left. He saw Rhiannon's house right at the point where the road turned, and followed that road to the field where he had seen them growing their crop. A handful of other houses dotted that road, but what surprised him was the number of homes back in the trees behind that row, as indicated by their lights shining out in the dark.

Dean and Sadie crested the hill first, and took in a dire situation. Down that road to the field was where the shootout was happening between what he assumed were VYPERs and townsfolk. Two structures were already on fire with a handful of people doing all they could to douse it. Light was limited to house bulbs, stars, and the moon but he could make out more people moving from the houses in the trees toward the conflict.

Rhett caught up with them and pointed toward the fight. "We cut across this field here, we can sneak up on them from behind," he said. "But maybe we don't all go that way-just in case they see us."

Dean saw what Rhett was trying to do. He wanted to get there first, get his target. The man who shot Tina. Because Dean could identify with that, he said, "You and Quincy go that way. Sadie and I will provide support to the Switchbackers."

Rhett nodded, and they rushed on.

Stone heard the shots before he saw the flames. He was coming down a slope (from the opposite direction of Dean and his group) and was still hidden by the trees. It was dark, but he had lots of experience hiking after the sunset. Still, he almost didn't see the small house that seemed to appear out of nowhere in front of him. Looking to his left and right, he saw rows of tiny homes. Far more than their assessment had identified.

That meant that Withers was going to find more resistance than expected.

Stone smiled, then kept moving.

Near the edge of the woods, he found a boulder and dropped behind it to check his weapon. Didn't want it jamming in the heat of battle, after all.

He also hadn't yet decided what he was going to do. He was definitely going to help the townspeople, but did he do that by killing Withers and his old squad? Or by wounding?

Or just trying to get people to safety?

He'd given up hope of convincing any of his squad to try a different path. Even Benton seemed resigned to his choice.

Stone lifted his rifle and looked through the night vision to get the lay of the land. He saw Sharpe and Trant sneaking around behind one of the inflamed buildings toward the rest of the small village- a flanking maneuver. Simmons and Benton were laying down fire on anyone who dared approach their position at the end of an open field beside the road leading into the village. None of them were firing on the people trying to put out the fires, and that made Stone lean toward 'wound' rather than kill.

But where was Withers?

Stone began to scan the field, but he couldn't see him anywhere. He did see Rhett Windsor and another man- a large deputy- rush Benton and Simmons' position, forcing them to address that assault.

Then he saw movement back toward Sharpe and Trant.

Remington Dean and the red-haired detective were walking casually toward the two VYPER men, but didn't see them. Stone was about to raise his rifle to fire when he heard a click behind him.

"Withers?" Stone asked.

"Nope."

Starr.

"So, you here to kill me?"

"Depends," Starr said. "On whether or not you want to be smart and help me out, or be stupid and get in my way."

"So, this has nothing to do with me shooting you?"

Starr shrugged, and lifted the arm he'd been shot in. "That was business. You had to prove yourself to your bosses and I to mine. Back when they wanted to maybe play nice with each other. They don't want to play nice, and my associate and I want to take advantage of that."

"Associate?"

"Hesse," Starr said. "He speaks highly of you, by the way."

Stone looked back at the shootout. Dean had spotted Benton and Simmons, taken a shot or two and driven them back. Dean and the detective were wading into oncoming fire, trying to protect the people of the village.

Being heroes.

Doing good.

It was why Stone had joined the military. Not just to kill for money.

To help.

To protect.

He swore under his breath, and turned his gun on Starr.

Dean and Sadie came up the main road, either unseen or deemed not a concern to the VYPER team assaulting the Switchbacks. Rhett and Quincey were already rallying the handful of locals to push the two men at the edge of the field back. One was laying down fire as the other moved back for cover.

And they knew of the two men on the other side of the small building they were approaching because Sadie had seen one of them just before he disappeared behind the inflamed wall.

"Pretend we don't see 'em," Dean said, moving out from the wall and exposing himself to the soldiers' line of fire. He secured the stock of his H & K in his shoulder, and walked forward.

A man with a black balaclava fired from a crouched position, and Dean drew down on him. He pitched backward as a shot from Sadie hit him center-mass. The other man hesitated briefly, considering if Dean or Sadie was a bigger threat, which allowed Dean to get his shot off on him. He was also struck in the chest, and went down. Both men began to squirm on the ground, crawling for cover. Wounded, but not dead.

"Stupid body armor," Sadie said, moving in with a look in her eyes that Dean knew all too well. She intended to finish them off.

"They're down, Sadie," Dean said. "Get their guns, and hold them. I'll see if I can help round up-"

BANG!

At first, Dean thought Sadie had shot one of the men, but he quickly realized the shot came from somewhere else, off to his right. He turned and saw a man in a beret- Stone- firing at a man in a suit.

Starr.

"Stay with them- and don't kill 'em!" Dean yelled, running toward Stone and Starr.

Both men were trying to get to cover, and Dean heard Starr shouting, "Wrong choice, Stone! You could have been a wealthy man!"

Stone shouted in reply, "I've recently remembered that honor means more than wealth. Something you forgot- or maybe never knew."

Dean went to Stone, who had not seen him approach. The soldier almost jumped from his cover when he saw Dean, who also ducked down with his back to the boulder.

"Things are bit different from the last time we met, huh?" Dean asked.

"Just a tad," Stone replied. "It's just Starr. But I have not gotten eyes on Withers- the guy who took my command from me. You seen him?"

"We got two under over by the shed, and two more on the run at the edge of the field," Dean said. "What's Withers look like?"

"Blockheaded son of a-"

A bullet ricocheted off the boulder they were crouched behind.

It had not come from Starr's direction. Dean looked up the hill to his left, in the cover of trees, and saw a hint of movement.

"Move!" Dean shouted as a second shot rang out. He raised his rifle and fired a burst toward the movement, and Stone raced for new cover.

Starr rose from his position and began firing at Stone, who ran in a crouched position and fired sideways- more for distraction than any actual attempt to hit Starr.

No more shots came from the treeline, so Dean turned toward Starr. Their eyes met, and an understanding passed between the two men. Dean dropped the rifle to the ground, and his hand hovered near his Colt. If Chris Starr was the man who had killed Amy, it would *have* to be the pistol that took him out. Dean's face was a mask of calm. His eyes coldly stared down the rogue FBI agent, his lips set in a thin grimace. His breathing slowed, and grew shallow. He waited. Starr had to go for the shot, first. In Dean's morality, it was the only justification for shooting the man. Even if he had been the man behind her death, Dean wouldn't- couldn't- murder him. But he could defend himself. Then the shoot would be justified.

Then, maybe, Dean would *feel* justified.

But Starr didn't go for the shot. "It wasn't me, Dean. I know what you think, what you've been putting together since we met last month. I know you recognized me. I know you connected me with Kolbe and Hesse. And I was there that night, but I did not kill your wife."

His breathing was still controlled. The sounds of the shootout were dying out around him. Calmly, coldly, he said, "Why should I believe that?"

"I know you've seen my file, Dean," Starr said, raising his hands. "You know my specialty. I was trained as a sniper by the bureau. I was there that night. But I wasn't at your house."

Dean's eyes narrowed. "Royder?"

Starr nodded. "And I suspect you know it wasn't Kolbe- seeing as you killed him already and haven't stopped digging."

Dean was still focused on Starr, but he heard footsteps behind him.

"It's me, Dean," Sadie said. "Got the two guys cuffed and with me. Do I cuff Stone so you can deal with Starr?"

"Stone's free. For now. Quincey and Rhett?"

"Looks like they have one of theirs, the other is gone."

"You find Withers? Big chin, shaved sidewalls?" Stone asked.

The man in the balaclava laughed.

Dean heard Stone run to the man and grab him, but he kept his eyes on Starr. Stone was yelling, "Where is he, Sharpe?"

The man simply said, "Right here, Nathaniel."

Then three explosions ripped through the night, pillars of flame rising from three more buildings in the Switchbacks. Including Rhiannon's clinic.

Dean finally turned from Starr, and as he did, he saw two things fly through the air toward them. Both small and cylindrical.

"Flash bang!" someone shouted. They all looked around and it landed in their midst and exploded.

Then the world went white.

Before they lost sight of each other, Stone drew to fire, but Dean was faster. He knew the shot wasn't a killshot, but he also knew he hit him. Starr yelped in pain, and Dean guessed he hit the same shoulder he'd been wounded in before.

Dean had tried to close his eyes, and had almost been successful. When he opened them, the world was still too bright- especially for night- and the shapes too blurry. Foggy. The second canister must have been a smoke grenade. He looked around to where Starr had been, but he was gone. Sadie was standing alone, her two captives running away in the once again gathering dark. Sadie hadn't been able to shield her eyes, apparently, and was wandering aimlessly.

The man in the mask- apparently Withers- was shouting orders as his voice grew more distant. Headed toward the woods.

Stone, crouched on the ground near Dean, yelled out, "Withers- I'll find you!"

Then, from across the field, a rage-filled roar rose over the entire chaotic scene.

"WITHERS!" Rhett bellowed.

Dean knew the kind of rage that caused that sound.

He knew it because he'd felt it.

He'd let it out himself.

Kolbe ran too fast for a man not accustomed to hiking, and fell down an embankment, rolling until he struck a tree.

Dean came up upon him as he was climbing back up to the trail, and drew his Colt. He stood there, waiting for Kolbe to climb up.

"You gonna shoot me in cold blood, Ranger?" Kolbe asked, wincing and breathless.

Dean cocked his head to the side. He wanted to. God knew the man deserved it. Then Dean caught himself. In his anger, his grief, he had begun to see himself as an agent of vengeance. The man of God had become an angel of death. The process had been subtle but fast, and now, standing on that trail in Colorado, looking at the man who had a hand in killing his wife, all that was needed to complete the transition was a little pull on the trigger.

But Dean heard a voice in his head.

If something happens to me, please…leave the Rangers. Leave law enforcement. Do something that brings light to the world- get out of the darkness.

Promise.

Amy.

One breath at a time…

He blinked fast, tears stinging at his eyes.

She wouldn't want him to become a killer.

Even to avenge her.

"No," he managed, his voice cracking. "I won't become you. Killing an unarmed person." He looked away from Kolbe, taking in the morning glow driving out the shadows from the trees. "She fought for you, you know? She believed you. Believed *in* you. And you just…used her. Used me. Then killed her when she wasn't useful anymore."

"I didn't kill her, Dean," Kolbe pleaded. "I wasn't there."

"You ordered it," Dean said flatly.

Kolbe licked his lips and sighed. "I *passed down* the order. There are people far scarier than me out there, Dean. I do *their* bidding."

"Denver mob?"

Kolbe blinked. "Them. And others."

"Like who?"

"I talk, I die. They have tentacles everywhere. In Texas. Colorado. The government-"

"You sound like a conspiracy nut," Dean said.

"It's no conspiracy. It's a business. It's run like one. And the mob- even they have no idea what's coming."

"Tell me about it- tell about what's coming, Kolbe."

He seemed to consider it. Then he smiled. It wasn't a cocky smile, and definitely not a cheerful smile.

It was a smile of resignation.

His gaze went to the trees, to the sky.

"Screw it. I'm dead either way." Kolbe pulled a gun.'

And Dean fired faster.

The bullet entered Kolbe's chest before his gun was level. It fell to his feet, clattering on the stone forest floor. Kolbe went to his knees, already gasping.

Dean went to him, gun still drawn. "Why'd you pull, Kolbe?"

He gurgled, unable to form words.

As Dean looked at him, he was struck by something. He didn't feel anger at the man, definitely not rage.

He felt sad.

Kolbe had lived a life of crime and poor choices. His life was ending because of both.

And because Remington Dean had a quick hand.

Had Grant Kolbe ever had another choice? A choice to look for hope and good in the world? Had he ever had an Amy that reminded him there was more to the world than darkness?

Over Kolbe's gasping, Dean asked, "Do you mind if I pray for you?" He wasn't sure what had urged him to do that, then and there. Maybe it was God, prompting the former minister to embrace that calling that remained on his life to share the message of hope for the condemned. Maybe it was Amy's words, letting him find a way to still serve and protect and keep out of that darkness.

Kolbe nodded, and Dean began to pray for Kolbe. For God to forgive him, for his soul to find rest in Christ, for there to be one more chance at redemption. "And I don't mean about who killed Amy. I'll find that. Right now, I want you to have a chance to get right with the only judge that matters."

Kolbe nodded, words beyond his capacity to make. And Dean prayed the Lord's Prayer.

Somewhere in that recitation, Kolbe died.

"That was…something…" Pickett said, declaring his presence.

"How long you been there?"

"Long enough to see he pulled on you, and you were justified in shooting him."

Dean shook his head. "I'm not justified. I still killed him in anger."

"That why you prayed with him?"

Dean shrugged. "Maybe. Or maybe there is still a part of me that wishes my job was still savin' souls rather than sendin' them to meet their Maker."

Pickett rubbed his chin. "While you consider that, you wanna track down Koskoff's brother? Give him the bad news about his brother? See if he knows anything?"

Dean looked down at Kolbe's body. "Someday, Amy. I promise. Just not today."

One breath at a time…

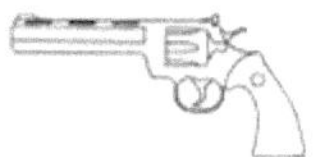

Rhett and Quincey had driven the men back, and one had taken off for the trees. Out of their range. But they had the big African American guy on the ground at their feet with his hands up by the time the shooting stopped over where Dean and Sadie were.

"I don't want to fight," he was saying. "I got trapped in with these guys, but I helped Stone get away earlier. Ask him."

Quincey was the one who spoke- Rhett was still wanting to kill him. Unlike other Windsors, his hatred for the man had nothing to do with the color of skin- just his connection to the men who killed his unborn child. "Who's in charge? Who's your CO?"

"I guess it's Withers, now," the man said.

"Where is he?" Rhett demanded, suddenly concerned about what the man could tell them.

"He's the one in the mask," he replied. Then he stopped. "Wait. He switched with Sharpe so Sharpe could go plant charges. They are gonna blow-"

The triple timed explosion went off just then, and Rhett heard a loud pop, followed by the explosion of white light up the hill.

The soldier stood up and scanned the tree line, then he cursed. "Your people are about to get ambushed. Someone else is here-"

There was a whistling sound, then another, and the man stopped speaking. He looked down at his chest, and saw two pools of blood begin to widen out from holes in his vest. "Armor piercing..." he said. "Hesse...?" then he fell back, dead.

"Withers!" someone yelled from up the hill as Quincey and Rhett ducked for cover.

But upon hearing the name, Rhett went into a rage. He didn't care about the sniper- he ran for the tree line. Withers was going to die by his hands- of that he was certain.

Chapter 22

The Fort Collins safe house was in the Old Town portion of the municipality, set up as an apartment above a local Homeland office. They parked a block down and sat quietly in the car.

Well, Ben and Walt did.

"Why are you just sitting here? Aren't we just sitting ducks? What if they make another go at me?" Fletcher asked rapidly.

"You ask one more question and I'll make a go at you myself," Walt said. "We are waiting because there is a code we offer to the agents in that office. If they give the right code back, we go in. They don't? Well, we got a big problem."

Ben's phone buzzed. He looked down at the message, from a private number. "Code is good."

Fletcher started trying to get out, but of course, he couldn't.

"Quentin, have you ever been in a police car? Or seen a movie with police in it?" Walt asked.

"No, and yes."

"Alright. Then you still should know that only we can open your door, as you are in the seat where the criminals go," Walt said patronizingly. "Wouldn't make much sense if we let folks just get out when they felt like it, now would it?"

Fletcher grumbled something.

"And just because it's good in the safe house doesn't mean it is out on the street," Ben added. "Or do you not recall our run-in with the Tolberts?"

After that roadside encounter, they had seen nary a hint of a follow or even another car remotely looking interested in them. And that made Ben nervous. He knew it was bothering Walt, too.

"I'll go first," Walt said. "Check it out first. I have more experience spotting ne'er-do-wells and I've lived a full life." That was how Ben knew Walt was worried. Gallows humor.

Walt got out and walked nonchalantly across the street, hands shoved in his jacket pockets as the cool fall wind picked up. His head turned and looked up and down buildings, down the street in both directions and in the alley next to their building all while looking like a normal pedestrian. He got to the door, paused, looked back, and gave a head nod.

"Now we go, Quentin," Ben said, getting out of the car and unlocking Fletcher's door at the same time. He helped the hefty man out of the car, and began walking him across the street.

"How do you know the safe house is safe?" Fletcher asked.

"It's in the title, man," Ben said, very ready to be done with the realtor for the night.

"But if the mob has people in the FBI, how do you know they don't have people in Homeland?"

How had he not thought of that?

At the door, Ben ushered Fletcher in, and then turned to Walt. "I think we need to stick around. Make sure these guys are legit."

"Agreed," Walt said. "Kho is on her way, too, so let's wait until she gets done with her part. Besides, I hate it when things are too easy. And after our encounter with the Mountain Men, everything seems downright simple."

The flashbang wore off, but Dean could still smell the acrid smoke lingering in the air. All the members of the VYPER team were gone, save

Stone. Sadie stood up, rubbing her eyes, then saw her two prisoners were gone, and cursed. Quincey was walking toward them, alone.

"You guys okay?" he asked, eyeing Stone carefully.

"He's with us…for now," Dean said. "And I think we're okay."

"Other than losing our prisoners, that is," Sadie clarified.

"Where's Rhett? And your two guys?" Dean asked.

"We had one guy, seemed a nice enough fella," Quincey said. "As we were making our way to you, a shot rang out from that ridge up there," he pointed to an outcropping of stone above the first crop of trees. "Two shots in the chest, and he's down."

"They have vests," Sadie pointed out. "Unfortunately."

Quincey shook his head. "Armor-piercing rounds went right through whatever he had on. Last thing the guy said was…" he looked at Dean. "Hesse."

Dean felt that rage burn again. If what Starr had said was not a lie, then Hesse had killed Amy. And he was there, not far away. "Where did Rhett go?"

Quincey pointed to the same spot. "He tore off after them, and they headed for the sounds of those shots."

Dean turned and began trotting off after them, as well. "Quincey, call it in. Stone, stay put. Sadie-"

She was at his elbow, keeping pace, "I'm with you, Dean. We get him together, right? For Amy? For Ashleigh?"

Dean nodded. And they ran faster.

Rhett could hear them just ahead of him. He hadn't thought through any of his pursuit, and was realizing at that moment that his query had automatic weapons, and he had a pistol and a shotgun.

They had training, but he had mountain living. He had to use that to surprise if he wanted to avoid getting killed. And he knew the land better than-

"Hesse! Where have you been?" one of them yelled out. If Rhett could hear them that clearly, they were close. He slowed his pace, cautiously stepping around downed branches until he could see them, then he made himself as small as he could.

Which wasn't very small.

They had come to the clearing beneath the outcropping they called the Shelf, and the four military men were standing side by side, looking up at a man in gray fatigues.

Robert Hesse.

Hesse had a rifle propped on his leg, not a sniper rifle but a semi-automatic with a scope. The kind that fired armor-piercing rounds just fine. And Rhett could smell gasoline, for some reason.

"Clearing things up," Hesse replied to the man who spoke.

The man with a mask rolled up just enough to see the shaved sidewalls of someone with brown hair. And a square jaw.

Withers.

Rhett wanted to rush, knowing that was suicide. But he also didn't know what he was going to do. And dying without reaching his objective wasn't an option.

"Clearing things up?" Withers repeated. "What's that mean?"

Hesse shook his head. "It means you're done, Withers. VYPER is terminated. On Voight's orders. Stand down, turn yourselves in, and take the fall for all of it. The shootout, the couple up on the ridge," he waved his hands around. "This. I mean, what were you thinking, Withers? Five of you taking on a town of hillbillies?"

"Voight wants this land," Withers protested. "He ordered it!"

Hesse smiled. "That information is no longer accurate. And he'll have it. But not like this. Because your team blew it. Brought too much attention to yourselves. To Voight. You know we have the Windsors- the other ones- in our pocket now? They'll get it for us with no bloodshed. Or, well much."

"You love bloodshed, Robert," Withers countered. "Wasn't it you who bragged to us about that cook you killed and made it to look like a serial from back east, then dropped it for the Ranger to find? Didn't you say you enjoyed it?"

Hesse nodded. "I enjoyed the game. And the skill it took to find him and kill him. What you tried- and failed- to do in the Switchbacks was like shooting fish in a barrel. And you still missed."

"So what, you gonna take us in?" another man asked.

"Nah, I'm no cop," Hesse replied. "You're gonna turn yourself in, like I already said, Simmons."

Simmons cursed, bringing his weapon up. "Nope, not doing th-"

POP!

Simmons' head snapped back in a spray of blood and brain. Just as quick as he dispatched Simmons, Hesse dropped his gun and rushed the other three. As Rhett watched, the two who weren't Withers were felled by a slashing knife to the throat and a snapped neck. As their bodies fell, Hesse turned to Withers.

And Rhett burst forth from his hiding spot.

"Wait!" he yelled. "He's mine."

Hesse looked at him, seeming to consider if it was a trick and if Rhett was a threat. Then he stepped aside.

Withers had a gun, but seemed to have forgotten about it. He began to back away from Rhett. "Listen, man, I've got no beef with you," Withers pleaded.

"You ever lost someone you love?" Rhett asked.

Withers looked confused, and looked to Hesse. Hesse had walked over to a gas can and picked it up. "Don't let him out of the circle. And I'd make it fast, if I were you." Hesse struck a match and dropped it on the forest floor. Ribbons of flame shot out from that point, tracing the gasoline Hesse must have poured before they arrived.

Rhett stepped over a line of flame. "I said, you ever lose someone you love?"

"N-no," Withers said. Apparently, he remembered he had a gun, and tried to pull on Rhett. Rhett fired the shotgun first.

Withers' body stumbled back into a tree with the shot and he dropped his rifle. Rhett advanced, dropping his shotgun. The flames were growing higher and hotter all around them. "You killed my child," Rhett said.

"I don't know what you're talking about," Withers countered, coughing. "I don't kill kids."

"The woman you shot- she was pregnant," Rhett said. "My child."

Withers sized up Rhett and seemed to see the situation. "Oh. My bad." Withers lunged at Rhett, drawing Rhi's Luger while Rhett drew the pistol from his waistband, firing point blank into

Withers' forehead. The body fell at Rhett's feet, the pistol still in his hand.

"Rhett…" Dean and Sadie had just walked up and saw what happened.

Rhett looked at the Ranger, but neither said a word. They knew. Vengeance united people. It was a kinship they would share, but never desire.

Rhett pulled the pistol from Withers' hand and said, "Hesse ran up the mountain. You pace it right, you can catch him."

Dean nodded, and he took off, Sadie trailing behind.

Rhett walked out of the ring of flames and started back down the mountain.

Hesse reached the small service road where he had parked his bike and started to cross the gravel to get to it. It wasn't the Hessian, just a dirt bike he used to get around the mountains more efficiently. The motorcycle was parked on the edge of the road, and he paused to look down the steep incline down to the river running below it.

He never saw Ashleigh.

She had parked her car just out of sight of Hesse's bike, having followed him using a GPS marker she placed on him at the hospital when she shoved him. She'd had the marker for Voight, wanting to follow him for her story, but hadn't gotten the chance to use it. She had left the hospital after Rhett, gone home and changed, intending to head to the Switchbacks to get the story. Then she saw the gunfight, saw what looked like Hesse shooting at Dean and the man she thought was Stone, so she drove up the only road not under fire, happening upon the dirt bike. She knew it was Hesse's.

She made her way down the slope, to the rock formation that looked like a shelf, and saw the end of VYPER transpire.

"Do you ever tire of hurting people, Robert?" she asked.

He didn't jump, or act surprised, but she knew that was because he either couldn't let her have that small victory or his sociopathic lack of emotion prevented him from even the small startle reflex that a normal person would have at the sound of an unexpected voice. Instead, he slowly turned, and his lips contorted into that dead smile of his. "Seems you never tire of me, love," he said.

She shook her head and stepped toward him. "You know what you make people feel, Robert? When they meet you?" she asked, expecting no answer. "You make their skin crawl. Unless you've affected your human skin appropriately. Then that creeping feeling is almost charming. I never understood how I *couldn't* see the real you. How you fooled me. *Me!* A reporter who prided herself on having a nose for the truth. While you were away, in prison, I figured it out, though. I didn't *want* to see you for who you were in the beginning. Because even though you made my skin crawl, I kinda liked that. You were different from other guys. You were dangerous. Just not…the right kind of dangerous."

"You hitting on me, Ash?"

She shook her head. "Don't call me that. Don't speak my name, ever again. See, when I first saw you again, I was terrified. That you'd hurt me- maybe kill me this time. But I was more afraid that I'd fall under your spell again. That *I'd* kill me by making that same stupid choice. That thought was fleeting, a whisper. But tonight, at the hospital, something changed. My skin didn't crawl. You didn't scare me anymore. I grew while you were away, Robert. And the thing I grew was a spine, and a brain. A brain that *knows* you are a dangerous man. But you are a weak man."

He laughed uncomfortably. He didn't like being called that. *Weak.* "You kept saying that, but what did I just do, Ash? I killed an entire team of special forces, some with my bare hands. That sound weak?"

Now she smiled. "No. That sounds like cover. You are no doubt physically strong. Strong with weapons and violence. But you kill because you are *weak.* You hide behind that, don't let anyone really know you, because *you*- the real you- is weak. And scared of being exposed. And you hate it. So you kill. And you hit."

Hesse bowed up, trying to make himself seem big. He took a step toward her, but she didn't back down. "You think you're something now, huh? Getting attention for your writing, got a new boyfriend who is also pretty tough when he waves that gun around. I'd like to take a shot at him myself someday."

She chuckled. "You don't think I can stand up to you on my own, do you? You gotta bring Dean into this. Who, by the way, is not my boyfriend."

She saw his hand reach around behind his back. "No matter. Someone needs to teach you some manners again. Guess you forgot how to speak to people while I was away. Got too big for your own good." He drew his knife and started toward her. "Gonna teach you real good this time."

She smiled.

"I'm so glad you said that," she said, reaching behind her back and drawing out the pistol Sadie had loaned her. "And that you brought your toy, too."

She fired.

His shoulder jerked back, and a look of shock washed over his face. That shock turned to anger, and he started forward again.

She fired again.

And again.

The first shot hit him in the gut. The second in the chest. Ashleigh knew it was body armor, but it didn't matter. It was *hurting* him. Hesse stumbled backward, and he turned away from her, moving toward his bike.

Ashleigh followed him, gun still up. He reached down to the side of the bike, his body turned sideways to her. He began to raise up, and she saw he had drawn a gun of his own. She fired again, and again, and again. His body jerked with each blow, but the second shot also drew blood. She saw it arc out from his armpit, where she must have hit him, instead of his body armor. The last shot hit the vest again, but he was teetering on the edge of the drop off, losing his balance on the shale and gravel.

"You won't ever scare me again, Robert," she said between clenched teeth.

"Ashleigh!"

She heard Sadie call her name, but didn't turn. She couldn't. She had to finish it. Robert raised the gun- not at Ashleigh but toward where Sadie's voice had come from.

Ashleigh fired again, and Robert's feet went out from under him. He tumbled over the ledge, falling and rolling down the steep slope. He bounced off rocks and trees, until his body splashed into the river below.

She looked at the empty space where the man who had haunted most of her adult life no longer stood.

And she felt relief.

"Ashleigh."

That voice was Dean's. And he was right there. Finally, she broke her stare from where Robert fell, and turned to Dean. His gun was drawn, but at his side. In his eyes, she saw compassion, concern. And something else that might be love or empathy. Or both.

"Put the gun down," he said calmly.

She dropped it, the world a fog. Like she was waking up from a dream.

No.

A nightmare.

But one where she beat the monster.

Finally.

Chapter 23

Pickett arrived via helicopter about thirty minutes after Dean and Sadie drove Ashleigh down from the service road to the Switchbacks. Pickett was directing the new arrivals from local and volunteer Fire and EMS with help from Quincey. Rhett had left, making his way back to Tina and Rhiannon at the hospital. There was a chaos feeling in the air, and Dean wanted to keep Ashleigh out of it for the time being.

"In the moment, I did it so I would know where he was. So he wouldn't ever just show up again," Ashleigh explained while they sat in the car. "Honestly, it wasn't a setup. I wasn't coming up here to shoot him. I was coming to get the story. But I saw him…saw him kill those men. And I couldn't…I couldn't let that kind of man just ride away."

"The gun?" Dean asked.

"Uh, that's mine," Sadie said. "Loaned it to her. For protection."

Dean shrugged, "Well, it worked." He looked out the window at the bustling rescue workers under the moonlight and headlights. "I don't think anyone will look too hard into the shooting. But we do need to find his body. I've called search and rescue in-"

"Body? You think he died?" Ashleigh asked, surprised.

Dean looked at Sadie and then back to Ashleigh. "Uh, well, you said you saw blood, right? And he fell, what, fifty feet? Into a river. Unless he's Rasputin, he's pretty likely dead."

"Rasputin?" Sadie asked.

"Russian monk, pre-Russian Revolution. Too tight with the tsar. Supposedly he was poisoned, stabbed, shot, thrown in a river and still lived for a bit."

Sadie looked confused.

"Villain in the cartoon Anastasia," Ashleigh said.

"Ooooh," Sadie replied. Then she looked outside the window. "Abel and Grace are here now, it looks like. I need to help them with the clean-up. I'll leave you two to talk." And she got out of the car, but stopped. "And you can keep the gun, Ash."

Dean looked at Ashleigh. She was so calm, so collected.

So beautiful.

She looked up at him, and he held her gaze for a moment before he spoke. "You okay?"

She offered a half-smile and a shrug. "As well as can be expected after committing murder."

Dean chuckled. "It's not murder. Self-defense. And I'll fight them if they go for anything other than that."

"Will they let you fight for me, Dean?"

He looked at her askance. "What d'ya mean?"

"Our relationship, whatever it is," Ashleigh answered. "We're close, friends. I don't know. Maybe more. But that would complicate your testimony, wouldn't it? In my defense."

Dean looked away. Ashleigh killed the man who had tried to kill her. In that moment, sure- but how many times before? He didn't know that- and he never would. Unless she offered. He knew better than to ask her about that part of her past. He turned back to look at her, those green eyes and auburn hair framing a face of a woman who had overcome so much. A woman that showed she could take care of herself.

And Dean realized that the only reason he had for not letting himself fall for her fully was gone. He had long feared she would be a target, she might get hurt like Amy had been.

But she had faced her villain, the man most likely to hurt her, and had emerged alive and victorious.

"Let Sadie testify," he said, then reached for her face, gently taking her chin in his hand and lifting it to his. He leaned in and kissed her, and he felt her body relax and lean into him. Her arms came up around him, and his free hand went to the other side of her face.

He pulled away and looked into her eyes, and she smiled. Then she leaned in to kiss him again.

And that was okay with him.

Stone was sitting on the ground, handcuffed. He didn't mind. He knew what he was guilty of, and was ready to face those consequences. Looking around at the devastation that just five men had inflicted for the sake of Xavier Voight's greed washed away any remnants of resistance to turning himself in and standing against Voight.

The Homeland agent, Pickett, walked over to him and stuffed his hands in his pockets. "So, you wanna talk?"

Stone looked at him, instantly judging his tone, demeanor, and attitude to be a typical condescending Fed. "I'll talk to Dean."

"Heh," Pickett scoffed. "For a guy who is such a loner, people sure seem to like to talk to him."

"He treats me like a person," Stone said. "And I've gone to guns with the man. He's fearless. He's honest. And he's a good man."

"You sure about that?" Pickett asked.

Stone looked at Pickett. "You mean that he's killed at least one man involved in his wife's death? That he is actively seeking to put down the others? That doesn't make him an evil man, it makes him a man put in an untenable position and making the best of it. If he wasn't a soldier, he'd have made a good one."

"So you know about all that?"

"Voight told me," Stone said. "Told me a lot of things. Things I'm willing to talk about. But not to you. To Dean."

"Well, you're in luck- here comes the man now," Pickett said, nodding toward the figure moving toward them. "You get Ms. Storms on her way?"

Dean nodded. "Sadie is takin' her back down in Ashleigh's vehicle. Figured I'd take Stone down myself." He looked from Pickett to Stone and back. "Looks like that was a good call?"

"He doesn't trust me, Dean," Pickett said. "Can you imagine that?"

"Yep," Dean said. Then he looked to Stone. "I shouldn't expect any ambushes this time?"

Stone smiled. "Not this time. Think you got them all."

Dean shook his head. "Not me. Robert Hesse."

Stone blinked. "What?"

Pickett interjected, which irritated Stone because he knew Pickett hadn't seen anything. "Yeah. Your old buddy killed your whole team, then set them on fire. Bet you're glad you ditched the VYPERs."

Stone looked down. The break with his team had been bad, but to be killed by your own former teammate- it was beyond sad. He knew Hesse was unstable, dangerous. But to so coldly execute his supposed friends? Then another thought struck him. "Hesse- did you get him?"

Dean and Pickett exchanged a look. Dean answered, "In a manner of speakin.' Don't think you'll hear from him again."

"And Starr?"

Another exchanged look. "He's in the wind. Again," Pickett said.

"Then get me to cover, now," Stone demanded. "Starr was a sniper. He's done hits for the Denver mob before-"

"Wait," Dean said, holding up a hand. "I thought you were working for Voight, not the Denver mob. Why would they want you dead?"

Stone shook his head. "Starr and Hesse, they were playing both sides. Hoping the mob and Voight took each other out so they could pick up the pieces. Don't you know that it's every man for himself up here?"

"I do. And I get that's why you are turnin' on them now," Dean said. "To save yourself."

"Yeah, I want to save myself," Stone said. "But not from punishment. I know I deserve whatever I get. I want to save my soul from the stuff I've done. From the betrayals and corruptions I've been a part of. I've killed a lot of wicked men, but since I took this job, I feel like

I've only hurt the innocent. And I can't abide that. Not anymore."

Dean looked at Pickett, who nodded. Then Dean said, "I think we can help you unburden your soul, then."

"Good," Stone replied. "Now get me in a car and get me out of here."

"How long are we gonna sit here?" Walt asked, sipping his second coffee.

"Until I feel certain that no is coming for Fletcher," Ben replied. They were sitting in their car, across the street from the safe house. Kho had come and gone, verifying the legitimacy of the agents. But Ben had an uneasy feeling in his gut.

"He's in Homeland's hands now. Let them take the hassle," Walt countered.

"It's something Fletcher said that's still bothering me," Ben said. "About how if the Denver mob had FBI agents on their payroll, what stops them from having Homeland?"

"It's been an hour of us sitting here," Walt said. "No gunshots, no strange cars. No unexpected guests-" Walt stopped because a car pulled up to the curb just outside of the office entrance to the Homeland office. "Okay, I'll take it back. That car look familiar?"

Ben leaned over the wheel. It didn't look familiar, but it was unique. A white sedan- plain and an older model. What made it unique is that it seemed to be trying to look inconspicuous, and in doing so, it became very conspicuous. "It's not Wagner's. But it feels…off."

A man got out, wearing a white suit. He ducked his head as he stepped from the car and donned a white fedora. He walked around the back of the car, and opened the trunk. He rummaged around a bit, then closed the trunk, moving to the opposite side of the car. They couldn't see what he'd gotten out. A second man got out of the car, and Ben recognized his odd-shaped bald head immediately.

"That's Wagner!"

Walt started to get out of the car, saying, "I hate when you're right- makes you insufferable to live with."

Ben was out of the car faster than Walt and drew his gun. "Wagner, hands up- CBI!"

The bald man turned toward them, but the man in the fedora just walked into the offices. Wagner raised a gun and opened fire. It was an automatic pistol, and the bullets began to spray all around them.

"Get behind the car, Samuels!" Walt barked as he returned fire from a crouched position behind the hood.

Ben turned and ran, staying as low as he could. Wagner was also ducking behind his car.

Then the sound of gunfire came from inside the office.

"The other guy is after Fletcher," Ben said.

"Really? You think?" Walt asked sarcastically. The gunfire stopped inside the building, and Wagner also stopped shooting. Then the sound of something hard and metallic bouncing on pavement broke the still of the moment.

"You hear that?" Ben asked.

Walt leaned over and looked under the car, and Ben followed suit. A small, dark, round thing was wobbling under the car, and it was Walt who recognized it first.

"Grenade!" he yelled, and they both dove away from the car. The explosion followed a second later, lifting the car off the ground as the sound of rending metal screeched into the night. As the flames licked the air against the dark night, Ben raised his head and saw Quentin Fletcher being led out of the building by the man in the fedora, and Wagner had his gun on him and Walt to make sure they didn't get up. Fletcher was shoved into the back seat, then Fedora rounded the car and headed for the driver's side. The distance was great, the flames distorted the surrounding air, and he was a bit shaken up, but as Ben watched the man take off the hat and get in the car, he felt certain he recognized him.

Edwin Jessup.

The lawyer.

The bumbling, lecherous fool.

Was he a hitman, too?

Or…

Was he the Ghost?

The white car tore off into the night, and Walt sat up. "You got your phone on you?"

Ben sat up. "Yeah. Why?"

"Cuz we need to call this in and I left mine in the front seat," Walt replied. Then, after a beat, "You think insurance will cover it?"

"You sure you're okay?" Sadie asked. Again.

"I'm fine, completely," Ashleigh replied. Again.

"It's just, you shot a man, Ash," Sadie said. "Might've killed him. Now, I don't want to sugarcoat it, so you need to know, you may be fine now, but in a few hours, the adrenaline will wear off and-"

"And if I need to talk, I'll call you," Ashleigh interjected. "Or Dean. Someone who has killed before. Sadie, I shot the man who beat me and destroyed me for years. I can't tell you how many times I wished I could have stood up to him, and finally I got a chance to prove I was stronger than him. And I did."

Sadie nodded. "Okay. Just know-"

"I. Will. Call."

"Okay," Sadie said. She paused for a moment, then asked, "So, what did you and Dean talk about?"

Ashleigh began to smile, and her lips kept spreading wider and wider.

Sadie looked over and began to laugh. "Or did you not 'talk' much at all?"

"We kissed," Ashleigh said, her smile at its apex.

And with that, they were just two women talking about life- not two women who just survived their second shoot-out together in less than three months.

A newly sober Brent Chase walked back into the home of Xavier Voight side by side with Charly. She hadn't said much on the drive out, during the…thing he had to do…or on the way back. He couldn't imagine what she was thinking of him.

Maybe it had to do with the Windsor boys being right there with them, every step of the way.

At the door, Charly stopped and turned. "You're free to go, boys. Job is done for the night."

Dutifully, Zeke and Nigel nodded, turned,

and left. Charly opened the door to the mansion and walked in. It was dark and empty, quite the departure from earlier that evening. Still in a daze, Brent walked in aimlessly, looking around. "Does he want to see my mud covered hands, too?" Brent asked.

Charly walked to Brent, saying nothing, and took his hands in hers. She pulled him toward the staircase, and began to lead him up. They passed two doors, and finally she turned to one on the right. She led him into a bedroom, but kept going to the attached bath. She walked to the sink, turned on the tap, and pulled his hands under it. She began to rub his hands, the dirt slowly washing away. Charly grabbed a bar of soap and rubbed them over his hands, then washed the suds away with water. All the while saying nothing.

Brent had been watching her clean his hands, but when he looked into the mirror, she was looking back at him. They locked eyes, and finally she spoke. "He owns you now. You realize that?"

Brent nodded. He'd killed his friend, buried the body, and come back to the scene of the crime. Of course, Voight owned him.

"Well, he's owned me for a while. I just had to do it once, maybe he'll only make you do it once."

Brent looked at her, shock all over his face.

"Yeah. It's how he traps those he thinks are valuable. Takes an innocent, has them commit murder, tapes it, and blackmails you into being his…whatever he needs." Charly shrugged. "I had to make peace with it, and you will, too."

"Did you know? That he'd planned this?"

She didn't answer right away, but finally, she uttered a quiet, "Yes."

Brent rubbed a clean hand over his face and turned away from her.

She grabbed his shoulder and turned him back. "I had no choice, Brent.He'd ruin me or kill me if I broke with him. I can't stand against him, and you can't either. At least…at least we can stand together." She rubbed a manicured finger down his cheek.

"Did Levi really rat me out?"

She shook her head. "I don't know. Probably not. He lies like he breathes. The person I killed, the friend he had me murder, he told me the same thing. I never really wanted to look too hard into it, you know?"

Deep down, he did. "Was any of this real? Any of his interest in my part in the incident? In my abilities?" He paused. "Your interest in me?"

She smiled sadly. "I don't know about the rest. But I definitely have interest in you." She kissed him.

At first it surprised him- no, shocked him. He wasn't expecting that. Not at all.

But he got over it fast.

He wrapped her up in his arms, pulled her close, and moved with her toward the bedroom.

Dean steered the Camaro down the main street of Eden Falls, the streets empty and dark.

"You should thank me, you know," Stone said.

"Why's that?"

"This car is much cooler than that Jeep truck thing."

Dean gave him a glare. For the entire trip down the mountain, Stone had been telling Dean about the inner workings of the VYPER system. How the branch Stone belonged to had been used in foreign affairs until the apparent joint venture between Voight and the mob. He'd explained the organization hierarchy, how Voight sheltered himself from the more 'controversial' elements of the business. And just before the comment about the car, Stone had begun to explain why both the mob and Voight wanted the Switchbacks- and a lot of other land.

"Back to the land grab stuff," Dean said, redirecting.

Stone sighed. "Okay. You remember the thing that started all this- the Windsor boy that got shot by my man, by Link?"

"Yeah."

"You lawmen all thought it was about the minerals, the lithium or gold or whatever-"

"But it wasn't- Rhett already told me that."

"Good. That saves some time. So you know it's about development. Modernization. A new type of living."

Dean looked over at Stone. "You mean it's about a housing development?"

Stone chuckled. "Kind of. You remember a couple years back, part of Seattle declared itself independently run?"

Dean recalled something of that nature, so he replied, "Yeah."

"Voight got it in his head that if the pothead extremists in Washington could do it, why couldn't his more like-minded associates do the same?" Stone pointed toward a mountain top. "The problem in Seattle is they were a bunch of peaceniks. Non-violent. So they didn't think about defense. And any good soldier or Star Wars fan knows the best position to defend from."

"The high ground."

"The force is strong with you, Remington Dean," Stone replied.

"You're tellin' me that Xavier Voight is an anti-government nutcase?" Dean asked incredulously.

"Not at all. I'm sure you know he works with the government all the time. It's just that…he prides himself on being a visionary. Like Elon Musk, but instead of electric cars and spaceships, it's guns and defenses." Stone pointed back at the mountaintop. "He thinks a civil war is coming in this country, and he thinks he can ride it out, and when the dust settles, he can pick up the pieces and rebuild America in his image."

"That's insane."

"Never said it wasn't," Stone replied. "But it is what the man thinks. He has no heirs, no children to pass things on, but he is obsessed with legacy and power. He want to possess and control them both."

"Senator Reece…"

"Yeah, he's one of the guys that Voight has in his pocket. See Voight has tired of waiting for this war- so he wants to push people into it. Stoke some fires, create some controversy. Put a bunch of dry powder in a small room and light the fuse. And none of it's political, mind you. He uses Democrats and Republicans alike. Whatever he needs that day to get what he wants."

"He's a terrorist," Dean realized out loud.

"I just realized that myself," Stone said. "Spent my whole military career and life after fighting terrorists, only to work for one. Irony sucks."

Dean pulled to a stop in front of the police station. "If half of what you just told me is true, we can't keep you here. He'll come for you- or send someone."

"Dean, I'm dead already," Stone said calmly. "The only thing that matters is that you were smart and recorded all that."

Dean smiled. "I may sound like a hick, but

I think good." He looked around, and seeing nothing, he got out and went to get Stone from the car. He helped the man out, and closed the door.

"Dean, I came to you not just because you're a good man," Stone said as they walked to the door of the station. "You're brave and tough and smart. If anyone can stop Voight- it's you."

"Well, you can testify with me at his-"
SSWWAK!

Blood sprayed in Dean's face as Stone's head exploded. Instincts kicked in, and Dean dropped down, drawing his gun. He took cover as best he could in the entry of the police station, and scanned for the shooter. No movement on rooftops that he could see, no one on the street. The shot was a perfect shot from an extreme distance- Dean knew that instantly. But since no other shots came, he pulled Stone's body into the police station, and shouted for help.

Chapter 24

One month later

Dean nailed the last board up and climbed down the ladder. "All yours, Walt," he announced as he stepped out of the older man's way.

Walt mounted the ladder and began to apply a copious amount of paint to the eaves of Rhiannon Windsor's newly rebuilt clinic in the Switchbacks.

Eden Falls had come out in force to help the small village get back on its feet following the VYPER attack of the month before. What resulted was that every damaged structure was fixed up, and a couple new homes were constructed. Small homes like those in the Switchbacks were assembled and in the dry quickly, so the tenants could live in them while the finishing touches were added. And just in time for the first snowfall to come.

Dean stood between Ashleigh and Rhiannon, watching Walt wobble on the ladder. "Good thing you're a doctor, Rhiannon," Dean said nodding at Walt. "He's either gonna fall and break his leg, or the wobble'll give him vertigo."

"One thing that still works is my hearing, you Texas hick," Walt said, then added a curse.

Rhiannon turned to Ashleigh and said, "Thank you. Your article- it made such a difference. Talking about what we stand for here…it dispelled a lot of myths about these folks."

Ashleigh, whose arm was wrapped around Dean's waist, smiled back. "I thought you might have meant the article about the shoot out. You know, people think Eden Falls is like a modern Tombstone or Dodge City, so the locals that made their way up here to help seem intent on disproving *that* myth."

Rhiannon laughed, and said, "Want me to show you the little schoolhouse we have going in?" Dean noted that Rhiannon had both of the Lugers again, courtesy of her brother.

Dean watched Ashleigh and Rhiannon walk away, and smiled. They had been seeing each other- not just talking daily- for most of the past month. Ashleigh had eventually hit that wall of grief- maybe even guilt- over her shooting of Hesse. Dean had talked her down from that, along with Sadie. But they had never found his body, so

Ashleigh wavered between guilt and concern that he might just show up again.

Her writing had been instrumental in her healing. She wrote about the attack, which led to a story about the lifestyle the Switchbacks were trying to create for lower and middle-income families with a generational connection to the mountains. Both garnered attention and accolades. The latter was up for a couple awards, and she had taken it upon herself to start up a fundraiser for supplies to rebuild.

Dean walked toward Ben and Sadie, who were putting the finishing touches on a small garden fence that enclosed bell peppers, onions, and carrots. "You two doin' okay with the tools? I mean, city folk that you are…"

"Do you think we are completely incompetent?" Ben asked good-naturedly.

"Just you, dear," Sadie said. They too had been dating for the last month, but the younger couple seemed to be moving faster. Dean ascribed it to his and Ashleigh's baggage that the two of them didn't have.

"How's the new job, Chief?" Dean asked Sadie.

"*Interim* Chief," she corrected. In the wake of Spitz's death, she was the highest ranking member of the police force in Eden Falls, so she got to take the big chair. "I really don't think it's for me, you know. In fact, Ben and I have been talking and…"

Ben turned from the chicken wire that was wrapped painfully around his arm and looked at Dean. "Sadie and I are considering applying for the FBI academy. Now that there is an opening in this region." He raised his eyebrows. Like Hesse, no one had seen a trace of Starr since that night at the Switchbacks.

Dean patted Ben on the back and said, "Well, good luck. But the bar is pretty low, so *you* probably won't need it."

"Jerk," he countered.

Dean walked away, leaving the lovebirds to flirt openly and unabashedly.

Fletcher's disappearance had put an end to the case that drawn them all together, but like Hesse and Starr, no one really knew what happened to him. Ben had shared what he thought he saw that night, Edwin Jessup, but no amount of digging turned up any connections to the Ghost.

And the murder of Collazo was unofficially attributed to Robert Hesse. Enough evidence had been collected to disprove the connection to the other murders in other parks, but nothing more than circumstantial evidence linked Hesse. But they all knew it was him.

Still, the other murders bothered Dean. Someone was out there killing people in the National Parks. It bothered Mike Williams, too. Dean was waiting on the call from Mike to make a run of investigating those deaths. Since the wheels of justice had ground to a halt on the Denver Mob- Voight case, Dean had been bugging his boss to let him look into it.

As for Voight, he was not anywhere near Eden Falls. But they knew where he had been- a month-long safari. And he'd taken his assistant and- to the shock of everyone- Brent Chase along with him. His shop was temporarily closed due to his absence and the sudden disappearance of his employee, Levi Montague.

No one knew where Levi had gone, and that was beginning to eat at Dean.

Dean turned his attention to finding Rhett. The big man had been scarce for the last month, mostly mourning the loss of his unborn child and nursing Tina back to health. She was doing well, physically, but the death of her child haunted her. Or so Rhiannon had said.

That fence had mended, too. Rhiannon had seen how Dean fought for the Switchbacks, and so she seemed to calm on his frequent jabs at men like Todd and Dell- who were poorly constructing a pen for some sheep up the road. When he met her, she had so reminded him of Amy, he had been instantly drawn to her. But he now saw that for what it was- a last grasp at his old life. Ashleigh was the woman for him- and since she had shot Hesse, he'd watched her closely. She was strong, and he'd always known that. But she now seemed free, unburdened.

Alive.

And that had an impact on Dean, too. He was friendlier, more open. He'd made it a point to reach out to Rhett several times over the month, but to little success. Then he saw him. Standing in the marijuana patch, looking off at the mountains.

Walking over, Dean announced himself. "Hey Rhett, long-time no see."

Rhett turned to him, his face cold. "Dean. I haven't much felt like talking. Sorry."

Dean could tell the man was still struggling with loss, with pain. And he had no words for that. Other than, "Rhett, I'm so sorry. I just want you to know, I'm here if you need me."

Rhett smiled sadly. "Thank you for that. You know, everyone has advice. Or a cliche. I don't need that crap. I need answers. I need justice."

"Killing Withers didn't-"

Rhett shook his head. "Didn't mean squat. He just pulled a trigger. It's Voight that killed my future. You know Tina cries every day? Every. Single. Day. And I have nothing to offer her for help. Nothing." He had been looking around, not at Dean, but now his eyes bored holes into Dean's. "You seen Voight? Heard from him? About him?"

Dean shook his head and kicked the dirt. "Nope. Out of town on a safari. Even with what we got from Fletcher's papers and Stone's confession, we can't get a warrant to force him back. Not yet. AUSA Kho is working to be build a strong enough case to go after him when he comes back."

"It true that Brent Chase is running his businesses now? With that blonde chick?"

"What I hear, anyway. But they went on that safari with him."

"And Starr?"

"Not a word."

"Hesse's body?"

Dean looked at Rhett, suddenly concerned. "Nothing. Why the questions?"

Rhett looked off in the distance again. "Bad men don't die, Dean. They find a way to come back. So you just keep knocking them down when they pop up. Hesse may be dead, but believe me, he isn't gone. Another man like him will come along soon enough. These mountains draw them. But you know how we win, Dean?"

"No."

"Can't be the way of the law. These men are too slippery. No. We do it the mountain way. They hurt us, we hurt them right back. They kill us, we slaughter them."

"That's not justice, Rhett," Dean said.

Rhett looked him in the eye. "You mean to tell me that if you saw Hesse, or Starr, or Voight up here in the deep solitude of the mountains- and you knew they killed your wife- you wouldn't just take care of them? No one looking, no one to see it?"

Dean didn't answer.

Because despite how good things were at that moment, a part of him agreed with Rhett.

Dean had dropped Ashleigh off at her house, then returned to his cabin. Without turning on a light, he made a beeline for the basement, where he at last turned a light on.

His board was rearranged, and the light workload had allowed Dean time to adjust it for the changes in Amy's case.

They had confirmed Bethea's replacement was intended to be Chris Starr, so that branch of the board was closed off. Starr, along with Fletcher and the mystery head of the Denver mob, the 'Ghost,' remained in their original location, but were marked with a yellow ribbon to indicate they were missing.

The Tolberts were on the board, but not because they were related to Amy's case- they were just making noise as to be a problem sooner rather than later.

Hesse had been marked out, like Kolbe. He reached up and took the picture down. He began to hesitantly rub the red X off.

What if he was still out there?

As much as that could affect Ashleigh, Dean still held out hope for some answers about Amy. Some closure he felt he was denied.

He looked down at the pile of pictures he had removed from the board. On top of the pile was Rhett Windsor. A reformed man. Dean reached down and picked up the photo. Slowly, he pinned it to the board. Something was nagging Dean about their talk. A deep, gut level feeling that Rhett was not done with his revenge, and that when he was, he wouldn't be able to stop. A lot of criminals were like addicts- they can quit, but one lapse and the urge rushes back faster and harder than before.

He prayed it wasn't the story laying out before Rhett.

His phone rang, and he pulled it from his pocket. "Mike, what's the word?"

"We got clearance," Williams said. "Pack your bags, the Park serial is yours. You fly to South Dakota from Denver tomorrow afternoon. Keep me in the loop."

"Will do boss," Dean said.

He looked at the board, and for the first time, he didn't feel like the Parks' job was impeding that investigation.

But a new pang hit him.

He was going to miss the people of Eden Falls while he was gone. Ben, Walt, Rhett. Sadie.

But above all, he would miss Ashleigh.

He smiled, because he knew she would miss him, too. And having someone waiting for him when he got back made the world a brighter place.

One breath at a time.

"Promise," he said.

And he knew Amy would be pleased.

After everyone had left, Rhiannon entered her clinic, and quickly walked across the room and lifted a rug off the floor. Beneath it lay a trap door, from the original cabin's design. It had been useful in the moonshine days, but lately she'd been forced to use it for another reason.

Harboring fugitives.

"It's me, coming down."

She stepped down the creaky stairs slowly, and as her eyes adjusted to the light, they fell on two figures. One was a blonde man with tattoos up and down his arms. Chris Starr. He was pale and tired, his arm in a sling from Dean's bullet. As always, he kept gun pointed at her as she came down the steps.

The other, laying in a bed with bloodshot eyes and bandages covering his bare chest, was Robert Hesse.

"Is it time for my meds?" Hesse asked.

Rhiannon nodded as she shakily got the pills ready for him.

"They suspect?"

"No," she managed. "They still think you're dead."

Starr asked, "And me?"

"Still no idea where you could be," she said. Giving Hesse his antibiotic. "Why won't you just take all the meds? I can get more. I don't want any part of this- keeping you two alive and lying to my family and friends. Just leave. They'd never find you. Get out of the country-"

"We are right where we want to be," Starr said. "War is coming to these mountains, and we intend to be here to pick up the pieces when all is said and done."

About The Author

Chad Lehrmann may reside in Texas, but his heart belongs to Colorado. It's only natural he would seek to tell stories of the mountains that inspire and terrify and invigorate. In addition to writing, he is a high school AP History teacher, husband and father to two daughters, adopter of two dogs, two cats and a rabbit he rescued from the weed eater.

Social Media

 Instagram- @chadlehrmannauthor
TikTok- @chad_the_writer
Facebook- Chad Lehrmann, Author
Website: www.chadlehrmann.com

Books by this author
Rocky Mountain Gothic Series:
The Ranger
Switchbacks

The Jonah Way
A loose cannon Houston cop takes on the gangs
and corruption in his city driven by his moral
code and lethal justice. He's a crazy good cop.

In The Fields of The Eagle 1930s Germany.
Fascism is on the rise, but a small band of
teenagers wants nothing to do with it. As their
personal tragedies mount, they must make a
choice- is it better to be free and live in the
shadow of death than to be trapped in the
certainty of it? Inspired by true events.

The Killogy Series

Killtown: One Road In, No Way Out Secluded Kingston, Texas is about to be visited by six vicious killers- all invited by a mysterious Host. They are coming to take part in a competition where the only way to win is to shed the most blood. Can a local sheriff and a handful of brave locals survive the night and defeat the sadistic murderers to win: Killtown?

KillU :   The survivors of Killtown learn a new meaning of terror on a college campus. The Host returns to teach a new class of killers the meaning of carnage.

KillState: The shocking finale to the Killogy! All will be revealed!

www.ingramcontent.com/pod-product-compliance
Lightning Source LLC
Chambersburg PA
CBHW061037310726
48969CB00004B/986